ALSO BY THE AUTHOR

Dear Kate—Dear Dad,
The Isle across Acheron

YOUNG ADULT FICTION

The Slip through Time

GALACTIC EATS

DENALI MAJESTO

HONOR SEQUITUR FUGI...TEM

DENALI MAJESTO'S
GALACTIC EATS

To Alton Brown, Samin Nosrat, and—most importantly—my mother-in-law, for molding my wife into the phenomenal cook she is today.

GALACTIC EATS, EPISODE #344:

"Narrow Egg–scape"

OFFICIAL TRANSCRIPT.
EPISODE SEGMENT RETRIEVED FROM ARCHIVE BLOCK 32D, THIRD
PLANET ENTERTAINMENT, INC.

A slender hand pushes aside the emerald-studded leaves of an indigo bala'bad tree. Sal Cantore peers through the gap and across the narrow jungle clearing. She points emphatically at the sheer cliff face on the other side, then addresses the camera with an excited grin. Stepping aside, she waves the camera forward for a clearer shot.

The camera zooms in on a nest of twigs perched in a crag a few meters off the ground. There is a flutter of movement, and the fist-sized head of a silvery creature rises into view.

Sal removes her coral-pink fedora in a show of reverence.

SAL
There she is! The native Ni'aruti call this rare and beautiful creature the *vivi-fa'ool,* the "bird of living silver." And—my!—she is gorgeous. But not half as gorgeous as those eggs she's sitting on.

Sal lets go of the bala'bad branch and faces the camera. She uses animated hand gestures to assist her explanation.

SAL

Because the *vivi-fa'ool* is revered by the primitive Ni'aruti as a holy
bird, we must be quick and cautious in our collection of the eggs. If
they catch us harvesting a clutch, there could be dire
consequences. So, in the name of secrecy, I've brought only a single
camera operator with me today. Not only is she my producer, she's
also now my baby boy's godmother: Mei-Li Tan.

The camera swivels to reveal the beaming face of the young woman
operating it. She gives a quick wave.

MEI-LI

Good afternoon, *Eats*-niks! I promise I'll do my best to capture this
special moment for you. For now, you'll have to be patient. Before
Sal can collect the eggs, we need the *vivi-fa'ool* to leave her nest.

The nest, still occupied, is shown from different angles. A time-lapse of
clouds and shadows indicates a long wait as day passes into late afternoon. Finally, the vivi-fa'ool flutters. It glances about, scanning for danger, then beats its four powerful wings and flies off.

SAL
(beckoning the camera to follow) Here's our chance. Let's go!

The camera bounces erratically behind her as she sprints to the base of
the cliff.

SAL

We're traveling light in case there's need of a quick escape, so I
didn't bring any climbing equipment. Since the nest is only about
four meters off the ground, I'll scale the cliff freestyle, nab the eggs,
and secure them in this specially designed creel.

Sal opens the basket slung around her shoulder. Inside is a cushioned
interior with separate chambers for each egg.

SAL

Then we'll hurry back to the *Eats Queen*, where we'll transform
these rare eggs into an even rarer crème brûlée.

Sal is seen scaling the cliff from a number of angles, choosing her hand- and footholds with care. At one point her boot slips, sending a shower of pebbles cartwheeling to the ground. She manages to keep her grip and regains her footing. When she reaches the crag which houses the large nest, she twists her upper body to face the camera. In her hand is a round egg, iridescent in the late-afternoon sunlight.

SAL

They're beautiful! I can't wait to show you up close. But first, I better stow them properly and climb down.

Sal gingerly places each egg into the creel. After zipping it shut, she descends the cliffside cautiously, taking care not to harm the eggs. With her feet back on solid ground, she unslings the basket and approaches the camera.

SAL

I guarantee, this is unlike any egg you've ever seen before. Check this out.

As she unzips the creel, Sal cries out with alarm. Embedded in the basket is a thin, feathered dart, still quivering. Sal's eyes widen, and she looks straight at the camera.

SAL

Ni'aruti! Run!

Sal tears across the clearing into the jungle. From somewhere off-camera, there rises a piercing cry of rage. As Sal weaves among the trees and vines, more angry shouts follow. She dives behind a large jungle tree and crouches there, catching her breath and grinning sheepishly.

SAL

(panting) I'm not sure I'm cut out for this anymore, Mei-Li. Your godson's been keeping me up all hours of the night! Do you think we lost them?

MEI-LI

(off-camera) No way. I think there was only one back at the nest, but he raised an alarm for the others. The sooner we find the *Eats Queen*, the better.

More shrill cries erupt, much closer than before.

> **SAL**
> Ready or not, here we go!

Sal leaps up from her position of safety behind the tree. She raises a wrist-comm to her lips and shouts into it.

> **SAL**
> Get the ship ready and make sure the boarding ramp is down.
> We've got company!

> **MALE VOICE**
> (*over wrist-comm*) Copy that, ma'am. I'd wish you good luck, but you already seem to have an endless supply.

> **SAL**
> Everybody runs out sooner or later, Ryder. Let's hope this isn't my day!

Sal's head jerks suddenly. She raises a hand to her ear and curses under her breath.

> **MEI-LI**
> (*off-camera*) You alright?

> **SAL**
> Fine, I think. The fletching from one of those darts grazed my ear.
> Seems my luck's holding out after all!

The camera turns, revealing a sweat-streaked Mei-Li. Behind her, visible through the patchwork of jungle trees, are the shadowy forms of the pursuing Ni'aruti. More unintelligible shouting ensues.

> **MEI-LI**
> They're catching up, Sal!

SAL
It's okay! I see the *Eats Queen!*

The camera faces Sal again. Ahead of her, splotches of bright sunlight are visible through the trees, marking a clearing among the dense jungle. The whine of engines overlays Mei-Li's gasps and the Ni'aruti war cries.

Sal bursts through the last of the trees into the clearing. Forty meters away stands the sleek form of the *Eats Queen*. Two armed women stand at the bottom of the ramp, sidearms in the combat position.

SAL
What are you waiting for? Shoot, dammit!

The guards open fire. Agonized shrieks are heard off-camera. Sal reaches the ramp and disappears into the belly of the *Eats Queen*.

The camera changes point of view, showing a close-up of Sal. She is lying on her side, propped onto an elbow. A trickle of blood runs down her nicked ear and along her jawline.

SAL
(grinning self-assuredly) Never a dull moment on *Galactic Eats*.
Although I'm worried our *vivi-fa'ool* eggs might've gotten
scrambled during all the excitement. Let's take a look.

The scene changes. Sal is in a well-lit kitchen, standing on the opposite side of an island counter. Her hair is still matted with sweat, face and arms marred by scrapes and dirt. On the island in front of her sit her fedora and the unopened basket.

SAL
And now, the moment of truth. Did our eggs remain in one piece?
Or will we be eating an omelet tonight instead of crème brûlée?

Sal unzips the basket and lifts the lid. She beams at the camera.

SAL
Luck is on our side once more! Not only did we find the *vivi-fa'ool,*

harvest its eggs, and outrun a bloodthirsty mob of Ni'aruti savages, but we also managed to make it back here with both eggs intact.

Sal lifts the eggs, one in each hand, from the basket. She extends them toward the camera. A close-up reveals two glossy spheres, each perfectly round. Their pink hue is streaked and swirled throughout with pastel shades of shimmering blues, greens, and violets.

SAL

The struggle makes the prize even sweeter in the end. Especially when you add the amount of sugar we're about to.

From somewhere in the ship, a baby begins to cry. The noise draws Sal's attention momentarily away from the camera.

SAL

But that sound means Baby Marq needs to eat, and when he's hungry, the rest of the galaxy has to wait.

Sal returns the eggs to the basket and zips it shut.

SAL

I'll meet you back here in ten, and we'll whip up the silkiest, most decadent crème brûlée you've ever tasted. That's your Sal Cantore guarantee.

END OF REQUESTED TRANSCRIPT.
DATE OF ORIGINAL AIRING: APRIL 14, 2198 CE.

SUNSET CITY, TERRA

– 2247 CE –

HIGHLAND HILLS FUNERAL HOME

WHERE ARE YOU?

I'm sitting, alone, in the front row of folding chairs. Chairs made of a material whose production was banned sixty years ago. Yet somehow, good ol' plastic keeps hanging around. They say it'll outlive the universe, but *they* obviously haven't seen the state of the chairs in this place. Most of them seem unlikely to outlive this service.

The modest room housing them isn't faring much better. Wood paneling is peeling away from the drywall beneath. The burgundy carpeting is threadbare and stained—and in a place like this, Cosmos-only-knows stained by *what*. Even the mortician—or director, or embalmer, or whoever the hell he is—might be old enough to have a couple plastic parts in him too.

Like its daily guests of honor, Highland Hills Funeral Home is already in a state of decay.

At least the casket is closed. Open caskets give me the creeps. The framed photos of the deceased balanced on top are more than plenty for my tastes.

Where are you? Stupid sonofabitch, you better have one epic reason for missing this.

I glance down at the tel in my palm. Nothing. Not from Cay, anyway. Plenty of outgoing messages. Zilch in return. Not for the last twenty-two days.

I swipe the screen, sending myself to a different message strand. Nothing new here, either. Every message is blue. Mine.

The eleven unread messages I do have can wait until later. Seven are from my dad, three from my mom, and one's from Gram.

I sigh and slide the tel into my pants pocket. I need more friends. And better ones.

The gaunt funeral director creaks as he saunters to the front of the casket. His somber voice matches the occasion, as he says, "Thank you all for joining us this morning as we celebrate the life of Marq Santore."

Cantore, I mentally correct him. Didn't even have enough budget to pronounce the dead man's name properly.

The director drones forth into the reading of an obituary. "Born in 2198 ... Raised by so-and-so ... Lifelong restaurateur ..."

But I'm too irritated to listen.

First you send the funeral home my way to make all these preparations, then you don't even have the courtesy to show up?

Assuming that I overlooked him somehow, I glance subtly around the room.

Only a handful of people have shown up for the memorial service. Two dozen at most, based on my quick scan of the crowd. Behind me, I see the restaurant staff of Marq's Eats, here to pay respects to their dearly-departed executive chef and employer—and all of them wearing their work uniforms.

Across the aisle sits an older Asian lady, snappily dressed and resting her fingers on the forearm of a much younger blond woman. So far, she's the only one I've noticed with tears in her eyes.

A couple rows behind them, a diverse four-person entourage snags my attention. Sitting furthest from the aisle is a red-tinted Vandreek *castrata.* She's dressed in drab, threadbare robes, and her dull eyes are cast deferentially toward her feet. Beside her is a lithe, serpentine Lai'oshan. Could be male, could be female. I never can tell the difference with Lai'oshans. Next is a human female who looks to be around twenty-five—my own age—and whose hair is pulled back into a tight brown bun. Finally, closest to the center aisle, sits a tall, distinguished gentleman who must be well into his seventies.

I frown, and not only because I'm the lone Black dude in the room. Something about the gray-haired gentleman seems vaguely familiar. I'm positive I've seen him before, but for the life of me, I can't figure out where or why.

Perhaps if I knew, it would also explain why he's watching the funeral proceedings with a condescending smirk.

But that's a mystery for later. Right now, my sole concern is the mystery of Cay's absence.

Not much of a mystery, is it? Selfish prick's probably halfway across the galaxy, getting himself sacked from another job. Par for the freaking course.

I fume for the remainder of the brief service. By the time the funeral director invites the guests forward to pay their final respects, I've vowed to tell Cay off, once and for all.

Marq's sous chef—I can't remember her name, only that she's a brusque but hardworking sort—approaches the casket first. She places a hand on the polished pine and mutters, "I'll keep an eye on her for ya," before relinquishing her position to the next member of the restaurant staff.

The last of them is followed by the older gentleman. He approaches the casket without his associates, sneering as he stares down at the closed box and photographs.

"*Auf Wiedersehen,* Marq Cantore," he says, his accent heavily European. Which district exactly, I can't be certain. "And give my best to your mother. Enjoy cooking your second-rate slop together."

Of course he would know Marq's mother. *Everyone* knows Marq's mother.

Sal Cantore. The swashbuckling host of the renowned culinary program *Galactic Eats*, who rose from general popularity to interstellar stardom when she vanished during her search for the Trees of Eden.

But that was almost fifty years ago—and Sal presumed dead for forty-eight of them. What could this fellow stand to gain by casting such disrespect at her now? And at her own son's funeral?

I want to say something. To speak up in their defense. But I know I won't. I come from a family of way-too-nice pushover types. We're bottle-it-up people. Stew-about-it people. Let-the-rage-simmer-in-silence people.

Why stand up when backing down is so much easier? The Hatch family motto.

It's also why I know I won't tell Cay to screw off when I do eventually see him. If I haven't lit him up already during the eight years we've known each other, I'm not likely to start now.

Save it for his eulogy, Jerricho. At the rate he makes enemies, you won't have long to wait.

The gentleman turns from the casket. His eyes meet those of the older woman across the aisle. In exchange for his smug grin, he receives a glare of smoldering hatred.

Another mystery.

And another that will have to wait. A stolen glance at my wristwatch tells me my funeral fun is at its end. The studio only gave me the morning off—and felt they were quite gracious in doing so—which means I have less than an hour to change my clothes, race across town, and have my camera ready for action.

Time to say my piece, then leave.

As I stand to approach the casket, the graying man struts proudly toward the exit, where his entourage is already awaiting him.

Someone else is also waiting there. *Two* someones, in fact.

A pair of musclebound, lizard-skinned, dragon-fanged Hekkra. Their black eyes bore into me as they meet my gaze.

At first I assume they're the older gentleman's bodyguards. Maybe even hitmen. But when they don't flinch during the strange quartet's departure, I realize they must be here for the funeral itself.

What could a pair of Hekkra want with Marq Cantore? Especially a *dead* Marq Cantore?

Maybe they're not here for Marq ...

I don't care for the way they're eyeing me up. While I'm sure there are plenty of nice ones on their native planet Hekk, seeing them around here carries certain implications, and none of them pleasant. They gravitate toward employment in the field of intimidation, enforcers for the kinds of people you don't want on your bad side.

I'm not sure why they're here, but I have the sense they aren't invited guests. Especially since I'm the one who arranged this affair.

At least I know they didn't come for me. Hekkra are the sorts of beings who hunt down escaped fugitives or debtors on the lam, and the only thing more spotless than my criminal record is my credit score.

Still, I don't relish turning my back on them as I approach the casket. I lay my hands on the cold lid and let my gaze linger on the largest of the framed pictures. I didn't know Marq Cantore well. We had only met a handful of times before he passed. But he had been kind to me. He seemed like a humble man and a hard worker.

How far the apple can fall from the tree.

"Goodbye, Marq," I say softly, giving the cherub-faced man wearing the chef's whites a reverent grin. "And rest in peace."

I can't help thinking he deserved better. Certainly better than what Cay gave him.

"Sorry your son's such a jackass."

With that final, heartfelt remark, I turn and hurry, head down, along the center aisle, carefully avoiding any further eye contact with the Hekkra as I depart the funeral home.

COSMIC BACHELOR PRODUCTION SET

"WHERE YA BEEN, HATCH?"

Dirk Plath—whose name would be more fitting if the *R* were swapped with a *C*—is *Cosmic Bachelor's* Director of Photography. And he's glaring at me.

"We don't pay you to be late," he growls.

I'm a big guy, a former high-school linebacker with at least five inches on Dirk, yet he somehow feels much larger than me. Suddenly aware of my exposed forearms, I unroll my shirtsleeves to cover them. I wince as my camera, a handheld ARRI Titan-SXT, bangs against the still-tender tattoo I'm hiding.

Don't need to give my DP any extra ammo.

"Two minutes," I say in my defense. "And I was at a funeral."

"Any idea how much two minutes cost on a set like this?" Dirk retorts. "I should take it outta your pay."

Looking around, I see that half the cast and crew are either still preparing for the scene or missing entirely. But there would be no point mentioning it. Dirk's had it out for me since day one. Arguing with him can only make life on the set of this crappy show crappier than it already is.

I sigh and say, "Sorry. Won't happen again."

"Better not," Dirk replies. "Set your ARRI for the scene. Dim, warm light. Cozy mood. Romantic. Couple's gonna be slow dancing in front of the fireplace, whispering sweet nothings. That kinda crap."

I'm still messing with my camera's settings—ISO, fps, shutter angle—when the "couple" arrives on set. Harrold Greve, the human protagonist seeking interstellar love during this season of *Cosmic Bachelor*, can't stand Inkla qi Paqwa. Everybody here knows it. And Inkla, a fair-skinned Candorian and the hands-down fan favorite of the three finalist bachelorettes, might hate Harrold even more.

Still, they're professionals. The moment this particular episode's director—I've forgotten her name—calls "Action!", Harrold and Inkla are all gooey grins and googly eyes, gushing the kind of chemistry that can only be faked. Each the last being in the galaxy the other would go to bed with.

Or maybe that's exactly what's happening behind the scenes. You never know with these actor sorts.

The afternoon drags on, each minute an hour as Dirk barks his orders. I'm third camera, which means I'm assigned all the awkward angles used to provide contrast for the main shots. Camera above my head. Camera at my shins. And everything in between.

A tough assignment for someone with my condition.

It's taking its toll on me today. One moment, my fingers and forearms are seizing so tightly, I wonder if I'll crush the camera between them. The next, they're so weak, I fear I'll drop this high-tech piece of equipment worth four years' rent.

But I've had worse days. I'll push through, like I always do. Like I have no choice *but* to do.

My mind wanders as I shoot, until I'm only half aware of the stage and furniture and players on set. It's easy enough to go through the motions when all you do is follow orders. I'm a drone here. Nothing more. Program me and let me do my thing.

At first my daydreams are filled with a tan, freckled face, punctuated by golden eyes under a sea of feathery cocoa hair. Natania, a stunt double I met during my previous project, is undoubtedly the most exciting girl I've ever dated. Half human and half Luatian, she's also the most gorgeous. I'd hang on to her even if she were on fire—which, I remind myself, she often has been.

I resist the urge to check my tel for a message from her. Besides, it's been over a day since she last said anything. She's the type who lives in analog, not glued to a screen.

I'm annoyed when my musings drift away from Natania. Like a stray cat that won't leave you alone once you've fed it, Marq Cantore's funeral keeps finding its way into my head. While I wonder plenty about the mysterious characters who were present this morning, I speculate even more about the one who *wasn't*.

I still can't believe he didn't come.

Cay Cantore and I have always had a tumultuous relationship, though you'd never know it if you asked his opinion on the matter. We met at the age of seventeen, when the housing algorithms decided we would make bang-up roommates at Sol 3 University. S3U—as it's affectionately known—is one of only two universities remaining on Terra, each dedicated to humanity's major contributions in the galactic arena. There's a tiny one in Nairobi focused on zoology, and then there's S3U, the galactic center of higher education dedicated to the arts in all their various forms: painting, sculpture, cinema, theater, literature, music—even food and drink.

Who knew humans were the only beings that cared about such stuff? But they all care now! We've taken our gluttony for sensory pleasure interstellar. Now you can find a McDonald's across the street from a concert hall on any planet in the Galactic League.

I'm yanked back into my surroundings by Dirk Plath. He's stabbing a finger at me and hollering, "Two-shot MCU"—shorthand for a medium close-up of the subjects' heads and shoulders—"with the fireplace directly behind them. Get to it."

I vomit my protest before I even realize I'm thinking it. *"Another MCU?"*

Dirk's head snaps toward me. His eyes narrow, and he says, "Yeah. Another MCU. You got a problem with that?"

I look away and shrug. "It's just—well, we've already done about a thousand MCUs. It's getting monotonous. What about a pedestal"—rising shot from feet to face—"to show off their full fancy getups and great body chemistry."

Harrold Greve and Inkla qi Paqwi blush and exchange guilty glances.

Like an Oggrian bear protecting its territory, Dirk growls as he says, "Jerricho Hatch isn't paid for his opinions. He's paid to hold a camera and do as he's told. MCU. Behind Inkla's right shoulder. *Now.*"

I shut my mouth and do as directed. Through my camera lens, I detect a hesitancy in Harrold and Inkla's words and movements. Ever since my comment about their chemistry, they've seemed off. Guarded.

They're *definitely* spending time in each other's dressing rooms. Or *un*dressing rooms, in their case. Hate and love ... two sides of the same coin.

So it was for me and Cay. Within five minutes of meeting him, I had submitted an official request for a roommate swap. Cay was selfish, tactless, arrogant, manipulative—everything you could hope to find in a classic narcissist. I've always avoided direct confrontation, so it was a quiet, seething contempt I harbored against him.

When university housing informed me that Cay Cantore was my only option if I wanted to live on campus, I resigned myself to tolerating the situation until another opening presented itself. Then we would part ways. Since Cay was in culinary school and I in cinematography, I'd never have to think of him again.

Of course, that all changed the night of the—

"Hatch!"

Once again, I'm jolted to attention by a very loud, very angry Dirk Plath.

"If you're gonna keep your head in the clouds," he sneers, "then you can use those new wings of yours to fly outta here and find a different gig."

Embarrassed, I glance at my arm to make sure my shirt sleeve is still covering my new tattoo.

Too little, too late. Now that Dirk has seen it, he'll never let it go.

From this moment until forever, I'll be the boy with the monarch butterfly tattoo.

"Sorry," I sheepishly mumble. "Won't happen again."

As I raise my camera, I make a mental note to update my resume. Time to find work at a different studio.

OUTSIDE REALITYFEED STUDIOS

THE STUDIO'S BACK lot is nearly empty when I emerge, backpack over my shoulders, into the fresh air. The sun has sunk behind the city's skyward buildings, leaving the few remaining vehicles steeped in evening's shadow.

I don't own a transport drone—or even an old-fashioned automobile—but there is an AirTram stop half a block down the street. Every morning and afternoon, six days a week, I cram myself between burnt-out shimmerheads and wannabe actresses for my commute to and from RealityFeed Studios.

It's not that I'm strapped for cash. For all my complaining, the studio actually pays a halfway decent wage. It's just that I'm saving my cash for something real. Something that means way more than a few extra meters of apartment space or hovering to work in my own *scabb*.

My dream project. One I'd be proud of, even if no one else ever cared.

The rotating RealityFeed Studios sign grabs my attention as I cross the large lot. Looming above the outer wall, with neon-red lettering on a blinding white backpiece, the sign is gaudy and loud. An attention whore screaming "Look at me!" without offering anything of substance.

Just like the twaddle we make inside.

My whole life I wanted to be behind a camera, telling important stories. Sharing things that matter—or so that they *will* matter. With over a thousand planets inhabited by sentient species in our galactic community, you'd think there might be something more meaningful than this.

Reality rubbish. Made by assholes, for assholes.

I suppose that makes me an asshole too.

My fingers are so shaky from the long afternoon, I almost drop my tel when I pull it from my pocket. I make a mental note to ice them when I get home.

I sigh. Eighteen new messages, and every one of them from family. None from Natania *or* Cay.

Don't let it bother you, Jerricho. There could be a hundred good reasons why. But at the moment, I can't think of any.

After a day like this, I think a visit with Gram is in order. Cay isn't the only one with a grandmother who could cook the blues away. Even better than her food is Gram's straight-shooting, no-nonsense brand of wisdom. She's always able to talk me through a tough time.

I'll return her message once I'm seated on the tram. A good icing followed by even better soul food—that's the Jerricho Hatch recipe to make it through another night.

Though I wouldn't mind dessert too. Hopefully Natania replies soon.

The back lot's security lights, grafted into the iron gridwork overhead, turn on with a uniform *pop!* as I approach the guard shack. Inside is Hank. He's much more focused on the novel pinched between his fingers than on catching any potential intruders. His official title is "Studio Warden." Really, he's a parking attendant with a badge and a taser. An electrified fence runs around the entire property, and old Hank is the gatekeeper. Nobody enters or exits RealityFeed Studios without his clearance—not from the back, at least.

I stop at his window. Hank finishes his paragraph, then looks up from the book. His pudgy brown face and bushy white mustache remind me of a walrus.

"Evenin', Mr. Hatch," Hank greets me lazily. "Mr. Plath workin' ya late again?"

He already knows the answer.

Drumming my fingers against the windowsill, I reply, "Certainly wouldn't be here at this hour by choice."

I nod toward the array of bluish lasers that make up the security gate. They're powerful enough to incapacitate any vehicle that passes through them, so there's no telling what they would do to a person like me.

"Mind dropping the gate?" I ask.

Hank seems momentarily surprised by the request, as if he hasn't been working at this guard shack for the past twenty-two years.

"Oh! Right. Studio badge, please."

Hank holds out a hand, and I lay it in his open palm. As he runs my badge through the system, he says, "Sorry 'bout that. Little brain hiccup. I just remembered that someone came by this afternoon askin' about ya."

I stiffen, recalling the Hekkra eyeing me up at Marq's funeral.

"Didn't let him in, of course," Hank continues. "Studio policy."

"He say who he was?" I ask, glancing toward the gate and fence.

Hank returns my badge. "Nope. He was a little antsy about it. Said he'd be waitin' outside fer ya. But that was a couple hours ago. Around quittin' time—fer everyone else, anyway. I can't imagine he's still hangin' around."

Hank presses a yellow button on his security console, and the gate beams disappear. He picks up his book and says, "Anyway, you have a fine night, Mr. Hatch. I'll see ya in the mornin'."

I hope you do, I think nervously. Who could have such urgent business with me that they'd be waiting outside the studio?

"Night, Hank," I mumble, and proceed cautiously through the gate.

Outside the studio lot, Sunset City looks alive as ever. Autos zip along the streets, drones overhead. Lights on in every café and shop. Silhouettes in the apartment windows above them.

Two blocks down, I see my AirTram settling onto the street. If I don't hurry to catch it, it'll mean waiting a half hour for the next one to come along.

There's a lull in traffic. I'm about to take my first step into the street when someone behind me calls my name.

I freeze. My throat feels like I swallowed a *kukua* egg whole.

I look over my shoulder. No Hekkra. Makes sense, I suppose. Hekkra speak in low, guttural grunts and growls. Their throats aren't designed to make the same noises as humans.

Instead, I spot a short, wiry fellow speedwalking toward me. Panting, he extends his hand and says, "Orlan Card. Marq Cantore's attorney. I have something important to discuss with you."

I raise an inquisitive eyebrow and shake his hand. As happens more and more these days, I hold on a little *too* long. Like my many ex-girlfriends have told me, sometimes I have a hard time letting go.

"Important like what?" I ask, still wary.

Orlan Card nervously wrestles his hand from my involuntary grip. "If you'll come with me, I can explain," he replies. Without waiting for an answer, he turns and hurries off the direction he came. "I've got a booth at Jack's. Little diner just over this way, so I could watch for you."

Down the road, my AirTram home takes off.

With nothing better to do for the next thirty minutes, I hurry to catch up with the mysterious Orlan Card.

Looks like Gram will have to wait.

JACK'S CORNER KITCHEN

THE TINY DINER looks like something from my grandparents' era. In that respect, at least, it matches Orlan Card's wardrobe perfectly. Now that I'm able to see him in better lighting, I notice his suitcoat lapels and cuffs are mildly frayed. His tie, wrapped into a tidy knot below his Adam's apple, might have come straight from a coat hanger in his grandfather's closet.

In stark contrast to the clothing is Orlan Card himself. With the rosy cheeks and smooth skin of a baby, he can't be more than a couple months past university graduation.

"Want anything to eat?" Orlan asks, offering me a menu.

"No. Thanks," I answer.

He looks relieved. "That's good. Marq was my first client, so I'm a little broke right now. Had to borrow this suit from my grandad's closet!"

I was right on the money with that one.

"Not to be rude," I say, "but I've had a really long day. What did you need to talk about?"

"Right. That." Orlan slams a scuffed leather briefcase onto the table and opens it. Before I know it, there's a rectangular sheet of translucent glass below my face.

I recognize it. It's a DocSheet. I've seen them around the studio before, usually in the hands of reality stars or the higher-up execs—or lawyers, like Orlan. Each is a one-of-a-kind, secure device used to transfer important documents from one being to another.

"It's already coded for your retina, fingerprint, and voice," Orlan informs me.

No surprise there. The Galactic League stores identifying information of all sentient species in their databanks. Not everyone can access it, but lawyers and law enforcement can pull certain information for official purposes.

Once the DocSheet has run the appropriate scans, its screen unlocks, allowing me to view the document.

My jaw drops a quarter inch.

On top, in bold letters, are two words: *PROPERTY TITLE.*

"Marq left it all to you, Jerricho. His entire estate."

I shake my head and slide the DocSheet back across the table. "There must be some kind of mistake. Marq has a son. This should go to him."

"No mistake," the lawyer assures me. "Less than a week before he died, Marq insisted the ownership of everything, particularly his restaurant and the apartment above it, be switched from Cay over to you."

"But—*why?*"

Orlan shrugs. "He didn't say. But it was clear he was in his right mind when he made the change."

Naturally, Orlan's revelation drums up my concern for Cay's well-being. He's always had a way of getting himself into trouble. Of mouthing off to the wrong people.

Will I have another funeral to plan soon?

"What am I supposed to do with it?" I ask. I'm a touch dazed. Everything's been thrown at me so quickly.

"That's for you to decide, isn't it?" Orlan Card replies. "You could live in the apartment. You could rent it out. The business would be easy enough to sell, I suppose. Unless you'd like to try your luck as a restaurateur?"

The baby-faced lawyer closes his briefcase. He stands and claps me heartily on the upper arm. "Either way," he says, "congratulations to you! I'll leave you to the rest of your evening, then."

Orlan turns to leave, then whirls around to face me once more. "Oh! I almost forgot to tell you! A pair of Hekkra came by my office early this afternoon."

My mouth goes dry immediately.

"They didn't say why," he continues, "but I figured I should mention it. Anyway, I'm off! If you have any questions, please contact my office. My information is there in the document."

As the energetic fellow speedwalks to and out the diner door, I retrieve my tel from my pocket. Still no messages, but this time I'm more interested in sending one.

Where the hell are you? I ask Cay.

The moment the message is sent, I stand to leave. But not for my own apartment.

I'm done waiting around for Cay Cantore to show up. It's time to pay him a long overdue visit.

Hopefully before the Hekkra do.

SKYLINE VIEW SUITES

Apartment 921

SHIT. SHITSHITSHIT. Oh, shit.

There's a two-inch gap of darkness between the front door of Skyline View Suites, Number 921, and its frame. Splintered bits of wood dust the carpeting beneath.

I'm too late. The Hekkra—or whoever the Hekkra work for—have beaten me to Cay's apartment.

Before I can think better of it, I shove the door open and step into the entryway. Why Cay pays good money for an upscale apartment on Terra is beyond my economic grasp. After all, he spends most of his time off-planet these days. The last time I asked him about it, he simply responded that he needed a sanctuary to come home to whenever he got fired. Which is often.

Now his "sanctuary" is in shambles. In the kitchen, every drawer has been wrenched from its track, silverware and utensils dumped crudely onto the floor. The living room is in better condition only because there was less to destroy here—the program monitor, in a thousand pieces on the hardwood floor, seemed to satisfy the intruders.

The intruders. What if they're still here?

This isn't a job for Jerricho Hatch. At once, I retreat into the hallway. Unsure what else to do, I use my tel to connect with the Sunset City Peacekeeping Department.

"My friend's apartment has been robbed," I say, once the bored operator has finished her greeting. "And he's missing. I'm at Skyline View Suites. Apartment 921."

The operator assures me someone will be here shortly.

I wait pressed up against the floral-patterned wallpaper outside Cay's door. Five minutes pass, then ten. Still no peacekeepers. Still no noise inside the apartment.

If anyone were inside, they would have run off by now. Right? Especially after they heard me tel the peacekeepers.

Summoning my meager courage, I push open the door and reenter Cay's apartment. This time I turn on the light, revealing the full extent of the carnage. As I meander through the one-bedroom unit, it strikes me how little sentiment Cay has. It's a strange realization at a time like this—after all, I've been in this apartment a hundred times. He has no pictures of his dad on the wall. No baubles or knickknacks from vacations with friends or family. Not a single poster of his famous grandmother's program, *Galactic Eats*.

Rounding the corner into the hallway, I feel a *crunch* beneath the sole of my canvas shoe.

It's a picture frame. Fallen, broken, and quite familiar.

I'd recognize it anywhere. After all, I gave it to him when we graduated. I spent hours picking out the right one—I cared more back then—only to hear Cay tell me he didn't think it would match the rest of his décor.

More conspicuous than the picture frame, however, is the photograph that went with it. The photo Gram took at our graduation from Sol 3 University.

A photo that's now missing.

"What the hell is going on here?" I whisper, kneeling to pick up the broken frame.

As if answering my question, a harsh voice from the exterior hallway yells, "SCPD! Whoever is in there, come out slowly and with your hands behind your head!"

SUNSET CITY HOUSING BLOCK 19
Apartment 12F

WHEN THE ELEVATOR opens to the twelfth floor of my housing block, I'm wrapping up a way-too-long video message: "I didn't have to deal with the peacekeepers very long. It was easy enough to prove I made contact, and they let me go. But this has been the craziest day of my entire life. Anyway, tel me back when you get my message. Miss you."

I stop outside my apartment door. Public housing is nothing glamorous—far from—but the rent is cheap and the city keeps it clean and maintained. Other than the occasional neighbor strung out on shimmer or blacked out in the hallway, life here is safe and quiet.

My front door's keycard is synced to my watch, so I raise my wrist to the reader. One blinking green light later, I'm pushing open the door and stepping into the dark entryway.

At once, goosebumps crawl up my skin.

I always turn on the living room lamp before I leave. *Always*. Did the bulb burn out? Or—

"Welcome home," a voice speaks in the darkness.

A flood of light fills the room. An intruder sits cross-legged on my sofa.

He has charming cobalt eyes. Immaculate, nut-brown hair, swooping like a wave breaking over his forehead. A cocksure grin turned up at the corners of his lips.

I'd know him anywhere.

"Cay!" I cry. Should I be relieved? Or angry? "How'd you get in here?"

"My keycard, silly," he says.

"I never gave you a keycard, Cay," I protest, dropping my backpack on the floor. "Although I do remember *losing* one last time you visited."

"Must've gotten mixed in with my things," he responds with his signature nonchalance. "Weird."

"Yeah. Or maybe not so much."

Cay Cantore rises from the couch. "Jerricho, Jerricho. Do you really want to spend this beautiful reunion splitting hairs about keycards? Or would you rather shut the door, lock it, and pile some heavy furniture against it so we can get right to the catching up?"

I slam the front door shut. No need to explain my urge to deadbolt it.

"Where the hell have you been?" I shout. "I've been trying to reach you for weeks. You made me plan your dad's funeral, then you didn't even show up for it. *And* there's a pair of Hekkra asking around about you!"

Cay raises his hands in a defensive posture. When he does, I notice he still hasn't undergone the surgery that would replace the missing middle finger of his right hand. He supposedly lost it in a crazy kitchen accident at culinary school.

Now I'm wondering who he pissed off that day.

"I may or may not have gotten into bed with some Malvudian businessmen," Cay admits, and without a trace of shame.

"Malvudians? You serious, Cay? They're loan sharks!"

"Jerricho Hatch! That's downright offensive. They can't help the way they look."

He's referring to the generally sharklike qualities all Malvudians share: bluish-gray skin, wide-set black eyes like eightballs, twin rows of serrated teeth.

"Besides," Cay continues, "they were quite accommodating when I approached them for the loan."

"How big a loan?" I ask, beginning at last to cool down.

"Only eight hundred thousand currents."

So much for cooling down. "Eight hundred thousand?" I yell. "What the hell did you need eight hundred thousand for, Cay?"

"I opened a restaurant. High-end cuisine for rich, slobbering Grinnuds. It was foolproof! Who could have foreseen the entire kitchen staff quitting on me within the first week?"

"It's 'cause nobody wants to work with you, Cay. That's why you've been fired from five restaurants in three years."

"Seven," Cay corrects me, "but who's counting? Anyway, now they want what I 'owe' them"—Cay puts air quotes around the word *owe*, like its strict definition is up for debate—"or else they say they'll collect it in blood. Such drama beings!"

"Why haven't you been answering your tel?" I ask, switching topics.

"I had to shut it off. Too easy to track."

"And why did that stop you from coming to the funeral?"

"Oh, come on, Jer," Cay responds. His tone suggests I've just asked the simplest question in the universe. "The Malvudians were already after me. I suspected they might have a friend or two waiting there in case I showed up."

Begrudgingly, I nod and say, "That is where I saw the Hekkra. I'm pretty sure they trashed your apartment, by the way."

"See? You should know by now that my instincts are always correct."

Of *course* that's the lesson Cay Cantore would take away from all this.

"It's why Marq changed his will, isn't it," I say matter-of-factly. "So I'd inherit everything instead of you. You put him up to it."

"Jerricho, you really are aging like a fine cheese," Cay replies. "Sharper every day!"

"The Malvudians could seize all his property if it went to you," I continue, fitting the pieces together as I go. "But they can't do that if it's legally mine."

Cay claps me heartily on the shoulder and, with a congratulatory smile, says, "Jerricho Hatch, restaurateur. Who'd a thunk it? Proud of you, buddy. I assume, then, that Orlan Card delivered the DocSheet right away?"

I nod, but before I can share any details of my meeting with the lawyer, an aggressive knock at the front door interrupts us. A series of angry, guttural grunts follows.

Cay's face betrays concern as he whispers, "Did the Hekkra know about the changes in the will? Anything that would lead them here?"

"I don't think so," I answer, panic rising in my chest. Then the realization hits me. "Our graduation photo. It was missing from its frame when they ransacked your place. They must have figured we were close. That you might come see me."

"How long you think that door's gonna hold?" Cay asks after another barrage of pounding.

"It's government housing. They reinforce the doors to withstand a beating. I don't think the Hekkra can get in."

"Good," says Cay. "Buys us time."

"Time to do what?"

"They're legal debt collectors, Jer," Cay explains, glancing frantically around my apartment, "and I'm technically a fugitive. All they have to do is man the door until the peacekeepers arrive. Then they'll be able to lay claim on me and haul me off for a visit with the Malvudians. We need to get outta here, and fast."

"No, *you* need to get outta here," I correct him. "They aren't after me."

"You sure about that?" Cay fires back. "What do you think they'll do once they figure out you're the new recipient of my father's estate? *And* my best friend?"

"I never said you were my best friend," I shoot back.

But Cay has a solid point. I can't deny it. The moment I opened Orlan Card's DocSheet, the legal transfer of Marq's property became public record. It won't take long for the Malvudians—and the Hekkra—to put two and two together.

"Like it or not, we're in this together, old pal," Cay whispers, readopting his confident grin. "Now, does your housing block have a trash chute in the common area, or does each individual apartment have one?"

"Individual. It's in the kitchen."

"Perfect." Cay points to my backpack beside the front door. "I assume the DocSheet's in there?"

"Yeah. What's the plan?"

Cay lifts my pack and cinches it around his shoulders. "We're going for a ride."

He hurries into my tiny kitchenette—a journey of about seven steps—and makes for the trash chute.

"You can't be serious," I protest. "You wanna take the chute? All the way down? It's twelve stories, Cay."

"I'm guessing the trash collects in the basement," he replies, "so technically thirteen."

"No, it's twelve. *Technically.*"

"Whatever. Point is, relative to the grand expanse of the universe, it's practically nothing."

"Yeah? And then what, Cay? They're already watching your apartment, and now they know where I live. Where do we go from here?"

Cay *tuts* his tongue at me. "Have you forgotten about your inheritance already? And thank you, by the way."

"For what?"

He holds up a flat disk. It's an access card, similar to those used here at Housing Block 19.

"For letting me have a key to the joint!" he cheerily exclaims.

The apartment above Marq's Eats. Of course. The one I just "inherited."

Cay opens the metal trash door. He peeks inside, then looks me up and down.

"I hope you fit in there," he says. "If not, give my warmest regards to the Hekkra. And remember, struggling will only make it worse."

With that heartfelt farewell, Cay climbs in, feet first, and slides into the darkness.

There's another vicious assault on my front door. It's obvious the Hekkra have run out of patience.

Cay's right. I'm in as much trouble as he is now. The Hekkra won't leave me alone just because they have no rightful claim on me. Once they're out of legal recourse, they won't blink before resorting to unlawful means for extracting what they want.

I have no alternative.

Down the chute I go.

MARQ CANTORE'S KITCHEN

THE OLD BATHROBE is a bit baggy, but at least it doesn't smell like soiled diapers, rancid meat, and overripe fruit. My own clothes are presently in the laundry, though I'm not convinced I'll ever wash out the stench I landed in at the end of my ride down the trash chute.

Things could be worse, I suppose. I could be in the Hekkra's claws, on a one-way trip to visit Cay's creditors.

Sitting safely at the square bistro table in Marq Cantore's kitchen, I massage my aching ankles as I listen to the din of the diner below. The garlicky aroma of savory food wafts through the shared ductwork into the upstairs apartment, and my angry stomach grumbles. I regret not taking Orlan Card up on his dinner offer.

"There she is!" shouts Cay. He's been rifling through Marq's cupboards, though I'm unsure what he's looking for.

"There's what?" I ask.

Cay responds by slamming a dusty bottle, half filled with dark liquor, on the tabletop. This is followed by the tinkling of two glass tumblers.

"*Oudang*," he answers. "This was my pop's most prized possession. Back when he ran a *real* restaurant, a Karthonian emissary gave him this to say thanks for his meal."

"What's so special about it?"

"This, my unrefined friend, is liquor."

"Yeah, I got that," I reply curtly.

"But not just any liquor!" Cay continues, flourishing his index finger like a melodramatic stage actor. "Oudang is fermented with the blooms of a lichen that only grows in one little cavern on the fourth moon of Idyos. Which makes it one of the rarest drinks in the galaxy."

Cay uncorks the bottle and pours a splash into each tumbler.

"Dad would drink half a finger once a year, on the anniversary of mother dearest running out on us. He said it was to remind himself how much beauty there is in our universe."

"Wow," I say. "That's ... kinda poetic, actually."

"It is, isn't it," says Cay with a wistful grin. "And now, we're going to finish the bottle."

"Technically, I think that's *my* bottle to finish," I remind him. But after the first glorious sip of fragrant liquor washes away every memory of the trash chute, I decide not to argue.

Cay downs the full contents of his glass. As he pours himself another, he says, "You know, Jer, that's the second time I've saved your life."

"Never mind that you're the one who keeps endangering it," I counter, glaring at him over the rim of my glass.

The first time Cay "saved my life" was when he rescued me from a dormitory fire. I was sleeping when the blaze started, oblivious to the smoke I was inhaling. By the time Cay found me, I was unresponsive. He hoisted me onto his shoulder and carried me to safety. After that, I was finally willing to overlook his many horrible qualities. The experience bonded us enough that we even became friends.

Of course, it wasn't until two months later that the investigation revealed Cay himself to be the cause of the fire. He had been experimenting in the common-area kitchen down the hallway. His "research" went awry, resulting in the quick-burning inferno. At first, Sol 3 University wanted to expel Cay for the damage he had caused, but in the end, he avoided punishment entirely.

His defense? "You can't be mad at a student for doing homework! Besides, it's not like I *killed* anybody."

And so, Cay Cantore was allowed to continue at S3U. He eventually graduated top of his class in the culinary college.

I, meanwhile, graduated well below the top of my class in film school. It's something I've always resented him for, considering I worked my ass off for four years, while he only opened his textbook if he'd written a girl's number in the margins.

"My professor told me I have my grandmother's extraordinary talent *and* her extraordinary arrogance," he said once during our third year at S3U. "I politely explained he was only half right."

Cay has always expressed a certain disdain for Sal Cantore's culinary abilities. "A short order cook with pluck and a personality," he'd say.

Now he sips the oudang, trilling it over his tongue and smacking his lips. Ever the culinary snob, he comments, "Floral, buttery smooth on the front. Spicy finish that leaves you begging for more. Speaking of, how *is* Josephina these days?"

I glower at him. He knows my younger sister has harbored a crush on him since the first time they met. I know Cay would never make a move on her, but that doesn't stop him from needling me.

"She's fine," I growl. "Working as an intern at an ad agency."

Cay raises an inquisitive eyebrow. "What kind of money does she make?"

"Not the kind you need."

"Pity. Then, it behooves me to ask: how's Gram?"

I freeze. Sip. "She's good. And don't even think about it."

Cay feigns offense. "Think about what?" he asks.

"You know what. Besides, she didn't win *that* much."

A few years back, Gram hit a big lottery drawing. Not the grand prize jackpot, but plenty to offer her the comfort and financial peace of mind a woman like her deserves.

"Why so defensive?" Cay says. He follows the question with a condoling grin. "Is it because she likes me better than you?"

"She only loves you for your food. If she knew the real you, she'd be backing the Hekkra."

"Speaking of which," says Cay, his face brightening with curiosity, "how *was* my dear old daddy's funeral?"

"Bleak. And poorly attended."

"Not surprising. The charisma gene skips a generation in my family."

"A bunch of the restaurant staff was there," I say. "Two women sitting together who I'd never seen before. There was an older man too. Gray hair, in his seventies maybe. Looked sorta familiar, but I couldn't figure out why. Anyway, it seemed like he might've known your dad—your grandma, for sure. Didn't exactly have nice things to say about either of them."

Cay's expression darkens. Rarely do I see this side of him, when his aloof immaturity and ego vanish, replaced by an authentic sort of dignity.

"Gustav Geiger," he mutters. "I'd bet anything. European accent?"

I nod once. I've heard the name, of course. Most beings have. He's arguably the most famous food personality in the galaxy.

"Son of a bisque," Cay growls. He swallows the last of his glass. "The *Food Fürst* himself."

Food Fürst. The "Food Prince." That was the name of Gustav Geiger's first galactic food program. To this day, it's the label he's best known by.

"Sal's biggest rival," Cay muses, cooling a bit. "Her only one, really. Even then, his ratings were light-years behind hers. If she hadn't disappeared, that caviar gargler would've ended up wringing out mops in a studio janitor closet. Her search for the Trees of Eden paid out well for old Gustav."

Before I can respond, I'm startled by an unexpected knock at the apartment door.

My first thought is: *Hekkra!* My second: *Where's the trash chute in this apartment?*

"Relax, Jerri," says Cay. "It's probably Trini from the restaurant. I put in a dinner order while you were showering."

My muscles don't relax. Not immediately. Only when Cay has looked through the peephole and unlocked the door can I finally take a breath.

"Hello again, Trini," greets Cay. "You look ravishing, as always."

A young woman enters, carrying a pair of to-go containers. She's Marq's sous chef. Her dark hair is pulled back into a sweaty bun, and an angry rouge fills her cheeks.

Trini dumps the containers into Cay's waiting arms.

"Warm evening in the kitchen?" he asks.

"And a busy one," Trini answers gruffly. "You need anything else? *Boss?*"

She apparently hasn't heard yet who Marq left the restaurant to, and Cay apparently hasn't corrected her false assumption.

He pops the lid off the top container. Like an actor in an air-freshener commercial, he takes a melodramatic whiff of its contents and says, "This smells almost as divine as you, Trini."

"Good," she barks. "Enjoy."

But before she can turn to leave, Cay winces and says, "Just one teensy weensy problem. I don't see the jalapeño aioli dipping sauce I requested."

Trini scowls. "I'll be right back with that."

"You're such a dear," says Cay. "Keep up the good work, and you may yet become a real chef someday!"

Trini slams the door behind her.

As Cay returns to the table, my tel chimes. I glance down at it.

Can u meet @ Harvest Moon b4 work tomorrow? 7:00?

Harvest Moon. The quaint coffee joint across the street from Natania's apartment. Little investment on her part. Much on mine.

"Booty call from Rishonne?" asks Cay, sliding the bottom container across the table.

I lift the lid, and a cloud of aromatic steam bathes my face. Cheeseburger and French fries, with all the fixins. Can't go wrong with a three-hundred-fifty-year-old classic.

"Rishonne was two girlfriends ago," I respond. "This is Natania. We've been dating for three months."

"Fixing to break the no-dump record, are you?" Cay takes two giant bites of his deep-fried Monte Cristo sandwich. "Mmm. That Trini sure knows her way around a cheese pull. I think I'm in love!"

I'm chewing my second bite of burger, ready to chase it with a fistful of fries, when there's another knock at the door.

"That'll be my dipping sauce," Cay says through a mouthful of sandwich.

He hurries to the door. Without checking the peephole, he throws it open.

"Uhhh, Jer?" Cay says with a sideways glance my direction. "Remind me to be nicer to Trini from now on."

Each carrying a sauce cup in its clawed hand, two Hekkra enter the apartment.

MARQ CANTORE'S LIVING ROOM

THICK, SCALY SKIN. Snub-snouted faces. Menacing fangs dripping saliva whenever they snarl at us. Now that I see them up close, I decide the Hekkra look like a cross between a tortoise and a *really* muscular bulldog.

As I stare up at them from the living room sofa, I'm fairly certain I'll die with their image imprinted on my retinas. They seem hungry, ready to pounce.

What does a Hekker eat? I wonder. If this is indeed the end, it's a strange last question to have.

The sweet intonation of melodic music surprises me. From the satchel slung at its side, the Hekker looming over Cay produces a vidcomm—like a tel, but larger and meant primarily for video communications. At the bottom of the dark monitor, a green button is flashing. When the Hekker touches it, the whimsical music stops, and the monitor pops with light.

Two Malvudians appear in it. They're sitting in high-backed chairs, onyx eyed and showing off their own toothy sneers.

The one on the left talks first. When he does, the vidcomm automatically translates his snappy, smacking words into Commonspeak.

"Clever boy, hiding from us as long as you did," he says. "But you should have known you couldn't hide forever."

Cay smirks. "Who said anything about *hiding?* Come now, Mr. Sawtooth. Surely you know me better than that."

"We know you plenty well," replies the aptly named Mr. Sawtooth. "Bloodgout here told me you would run."

"All the cowards do," Bloodgout adds with a disapproving shake of his hairless, rubbery head.

"Truly, I am offended," says Cay, appearing as hurt as possible. "You must have heard about my dear father's death here on Terra. I had to hurry home for his funeral."

"A funeral you didn't attend, according to our Hekkra associates," Bloodgout remarks.

Cay shrugs. "I ran into some travel difficulties."

"How convenient for you," says Sawtooth. "*And* for us. We've compounded interest on your payment each day we couldn't find you."

"That hardly seems fair," Cay replies.

Sawtooth slams his webbed flipper-fist-thing on the desk in front of him. "It's more than fair! If you want *fair,* I'll have the Hekkra rip you limb from limb while your friend watches."

"We gave you a loan, and we demand you make us whole," says Bloodgout. He's much calmer than his associate. "Either through full payment—with interest, of course—or through blood."

"I'm failing to see how murdering me helps your bank accounts," Cay argues.

Sawtooth chuckles. At least, I assume that's what his rapid jaw-snapping and guttural discharges amount to.

"You'd be surprised how valuable one mutilated corpse can be," he says. "You will buy us many prompt payments from future borrowers."

Cay flashes his cocky grin. "I'll get you your money, but my assets are tied up at the moment. It'll take me a while to liquidate them."

"We want double," says Bloodgout, cutting to the chase.

"*Double?*" Cay nearly chokes on the word. "You can't be serious."

"And we want it in one month," adds Sawtooth.

"Two months," Cay counters. "Two *Terran* months."

The Malvudians exchange a long look. Finally, Bloodgout says, "Two Terran months. But let's make it an even two million."

Cay must realize he won't broker a better bargain, so he says, "Deal. But only if you throw in an invitation to your daughter's wedding, Mr. Sawtooth."

"If you pay us the full two million, I'll even let you give the first toast."

"A decision you will not regret, sir."

"Remember," says Bloodgout, cutting into the pleasantries, "two million in two months. If full payment is even an hour late, you become our next motivational video."

"One way or another, I always knew I'd be famous," quips Cay.

The vidcomm goes dark, and the Hekker stuffs the device back into the satchel. It exchanges a look with its counterpart, as if it's disappointed the evening didn't end in at least *some* blood.

"Thank you for interrupting our meal," Cay says, daring to rise from the sofa. "If you don't mind, we'll get back to it before our food ices over."

With no further business—not for another two months, anyway—the Hekkra turn and exit the apartment.

MARQ CANTORE'S KITCHEN

61 Days to Payment

MINDFUL TO BRING his dipping sauce with him, Cay reseats himself at the dinette. Seemingly unfazed by our encounter with the Hekkra and their Malvudian bosses, he resumes where he left off with the Monte Cristo sandwich.

I rejoin him, but the idea of food repulses me at the moment. The few bites I took before the Hekkra's arrival are threatening to resurface. I slide the takeout container away in disgust.

"Not hungry?" Cay asks, as casually as if we just returned to our dorm room after a day of classes.

I ignore his question to ask one of my own. "How much money do you have in your bank account?"

"Jerricho," he says, casting me a stern glare, "that is a *very* personal question."

"You just signed up for *two million currents*," I retort, stressing each of the last three words. "How much ya got in the damn bank, Cay?"

"Minus the debt on my credit accounts? Negative eighteen thousand, give or take."

I bury my face in my hands and groan. How could he be so irresponsible? And how did I let him drag me into this fiasco?

Cay reaches across the table to squeeze my shoulder. "Fear not, sweet Jerricho. I've always been the master of the narrow escape."

From somewhere in the living room, a mechanized female voice speaks to us. "Now playing *Galactic Eats*, episode three hundred forty-four, 'Narrow Egg-scape.'"

As Cay continues devouring his meal—His way of enjoying food means demolishing it—I hear Sal Cantore's familiar voice. Cay must have inadvertently triggered the wall-mounted program monitor when he spoke the words *narrow escape*. Behind me, a *Galactic Eats* episode with a similar-sounding name has begun to play.

At least the background noise masks Cay's smacking lips and the weird purring sound he makes whenever he eats.

"*Welcome to Kili'a'an,*" greets fifty-years-ago Sal. "*Home to thick jungles, roaring waterfalls, winding canyons, and abundant life—most notably, the indigenous Na'umata peoples.*"

Ignoring the program, Cay engulfs the last of the Monte Cristo and declares, "You know, I think I'm in the mood for dessert."

He pokes at his tel, then holds it to his ear. Moments later, he says, "Would you mind sending Trini upstairs with two slices of your finest cheesecake? And no side of Hekkra this time. Please and thank you."

"I'm not hungry," I remind him.

"I know. Both pieces are for me."

"*These primitive beings, once unified, now exist in hundreds of smaller tribes around Kili'a'an,*" video Sal goes on. "*Though each retains the basic catlike features common to all the Na'umata, different tribes in different regions have, over time, developed unique physiological traits, as well as their own technologies and customs.*"

"You know," Cay says, glancing up at the monitor behind me, "this was the last episode Sal filmed before she went looking for the Trees of Eden."

"Yeah?" I reply, too tired to feign interest.

"Legend says their fruit is the most captivating food in the entire galaxy," he adds, shoving a handful of aioli-slathered chips into his mouth.

"*The scattered tribes are generally peaceable with each other, but they're a backward and superstitious species, who view all outsiders as a threat.*"

Staring at his grandmother with a mixture of adoration and pity, Cay says, "Sal had an incredible on-screen presence. That's why people didn't realize she was such a mediocre chef. And why Gustav Geiger resented her so much. He's twice the genius she was—maybe more—but he couldn't sell himself quite like she could. Not even close."

"*We will be landing,*" Sal informs us, "*in an area known as the Kalumma—the 'Needles,' in Commonspeak—in the mountainous rainforest region of Aruti, where the tribes of the Ni'aruti live. As does our quarry for this episode, a birdlike creature known by the locals as vivi-fa'ool.*"

"Is that why Geiger came to your dad's funeral? Petty spite?" I ask.

"A little, maybe." Cay savors a sip of oudang thoughtfully. "But I think he also saw Dad as a threat. The culinary gene only seems to improve with each generation in my family. In the kitchen, at least, Dad was light-years better than Sal. Unfortunately, he was a terrible businessman."

"The famed silver bird is intensely territorial, with razor-like talons that could make mincemeat of an overdone beef shank."

"How so?" I ask. "Seems like he did alright for himself."

"He kept getting into bed with all the wrong people, and I'm not just talking about my mom. People knew how to take advantage of him. He was too nice. Naïve. A pushover. His business partners took what they wanted from him, then figured out a way to screw him. It didn't take him long to lose the fortune Sal left him."

"Is that why he ended up settling for a smaller restaurant?" I ask, intrigued again. Cay never said much about Marq when we were at S3U.

He scoffs at my question. Gesturing about the apartment, he says, "A little diner for a little dreamer."

"At least he had a steady job," I say, more to offend Cay than to defend Marq. "And a restaurant staff who thought enough of him to show up at his funeral."

Cay's eyes flick toward mine. For once, he seems at a loss for a snappy retort.

We sip oudang and listen to Sal.

"The vivi-fa'ool builds its nests among the Needles' cliffs. But we aren't after the bird itself—not today, at least. We're on the hunt for its fabled eggs, which each female lays only once every three years. Vivi-fa'ool eggs possess one of the richest flavors in the entire known galaxy. We could use them to elevate a hundred different dishes or desserts, from carbonara to custard. In this particular episode of Galactic Eats, *I'll walk you through all the steps necessary to turn one of these worth-dying-over eggs into a to-die-for crème brûlée."*

"See what I mean?" Cay shakes his head with disappointment. "Master of the screen. Mediocre in the kitchen."

"I happen to love crème brûlée."

"Sure, who doesn't? But making a crème brûlée with eggs as rare as those? She's wasting half of her main ingredient! A proper crème brûlée only uses the yolk."

"And I suppose you could do it better?"

In that instant, such a gleam of realization awakens in Cay's eyes, I'm sure he's about to jump up and shout "Eureka!"

He doesn't. Not quite. But he does stand and cry out, "That's it! Jerricho Hatch, you're a genius. I know *exactly* how to scrape together the money I need."

I groan. It isn't difficult to deduce what's coming.

"I'll revisit some of ol' Granny Sal's most famous episodes, spaceship and all," he announces. "A brand-new show for a brand-new generation. But this time, I'm gonna get the food *right.*"

"And where the hell is this spaceship coming from, Cay?" I contend.

"The ship is the easy part," he replies.

He's staring at me with a hungry look in his eyes.

Now I know how his sandwich felt. I'm afraid to hear whatever's coming next.

"Finding someone to film it for me, *that's* the real stumper," Cay continues. "If only I knew a guy ..."

I shove my chair away from the table, shaking my head decisively. "Oooh, no. No no no no no. *No.* Not happening, Cay. Not in a million light-years."

"Come on, Jer!" he goads. "Think about it. You'd be the one calling the shots. Literally! And I've told you again and again how we should spend more time together."

"You've never said that."

"And Cosmos knows you could use a dab of adventure in your life."

"That's just insulting."

"Besides, you heard those Malvudians. If I don't come up with that money, I'm dead. It would be like you're helping them kill me."

"That's ridiculous."

"Don't kill me, Jerricho," he moans, covering his face as he fake-cries. "You don't want my blood on your hands. Think of what your sister would say! She'd disown you forever. At least until the Hekkra came for you next."

I hate that Cay can't take *no* for an answer. Never has.

I hate even more that his theatrical guilt trip is working on me.

"Even if you somehow got your hands on a ship," I protest, "neither of us has a clue about interstellar travel."

"There must be a billion video tutorials on Do-It-Yourself-Tube," Cay replies, waving off my objections. "Besides, how hard can it be? The navigation computer probably does ninety-eight percent of the work."

"Yeah? If it's so easy, how come Sal never came back from Eden?"

"Maybe the trees really are that gosh-darn captivating," Cay rebuts.

"And how are you gonna fund this enterprise with your negative eighteen thousand in the bank? There isn't a lender in this galaxy who'd give you a single *pip*—not with those Malvudians holding your debt over your head."

Cay grins. "Cullan Jonas."

"Who the hell is Cullan Jonas?"

"He's the chief exec over at Food Feed Studio. It's a division of Third Planet Entertainment. He's the one responsible for turning Sal Cantore into a galactic name. Maybe Jonas would be interested in backing her equally photogenic, much-more-culinarily-evolved offspring in a wildly successful reboot."

All those adverbs and adjectives are making my head spin. I try to formulate my next counterpoint but find myself coming up blank.

"Look," says Cay, "I don't need an answer tonight. Take a day. Think about it. I'll make some calls in the morning, see if Jonas is even interested."

A knock at the door, the third one tonight, saves me from a response.

Cay hurries to open it. Trini steps inside with two plates of cheesecake.

"They're both for me, thanks," says Cay. He dumps the cheesecake wedge from one plate onto the other, then hands the dirty dish to Trini.

"That all for tonight?" she asks, arms crossed.

"Almost," Cay replies. "I do have one question: why'd you rat us out to the Hekkra?"

"Because you're an arrogant ass-wipe," Trini replies in no uncertain terms. She looks like she's considering taking a swing at him. "You've always been an ass-wipe, right from the first day I met you in culinary school."

Cheesecake and straightforward condemnation delivered, Trini storms out the door. She takes special care to slam it shut behind her.

Cay stares a moment at the closed door, then looks over at me.

"I went to school with her?"

HARVEST MOON COFFEE

60 Days to Payment

MY LEFT LEG BOUNCES nervously beneath the stained hardwood tabletop. Warming my hands is a mug of the rainforest's finest. Black, of course. I don't know much about Cay's culinary world, but it's no mystery that quality coffee requires no additions. Across from me sits a frothy latte. Soon, it'll have the honor of meeting Natania's perfect lips.

I glance at my watch. 7:05. Fashionably late, as usual.

Yawning, I lean forward and rub my temples. Traces of last night's oudang are still coursing through my bloodstream. Cay wouldn't let me go to bed before finishing the bottle, and, after the scare with our uninvited guests, I was more than happy to oblige.

He was still asleep when I left. Typical Cay. Even on the morning of life-altering business, he snores on without a care.

How could I possibly consider working with him? He's condescending, aloof, and an undiagnosed sociopath. Everyone else who's worked with him the past few years has fled cursing into the furthest arms of the galaxy.

So ... why am I intrigued?

"Hey, Jerricho."

I glance up as Natania slides into the seat across from me. When I see her, any thought of accepting Cay's offer evaporates.

Natania smiles, but only with her lips. Not her eyes. Slightly larger than those of an unmixed human, her half-Luatian eyes are gaping windows into her soul. And her true emotions.

Something's up. But if there's anything I do better than camerawork, it's denial.

Reaching across the table to squeeze her hand, I say, "Morning. You always look this good at seven a.m.?"

"I get up at five to work out." Natania looks me up and down, appraising my hungover-ness, and asks, "What happened to you?"

"Late night with Cay," I answer.

"Oh? He's finally back on Terra?"

"Yeah. And brought trouble with him. I got to meet a couple Hekkra last night."

"Glad you're alright," she says, pulling her hand away from mine to take a sip of coffee. When she's done, both hands remain clasped firmly around the mug.

"He also offered me a job," I tell her. "Wants to fly around the galaxy remaking some of his grandma's old *Galactic Eats* episodes."

"And?" There's something unsettlingly hopeful in her tone.

But the walls of my denial are as thick as they are high.

"I'm not gonna take it," I answer. "I can't be away from my job that long. Or from you."

Her next words pour off her tongue like water breaching a dam.

"I want to break up."

My jaw drops. Part of me saw this coming. Still, I'm left speechless.

"I'm sorry," she continues, scrambling for some explanation. "There's just ... no magic left in this relationship."

"Is there anything I can do to bring the magic back?" I ask, perhaps with a bit more pleading in my voice than intended.

Natania shakes her head. "You're a wonderful boyfriend and a super sweet guy, but—Well, maybe that's part of the problem. For Cosmos' sake, you have a *butterfly tattoo,* Jerricho!"

She removes a pair of paper currents from her pocket and sets them on the table. "That's for the coffee."

I feel number than an anesthetized ice cube as I stand and mumble, "I should really be getting to the studio."

Natania grabs my hand and squeezes it. I stare down at her, wondering if she might be experiencing a sudden change of heart.

"You should go with your friend," she says. "It might be good for you to leave Terra. To have an adventure."

"Yeah. Maybe. Thanks for the advice. See ya around."

My hand slips free from hers. With a freshly broken heart, I stumble out into the budding daylight.

COSMIC BACHELOR PRODUCTION SET

"HEY! DIPSHIT! What part of *close-up* don't you understand?"

Jolted from the quagmire of my Natania-heavy ruminations, I glance up into Dirk Plath's scowl.

"Yeah, I'm talking to *you*, Hatch," he continues. "Don't know where the hell you are, but the rest of the crew is working here on Terra."

"Sorry," I mutter. "Had a rough night. And morning."

"I don't give half a shit what problems you've got outside this studio," he says. "Especially if they're making you *my* problem *inside* this studio. Get your shit together, or get the hell out."

"How 'bout *you* get the hell outta my face!" I fire back.

Dirk takes a step back. His eyes are wide with a mixture of surprise and anger.

So are mine. Apart from my own family, I've never spoken so boldly. Certainly not to a superior.

Yesterday's harrowing encounter, followed by this morning's heart-break, has left me riddled with stress fractures. I didn't know where my breaking point was, but Dirk's attitude apparently catapulted me straight past it.

And it feels ... *good*. Without a care for the consequences, I thrust my camera at him and say, "I'm done with you and your shitty show. I quit."

Without another word, I storm off the shocked set and into the hallway. Once in the locker room, I turn on my tel and press the icon bearing Cay's face.

He answers immediately. Like he knew.

"You in, or what?"

I don't wait to give him my answer.

"I'm in."

"Good," Cay says. "Go home and put together a reel of your best camerawork. Meet me in the lobby of Third Planet Entertainment at three o'clock sharp. Bring the DocSheet with the deed to my dad's place."

"Why so late?"

"Jonas will be well into his afternoon drinking by then. If we're gonna convince him to make a bad decision, we'll want him good and drunk first."

CULLAN JONAS'S OFFICE

"YOU OBVIOUSLY KNOW what you're doing behind a camera, but shooting a program requires multiple cameras from different angles. Maybe if you were a Squimmo you could pull it off, but you've only got *two* hands."

Cullan Jonas turns off his datapad. He takes a long sip from the highball glass welded to his hand. The ice inside clinks and cracks, melting rapidly in its whiskey environment.

"We'll find the hands we need," Cay assures the Food Feed exec. "Jer here could teach anyone how to use a camera."

It's a bluff, of course. Cay knows my teaching resume is shorter than a Hekker's temper.

Like Natania, Cullan Jonas is a mixed-race being. Once humanity discovered we weren't alone in the cosmos, it wasn't long before we started engaging in bedroom escapades with our new galactic associates. Like tigers and lions have enough common ancestry to produce hybrid offspring, humans learned—to someone's great surprise, I'm sure— that they could breed with certain races from beyond Terra. This all but confirmed the theory of panspermia, the idea that life spread long ago from star to star in our galaxy.

True or not, it's one possible explanation for the person presently holding our fate in his six-fingered hands. According to Cay, Cullan Jonas possesses all the ingenuity of a Rouzh and all the greedy ambition of a human.

Cay hopes he can leverage both traits to our advantage.

Jonas heaves himself up from his leather office chair. He approaches the wall of glass overlooking the city streets below and stares out, weighing our proposal against the potential risks. A black suit, crafted from some kind of shimmering fabric, hugs his seven-and-a-quarter-foot frame. With hair so brilliant white, it looks like it was slicked back by a bolt of lightning, Cullan Jonas is the very image of importance—even if he is a couple years past his prime.

After downing the remainder of his glass, ice and all, Jonas says, "It's an ingenious idea, of course. A Sal idea. But from a timing standpoint, it doesn't work. We're in the middle of a programming season right now. The studio budget's already set. Come back in a couple months. We'll talk then."

I hang my head, dejected—and maybe a tad relieved—at the dismissal.

But Cay isn't defeated so easily.

"I'm sorry, Mr. Jonas, but it's now or never," he says.

Jonas raises an electric eyebrow.

"These are the episodes I want to remake," Cay continues.

He hands Jonas a piece of paper. There's a short list scribbled on it. A list his head cameraman apparently wasn't privileged enough to look at first. Or approve.

"One of them is Sal's final episode—it's the one people will be most eager to see. But the egg-laying cycle of the vivi-fa'ool on Kili'a'an only occurs once every three years. I've done my research, and we're in the middle of that cycle *right now*. It only lasts another couple months. If we don't do this now, it'll be years before we can try again."

I'm unsure whether that's another bluff. If not, I'll color myself impressed by Cay's thoroughness.

Jonas's office door opens, and a PAD—Personal Assistance Drone—hovers through, carrying a silver tray laden with refreshments. The hexacopter drone deposits the tray on an empty corner of the oversized mahogany desk. Once its task is finished, its cylindrical, multi-appendanged body floats between me and Cay.

"Do you require anything further, Mr. Jonas?" the PAD inquires in its robotic voice.

Selecting the sweating whiskey glass between the two waters, Jonas replies, "Nothing now. You may leave."

Returning to our conversation, Jonas says, "The timing is unfortunate, but it doesn't change the facts. Not to mention, I don't have any footage of *your* screen presence, Mr. Cantore. Your friend's camerawork may be up to snuff, but you're asking me to take an awfully big risk on *your* ability to carry a show."

"All due respect to my grandmother," says Cay, taking a swig of water, "but I'm ten times the chef she was. Graduated top of my class at S3U. If there's anything I lack in screen presence—which I doubt—I'll make up for it in my chefsmanship. You won't be disappointed. And that's the Cay Cantore guarantee."

Jonas throws back his beefy head and laughs with such gusto, I wonder whether his ornate paintings might rattle off the walls.

"I like you, kid," he says, wiping his mouth. "Your swagger reminds me a lot of Sal herself."

"I've been told that before."

"But take a warning from me, will you?" the studio boss continues. "If you follow that ego too far, you might vanish from the galaxy too."

"So you're saying you'll buy our episodes?" Cay asks eagerly.

"Ho-ho!" laughs Jonas, now with less fervor as he collapses into his chair. "Not quite, Mr. Cantore. Not quite."

Cay frowns but doesn't speak.

"Here's my deal," the Rouzh-man says, leaning forward to adopt a powerful business pose. "You shoot five episodes, funded entirely by you. Return the finished product to me, and *if* I think those episodes might sell, I'll buy them. For five hundred thousand apiece. Two-point-five million total, if they're all useable."

Cay glances sideways at me, seeking my nonverbal opinion.

You don't have the money to fund this yourself, I reply telepathically. There could be no mistaking the look I'm giving him.

"Deal," he replies, to both my surprise and annoyance. "But only if you throw in a PAD to assist with the camerawork."

"A PAD?" says Jonas, unsure whether he might have misheard Cay in his buzzed state. "They're drones, not camerapeople."

"Have you ever tried programming one for camerawork?" Cay asks. "Like I said, Jer can teach anyone. Including a drone. It'll save us the time to find and train someone else. Whaddya say?"

Jonas must be a happy drunk. The entire room shakes once more with his laughter.

"Your spunk is inspiring," he says. "You really are Sal's grandson. I'll give you a PAD, but it'll have to be an older model. The studio's been looking to scrap a few anyway. Might as well let you use one."

Can't say I love the idea of training a defunct PAD unit, but it can't be worse than nothing ... right?

"By the time Jer's done with it, you'll be making it head camera-person on your next project," Cay assures him with a wink.

"Very well," says Jonas. "I'll have one wiped clean and sent over to your apartment."

"Better make that *Marq's* apartment," Cay responds. "A couple Hekkra trashed mine last night."

MONTROSE AVENUE

THE MOMENT WE exit the Third Planet Entertainment lobby, Cay breaks left down the sidewalk. He heads east along Montrose Avenue at a hurried pace, offering me zero explanation regarding our next destination.

"Where're we going, Cay?" I call after him.

Glancing over his shoulder, he shouts, "Keep up! We have to hurry, or it'll be closed."

"What'll be closed?"

He ignores my question. "Did you bring the documents I asked for? Dad's estate materials?"

Shifting my backpack from one shoulder to the other, I jog to catch up. "Yeah, I got 'em."

"Good," he says, approaching the intersection.

The crosswalk light changes, and I step into the street. Without warning, Cay grabs my arm and yanks me back onto the sidewalk. A split second later, an AirTaxiCab—an ATC—screams by in front of us.

"We also need *you*, if this is gonna work," he adds. "So no jumping out into traffic just yet."

OUTSIDE THE SUNSET CITY TRUST

"I CAN'T BELIEVE they didn't loan you more!" rages Cay.

We've just exited Sunset City Trust, one of the largest banks in the city. Evening shadows, cast early by the looming skyscrapers, envelop the busy streets as people flock home from work. The warm air is damper than usual for our high desert climate, and I feel instantly fatigued.

"Unbelievable," Cay continues. The weather couldn't be further from his mind as he raises a hand to hail an ATC. "You put up a whole restaurant and an upstairs apartment as collateral, and they barely gave you enough for a used *scabb!* Your credit must be utter crap."

"They loaned a lot more than if you would've cosigned," I grumble. "I'm sure your problems with the Malvudians haven't escaped the galactic banking radars."

Three cabs whiz by us, despite Cay's insistent arm-waving.

"Or the ATC depot's," I add.

"Yeah, well, let's hope the stellar dealership hasn't," says Cay. "Because we're gonna need something a lot bigger than a *scabb* to pull this off."

"So? What's the plan?"

He sucks in a deep breath and looks thoughtfully at the sky. Finally, he answers, "I'm thinking ribeyes and mashed potatoes with a side of bourbon. Maybe two. Properly mourn the loss of your true love Rishonne."

"Natania," I correct him. "And how'd you know? I didn't say anything."

Cay chuckles and slaps my back. "Please, Jer, it's written all over you. There are no secrets between best friends."

"I never said you were my best friend."

"Your denial is adorable," he says. "You don't quit your job to fly around the galaxy doing free labor for just *anybody*."

"Free labor? I thought I was getting half."

"Tomorrow's visit with Jonas will determine that," Cay responds.

"We're going back?"

"Only if we want to get our hands on a decent ship. Fortunately, I've still got one more card left up my sleeve. *Un*fortunately, it'll have to be when he's hungover. But if I play him right, I think I can pull this off."

At last, an ATC slows and eases itself onto the ground in front of us. The door swings open, and Cay jumps inside.

"Your place or mine?" he asks, flashing me the same cocky grin I see in my nightmares.

"Mine," I sigh, climbing into the cab. "Yours is trashed, remember?"

"Yes, that's right," mutters Cay, appearing deep in thought. Then, to the ATC operator, he says, "Skyline View Apartments, please."

"But that's *your* building," I protest.

"It sure is. Do you prefer vacuuming or sweeping?"

THIRD PLANET ENTERTAINMENT

59 Days to Payment

"WHAT THE HELL are they doing back here?" Cullan Jonas bellows at his assistant.

Jaque Spinder is a balding, middle-aged man. The only feature snootier than his bowtie is his upturned face, which has the look of someone who's been sucking on a lemon.

"I didn't want to let them in, sir," Jaque replies, fiddling with his glasses rim. "But *this* one"—He motions toward Cay—"insisted upon seeing you. Said it was urgent."

Jonas sighs. He waves a hand to dismiss Jaque, then narrows his bloodshot eyes at Cay. "I thought we concluded our business yesterday. I have a full morning of—"

"Relax," Cay interrupts. "It'll only take a couple minutes. I came back to give you something. Well, *sell* you something, to be accurate."

"What the hell else do *you* have that *I* would want? I'm not interested in joining the restaurant game, if an investor is what you're after."

"No restaurant," Cay assures him. He approaches the desk and takes a seat across from Jonas. "The Trees of Eden."

"The Trees of Eden?" Jonas echoes. He sits up a bit straighter.

"And Sal, if she's still alive," says Cay. "It'll be my fifth and final episode."

"Hmmmm," Jonas muses, a greedy smile creeping over his lips. He's surely aware of the cultlike following Sal still possesses. The centuries-old Amelia Earhart mystery finally became obsolete after the *Galactic Eats* host's disappearance.

Cay mirrors Jonas's hungry grin. "Everyone in the galaxy would tune in," he says.

"And what do you want in return?" Jonas asks. "What's your price?"

"If I'm successful, I want double. Five million currents."

Jonas gives him a long, probing stare, then bursts into booming laughter—which he cuts short when it reminds him how hungover he is. Extending a meaty palm, he says, "You've got yourself a deal, Mr. Cantore. My board's gonna shit a brick when I tell them, but if you pull this off, at least it'll be a solid gold one."

Cay grips Jonas's hand firmly and says, "One more teensy thing."

"And what's that?"

"Can I get our agreement in writing?"

"Why?" Jonas asks.

"Leverage. Don't worry, not leverage against you."

Jonas eyes Cay suspiciously, then shrugs and says, "I'll have our lawyers send the docs to your tel within the hour."

"You're a saint, sir."

"And here's an up-front bonus for you," Jonas continues. "Call it a bit of advice. If you're trying to find Sal, you'll want to hunt down her old producer first. Name's Mei-Li Tan. If there's anyone who can shove you in the right direction, it'll be her."

"Any idea where I can find this Mei-Li Tan?"

"Not on this planet, unfortunately. Last I heard, she was puttering around somewhere in the Sagittarius Arm. But I'll scrape up her contact data and send it to you."

"Mr. Jonas, you are a wonderful and kindhearted being."

"Of course I am. Now, get the hell outta my office. Next time you drop by without an appointment, I'll let my security team have some fun with you. In the room *without* cameras."

"Getting the hell out right away, sir," says Cay. "I eagerly await our next meeting. And your five million currents."

Behind his triangular slate desk, Jaque Pinder scowls as we sweep past him into the elevator.

Cay presses the button for the ground floor.

Now that we're finally alone, I hiss, "What the hell are you thinking, Cay? The Trees of Eden? Sal? You can't exactly cast someone to play her! Or build a set for that!"

"No set, Jer," Cay agrees. "And no cast. Just space. And planets. Lots of 'em, from what I'm told. One of those planets is called Eden, and it has trees on it. Maybe not fruit trees like the legends say, but trees all the same. Could be treehouse trees or Truffula trees or taco trees, for all I know. Wherever and whatever they are, though, we're going to find them. And they're going to make us famous."

We arrive at the ground floor, and the elevator opens to the lobby. We haven't gone far across the sunshine-flooded atrium when a gray-haired man approaches us. He's tall and thin, dressed from toe to torso in black, and emits an aura of self-importance. I recognize him instantly as the irreverent gentleman from Marq Cantore's funeral.

Behind him, her arms stacked with files and paperwork, is the young woman I saw with him at the memorial service. She's about ready to tip over under the weight of everything she's carrying.

The man in black stops in front of us. With a derisive smirk, he says, "You must be Cay Cantore. You bear quite the resemblance to your late father."

Cay's response is thick with faux geniality. "And *you* must be Gustav Geiger, the esteemed Food Fürst. Translates to Food *Prince*, if I'm not mistaken? Catchy! And very pompous!"

"When one comes from nobility, he wears his heritage with pride," Geiger says imperiously.

"I come from a failure of a father and a skank of a mother," Cay replies. "One is dead, and the other is probably OD-ing on shimmer as we speak. But I'm still a Cantore, so you can keep your title of *prince*, 'cause I'll always be *king*."

"I see you inherited Sal's tongue," Geiger replies. "Be careful that it doesn't get you into too much trouble."

"Only with the ladies," says Cay. "Speaking of which, I heard you showed up with three of them at my dad's memorial."

"Yes. I had little respect for Marq, but apparently more than you did. Who doesn't show up to his own father's funeral?"

"I had certain things dissuading my attendance."

"Ah, yes," says Geiger, stroking the silver stubble on his chin. "The Hekkra. I do remember seeing them. From what I hear, you like to get in over your head. Just like your lovely grandmother."

"It's the best way to learn how to swim," Cay retorts.

"Let's pray you didn't also inherit Sal's sense of navigation. We wouldn't want another Cantore lost among the stars." Noting Cay's look of surprise, he says, "Yes, I heard about your deal with Jonas. He told me himself. Not too shabby for a novice."

"It just got not-too-shabby-er," Cay gloats. "But I'm sure someone as important as you will hear all about it upstairs."

Geiger leans in close to Cay. "The galaxy is far more dangerous than a blender. If you aren't careful, it will be more than a finger that goes missing."

"It was a food processor," Cay says. He raises a four-fingered fist, so that the scarred nub of his missing middle finger sticks up at Geiger. "And for the moment, I'd like you to imagine it's still there."

Gustav Geiger grins bemusedly, then turns to address the young woman flanking him. "You were in that class, weren't you?"

She nods briskly, timidly, without taking her loamy eyes off Cay.

"This is Ameliana, my granddaughter," says Geiger. He looks sideways at her with the expression of someone who's just spotted a fly in his drink. "Though I wouldn't expect you to remember her. She's quite forgettable, in my opinion, and a perennial disappointment. How she graduated second place to a maimed Cantore is downright unforgivable."

Ameliana's cheeks glow red. She lowers her face and clutches the stack of files tighter against her chest.

"You're very lucky to have such a sweet old grandpa," Cay tells her. "I bet you have an adorable nickname for him. Something like Pop-Pop or Babu. G-Tiger, maybe?"

The glimmer of a grin tugs at Ameliana's lips, and her cheeks burn even brighter.

If not for a timely interruption, the exchange of backhanded pleasantries might have gone on indefinitely.

"I apologize, sir," speaks a meek female voice behind me, "but you have an appointment waiting upstairs. Drummond Paetski is here for his interview."

Turning, I see the Vandreek *castrata* from Marq's funeral. The indentured servant—or *slave*, for all practical purposes—is easily identified by the two metal rings implanted into her flesh. One on each side of her neck, these silver circlets don't merely serve to brand a castrata. They're also paired to a controller, a remote device used to track them if one should run away. Or torture them, if one should disobey.

Humanity may have taken two steps forward when it joined the Galactic League, but this Vandreek castrata is a reminder that, in certain ways, we took just as many steps back.

"Tell him to be patient," Geiger orders sternly. "You may go."

The melancholy castrata does as her ruler tells her, because she has no other choice. Like a car or personal assistance drone, she is his legal property. And if she's anything like ninety-nine percent of the galaxy's castratae, she always will be.

"Well," says Geiger, returning his attention to Cay, "you heard her. I have an appointment to keep. Good luck with your little project. Say hello to Sal for me."

"I won't need to. Once I bring her back, you can say it yourself," Cay replies.

"I look forward to it," says Geiger. "If you'll excuse me."

With that, he sweeps toward the elevator, Ameliana trailing behind him with her mountain of paperwork.

She casts a fleeting glance backward at Cay and grins. Then she, too, enters the elevator.

Cay's gaze lingers after her, but only for a moment. When she disappears behind the closing elevator doors, he elbows me and says, "Come on. Time to find ourselves a ship."

AQUARIUS STELLAR DEALERSHIP

SLYCE COBB, OWNER AND SALES—that's what the placard on the reception desk says, anyway—runs his fingers through greasy shoulder-length hair, pushing it away from his eyes. He seems surprised to see customers walking through the front door of his stellar transport dealership.

"Good morning!" he greets us, jumping up from his chair and extending a hand. "Or is it afternoon? Anyway, welcome to Aquarius Stellar. I'm Slyce Cobb, here to find you the best vessel at the best value."

Cay beams his warm-syrup grin and gives Slyce's hand a hearty pump. "If that's true, then you and I are about to become best friends. I'm Cay, by the way."

A gang of houseflies buzzes against the window behind Slyce Cobb. My quick glance around the shabby room leaves me hesitant to shake his outstretched hand.

"And I'm Jerricho," I say.

"Well, Cay and Jerricho, how can I get you into the perfect ship this afternoon?" Slyce asks.

"We need something capable of interstellar travel," Cay explains, "where we can both live comfortably for long stretches of time, and which has a really, *really* nice kitchen. And, if possible, a sixteen-person hot tub that shoots lots and lots of bubbles."

Slyce raises a nervous eyebrow. "Well, I don't know about the hot tub—You might need to visit a luxury dealership for something like that—but if you can go without, I've got the perfect fit in the back lot."

Cay clucks his tongue. "Drat it all! I'd have to leave my Volcan thermalfish at home with a sitter, but I suppose we'll take a look anyway."

"In that case, follow me!" Slyce exclaims.

We exit through the back door into a spacious lot. Rippling with the heat of the year's warmest afternoon yet, the shipyard looks a lot more like a junkyard.

Masked by Slyce's cheery whistling, I whisper to Cay, "Look at these ships. I told you coming here was a dumb idea."

"Why? Just because this is the lowest-rated dealership in Sunset City?"

"Seemed like a pretty good clue to me, Cay. We'd be lucky if any one of these made it into orbit!"

"Did you even read the reviews? All the bad ones were either about the owner or about how filthy the place was. The people who actually bought ships here rated it pretty high. Mostly."

"We keep the good stuff in the back lot," Slyce calls over his shoulder.

That's just bad business sense, Slyce.

"Everything here is used," he continues. "Might look a bit rough on the outside, but I guarantee you everything's in working order. My cousins Ernie and Fineas do all my maintenance and refurb."

"Hear that, Cay?" I whisper. "His *cousins*. Come on, stop wasting our time."

"If your cousins are anything like you, Slyce," says Cay, for no reason other than to badger me, "I'd trust 'em with my house key."

"You shouldn't," Slyce replies. "They're criminals. But that doesn't mean they can't be damn good mechanics too. They could make even the most broken-down ship flightworthy again."

Slyce Cobb is true to his word. The further we proceed toward the back of the lot, the bigger and sleeker the ships become. Before long, he leads us up a ramp and into the belly of a cigar-shaped vessel with a quicksilver hull.

Inside, he raises his arms and spins a full circle, showing off what is, I must admit, an impressive interior. The ample windows running lengthwise along the ship's body allay any concerns of claustrophobia I have about traveling through space. Against one wall is a kitchen area, both eye-catching and tidy—by my standards, anyway. There's also a dining table with chairs and an entertainment corner, complete with program monitor and sofa.

I could live comfortably aboard a ship like this. Which means it's too good to be true.

"She's twenty-six meters long, eleven wide," Slyce informs us, summoning the numbers from memory. "Two small bedrooms and a washroom through that rear door, cockpit through the front. All the engine housing, electrical hubs, and X-space quantum drivers are hidden beneath the flooring, out of sight and out of mind."

"I have to hand it to you, Slyce," says Cay. "*Sexy* is the only word to describe this bird."

"Care to take her for a simulation flight?" Slyce asks, rubbing his hands together hopefully.

"Before I do, I have to ask how much she costs," Cay replies.

"I only require fifteen percent down," Slyce says, dodging a direct answer. "Most dealers ask twenty-five. After that, eight percent interest over the next twelve galactic years. That said, I've got this one listed at eight-point-eight million currents."

Yep. *Definitely* too good to be true.

Cay whistles through his teeth. "I can't imagine you'd take two?"

Slyce chuckles. "No, I can't imagine I would."

"What about two-point-four, and I throw in a date with Jer's sister?" Cay counters.

I shoot him a venomous glare and interject myself into the dealmaking. "We'll look at something a little closer to our price range, thanks."

"Okay," Slyce concedes, "but you'll have to rethink your wish list. *Kitchen* might need a downgrade to *scullery*."

"I can work with scullery," Cay responds enthusiastically.

We backtrack a depressingly long way toward the main office before Slyce leads us into another ship—one that looks like it was designed after my youngest brother's latest Lego creation.

The interior isn't any better. Its square living space isn't much larger than a boxing ring, with furniture and fixtures that look like they belong in a museum instead of outer space. And, except for the cockpit and a few plate-sized portholes along the hull, there are no real windows.

"You weren't kidding about that kitchen, were you!" says Cay, grimacing at the double-burner stovetop like he's stumbled upon a corpse. He opens the oven door and peers inside. "I'd have to fold a pizza in half to fit it in here. And this sink! I'd be better off with a watering can."

Further along the wall, Slyce opens a door to reveal a no-frills room about the size of my closet at home. Inside is a bunk bed and dresser.

"Toilet and shower are in here," Slyce says, opening another small door. "The toilet uses a vacuum flush, so for the bigger loads, you'll want to dump some water from the kitchen sink—which is where you wash your hands, by the way."

My nose crinkles. "What about the engine?" I ask.

"She'll get you where you need to go," Slyce answers. "There's a little mechanical closet in back for replacing and storing fuel rods, but most of the ship's moving parts and electrical equipment can only be accessed externally."

"And what's in there?" Cay asks, pointing to yet another door.

"That's the airlock, in case you need to dock with an orbital station or another vessel."

There's no way this ship could work for us, and I have a sneaking suspicion we won't find better clash for our currents elsewhere. Cay has no choice but to scrap the whole plan and devise a new way to pay the Malvudians.

But what's plain to me is rarely so obvious to Cay.

"Can we take a closer look at the cockpit?" he asks.

His satisfied expression concerns me.

"Absolutely," Slyce replies. He himself seems surprised Cay would want to see more.

Together with the ship's main cabin, the cockpit forms a single, contiguous room. Partial walls, only a couple meters long, protrude inward between the two areas, creating a dedicated space for the ship's controls. The narrow strip of cockpit is also sunken below the level of the main cabin, accessed in the middle by a pair of stairs.

It's down those stairs that Slyce now ushers us, saying, "Check out those humongous pilot chairs! Sit down, see how it feels!"

We do. I sink back into the plush fabric and look around the cockpit. This, at least, I could live with. On all sides, the ship's flawless wind-screen curves back toward the stern, creating a one-hundred-eighty-degree field of vision and giving me the sensation I'm sitting in a dry fishbowl. This cockpit is a surefire cure for any claustrophobia I might experience in the main cabin.

The control console in front of us is less inviting. An overwhelming array of buttons, gauges, instruments, joysticks, and monitors triggers a wave of anxiety—and we aren't even moving yet.

"What the *Tantalus* lacks in livability, it makes up for in avionic sophistication," Slyce informs us.

"The *Tantalus?*" I ask curiously.

"That's the ship's name," he clarifies. "The *Tantalus*. She's old, but her technology was ahead of the curve in her heyday."

"Do we have to stick with *Tantalus?*" asks Cay. "Or can we rename it something cool, like *Space Shark* or *Demon Star Eater?*"

Slyce shrugs. "You can name her whatever you want, but reprogramming for voice commands and automatic call signatures is a real bitch. It'd take a few days and a lot of money to do it right."

"Then the *Tantalus* it shall be!" Cay exclaims. "How much?"

"Two-point-five million."

"What about two even? And I keep Jer's sister on the table?"

Before Slyce can counter, I turn to him and say, "Would you mind if I had a few words with my associate? In private?"

"Sure. Take all the time you need. I'll wait in the back."

As soon as Slyce is out of earshot, I whisper, "What are you thinking, Cay? Do I need to point out the obvious? There's no damn kitchen on this thing! Kinda hard to shoot episodes for a *cooking* show with half an oven."

Calmly, Cay rests his hands on my shoulders. Looking me square in the eye, he says, "Jer, it's time you learned something about chasing dreams. If you dream of being a butterfly someday—Yeah, I saw the tattoo—you'll be a butterfly! And if this kitchen-less ship dreams of having a kitchen, someday, a kitchen-having ship is exactly what it'll be."

"Even if this rust bucket magically sprouted a kitchen overnight, how are we gonna pay for it?" I argue. "It's still too much!"

"We have enough for the fifteen percent down payment, and with twenty thousand to spare! That's right, I did math. In my head."

"Yeah, but Slyce is gonna make sure we've got assets and income to make payments. We have nothing to show him!"

"Oh, dearest Jerricho," Cay replies, holding up his tel, "that's where you're wrong. I have a contract with Jonas. He owes me five million currents in two months, remember?"

Snatching his tel, I begin scrolling through the document. It doesn't take long to find my rebuttal.

"Here!" I triumphantly whisper, still keeping my voice low enough to hide it from Slyce's ears. "The contract says you only get paid *if* we find the Trees of Eden and *if* Jonas wants the episodes. That's a lotta *ifs* he might notice, don't you think?"

Cay looks at the tel again. He frowns, but only momentarily, before his fingers start dancing upon the screen.

"You're right," he says. "There *are* a lot of *ifs*. But if this contract dreams of being *if*-less, it can be whatever it sets its iffy mind toward."

"That's fraud, Cay."

"It's only fraud if we don't pay up, which we will," he responds. After another few seconds doctoring the contract, he says, "Aaaaaaand ... done!"

Sidestepping me, he exits the cockpit and says, "We love it, Slyce. So, how about that two-million-current offer?"

"Two-point-four."

"Two-point-three. But that takes Jer's sister off the table, I'm afraid."

Slyce extends a hand. "I think I'll live. Two-point-three."

Cay grabs it and shakes. "You sure? You haven't seen his sister."

"Let's go back to my office and sort out the paperwork!" Slyce exclaims.

Forty minutes, sixty signatures, and a three-hundred-forty-five-thousand-current bank transfer later, our business is concluded. Since I'm the one who got the loan and made the down payment, I'm technically the new owner of an ancient ship.

As all three of us stand in unison, Slyce Cobb asks, "Anything else I can do for you today?"

"Just one. Do you make deliveries?" Cay asks.

"I'll deliver her myself at the end of the day," Slyce promises. "Where to?"

Cay snags a pen and business card from the reception desk. He hastily scribbles something on the back, then hands it to Slyce.

"She'll be there this evening," he promises.

With a flattering wink, Cay says, "I *knew* we'd be best friends by the end of the day."

Outside, immersed again in the brutal heat, I ask, "What now?"

"We have one more stop to make," Cay answers.

"You wanna tell me where?" My irritation is ready to boil over. I'm remembering why I call him a "small doses" sort of person.

"And ruin the surprise?" says Cay. "I wouldn't dream of it."

1300 PINEWOOD TRAIL

"OH, HELL NO." I've just opened my eyes—must have nodded off during the ATC ride from Aquarius Stellar Dealership—to see that we've stopped in front of a colonial, red-brick home in Kingspoint Estates.

I know exactly where we are. After all, I've been visiting this suburban neighborhood for the past sixteen years.

"Surprise!" Cay cries. "It's Gram's house!"

"What're we doing here, Cay?" I demand, rubbing my eyes. "You are *not* fleecing my grandma. No, Cay. This is where I put my foot down."

"Who said anything about fleecing?" Cay jerks his head toward the ATC driver. "Now, be a decent fellow and tip the man. You *did* just inherit an estate, after all."

Scowling, I drop a handful of currents into the driver's waiting hand, and we exit the cab into the cool evening air. From the landing pad, we march up the long walkway toward the two-story house.

Jolene Hatch, better known as "Gram" to her family, has enjoyed her lottery winnings. I'm glad for it, too. She's one of the best people I know. The money is small consolation for losing my grandfather so young, but it's a consolation nonetheless.

"You promise you're not here to beg for money?" I ask. For someone I call my best friend, I'm never unsuspicious of Cay's motives.

"Cross my heart," he assures me. "Can't a guy make dinner for his favorite septuagenarian without getting the third degree?"

"Fine. But I'm not leaving you alone with her, Cay. Not for a single minute."

We climb onto the front stoop, and Cay raps his knuckles against the espresso-stained oak door. When there isn't an immediate answer, he presses the glowing doorbell.

"Hold on to your panties, I'm coming!" calls an annoyed voice. "Give an old lady half a second, will you?"

The door opens a crack, and one of Gram's dark eyes peers out at Cay.

Beaming his cocky grin, Cay says, "I don't think anyone who looks as good as you should call herself an 'old lady' just yet. Not 'til you're eighty. At *least.*"

"Cay Cantore." She speaks his name fondly, then cackles with delight. "I always knew you'd show up for a booty call sooner or later."

"Uh, I'm here too, Gram," I say, stepping into her line of sight with an awkward wave. "Though I might need to excuse myself so I can puke in the bushes."

"Jerricho! My sweet baby boy!" Gram cries, flinging open the door and throwing her arms around my neck. "How come you haven't come by lately? And your parents say you haven't been returning their messages." She narrows her eyes, studying me. "I know what's going on. You're getting too obsessed with that Natania girl. I don't like it."

Cay doesn't stifle his laughter. "Neither did she, apparently. Broke up with him yesterday."

"Good," Gram replies. She steps back, looking me up and down like a museum curator examining a famous painting. "You can do much better than her, if you ask me."

"Sorry to drop by unannounced," Cay says, taking his turn to hug her, "but it wouldn't be a proper visit to Terra without stopping to cook Gram dinner."

"Then, by all means, come in!" she exclaims. Shuffling aside, she waves us past her into the front foyer. "I had an early dinner, but I see no harm in an early-evening snack. Especially one prepared by a Cantore."

"Keep up the flattery, and this might turn into a booty call after all."

Gram follows us through the darkened foyer into her well-lit kitchen. She's already wearing her baby-blue evening gown, the one she seems to don a little earlier every time I see her. At the base of her throat, hanging from a dainty gold chain, is a milky gemstone. It once belonged to my grandfather, Jephthah Hatch, until his tragic death. Now the ovoid jewel hangs around Gram's neck, such a constant presence it forms its own tan lines.

"Have I ever told you how beautiful your kitchen is?" says Cay, feasting his eyes on the hardwood cabinetry, granite countertops, and state-of-the-art appliances.

"Only one or two *dozen* times," Gram answers, taking a seat at the sturdy kitchen table.

"Like a woman, you can never compliment a kitchen too often," Cay remarks. "Now tell me, what do you have for me to work with tonight?"

Gram motions toward the pantry. "Use whatever you can find in there. But check the expiration date first, would you? Old birds like me don't tear through food like I used to."

A bolt of inspiration must strike Cay immediately, because he re-appears from the pantry seconds later. Piled in his arms are a pair of onions, a bulb of garlic, a wedge of wrapped cheese, and a partial bottle of some sort of red wine.

"Please tell me you have a carton of beef broth somewhere," he says.

"I've got beef broth, but it isn't in some *carton*," Gram replies, offended at the notion. "I do it the proper way and make it myself. Look in the freezer."

As Cay goes to work gathering the proper spices and utensils for— well, for whatever it is he's making—Gram asks, "So what's the real reason you're here? I know something more's going on. You didn't come just to make an old lady dinner."

Cay stops slicing the onion. He glances at me and says, "We're caught, Jer. No sense hiding it any longer."

I know exactly what comes next: the monetary request he promised he wouldn't make.

To my surprise, Cay says, "We came to tell you about our big break."

"Big break?" Gram echoes, shifting her gaze toward me. "What's he talking about?"

"We're gonna remake a few of Sal Cantore's old *Galactic Eats* epi-sodes," I explain. "Only five for now, but Cullan Jonas from Third Planet Entertainment is willing to pay well for them. *If* we finish the job and make it home alive."

Gram doesn't reply with the enthusiasm I expected. Squeezing my tingling fingers with her gnarled ones, she says, "Are you sure you're up for something like this, Jerricho? If you're remaking *Galactic Eats,* I assume it means leaving Terra and flying all around the galaxy."

I lower my eyes. I'm really *not* sure I'm up for it. Trouble is, I've already signed on the dotted line. Cay's counting on me. If I back out now, he might as well hand himself over to the Malvudians before he's finished slicing Gram's onions.

And I probably wouldn't be too far behind him.

"I—yeah, I think so," I stammer.

Gram casts me a glare of obvious doubt. I can't blame her. I couldn't even convince myself with that milquetoast response.

"What do your parents think?" she asks.

I sink even lower in my seat and mutter, "I haven't told them yet."

"And why not?"

"I wanted to tell them in person." It's a lie, of course. I haven't told them because I know exactly how they'll react. Since Gram is staring at me, waiting for more, I add, "I'll go home tomorrow, tell them then."

"Good," she says, and with a note of finality that lets me know she'll hold me to it.

Addressing both of us again, Gram asks, "What's the reason for this new venture of yours, if you don't mind me asking?"

"I took out a loan to start a restaurant," Cay casually answers. He drops a generous glob of butter into a hot pan. "Turns out it was a bad investment. Now a couple Malvudian loan sharks are getting nasty about repaying them. Where do you keep your cheese grater?"

"Below the countertop. Second drawer from the left."

Cay adds the onion ribbons to the pan, then goes in search of the grater.

"I assume you're borrowing a ship from someone?" says Gram, continuing her line of questioning.

"Bought one," I answer. "Though I'm not sure you can call it a proper *ship*. More like a flying hardware bucket."

"Oh, don't be such a pessimist," Cay calls over his shoulder. He unwraps the cheese wedge. "It may not be pretty, but my dear friend Slyce Cobb assures me it'll get us where we need to go."

"It doesn't even have a kitchen, Cay," I argue. "Remember that little detail?"

"You're filming a food show without a kitchen?" Gram asks. She doesn't try to hide her incredulity.

"That *is* one tiny problem," says Cay. He begins grating the pale cheese. "We'll figure something out, though. Always do!"

Gram throws back her head and laughs from her belly. "Cay Cantore, you sure know how to pull one over on an old woman, don't you? You come here, offer to make me dinner, slather more butter on me than those onions you've got cooking. Well, I'm onto your games, young man. I may be old, but I'm still sharp as an Andorsk hedgepig."

Cay casts her a sideways grin, then silently returns to grating cheese.

"How much do you need?" Gram asks. "To outfit your flying hardware bucket with a proper kitchen?"

Cay turns, cheese and grater in hand, to face her fully. "Fifty thousand ought to do the trick. Maybe sixty to make it real camera pretty."

"You promised, Cay," I object. "You told me you wouldn't ask her for money."

"Jerricho! Such an unfounded accusation!" he protests with a look of wide-eyed innocence. "I haven't asked Gram for anything at all!"

I open my mouth, ready to launch a tirade.

Gram raises a stern finger to shut me up.

"I'm a grown woman and can make my own decisions, Jerricho. Especially my own *business* decisions."

She stands, smooths down her robe, and waddles to the stove. Inhaling a deep whiff of the onions glistening in their butter puddle, she says, "I'll expect repayment, of course."

I groan, shaking my head in disbelief. I don't know how much Gram still has of her lottery winnings, but I imagine Cay's dream kitchen constitutes a fair chunk.

"I want *double,* in fact," she says. "A hundred and twenty thousand, as soon as this Cullan fellow pays you for those episodes."

"You might have to stand in line behind the Malvudians," I warn her.

She ignores me. So does Cay. "Double is too much," he replies.

"Fine. An extra fifty percent, then. But I also want you to be my personal chef for a whole week. Three meals a day, seven days."

"Deal," Cay agrees, extending a hand.

Gram shakes it firmly.

"Now, if you'll permit me," says Cay, "I'd appreciate a visit to the wine cellar. This pinot noir I found in the pantry is fine for deglazing caramelized onions, but if we want to celebrate our partnership properly, I'm afraid we'll require something a bit fancier. A bottle of Pauillac should pair beautifully with my French onion soup."

Whether it's the food or the drink, I'm not certain. But by the time I've drained every drop from my wineglass—twice—and peeled every morsel of cheese crust from my soup crock, I'm convinced we have a legitimate shot at pulling off Cay's crazy plan. For the first time in days, I feel—dare I say it?—*good.*

"Delicious," Gram mutters, sucking a gob of melted gruyere off her index finger. "That might be the best soup I ever had. Although with all that cheese on it, I'm not sure it was a fair fight. What's your secret?"

"Time," Cay answers.

Gram chuckles. "Time? How so?"

"It's the secret ingredient for nearly everything. In this case, it was the time dedicated to caramelizing the onions until they were just right. When I'm cooking a steak, it's the proper amount of time needed for the perfect sear. Time can be the chef's most flavorful—or most regrettable —ingredient. In the kitchen, both patience *and* haste can be virtues."

"Ooo!" Gram squeals. "On top of everything else, he speaks like a poet. I'm thinking I made a fine investment in you. You'll be as good a host as your grandma ever was. Maybe better!"

"Usually I end up kissing girls who flatter me so much," says Cay. "Good thing I didn't have that third glass of wine!"

"Stop flirting with my grandma, Cay," I say, but without any edge to my warning.

"Oh, she knows I'd never try anything. Besides, I have a strict rule about getting into bed with business partners."

"I'd let you break that rule with me!" Gram exclaims. She follows her suggestive remark with a burst of raucous laughter.

"I also have a rule about dinner," says Cay, grinning slyly my direction. "If you ate it but didn't make it, you get to do the dishes."

Despite my exaggerated eye roll, I gather the empty soup crocks. I'm carrying them to the sink when a sudden commotion outside startles me, causing me to bobble and nearly drop all three.

Over a high-pitched whine and the rattling of her kitchen windows, Gram yells, "What's going on? What is that?"

Moments later, everything has settled back into silence.

Cay stands. He wipes his hands on a napkin, crumples it, and drops it on the table.

"That," he announces, making for the front door, "would be Slyce Cobb. I've been expecting a delivery."

THE HATCH RESIDENCE

58 Days to Payment

IT'S THE HOUSE I grew up in, but as I step onto the front porch, I feel oddly like a stranger. Usually returning home is familiar. Healing. I'll eat the same food Dad's been making for years. I'll laugh at Mom's corny jokes or cringe while she yells at the twins. I'll cozy up for the night beneath bedsheets that smell like childhood and better days.

But this particular evening, it's like I'm showing myself before a tribunal. And I know I'm guilty.

Do they really need to know what I'm up to? Should I put that worry on them? Wouldn't it be easier—kinder, even—to fake extreme busyness, send them a few messages from the far side of the galaxy, and return home like nothing ever happened?

If only Cay hadn't taken us to Gram's house ...

Get it over with, Jer. You'll feel better once you do.

I knock as I open the front door. The aroma of spaghetti and garlic bread—a Daryus Hatch staple—fills my nostrils, putting me immediately at ease.

"I'm home!" I call toward the back of the house. That's where the kitchen and dining room are, so that's where my family will be.

"Jer?" my mother's familiar voice calls back. "Is that you?"

"Yeah, it's me," I answer. I drop my bag inside the door, then proceed through the empty living room to the kitchen.

Maura Hatch meets me there with open arms. After a solid eight-second embrace, my mother steps back and stares up at me with dark, searching eyes.

"What're you doing here? Why didn't you call?" she asks worriedly, even as four siblings and one father hail their greetings from the dining room. "And why don't you ever reply to our messages?"

"I wanted to surprise you." It isn't a total lie. They'll definitely be surprised when I share my news. Glancing at the rest of the family, I ask, "Is there room at the table for one more?"

"Yeah, sure," answers Turin. "There's room."

"Not enough *food*, though," quips Alric.

Turin and Alric, my nineteen-year-old twin brothers, play off each other like a classic sitcom duo. They're also dyed-in-the-wool mischief fanatics. They've spent more time grounded than a whole fleet's worth of Boeing starliners.

Mom scowls at Alric. To me she says, "You grab a seat, and I'll grab you a plate. What'll you have to drink?"

"Just water. Thanks."

I sit in the empty seat between my two youngest siblings. Zinnia is a typical boy-crazed teenage girl, while Zephyr, the "oops!" child of the family, leans more into sports. Roughly once each week, they alternate from best friends to worst enemies. I figure they must be in the latter stage at the moment, hence the reason for the lonely chair between them.

Setting the pot of spaghetti noodles in front of me, my father, Daryus, asks, "What brings you home, Jer? Clock out of work early?"

"Actually, I quit a couple days ago," I admit.

Dad's fork pauses halfway between plate and mouth. "Quit? How come? I thought you were making good money there."

"Decent. But I hated the trash we were making, and I hated my boss even more."

"You shouldn't *hate* anyone, Jerricho," Mom scolds from the kitchen. She slides through the doorway with my dinnerware and glass of water.

"So you're moving back home?" Dad asks hopefully. He never wanted me to leave Coral Sands in the first place. If he had gotten his way, I'd be selling insurance alongside him until retirement. Maybe longer.

"No, Dad," I say, unable to hide my irritation. "I came home because I need to tell you something, and I wanted to do it in person."

Liar. I came home because Gram made me. But they don't need to know that.

"Did you get engaged?" Zinnia squeals excitedly. My family only met Natania once, but it was enough for my sister to fall in love with the badass stunt performer.

"No. We broke up, actually."

Zinnia frowns. "I knew she was too cool for you."

"Wow! Your life is really falling to pieces, isn't it!" Alric exclaims. "Kinda like the walls of—of—oh, what *was* that city?"

"Jericho!" Turin cries emphatically, supplying the punchline. Like professional volleyball players, one sets, the other spikes.

"Yes! Your life is crumbling like the walls of *Jericho*," says Alric.

"Leave him alone," Mom snaps. She passes a slice of garlic toast across the table to accompany my spaghetti. "I assume you're looking for a new job, then?"

"That's what I came to tell you," I sheepishly answer. "I ... already have one."

"Great! Why didn't you lead with that?" says Dad.

"I'll be working on a project ... with Cay."

My parents' not-so-subtle exchange of uncomfortable glances doesn't go unnoticed.

They've never held a particularly high opinion of Cay Cantore. He's more tolerated than welcomed around here.

Dad replies first. "You know, my insurance group is looking at shooting a couple commercials for the local market. It's nothing big, but it could be a step in a new direction."

I shake my head. "That's not for me, Dad. Sorry."

"So? What's the project?" Alric asks. He and Turin think Cay's the coolest shit since polar bear poop. Probably because they're jackasses, all three of them.

"We're making a program together," I answer. "A food show."

"Yeah?" says Zinnia, sitting up straighter in her chair. Perhaps my venture will be a steppingstone to her own future stardom.

"Actually, we're *re*making a program. *Galactic Eats*. Cay's grandma's old show."

"What do you mean?" Dad asks. He's stopped eating altogether. "How will you do that?"

"We ... bought a ship."

"A *ship?*" Dad is already losing his mind. Not with anger, but with angst. "You mean you'll be flying all over the galaxy? Taking off and landing on different planets? Traveling through *X-space?* Do you have any idea how dangerous that is, Jerricho?"

"I know, Dad," I say through gritted teeth. The anger is boiling up. Usually my default setting is to keep my aggression at bay, but the last few days I've been a rage volcano, spewing as soon as the pressure builds.

"You can't go," Mom says with a note of finality. "Not in your condition."

"I can, and I will."

"You'll stay with us 'til you get back on your feet," she continues, undeterred. "Dad's insurance commercial pays—"

I drop my fork. It clatters against my plate. Shoving my chair back, I stand above the table and its surprised diners.

"Stop trying to shelter me!" I say, raising my voice at last.

"We're only trying to protect you, Jer," Mom replies soothingly. "You're our son. We don't want to see you get hurt."

"I'm already damaged goods," I respond. "Staying here—or anywhere—isn't gonna fix me."

"We're just scared for you," Dad assures me. He seems quite taken aback by his passive little boy's outburst.

I throw up my hands in frustration and storm toward the front door.

"Where are you going?" Mom calls after me.

"I'm taking a walk."

For good measure, I slam the door when I leave. That'll show 'em.

CORAL SANDS TOWNSHIP

THE GLASS-CLOAKED skyscrapers of Sunset City gleam like oozing volcanoes in the distant eastern horizon, reflecting the last gasps of the evening sun. I'm walking familiar paths toward a familiar place, yet I can't shake the feeling I've become a stranger to Coral Sands—or, at the very least, like some unwanted houseguest. It'll tolerate me for now, then throw a party when I leave.

My parents are right, and I know it. Blasting off into the galaxy's extremities, parrying countless dangers to track down exotic foods—it's a miracle I'm not dead just thinking about it. And in my condition, I'm bound to be a burden more than anything. Even if Cay and I manage to figure out where these Trees of Eden are, there must be a reason Sal never returned. So what chance do we possibly stand?

The worst fear of all, though, is that I might fail. That my filming or editing or both will be rejected. That I'll be exposed as the wannabe fraud I know I must be.

That's probably why I'm so furious at Mom and Dad. I'm a reflection of them and their riskless suburban life, and I know it. Cut from the same cloth as Maura and Daryus. Which isn't all bad—don't get me wrong, there's lots to admire in my parents—but it's their DNA that's kept me pressed beneath Dirk Plath's miserable bootheel the past two years.

Maybe that's why every girl I date, and inevitably fall for, ends up walking out on me. I'm too safe. Too careful. A Nerf boyfriend. When I finally work up the courage to reveal my rare condition, they stick around just long enough not to look like shallow bitches, then come up with some excuse to bail.

For Natania, it only took six days.

My mopey musings are cut short by my arrival at the Coral Sands Butterfly Oasis. Three modest glass domes and a science hall comprise the city-funded wildlife refuge. Here, moths and butterflies, many of them extinct in the wild, are preserved so that future generations might not forget them. More importantly, hardly anyone visits it, which makes it one of the quietest places in town. This, and the fact that it's only a five-minute walk from my parents' house, made it the perfect place for a teenaged Jerricho Hatch to escape and ponder life.

I glance at my watch. Almost seven o'clock, which means the Butterfly Oasis is about to close.

The plexiglass door slides open as I approach. Leaving the warm evening air behind, I step into the cool—and empty—science hall. Display cases, most of them home to dead insects and informational placards, line its walls. Exhibits that few people see, and even fewer pay attention to.

A hunched woman, with more stubble on her gray chin than I could grow, is mopping the epoxy floor. Without glancing up, she croaks, "Oasis is closing in two minutes."

"Even for your most loyal customer?" I ask.

She looks up at me. The lower half of her face breaks into a grin so wide, I can see all six of her teeth.

"If it ain't Jerricho Hatch!" she exclaims, leaning against the mop handle. "Been a few months. Maybe a year? Thought the city rats might've eaten ya."

Oakey Greaves has worked here since before I was born—maybe before my parents were born. I didn't start frequenting the Coral Sands Butterfly Oasis until I was halfway through high school, but I quickly became Oakey's favorite visitor. Some days her *only* visitor, if you took her word for it.

"They've nibbled off a few toes," I reply, "but left me alone otherwise. How ya been?"

"Creaky," she answers. "And leaky. My kids have got me in adult diapers now, Jerricho. Adult diapers! Won't be long before they put me out to pasture."

"When they do, make sure I get an invitation to your retirement party," I tell her.

"Ya don't get a party at my age. Just a gift basket with pudding cups and coupons for the nearest assisted-living facility."

I chuckle. Old Oakey hasn't taken herself seriously a day in her life. I admire her for it. Sometimes I wish I were more like her, minus the gum rot and hunch.

"Well, I'll be mopping awhile," she goes on, "so ya might as well keep the butterflies company. But not too long, mind you. I've got a date tonight."

"Yeah?" I reply, more impressed than surprised.

"Believe it or not, there's a market for this!" she says, shaking her hips provocatively. "My ninety-year-old neighbor can't wait to get a piece!"

I'm still listening to her cackles—and chuckling a bit myself—as I trade the science hall for the small airlock separating it from the domes. On my way out, I'll stop here to check myself for hitchhikers, but for now, I parade on through.

Animals have interested me for as long as I can remember. I could have spent weeks at the Sunset City Rescue Zoo when I was in elementary school. As I grew older, my enthusiasm waned somewhat—girls, sports, and video games took the limelight then—but I still enjoyed the occasional zoology program once my evening homework was finished.

Lately, though, I've been drawn only to one. It's a fascination that has ballooned quickly into obsession.

The monarch.

They're a dying breed of butterfly. One of many. Long ago, millions of these amazing creatures used to undertake what might be Terra's most impressive animal migration. Today, scientists estimate those numbers to be in the few *hundreds*.

But no one cares. Why should they? A hundred and fifty years ago, the Galactic League introduced artificial pollination to our planet. Like the honeybees I see pinned up in the science hall's display cases, the monarch's usefulness dried up, and so did our protection. I fear that, someday soon, the amazing monarch will hang beside the honeybee in humanity's Hall of Extinction.

A short distance along the walkway, I stop and lean against a railing. It overlooks a sunken area in the dome floor, home to a forest of milkweed. The errant white specks scattered about the broad leaves are no bigger than the head of a pin, but my eyes have grown attuned to spotting them over the years. There are hundreds—thousands, maybe—and each one a future monarch.

Their parents swarm above them, a liquid kaleidoscope of burnt orange and black. Soon they'll be released into the wild to live out the rest of their short lives in the free and fresh air. Long-dormant instincts will set them on their ancestral migration routes, but they won't get far.

Still, my monarchs will give it a hell of a go before they die.

I think that's why I'm so drawn to them. It's the sheer tenacity. Such fragile creatures, yet such fighters. Despite all the adversities stacked against these insects—storms, predators, parasites, and the ever-scarcer milkweed they require for food—these winged warriors journey some five thousand kilometers each year. In their epic travels, some will soar up to four kilometers above Terra's surface! Call me crazy if you want, but for something that weighs less than a paperclip, that's downright admirable.

"You'll be flying a lot higher than that," I say out loud to the full-color tattoo on my forearm. "And a lot further."

Am I tough enough to do it? Can I really stand up against the pressures? The dangers? Or are my parents right? Am I kidding myself, thinking I'm up for such a task? Especially one so daunting as this? And in my condition, to top it off?

I received my medical diagnosis a little over a year ago, but the symptoms started showing up long before, during my final year at S3U. Due largely to a misguided sense of pride, I kept the pain hidden from everyone around me.

Stupid. If I had come clean right away, doctors could have caught it early. They might have slowed or even stopped progression.

Clarion-Burgess Syndrome—CBS, for short—first showed up in the human genome a little over a century ago. It's rare, but fully treatable if caught early.

Mine wasn't.

Now the muscles in my extremities are out of control. One moment they seize and go rigid. The next, I can hardly feel or move them at all. Tremendous pain, akin to shoving my hand or foot into a bonfire, accompanies the bouts of rigor. During the numb spells, it's a crippling fatigue that can linger for hours.

Beyond my family and my last couple romantic pursuits, no one knows I have the disease. Not even Cay. But, month by month, my CBS progressively worsens. It used to be my fingers and toes. Now it's my hands and feet. Soon, my legs and arms will fall victim. Then the muscles controlling my bladder and bowels. My shoulders. My abs. My diaphragm. My organs.

I don't need to explain what happens when it reaches that stage.

Not so long ago, I was making craters out of quarterbacks on the gridiron. Now I have to ice my wrists after holding a camera.

I sigh. If only I could take a mulligan. Seek treatment before it was too late.

But there is no turning back the cosmic clock. All that's left is to live in the present, trying my best to ignore what the future holds for me.

Speaking of clocks, I'd better head out. Don't want to keep Oakey's date waiting.

THE HATCH RESIDENCE
Front Porch

I'M NOT READY to face my parents yet, so I detour to their porch swing. There I sway, back and forth, a reed caught in a confused breeze. Inside, Mom plays the piano, and my swinging falls into her music's rhythm. Far on the western horizon, the jagged spine of the Santa Maria Mountains forms an inky skirt for the darkening sky.

Of course, *far* is only relative. Give me two months in space, and those mountains might seem as near to this porch as my right hand to my left.

In history class, I learned that this place was once called *Arizona*. And it wasn't a Terran district like we have today. Back then, people called it a *state*, and it was in a country named the United States. Apparently there were hundreds of countries back then, all of them squished into this one tiny globe. We bickered with each other over trivial disputes, were even willing to sacrifice millions of our own race to the major arguments.

Now we have a whole galaxy to bicker with. All in all, we humans get along pretty well amongst ourselves these days. Although that theory might be put to the test after I've spent a few weeks in space with Cay.

The front door swings open, and Dad exits with a compacted trash cube. He walks past without noticing me, making for the round landing pad. After depositing the trash for morning pickup next to the one-seater *scabb* he uses to commute to work, Dad turns to head back indoors.

"Jerricho!" he cries out, clutching his chest with alarm when he sees me on the porch swing. "Good Cosmos, son, I didn't know you were out here."

"Sorry," I reply. "Didn't mean to scare you."

Dad sits beside me. He crosses his arms and stares out at the mountains. "I'm the one who should be sorry. About before."

I look down, but I'm still too upset to say anything.

Dad goes on. "Did you know I spent a year in flight school?"

"Really?"

"I did. Right outta high school, before I met your mom. My whole life, I dreamed I'd be an intergalactic yacht captain, just like your granddad. I wanted to rub elbows with the rich and famous, the way you get to do at your studio."

I stifle a scoff. He apparently hasn't watched much of the low-grade garbage I've been involved in. Someone ought to compact *that* into a trash cube and leave it out for pickup.

"So? What happened?" I inquire with genuine interest. This is a chapter of Dad's story I haven't heard before.

"I dropped out when your granddad died. He was on a routine client pickup—at least, it *should* have been routine. According to the official investigation, their nav computer must have miscalculated the coordinates by a tiny fraction. The ship dropped out of X-space too close to a neutron star. Barely had time for a distress signal before the gravity ripped them apart."

I lower my eyes. I've heard the tale of Jephthah Hatch a hundred times before tonight. The pain in Dad's voice is audible every time, even decades after the fact.

"Anyway, I got cold feet after that," he says. "Couldn't step foot in a flight simulator without breaking into a cold sweat. The insurance gig I ended up with seemed a lot safer. And it was. For a while, I was okay with the decision to drop out of flight school. After a few years, though, I started regretting it. But by then, you were a toddler, and life was already in full swing. There was no going back for me."

Dad glances sideways at me, a reluctant grin decorating his lips.

"Earlier in the dining room, I think I was projecting my own fears onto you," he says. "Maybe even my regrets. Don't get me wrong—I'm scared for you. Any father would be."

"I won't be alone, Dad," I remind him. "Cay's gonna be there too."

"Not helping, Jer. But I *do* know that a person has to take some calculated risks in life."

I swallow a lump of guilt. It's probably best I don't share how little of this I've actually calculated.

Dad drapes an arm over my shoulders and hugs me to his side.

"I'm proud of you for having the courage to go."

"Thanks," I mutter. "I needed to hear you say that."

Without another word, my father returns indoors, leaving me alone once more on a gently rocking swing.

For a second time this evening, I study the monarch tattoo on my forearm. I think of them, dancing in a cloud above me in the dome. None of them knows whether it will survive its migration. But they don't care. They just go, because that's what they have to do. What they were born to do.

And so will I. Besides, we all die sometime, right? Why wait for a slow, painful end, lying helpless in my bed?

No thanks. If I'm gonna die, I'd rather go out like a monarch.

In the midst of a beautiful flight.

THE *TANTALUS*

56 Days to Payment

"WHERE ARE WE supposed to sleep, Cay? The shower?"

Indignant, I glare around the *Tantalus'* cabin, now parked in Gram's landing pad. Since my departure for home, Cay has ripped out everything but the cockpit and lavatory, replacing it all with a state-of-the-art kitchen.

Cay winces ruefully at my question and says, "Actually, I repurposed the shower into a pantry. The spray nozzle is still in there, but I'd caution against ruining our dry goods. Might need those."

"You expect us to go *two months* without showering? Are you crazy?"

I open the lav door to make sure Cay isn't messing with me. He's not. "It's half booze in here!" I holler at him.

"Sure is! I had a little money left over. Bought the good stuff, too." He reaches past me to grab a bottle of caramel-colored liquor from one of his new shelves. "Speaking of, we should celebrate my updated kitchen with a toast."

I'm not over the shower thing yet. "You realize how bad we're gonna smell? I'm not living like that, Cay. I'm not an animal."

"It'll be just like our dorm room freshman year!" Cay cries with wistful enthusiasm. "Remember when you got that foot fungus? Ah, memories."

Cay opens a sliding drawer beneath the granite countertop. As if this should appease me, he points inside and says, "Besides, look at all this deodorant I bought. Three sticks apiece! And this gorgeous sink—you could practically swim laps in it!"

"You're nuts," I bark, wagging a finger at him. "Absolutely nuts."

"No, nuts would be leaving without sleeping bags and pillows," he says, offering the galaxy's flimsiest-ever defense. Crossing to the other side of the kitchen, he throws open a cabinet door to reveal a pair of flower-patterned pillows and two rolled-up sleeping bags.

"Gram pulled these up from the basement," says Cay. "I already called dibs on the blue one."

I sigh in defeat. Has arguing with Cay ever been anything *but* pointless? Besides, it's not like we can change anything back, so I might as well get used to it.

I vow to let it go. At the same time, I know I never really will.

Trying to distract myself from the two-month discomfort to come, I turn my attention to the kitchen. For a rush job, it really is something. As a videographer, I know how important aesthetics are if you want to sell a program, and Cay's sophisticated tastes have delivered exactly that. The light fixtures give me the sensation that I'm bathing in soft firelight, rather than being assaulted by harsh beams of it. Our appliances—ice chest, oven, toaster, and company—are enamel finished and match the color scheme. *Much* more camera friendly than the industrial aura cast by stainless steel. He even added a tile backsplash on the walls most likely to see camera time.

"I can work with this," I mutter to myself.

Even so, it isn't half as luscious as Sal's kitchen studio. Maybe after finishing a couple hundred episodes, we'll be eligible for an upgrade.

"The only thing left to do is learn how to fly it," Cay says.

"I've been with my parents the last two days, and you didn't use any of that time learning how to fly?" I ask in disbelief.

"New kitchens don't pick *themselves* out, Jer," he protests.

"That took—what—all of fifteen minutes?"

"Relax. There's video tutorials galore on Axon. *Thousands*, probably. It didn't become the intergalactic informational highway for no reason. Besides, the *Tantalus'* autonav system does most of the work for us. Adjusts everything to make flying in space feel exactly like terrestrial travel for the person behind the controls. That's what Slyce said, anyway."

"Yeah, except we don't use X-space when we take a scabb to the grocery store," I remind him. "We mess that up, we could wind up spaghettified in a black hole."

"As someone who adores spaghetti, I can't think of a better way to go."

No one is certain anymore how X-space ended up with its name. In my eighth-grade history class, my teacher claimed it was shorthand for "*ex*-tra space."

Then, in high school physics, a different teacher, Mr. Zepp, professed it was named after Xavior Barclay, the lead scientist whose team discovered and perfected our interstellar mode of travel.

What nobody disagrees on is how X-space works. It's essentially an interdimensional mode of shortcutting one's way from Point A to Point B. To this day, I still remember how Mr. Zepp explained it. He placed a beach ball and ping pong ball next to each other on his desk.

"Let's say I placed a beetle on top of this beach ball," he said, "and timed how long it took to crawl all the way down to the bottom. Then I took the same beetle and performed the same experiment with the ping pong ball. Which would take less time for our insect friend to travel? Beach ball or ping pong ball?"

In unison, the class gave the obvious answer: "Ping pong ball."

"X-space," he went on to explain, "allows a vessel and everything it contains to travel across the beach ball, but in a ping pong ball's amount of space and time. When you're dealing with the magnitude of inter-stellar travel, though, it's more like a beetle traveling from the North Pole to the South Pole in a ping pong ball's amount of time. In X-space, you drop down from the normal, everyday plane of existence to travel quantum roadways, thus making mammoth distances relatively short. It still takes *some* time, but we're now able to travel from one end of the Milky Way to another in just a few days. A couple centuries ago, that would have taken a hundred thousand *years.*"

"So people in X-space shrink down really, really small?" one student asked.

"Don't think of it like that," Mr. Zepp answered. "Because even really, really small things still exist in our three-dimensional plane. Think of it more like leaving one room and entering another. The room you just left—you aren't in it at all anymore. When traveling through X-space, you literally cease to exist here, along with whatever lies inside the bubble of your vessel's Barclay field."

Nobody asked about the Barclay field. We could tell from context that this was some kind of mysterious, quantum energy blob none of us would ever understand.

"X-space," Mr. Zepp concluded, "has forever changed the way we travel. It opened up the stars to us."

It also opened up the Galactic League to us. Apparently, Terra—called *Earth* back then—was under close observations. On the very same day Xavior Barclay confirmed his X-space success, the Galactic League of Advanced Beings paid our planet a visit and offered us admittance into their federation. In the hundred and fifty years since, we've gone from "alone" among the drifting planets to become a blossoming partner in the economics, politics, culture, and other general affairs of the Milky Way.

But it's not the affairs of the Milky Way I'm concerned about right now. I'm concerned Cay and I have bitten off more than we can chew. *Way* more. We're garden snakes trying to swallow an elephant.

"How can you think we'll be ready to leave tomorrow?" I ask, addressing the elephant in the room. The elephant we're supposed to gulp down in one bite.

Cay waves off my concern. "Like I said before, video tutorials. And don't forget about that personal assistance drone Jonas promised us. It should be arriving any minute now." He checks the time on his tel, then adds, "A little late, actually, but what's a few minutes? Once it's here, I'll plug it into Axon to download everything there is to know about interstellar travel. Between our autonav system and the PAD, X-space will be simple as syrup by the time we take off tomorrow."

As if on cue, we hear a female voice behind us. "I'm here with your PAD. The one from Cullan Jonas."

Cay and I turn as one to view the intruder. I recognize her instantly. Last time I saw her, Gustav Geiger was lamenting her inadequacy as a granddaughter.

"Ameliana, right?" says Cay, brandishing his pearly smile. "I never forget a face, especially one as pretty as yours. Names, on the other hand, are a bit trickier for me."

"Oh, you're good," Ameliana replies in an accent that mirrors Geiger's. She exudes a lot more confidence when she isn't smothered underneath her grandfather's shadow. "How many girls has that line worked on?"

"None, actually," says Cay. "I should probably come up with some new material."

"I would," she playfully agrees.

"Why are *you* dropping off the PAD?" I ask. I don't bother hiding my suspicion as I gesture to the drone whirring beside her. "I can't imagine Gustav wants to play nice all of a sudden."

"No, I can't imagine so," Ameliana concurs. "When he heard Cullan Jonas was lending you a PAD, he volunteered to bring it here himself. Probably wanted one more opportunity to intimidate you into quitting. Then more pressing business came up, so he sent me instead. His little errand girl." She faces the PAD and says, "This is Cay Cantore. I'm releasing you from my care and turning you over to him."

The PAD hovers toward Cay. With a warm, eerily human voice, it says, "Nice to meet you, Cane Cannoli. I look forward to all the ways I might assist you."

"Okay, first, you can take the formal thing down a notch," Cay says. "Also, my name is *Cay Cantore*. Although, I do love cannoli, so if you're going to insist on saying my name wrong, you could do worse."

He faces Ameliana again. "Thanks for dropping it off. I'm glad you came instead of your grandpa."

Ameliana scuffs the toe of her right boot against the floor. Her cheeks flush pink as she says, "I'm sorry about him. He's an ass. To tell you the truth, I have always admired you, ever since university. My grandfather may look down on me for it, but I'm actually proud I came in second to you."

I look around for a trash can to puke in. This is exactly what Cay needs, someone further inflating his ready-to-pop ego.

"Uh, thanks?" Cay replies. He's a constantly cool person, but even he seems taken aback by Ameliana's flattering candor.

She gives an embarrassed chuckle. Buries her face in her hands. Then flashes him the same flirty grin as before. "Sorry. That was awkward, wasn't it. True, though. You were top of our class for good reason. I only wish my grandfather would stop rubbing my nose in it."

Ameliana steps around us to admire the kitchen. An impressed whistle slides through her lips.

"You know, when I was walking up to the ship, I couldn't believe you were planning to make a food program in it. But, I have to admit, this could work."

"Picked the colors myself," Cay brags. "Jerricho here was no help at all."

Ameliana speaks in a dreamy, almost melancholy tone, as if she didn't hear him at all. "Maybe this is what I need. Nothing big. Nothing fancy. Just a ship and a halfway decent kitchen to film in."

"What do you mean?" I ask. There's no way we can take on a *third* person in this cramped space.

"Ever since I started university, I've been hoping I'd take over the Geiger empire someday. I even minored in acting at S3U, so I could get used to being in front of an audience. But the way my grandfather treats me, I think he'd rather hook it all up to a self-destruct button. One that blows the whole thing up the second his heart stops beating."

"As a Cantore, I would be okay with that," admits Cay. "But you seem like less of a butthead than Gustav. Maybe someone like you taking over would be alright."

Ameliana giggles. "On the off chance that happens—and you don't kill yourself first—give me a call."

"Give me your contact data, and I will," Cay replies.

Ameliana reaches into her pocket. Like she expected him to ask for it, she hands him a contact card. "I hope to hear from you sometime."

"And I hope to be heard."

Seriously. Trash can.

"Do me a favor," says Ameliana. "If you see my grandfather sometime, tell him I spit in your face when I dropped off the PAD. He doesn't need further reason to keep me on the sidelines. If he finds out I was making nice with a Cantore, I'll be junior staff forever."

"Deal. I'll tell him you were so mean, you made Jerricho cry."

Ameliana waves and backs her way toward the boarding ramp. "See you. And, seriously, good luck."

When she's gone, Cay gets right to business. He faces the newly delivered drone and says, "PAD, I want you to plug in to Axon. Learn everything you can about X-space flight. Be ready to take over all navigational responsibilities in the event Jerricho and I find ourselves incapacitated."

Then, uncorking the bottle of booze he snagged from his new pantry, he says, "Now, about that toast ..."

1300 PINEWOOD TRAIL

55 Days to Payment

GRAM SCOOPS ANOTHER helping of eggs Florentine onto my plate. Now my two buttermilk biscuits, smothered beneath enough sausage gravy they could survive a nuclear blast, have company.

"Don't stop eating!" she admonishes. "You've got a long trip ahead of you."

"It's not like there's no food on the ship, Gram," I respond.

Our whole shower is food ... and booze, I recall through my brain fog. I may be sitting at Gram's table, but my mind is still tucked in bed. Most of my night was spent watching flight tutorials, and my morning alarm greeted me way earlier than it should have. Rude.

Cay stumbles into Gram's dinette. He looks even worse than I do. Without a word, he sits across the table. Gram slides a full breakfast plate in front of him. When he opens his hand, Gram places a fork into it.

Biscuits and gravy are sliding down both our gullets when my grandmother clears her throat importantly. I notice she's fingering her necklace.

"I have something for you boys."

Cay looks eagerly up from his food.

"Not a gift," she says. "A loan."

"You'ff loaned uff ... more den ... 'nough," I reply through an intermittent bite of eggs.

Gram removes her necklace with the milky gem. She lays it on the table in front of me.

I swallow. "Gram, I can't take that. *You* need it."

"No," she says, backing away. "No, I need you to have it. Take it, Jerricho. Please."

Cay grabs it. Holds it up to the light.

"I don't know what it is," he says, "but okay."

"It was my granddad's, Cay," I retort, snatching it away. "It's an Azazule diamond. They're supposed to resonate with a parallel universe. One where everything goes right."

"So it's a good luck charm?" says Cay.

"I used to give it to my Jephthah every time he left on a flight," Gram tells him. "Then, when he came home, he'd return it to me. It was our little ritual. But the morning he left for his final voyage, I couldn't find it anywhere. It was in his pants pocket, and I'd put them in the wash. That one time he didn't have it ... was the one time my Jeph didn't come home."

Gazing into Gram's teary eyes, Cay says, "Jer's right. We can't take it. I'd feel terrible if we lost it."

But Gram backs away further. "My payday is riding on your success. Take the damn necklace."

"It *does* go swell with your butterfly tattoo," Cay teases.

Still reluctant, I clasp the gold chain around my neck. For someone who's never worn a necklace in his life, I'm surprised how comfortable the gem's weight feels against my breastbone.

"I'll bring it back in one piece, Gram. I promise."

Later, after Cay and I have said our goodbyes, we walk side by side down the stone path to Gram's landing pad.

Cay notices me toying with the Azazule diamond hanging from its chain. "You really think that rock's gonna do anything?" he asks.

"Not sure," I reply. "But I do know Gram's only bought one lottery ticket her entire life. When she did, she was wearing this."

THE *TANTALUS'* COCKPIT

LIKE A PANORAMIC movie screen, the *Tantalus'* oversized windshield fills my vision. We haven't left Gram's landing pad yet, but I'm already imagining the things I'll soon see through it.

Strapping myself into the copilot's chair, I ask, "How much time did you spend watching videos last night?"

"Ugh. That was the worst half hour of my life since the *Cosmic Bachelor* season premiere," Cay answers. "Such sloppy camera work."

I decide not to give voice to my annoyance. My death stare is doing the job for me. Once again, Cay has shown the expected amount of dedication to a task that didn't wholly interest him.

"Relax," Cay assures me. As if they're old drinking buddies, he drapes an arm around the robot at his side. "PAD spent all night interfacing for X-space flight. He'll be right next to us, offering whatever assistance our autonav might need. Which is probably none."

He flourishes a hand toward the control console's magnificent array of gadgetry.

"Do or die time. Care for honors, my dearest Jerricho?"

THE *TANTALUS'* COCKPIT

"SEE? THAT WASN'T so hard."

I hardly hear Cay. I'm too mesmerized. Sure, I've seen stars before. When I was young, my family would sometimes drive into the desert, far from the suburbs. We'd wrap ourselves in blankets and admire the luminescent tentacles of the Orion Spur and Sagittarius Arm, reaching out from the Milky Way's Galactic Center toward the infinite universe.

But that could never prepare me for how I'm seeing those stars through the *Tantalus'* windscreen.

Incredible. Absolutely incredible. For some reason, I ache for Natania, wishing I were sharing this moment with her instead of Cay.

"You all there, buddy? Hellooooo!" Cay says, flapping an arm to get my attention.

"Huh? Yeah, I'm here," I reply, as my consciousness returns from the stars to the *Tantalus.* "And don't get too cocky, Cay. Remember, it took us six hours just to figure out how to turn on the damn ship. We might've made it out of the upper atmosphere, but we aren't exactly bouncing from star to star yet."

Still, my trademark skepticism feels a bit flat. I have to admit, the last forty minutes have been an absolute rush. And *very* cool.

"I think it's your job to send us on our way to Tarrkanna-Rrui," says Cay. "Between the two of us, you *are* the X-space expert."

"Only 'cause I actually watched the videos last night," I grumble. Putting forth no further protest, I explain the steps out loud—at least, as well as I remember after only four hours of non-hands-on training. "Tarrkanna-Rrui is a heavily trafficked League member, so it should be a piece of cake. First, we need to tell the ship's autonav to load coordinates from Axon."

Cay stares at me and gives two slow blinks. I might as well have explained that to a cow.

"Uh, Autonav?" I speak uncertainly, like someone trying to communicate with a ghost or a spirit. "Will you please load the coordinates for Tarrkanna-Rrui?"

"Nice. Very polite with the *please*," Cay whispers.

After a moment without any response, I say, "Did something happen? Is the system asleep?"

"Maybe you have to use its proper name," suggests Cay. "I called it 'Tantalus' when we were taking off earlier."

I try again. "Okay. Tantalus, load the coordinates for Tarrkanna-Rrui."

"Please and thank you," Cay adds. He casts me a disapproving look.

This time, the response is immediate.

"Loading coordinates for Tarrkanna-Rrui," speaks the ship's metallic voice.

A string of numbers, letters, and symbols, hundreds long, appears on the rectangular monitor in front of me.

"Coordinates loaded. Match rate: 99.996 percent," Tantalus informs us. "The other four-thousandths percent were all adjusted to match."

"What's it talking about?" asks Cay, raising an eyebrow.

"It's a safety measure, I think."

The image of Jephthah Hatch wearing his pilot's uniform materializes in my mind. The same one hanging in a frame on Gram's living room wall.

"If the coordinates are even the slightest bit off," I explain, "there's no telling where you'll end up. Which is exactly what used to happen. There were too many ships disappearing during X-space flight. So, a couple decades ago, the Galactic League finally implemented new safety standards. This is one of 'em. When Tantalus loaded coordinates for Tarrkanna-Rrui, it also cross-referenced them with the coordinates used by every other ship that's traveled there. That last bit about the four-thousandths percent means everyone who got it wrong the first time adjusted their coordinates to match what we're seeing on the screen right now."

"So it's certain?" Cay asks.

"Either that, or everyone who's tried going to Tarrkanna-Rrui ended up lost."

"So it's certain," Cay repeats, this time with confidence.

I nod. "Next, the ship needs to map our X-space path from here to Tarrkanna-Rrui."

After I give the command, Tantalus responds. "Mapping X-space. Action will take approximately two minutes to complete."

"While we're waiting, we can get PAD ready to input his coordinates," I say.

"Why do we need coordinates from PAD?" Cay asks. "Isn't that what the ship is doing?"

I shake my head. "You also have to plug an outside device into the X-space module. The *Tantalus* will only jump if they *both* agree on the coordinates and path. It's a failsafe in case of a glitchy onboard computer."

"Whatever you say, my captain."

I turn in my chair. "PAD! Come here, please."

PAD's four rotors whir to life, and the drone is soon hovering behind my left shoulder.

"Download coordinates for Tarrkanna-Rrui, then map an X-space path," I order.

"I'm sorry, but I cannot complete the task as desired," the robot replies.

I shoot an angry glance over my shoulder. "Why not?"

PAD sinks an inch, like it's ashamed of itself. "I haven't downloaded the proper software or performed the required simulation trainings. Thus, I am unable to aid in X-space flight at this time."

"I told you to do that yesterday!" Cay yells. "What were you up to all night?"

"I performed extensive research and simulated trainings on the art of escape flight," PAD answers. "I am now well-versed in every evasive maneuver known on Axon."

Cay groans. "I said *X-space* flight, not *escape* flight. Can't you hear?"

"Buggy audio receiver," I mutter. "It's an older unit, remember? But it's not a big deal. There should be an X-space cartridge around here somewhere. Black rectangle, about the size of a tissue box. We can connect it to one of our tels and map X-space that way."

"No, we can't."

"Why not?"

"When Slyce dropped off the *Tantalus*, I told him he could keep the X-space cartridge. Knocked almost a thousand off the total price! How did you think we got our booze money?"

"Dammit, Cay! No cartridge? That means we gotta wait for PAD to learn X-space!"

"A minor setback. It'll give us time to get to know each other better. PAD, how long to do all that X-space stuff?"

"Five hours and four minutes, minimum," the drone answers. "More, if you want me to run expanded simulations for extra security."

"The minimum should be fine," says Cay. "And remember, you're learning all about *X-space* flight this time. Say it back to me."

PAD does, then whirs into a corner and lowers itself to the floor. By shutting down its other components, it'll be able to spend more energy downloading and implementing all the necessary X-space technology.

"Well? What do we do for five hours?" I ask, admiring the field of stars beyond the windscreen once more.

"We could vidcomm Josephina," Cay suggests. "I'm sure she's aching for one last look before I take off to the stars."

"We aren't talking to my sister, Cay."

"Your parents, then," he says. "You've been sending them messages nonstop anyway."

I scowl and shove my tel deeper into my pocket. "My dad knows a lot about flying. He's the reason we were finally able to turn on our engines."

"And all the messages you've sent since?"

"They're worried. It's called being a good son, Cay."

"Afraid I wouldn't know much about that," he admits, unbuckling his safety harness and vacating his pilot's chair. "If you won't let me talk to your family, we might as well do a bit of episode prep."

"Episode prep? What do you mean?"

Cay doesn't answer me. Approaching the tiny program monitor mounted on the cabin's rear wall, he says, "Play program: *Galactic Eats*. Episode title: 'Frozen Yogurt.'"

The dark monitor bursts to life.

GALACTIC EATS, EPISODE #23:

"Frozen Yogurt"

OFFICIAL TRANSCRIPT.
*EPISODE SEGMENT RETRIEVED FROM ARCHIVE BLOCK 32D, THIRD
PLANET ENTERTAINMENT, INC.*

Two-second clips parade by in rapid succession, depicting a landscape of snow and ice. The moan of a steady gale accompanies them.

SAL
(narrating) **Tarrkanna-Rrui. A world of snow and ice. Of glacial temperatures and brutal conditions.**

The image steadies over a calmer scene. Distant peaks create a jagged horizon. The narrow arc of a violet sun rises above them, looking out over an empty world.

Next, the ice planet is seen from orbit through a broad viewscreen. One half of Tarrkanna-Rrui is light blue, awash in sunlight. The other is dark, cloaked in its own shadow. In the foreground, the silhouette of a young woman approaches the viewscreen, gazing out.

SAL
(narrating) **It seems impossible life could exist on this tidally locked world. Tarrkanna-Rrui doesn't spin on an axis, which means the half facing the sun remains constantly exposed to harsh and deadly radiation. On the other half, temperatures range**

**between one-seventy and two hundred ten below zero, creating a
stiff competition between death by frostbite or death by
hypothermia.**

The scene zooms in on the equatorial line dividing the planet's two
halves.

SAL

(narrating) **But at the place where light and dark meet—the
"Twilight Zone"—life has found its sweet spot.**

Another rapid montage shows a dozen types of animals, ranging from
large, lumbering beasts to skittering invertebrates.

SAL

(narrating) **And, overseeing it all, are the guardians of the planet:
the Tarrkarr.**

The picture is filled with a half dozen faces. They have wide, black eyes
and sleek, chocolate-colored fuzz. More scenes depict Tarrkan children
playing together, a family enjoying a meal, laborers working in a smelt-
ing plant, and a pair of herders wandering their icy range.

SAL

(narrating) **Most impressive, perhaps, is Tarrkan-Uffrra, the great
city of the Tarrkarr peoples.**

A series of clips reveals buildings like giant crystals rising from the
planet's icy surface, vehicles zipping along the streets between them, an
interstellar vessel landing at a spaceport, and a handful more shops and
restaurants. Following this, in rhythm with Sal's descriptive narration,
are more shots of the Tarrkarr.

SAL

(narrating) **Although small compared to some of the galaxy's great
metropolitan centers, Tarrkan-Uffrra is a thriving home to fishers
and architects, mothers and fathers, interstellar business Tarrkarr
and day-laborers, squeaking infants and their graying elders. And,
certainly not least of all, the *shepherds*.**

A lone Tarrka, carrying a metal staff twice as tall as himself, trudges up an icy slope in the twilight. He tightens his anorak hood around his face, protecting himself from the wind and drifting snow.

> SAL
>
> *(narrating)* **These Tarrkan shepherds endure the harshest of conditions. Most beings wouldn't survive unprotected for more than a few hours, yet this shepherd submits himself day after day to the biting cold of Tarrkanna-Rrui's windswept plains. After all, it isn't only his livelihood at stake, but also that of the great *gurrffa*.**

The shepherd reaches the crest of the hill. On the other side of the rise, basking in a thin crescent of direct sunlight, is a herd of shaggy, horned quadrupeds. They dwarf the Tarrkan shepherd approaching them.

> SAL
>
> *(narrating)* **Under an eternal sunrise—or sunset, if you prefer—the shepherd keeps vigilant watch over his gurrffarr. For untold thousands of years, these creatures have provided the Tarrkarr with the wool, oils, bone, and meat necessary for survival.**

The scene changes. Sal Cantore, bundled in a Tarrkan anorak, approaches the camera between two gleaming buildings.

> SAL
>
> **But those aren't what we're after—not today, anyway. From the warmth of your living room, join me on another *Galactic Eats* adventure as I risk losing my nose, toes, and fingertips here on Tarrkanna-Rrui ... and all of that for a gallon of milk. *Gurrffa* milk.**

The location changes again. Sal is sitting at a stone table in a Tarrkan pub. On the table in front of her is a crystal goblet filled with bluish liquid.

> SAL
>
> **In its raw state, gurrffa milk is toxic, both to Tarrkarr and to humans like me. But when the milk is simmered over a long period of time, those toxins break down. Much of the liquid also**

evaporates during this process, leaving behind a creamy, savory yogurt.

Sal raises the glass of milk. She gives it a look of dissatisfaction, then slides it across the table and out of sight.

SAL
But my Nana always told me you should know exactly where your food comes from. That means we'll be skipping the supermarket today. Instead, we'll journey to the ice fields outside the city, the desolate hills where the gurrffarr live in their vast herds. After all, if we want the freshest milk possible, we've got to go straight to the source.

Now inside a cozy, firelit home, Sal and a Tarrka sit opposite each other in a pair of plush chairs. Between them hovers a frisbee-shaped translator drone. When Sal speaks, she addresses the camera.

SAL
Assisting us on our quest to the ice fields is Rumrra. Although the vast majority of shepherds are males, Rumrra, a female, is among the most highly respected in all Tarrkan-Uffrra. Rumrra, would you mind sharing a bit about your experience as a gurrffa shepherdess?

Rumrra speaks with a mixture of guttural consonants and shrill squeaks. *(Note: For purposes of this episode transcript, Rumrra's portion of the conversation has been translated into Commonspeak.)*

RUMRRA
It is a hard, dangerous life, and often a lonely one. But it is beautiful and rewarding nonetheless.

SAL
What dangers are involved in it?

RUMRRA
Most gurrffarr are gentle and friendly, but sometimes one may turn wild. Because they are so much larger than Tarrkarr, we are easily injured by those which go mad. Besides the gurrffarr, we must also

worry about sudden ice storms or falling into deep crevasses buried
beneath the snow.

SAL

If the ice fields beyond Tarrkan-Uffrra are so dangerous, why not
build fences for them closer to the city?

RUMRRA

It has been tried in the past. But the gurrffarr do not thrive in
captivity. They become weak and sick. Their meat grows
exceedingly tough, and they soon stop producing milk.

SAL

Can you explain where you'll be taking us and what we'll do there?

RUMRRA

We will travel by *krrukka* far beyond the city—

SAL

Sorry, what's a krrukka?

RUMRRA

It is a small, protected vehicle Tarrkarr use for planetary travel.

SAL

Thank you. Go on.

RUMRRA

With the krrukka, we will skim over the *Mrrunkakarr*—a maze of
jagged ridges and crevasses—to the ice fields beyond. There, we
will locate a suitable gurrffa, and you will extract its milk.

SAL

I will?

RUMRRA

(squeaking with laughter) Of course! If you truly want the
shepherdess experience, you must be willing to get your hands
dirty.

SAL
I guess that's settled then! Shall we head out?

The scene changes. Sal is bundled and shivering beneath many layers in the rear seat of a glass-domed krrukka. Through chattering teeth, she shouts over the din of the vehicle's engines and rushing wind.

SAL
The Tarrkarr enjoy a roaring fire in their homes, but apparently no one's had the novel idea to introduce heaters into their vehicles. I'm freezing my ass off in here, and we haven't even stepped outside yet!

Seen from an exterior angle, the krrukka settles onto the snow. A door opens, and Rumrra jumps out, followed by Sal and a cameraman. Next is a close-up of Sal facing the camera. Behind her are a dozen gurrffarr, lowing peacefully. Rumrra approaches them, speaking in gentle tones.

SAL
We've made it safely to the ice fields. And, I must admit, these are some spectacular creatures. They almost remind me of humpback whales! Whales with flipper feet and shaggy gray hair.

Sal points toward Rumrra, who is stroking one gurrffa's lowered head. A second gurrffa, seemingly jealous of the first, is vying for Rumrra's attention.

SAL
As you can see, they're very social creatures. Not only with each other, but also with the Tarrkarr. During the trip out here, Rumrra explained that the gurrffarr can be quite protective of their shepherds. Although she's never experienced this herself, there are documented instances in which gurrffarr have rescued lost or stranded Tarrkarr, even returning them all the way back to Tarrkan-Uffrra. You wouldn't guess it from how hefty they are, but a gurrffa can haul ass when the need calls for it, and they're experts at navigating the crevasses between here and the city—including those hidden beneath the snow.

Sal shudders against the cold. She laughs in spite of herself.

SAL
Okay. That's enough zoology for today. Let's find a ready-for-milking gurrffa, take care of business, and get the hell outta here.

In the next scene, Sal and Rumrra stand side by side, facing the gurrffarr as they converse.

RUMRRA
The goal is to find one whose udders are plump but not overly swollen. Swollen udders mean a gurrffa has lost her calf. Such a gurrffa can be unpredictable and dangerous. One whose udders are merely plump most likely has a calf nearby but has not recently fed it. We can extract the most milk from these gurrffarr, and they will be quite pleased with us for relieving the pressure.

SAL
But with all that hair, how can you tell the difference? I can't see *any* udders behind that shag curtain!

Rumrra laughs. She pulls aside the "curtain" of hair hanging from the gurrffa's abdomen, then motions Sal forward.

SAL
(skeptically) You want me to crawl underneath? Is that safe?

RUMRRA
Don't tickle her and you'll be fine.

Sal crouches and wriggles her way underneath the gurrffa's stomach. Rumrra and the camera follow her until they arrive at a plump udder with ten protruding teats.

SAL
It seems I have plenty to choose from. Is there a trick for choosing one that works best?

RUMRRA

Find one that is already leaking. This indicates the gurrffa's most natural milking channel.

A close-up reveals one teat oozing bluish milk. Rumrra hands Sal a stout container with a tube attached to its lid.

SAL

I'm assuming I attach the free end to the gurrffa? Do I even—you know—have to *yoink* on it?

Sal sets the container on the snowy ground, then uses both hands to fasten the tube to the teat.

RUMRRA

Long ago, a shepherd might remain beneath a gurrffa for nearly an hour to extract the milk, praying she would not grow tired and lie down for a nap during that time. Now all we do is press the green button on the pail, and the machine extracts the milk in only a few minutes.

Sal chuckles as she presses the proper button. The machine hums to life, and milk begins flowing through the clear hose.

The next shot is of Sal, Rumrra, and the camerawoman emerging from beneath the gurrffa into the open air. Sal raises the milk container triumphantly.

SAL

Look at that! If my food program gig doesn't work out, maybe I'll try a career as a shepherdess. What do you think, Rumrra?

RUMRRA

You are a natural! When you return someday, I will teach you how to shepherd them where they can find food. That requires many days outside.

SAL

Oof. On second thought, I'll pass!

Sal hands the pail to Rumrra, then approaches the camera to address her viewers.

SAL
Now that we have what we came for, it's time to return to our ship. I hope you don't think we came all this way just to drink a refreshing glass of milk. I'll show you what comes next—but only after we're back in orbit. *And* blasting every heater the *Eats Queen* has onboard!

END OF REQUESTED TRANSCRIPT.
DATE OF ORIGINAL AIRING: DECEMBER 14, 2191 CE.

THE *TANTALUS*

IN OBEDIENCE TO Cay's command, the wall screen fades to black.

"Why'd you turn it off?" I ask. "Don't you want to watch the rest?"

"No. Why would I want that?" Cay replies, as if the answer should be as obvious as two plus two. "I've seen it before, and I remember what she made. It was a bland yogurt that she mixed with sliced fruit and *fleur de sal*. I've got something bigger in mind than a friggin' *parfait*." He spits out that last word like it's a wormy bite of apple.

"Then why'd we watch the first half?"

"Tips. Sal was popular for her show-womanship, not her culinary genius. I can't learn much about *food* from her, but I can learn plenty about standing in front of a camera."

"You don't think you could learn that from me? The film school graduate?"

Cay ignores me. "We can also learn a little about the planet we're headed to."

"Couldn't we just look it up on Axon?" I argue.

"Watching Sal gives us an up-close, personal look at Tarrkanna-Rrui. Better than we'll get from Axon's analytical breakdown. But since you mentioned it, it can't hurt to do that too."

Cay returns to the cockpit. "Tantalus, give us an analysis of Tarrkanna-Rrui. The encyclopedia version, please."

The ship's mechanized voice responds so quickly, I could swear it was listening all along.

"Tarrkanna-Rrui is classified as a cold eyeball planet. It is the second planet from the star Rrui, a red dwarf formerly known to Terrans as Kepler-1652. Tarrkanna-Rrui is tidally locked, meaning the same half of the planet always faces the star as it orbits. Because of the dangerous radiation on one half of the planet and dangerous cold on the other half, there is only a narrow habitable strip, approximately seventy kilometers wide, called the Twilight Zone.

"Tarrkanna-Rrui's air is breathable for humans and is composed of approximately 76.4% nitrogen, 21.8% oxygen, 0.66% argon, 0.039% carbon dioxide, and 1.1% other gases. Because Tarrkanna-Rrui's mean temperature in the Twilight Zone is around thirty-four degrees Celsius below zero, it is highly recommended that humans wear thick protective gear and cover all exposed skin."

Tantalus goes silent. It has arrived at the end of its "encyclopedia version" analysis.

"You couldn't have picked someplace warmer?" I contend, shuddering to imagine what such extreme temperatures—plus wind chill—will do to someone with Clarion-Burgess Syndrome. "There's still time to switch it up."

"Getting *cold* feet?" Cay says, and he laughs at his own pun. "The reason I chose Tarrkanna-Rrui is because this was one of the least dangerous foods Sal ever showcased. Believe it or not, Jerricho dearest, this is our breaking-in location."

Unable to hide my discomfort, I frown and look away.

"But don't worry," Cay continues, opening a small compartment next to his copilot's chair. As he rummages about inside it, he says, "When I told good ol' Slyce Cobb what we were up to, he insisted on sending a couple of these along."

Triumphantly, he holds up a clear mask. Tangled together and dangling below it are an elastic band and pair of thin tubes.

"It's called a *TARM*," Cay says, tossing it to me. "Can't remember what it stands for, though. I was distracted by the mole on Slyce's neck when he was explaining it."

"Terran Atmospheric Replication Mask," I inform Cay. He seems impressed until I point out the corresponding words on the mask's adjustable strap. I also notice a rectangular device fused onto it.

"Anyway," Cay goes on, "he said that black box thing on the side controls everything so that the air you breathe is exactly what you'd find on Terra. It filters out all the bad stuff, keeps the good stuff. *And* you can set it to adjust the temperature of the air you're breathing."

It isn't much, but I guess a *little* something is better than nothing at all.

Returning to my seat in the cockpit, I ask, "Do we have a guide lined up? Someone to take us to the ice fields?"

"Not yet," Cay answers. "While you were enjoying leisure time with your family, I had my hands tied with the remodeling job. But once we land in Tarrkan-Uffrra, I'm sure those adorable sea lion people will point us in the right direction."

I snort something close to a laugh. Cay's right. The Tarrkarr do resemble the sea lions we have on Terra.

"PAD still has a few hours left before we can jump into X-space," says Cay, "so I'm gonna try contacting Mei-Li Tan on the vidcomm."

"You think she'll help us?" I ask doubtfully.

Cay shrugs. "Cullan Jonas seems to think so. Besides, she was my dad's godmother. That makes her my *grand*-godmother, right? Who wouldn't help out her own grand-godson? Especially one who looks as tasty as me!"

I roll my eyes and stand. "Whatever. I'm taking a nap. One of us was up all night learning about X-space."

"Glad you're finally pulling your weight," remarks Cay. "You know, the floor of the mechanical closet might be big enough for you. It'll be warm and dark in there, and probably loud enough to drown out the music from mine and PAD's dance party."

"It'll be like sleeping on a down mattress," I reply, my tone laced with sarcasm. "Thanks for the upgrade in sleeping quarters."

"You're quite welcome. Don't forget your complimentary pillow and sleeping bag."

THE *TANTALUS'* "SLEEPING QUARTERS"

54 Days to Payment

I'M UNSURE WHICH comes first, Cay shouting "mother of pearl!" or my being slammed violently against the mechanical closet's metal panels and tubing.

Either way, my body explodes. Almost, anyway. My vision swims, and I fear my skull has cracked open and is oozing brains like a dropped melon. The force of collision would have brought an Inshiri prizefighter to her knees—or whatever it is they fall onto. For a human suffering from CBS, the agony is downright hellish. Even after the initial impact, it feels like some giant hand is trying to squash me into the wall.

The abrupt change in inertia lasts only a moment. As soon as it releases me, I open the door and half-crawl, half-roll into the *Tantalus'* main chamber. Which is, I remember, a kitchen and not a hospital. Unfortunate for me.

"What the deviled egg was *that*, PAD?" Cay yells, berating the drone hovering above the *Tantalus'* control console. "You ancient, stupid, robot idiot! You could have killed us!"

I don't hear PAD's response. I'm too mesmerized by what I see on the other side of the cockpit's windscreen. We seem to be immersed in some sort of luminescent, lavender sea foam. Bubbles—or ripples?—bathe the *Tantalus* in their otherworldly aura.

For a moment, I wonder whether we crashed into the ocean. Then it hits me.

This is X-space.

My marveling over the ethereal spectacle is short-lived.

A spasm racks my abdomen. I cough. Stare at the gob of dark red ichor that has appeared on the floor below me. Think, *Someone really ought to clean that up.*

Then my face is *in* the gob. It's sticky, but I don't mind. It feels warm against my cheek. Cozy.

As my world disintegrates to black, the last image I register is of Cay. He's flying up from his seat. Racing toward me. Yelling.

"Jer! You alright? Jer? Aw, *shitballs!*"

Then, nothing.

TARRKANNA-RRUI

– PERSEUS –

THE HEALERS' *IRRKUU*

I'M OUTSIDE. IN THE SEA FOAM. First it's lavender, like I remember from earlier. Then it's dainty blue, the color of a springtime flower in the hills near home. On and on, the shades and hues change. Morphing from one into another. Circulating through the infinite possibilities within a rainbow, and beyond.

How can I be alive? I wonder. Actually, I tried to speak the words aloud but couldn't. Something must be wrong with my voice.

X-space, I decide, is surprisingly warm. And relaxing. Like soaking in a tub with thousands of tiny bubbles massaging your skin all at once.

"Grrun arrkaan eemrrarr."

Huh? What's that noise? It sounds vaguely familiar, yet somehow totally foreign at the same time. Is someone else out here with me? Riding the quantum pathways of X-space?

"Krruumarr teemrreet affman rrakrrau."

Hello! I shout, but with my brain only. I don't know if I have a mouth anymore. Or maybe I never had one to begin with?

The color-fluid foam enveloping me grows brighter. Dark shapes, moving shadows, appear. Three? No, four of them.

"Grrun olmrree. Uff! Grrun olmrree."

"He's opening his eyes. See! He's opening his eyes." Words, spoken by a voice I know. At least, I think I do?

The shadows take solid form. They're seals. Something like seals, anyway. Sea lions? The light behind them is terribly bright, so it's difficult to tell anything for certain.

Another shape floats into view. This one has a cylindrical body and four whirring arms.

PAD. It was his voice I recognized.

"What happened?" I whisper, closing my eyes. I can't endure the light any longer. "Where are we?"

"You suffered life-threatening internal injuries, due to remaining unrestrained during the *Tantalus'* jump into X-space," PAD informs me.

Yes. Yes, I remember. It's coming back. Cay was yelling at PAD. That was right before everything disappeared.

"Presently, we are inside an *irrkuu*," PAD continues. "The healers of Tarrkanna-Rrui have been attending to you."

"Am I—you know—gonna die?"

One of the seals—a Tarrka—mutters something in her guttural tongue, and PAD translates. "You are in some of the most capable paws in the galaxy. Your injuries will not kill you."

"It ... hurts," I say with a groan. "Hurts a lot."

In response, another Tarrka opens a glass jar. Using one of the rubbery digits on the end of his webbed paw, he rubs some kind of paste between my nose and upper lip.

A sweet scent fills the air, reminding me of December spices and my dad's Christmas punch. At once, the pain starts leaking out of me, like it's draining through holes drilled into my back. The harsh light above likewise begins to fade, along with the chestnut faces of the whiskered healers.

Before I'm able to ask where everyone is going, my world is swallowed again in darkness, and my consciousness flies far, far away.

THE HEALERS' *IRRKUU*

THE NEXT TIME I wake up, the Tarrkarr are gone, the lights above me mellower. After a few groggy blinks, I force myself to sit up. Through no small amount of lingering pain and stiffness, I swing my legs over the side of the bed and place my bare feet flat on the ground.

Big mistake. I recoil instantly, yelping with shock.

"Cold, isn't it," a voice behind me says.

I jump, startled, and turn in my bed to face the intruder.

"Cay!" I cry. I'm surprised how relieved I am to see him.

"This entire city is civilized," says Cay, leaning forward in his chair, "but these *irrkiitaa*—the healers—insist on working in their traditional igloos. Very annoying."

One after another, my questions come vomiting out. "What happened? How'd we get here? How long have I been out? Does my family know what happened?"

Cay jerks an accusatory thumb at the drone hovering beside him. Answering the first question, he says, "Once PAD was finished downloading, I told him to *get ready* to jump into X-space. Apparently, all he heard was the last part: jump into X-space. So he did."

"And you kept going to Tarrkanna-Rrui? Why didn't you turn around?"

"Because my X-space expert was comatose," he answers. "Besides, you don't 'turn around' in X-space. It's not like an ATC when they've missed your street. As soon as we came out of X-space again—Not easy to buckle your giant butt into your restraints, by the way, so a *thank you* might be in order—we landed here and I called for medics. As for your other question, whether your family knows anything ..."

Cay removes a jumble of loosely connected wires, buttons, and fiberglass from his pocket.

"Is that my—?" I can't finish the question.

"Your tel. Yeah. It handled the jump to X-space even worse than you did."

I can't believe it. My lifeline, my connection to everyone I know and love back on Terra ... gone.

"It's okay, you can use mine!" Cay reassures me. "I've been itching for Josephina's number anyway, so this works out well for both of us."

"Thanks," I mumble. Sure, I'll be able to reach my family in a pinch, but not with any amount of privacy. Who am I supposed to vent to about all Cay's stupid antics now? PAD?

"You can thank me by getting dressed," Cay says. He lifts a bundle from the little table beside his chair. It's my backpack. He tosses it to me. "We've already wasted six days waiting for you to rest up, and I don't think Sawtooth and Bloodgout are likely to give me an extension for something as trivial as near-death experiences."

He faces the wall to give me privacy.

"Any luck reaching Mei-Li?" I ask, stripping off the poncho-like gown supplied by the healers.

"I left a message," he says, "but she hasn't sent a response yet."

"What about a guide? Did you find someone to bring us to the ice fields?"

"Four days ago," Cay answers. "Seems like a bit of a sleaze, but on our budget, we take what we can get."

"Where'd you find him?"

Cay chuckles. "The only place to find any budget-friendly guide for hire—the bar!"

TARRKAN-UFFRRA

48 Days to Payment

THE CITY BEYOND the *irrkuu's* walls is, in a word, breathtaking. The cluster of ice domes where Tarrkan-Uffrra's physicians labor is set among a gridwork of far more impressive gems. Although none of these buildings can rival Terran skyscrapers in terms of height, their architecture is far more harmonious to their environment.

"Buildings of stone and ice," I marvel out loud, my stiff joints attempting to match Cay's pace. "I've never seen anything like it."

"And you still haven't," Cay casually replies. "It's stone and *glass.*"

"How do you know?"

Even in my post-coma brain fog, my instinct to bicker with Cay is making a quick comeback.

"Ice always shrinks over time. It's called *sublimation,* my unscientific friend. It's what happens to your ice cubes in the freezer. These buildings would be falling over left and right if they were made of actual ice."

"How far are we going?" I ask. Already I'm shivering against the cold.

"Only a few more blocks," Cay answers. "But after all that rest you got, I'm sure you've got a hundred miles in you."

As we pass by one long building's street-level entrances, I notice strange symbols carved into the stone above the doors. Some kind of writing, I'm sure, but I can read neither vowel nor consonant of it.

I'm not on Terra anymore. That much is certain.

A boxy carriage atop two broad skis passes by us on the ice-paved road. It's being pulled by four shaggy beasts, like horses but with half the snout, thrice the eyes, and twenty times the hair.

It strikes me—I haven't seen anything with an engine along the streets of Tarrkan-Uffrra. Not a single, solitary scabb. On Terra, the noise of a large city could be deafening. Yet here, even surrounded by such grand buildings, the world is hushed. Calm. Like a Norman Rockwell Christmas if he'd painted sea lions in place of humans.

Reading my mind, Cay says, "They don't allow engines inside the city. Even walking around with PAD earned me a death stare from an elderly Tarrka."

"It's ... nice," I say. At the same time, I wish I weren't traipsing about in way-below-zero temperatures.

Eventually, Cay leads us off the main road, down a wide alley between two high-rises of polished stone. Here we arrive at a dark doorway. Above it hangs a stone placard bearing more of the foreign symbols.

Cay throws open the door and says, "Welcome to the Hot Shot Hothouse."

Hothouse is an apt name for it. The moment I step inside, I uncinch my parka and lower the hood. The bar's interior is brightly lit and vivid blue, like the underside of a sunlit glacier. There are only a handful of patrons present, a couple bellied up to the bar, the others hunched over tables pushed against the wall. I can tell they're serious drinkers, because they're all drinking alone.

"These Tarrkarr all look the same to me," Cay mutters, scanning the room.

Fortunately, one of the Hot Shot's denizens waves a paw at us.

Cay's million-current grin reappears at once. "There he is!" he exclaims. "The handsomest gurrffa shepherd money can buy. With my bankroll, anyway."

· PAD translates Cay's words into Tarrkan grunts and squeaks.

The Tarrka stands to greet us. He's wearing a bulky, fur-lined coat and matching gloves. Strapped to his waist is a holster, and in it, a sidearm. I have little experience with guns—never even touched one—but I do know a single squeeze of its trigger will produce a laser blast lethal to most beings. Certainly so for a human like me.

Why a gurrffa shepherd would need such a thing is beyond me. But, so long as he's on our side, I guess I have nothing to worry about.

The energetic Tarrka gestures toward the empty chairs at his table. "Sit! Sit!" he says—through PAD, of course. "I am glad to see your friend alive and awake."

"Jerricho, this is Turrfurrkrro," says Cay, "but he has mercifully agreed to let us call him 'Turf' while under our brief employ."

"Let me buy you a drink," Turf says. He hollers something at the bartender. "Here on Tarrkanna-Rrui, it is impolite to eat or drink in the presence of friends without offering them what you have in front of yourself. Besides, I could use one more *ullurr* myself."

"Thanks," I reply with a nervous grin. I'm not sure I'm ready to try Tarrkan booze. What if their tolerance is way higher than a human's, and I end up flat on my ass in an *irrkuu* for another six days?

"You'll love it," says Cay, offering a reassuring nudge. "Reminds me of your sister's perfume. Turf and I had six or seven the other day."

The bartender brings three tankards to the table. The steam pluming up and out of them does, I admit, smell appetizing. Floral and piney, like someone juiced an alpine meadow into a glass.

When I take a sip and don't feel immediately lightheaded, my shoulders relax. The warm ullurr is sweeter than tea but not cloying, and it raises my still-shivering innards a few degrees.

"It will keep you warm in the ice fields," says Turf. Gesturing crudely with his flippers, he adds, "There are many heavy-titted gurrffarr this time of year, plump with milk for their newborn pups. But it is also the coldest time of the year, when my planet is furthest from Rrui, our parent star."

Great. We came to Antarctica. In winter.

"Turf's herd isn't too far outside the city," Cay says, "so we'll fly there in his transport. We'll do a few informational shots to explain what we're up to, like Sal did with Rumrra. Then I'll milk a gurrffa—by hand—and we'll hurry back to the city before our nippies freeze off."

"Why milk by hand? Why not use one of those milking machines like Sal?"

"The mechanized suction causes the gurrffarr to release a slightly bitter hormone into the milk. Apparently the machine pleasures them too much. It's not a huge difference—probably why most Tarrkarr still use the machine version—but we're a step above Sal on *Galactic Eats Reheated*. If we're gonna have the best eats, we've got to squeeze the teats."

"Save that line for the camera!" I reply with a chuckle. "And when did we decide on the whole 'Reheated' thing?"

"Came up with it while you were sleeping. Like it?"

I nod, genuinely impressed. It's a clever name.

"Good. Because I wasn't planning to change it."

I raise my tankard toward Cay. "Well, then. To *Galactic Eats Reheated*."

Cay taps his glass against mine, and we gulp down the rest of our ullurr.

"Let's head back to the *Tantalus* to pick up your camera equipment," says Cay. "Turf, can you meet us there in one hour? We're in Port B, stall forty-four."

"I can," he says, draining his mug. "And for you, I will bring my family's very best *krrukka*."

THE ICE FIELDS

"THIS IS YOUR best *krrukka?*" I holler over the rushing air. Instantly, I regret forgetting the TARM—the Terran Atmospheric Replication Mask —in the bag with my camera gear. At the rate we're traveling, opening my mouth to speak is like biting some supervillain's freeze gun and holding the trigger.

"No, the best one was undergoing repairs," Turf shouts back.

My heart sinks. If their *good* krrukka needs repairs, what does that say about the one we're jetting toward the ice fields in?

"Just pretend you're sitting on a beach somewhere, with a cool breeze blowing in from the sea," Cay advises.

"A *beach?*" I yell. "It's twenty below zero, and this piece of shit *scabb* doesn't have a roof!"

"Look on the bright side! At least we're keeping each other warm."

Warm, my ass. The krrukka doesn't have a rear seat, which means there are three grown beings and a robot shoved into space for two.

I sure hope my cameras function alright in weather this cold. At least I was able to seal them shut in a storage compartment.

"We are passing over the Mrrunkakarr," Turf informs us, pointing down.

Leaning as far as my restraining harness allows, I peer over the edge of the krrukka. Below us is a jagged labyrinth of glacial upheavals and crevasses. In Tarrkan-Uffrra, stone and ice—or, glass, I suppose—merge to form a raw symphony of architectural splendor. Out here, however, stone and ice seem locked in some grotesque battle, each wrestling to gain the other's territory. Cosmos help the poor soul navigating such a place on foot! The fact that the ancient Tarrkan shepherds once did exactly so fills me with deep admiration for them. It also makes me suspicious they were batshit crazy.

"When we arrive," Turf says, speaking through PAD, "we will seek out the gurrffa with the largest udders. They will be most receptive to our milking. Those with less milk can become violent, because they must save what they have for their pups."

I frown and replay Turf's words in my mind. Something isn't sitting right with me, but I can't put my finger on it. I know I'm likely suffering confusion and brain fog due to my coma, but the sense of unease lingers nonetheless.

Soon, the krrukka crosses over the last reaches of Mrrunkakarr. Ahead are the gentle, rolling slopes of the ice fields. A dense cluster of dark shapes appears, a singular body of lazy beasts writhing in slow motion as they jostle for interior—and, I'm guessing, warmer—positions among the rest.

"That is my family's herd," Turf informs us.

The krrukka decelerates—I know, because the wind's brutality is subsiding—as we approach the groaning mass of gurrffarr. Turf lowers the vessel gently onto its skis. He leaves the engine running and clambers out. In conditions this cold, it might be too great a gamble to hope the vehicle will restart.

I retrieve my bag from the krrukka's storage box. Before dealing with anything camera related, I strap the TARM to my face. It engages automatically. At once, I'm sucking down warm air.

Small relief when the rest of me is turning to ice.

Next, I remove a camera from the bag. Waving PAD over, I hand it to him. He grasps the camera firmly in one of his many appendages, appraising it thoughtfully with his electronic eye.

"You're gonna be first AC—assistant camera," I explain. "I want you to hover above the herd and take shots of the landscape only. Do that for a couple minutes, then switch to long takes of the landscape *with* the herd. You got that?"

"Yes, Mr. Hatch."

Remembering the problems we've experienced with his listening skills, I tell PAD to repeat my commands back to me. He does.

"Good. I know it's windy, but stay as steady as you can for those shots."

While PAD floats upward to carry out his role, I remove my ARRI Lite from the storage compartment. This camera doesn't possess anywhere near the production value of the Titan I wielded on the *Cosmic Bachelor* set, but it's half the weight with twice the versatility. A fair tradeoff for the task at hand.

I had the genius idea to shoot a "meeting" scene between Cay and Turf back in the warmth of the *Tantalus*: "This is our guide ... comes from a millennia-long line of shepherds ... taking us to the same ice fields Grandma Sal visited fifty years ago ..." And so on, and so forth. With so much lead-in footage out of the way, I'll supplement with a few contextual shots, watch Cay milk a gurrffa, and call it a day. With any luck, I'll be thawing in front of the *Tantalus*' heater within the hour.

"Cay, come put your lapel mic on. Then stand in front of the krrukka and explain what it is and how it brought us here," I order.

Cay crunches toward me through the snow. "Listen to you, taking charge and bossing me around. Put a camera in your hand, and you turn into my apartment manager when she's breaking up one of my parties. I'll tell you the same thing I told her: You're kinda turnin' me on right now!"

But the moment the camera is rolling, Cay becomes a different person. A better version of himself, if you ask me. He sheds his oppressive immaturity while maintaining all the charming swagger. He oozes earnestness yet continues to glow with his lighthearted and playful aura. It's almost like he's flirting with the camera.

Exactly the way Sal did when she was on-screen.

Once Cay is finished narrating the krrukka's role in our adventure, he approaches Turf and the gurrffa he has chosen for the milking demonstration.

The largest of the hefty creatures are about the size of an adult elephant, though most are smaller. They look something like snub-nosed whales, albeit ones who sprouted thick limbs and went splashing about in a sea of radioactive hair-growth serum. They seem mindful of us, perhaps even curious, but not threatened or agitated by our presence.

"Now the real fun begins," Cay tells the camera. "Turf has found a gurrffa with a swollen udder."

Swollen. The word triggers that same sense of discomfort I felt on the krrukka.

"Perfectly ripe for the milking, according to our resident expert." Cay spins the milk bucket in his hands like it's a child's play ball. "That also means it's time to take a deep breath and dive straight into the belly of the beast. *Under* it, anyway."

I remember how Rumrra pleasantly held aside the gurrffa's hair for Sal, even accompanied her underneath the animal. Turf does neither. He backs off without a sound, other than his leather shoes stamping through the top layer of crusty snow.

Following Cay as best I can while keeping my camera in a steady position, we edge our way beneath the gurrffa. It bellows an agitated cry, then stamps and grinds its thick hind paws.

Like a bull ready to charge.

My reaction is a moment too late. Cay has already grabbed the gurrffa's teat when I realize why Turf's comments made me so uneasy.

"Cay!" I scream. "Get out! Now!"

A rush of frigid air envelops us as the gurrffa rears up onto its hind legs. Cay yells and dives out of the way. I do the same, but it isn't enough. The gurrffa's forelegs stamp down into the ice-crusted snow, mere inches from my face. Like it's my child, my instincts are to protect the camera. I tuck it into my parka and roll once, twice, three times to the side.

I'm clear of this particular gurrffa's rampage. But the rest of its friends and family have begun joining in. One angry gurrffa upsets three of its neighbors, creating a chain reaction. On two knees and one arm, I crawl frantically in the direction of the krrukka.

Until, suddenly, the krrukka isn't there anymore.

Where did it go?

Fighting the stiffness of my long sleep and the chronic agony of my illness, I leap to my feet.

The gurrffarr are a brawling mess. A hundred me-sized legs tramp. Another hundred stamp.

Ten seconds pass. Then twenty.

Cay is dead. I'm sure of it. He's dead, which means *I'm* on the hook with the Malvudians.

Strangely, I find I don't care about that last fact. All I care about in this moment is my friend. The only real friend I've had the past few years.

What will I do without him?

Fortunately, I don't have to answer my morose question. Not yet, anyway. Channeling his inner action hero, Cay comes surging out of the chaos.

Sonofabitch even managed to hang on to his milk pail.

He grabs my arm as he runs, dragging me further from the danger.

"What *was* that?" he wonders, gasping for air as he watches the bickering gurrffarr herd. "She freaked out on me the second I touched her!"

"Turf lied," I moan. "I knew something was wrong, but I didn't realize 'til it was too late. He told us to go for the gurrffarr with the biggest udders. But those were the ones that *lost* their pups. In Sal's episode, Rumrra explained they could be unpredictable and violent."

"But why would he lie to us?" Cay asks. He wraps his arms around himself to ward off the cold.

"I'm not sure we'll ever hear an answer," I reply. I nod toward the imprints Turf's landing gear left in the snow.

The krrukka is gone. And with it, any hope of our survival.

To this point, PAD has been carrying out his task to procure aerial footage. Now he descends to eye level and hands me the camera, "I have secured the film you requested. How else can I be of assistance?"

I loop the camera's nylon strap around my neck. "Fly back to Tarrkan-Uffrra," I say, "and send help."

PAD gives my order only the briefest consideration. "I'm sorry, but I cannot. My battery will not last long enough in this extreme cold. I am already nearing reserve mode."

Our last shot at rescue, shot himself.

"Well?" I shout at Cay. "Any brilliant ideas now?"

"Cinch your parka tight," he replies, pointing westward. "I can see the city on the horizon. Maybe we can walk back."

"Are you that stupid, Cay?" I retort, bumping him angrily with my camera. "Remember the Mrrunkakarr? That maze of rocks and ice in between?"

"It's okay, I was really good at mazes as a kid. One way or another, we'll find our way out," Cay cheerfully replies. He raises the milk pail. "But, first things first!"

"You can't be serious!" I yell, incredulous. "You're still worried about the *milk?*"

"It's what we came for, isn't it? Now, to find a less homicidal gurrffa ..."

Cay approaches the nearest one, raises its fur curtain, and chuckles. "I don't think you'd like me milking *that!* Or maybe you'd like it too much? You sure know how to make a man feel *very* inadequate."

He turns to another gurrffa and has a look beneath.

"Bingo!" he cries. At once, he disappears into a sea of hair.

I hug my chest and stamp my feet, trying to produce and retain whatever heat I can. But out here, in such brutal chill and wind, it's about as effective as trimming a football field with fingernail clippers.

For some inexplicable reason, all I can think about in those dire moments is Gram. We promised Cullan Jonas five episodes, and here we are, about to die before we're halfway finished shooting one. Gram will never see a dime of return on her investment.

Her stupid fault, I guess. Betting on Cay is a sure loser. She should know that by now.

The gurrffarr are finally cooling off—no pun intended—and have begun returning to their bucolic laze. Perhaps we can shelter beneath some of the more peaceable ones for warmth? Wait until another shepherd swings by to check on the herd? After all, it *is* milking season.

But ... no. A bitter shiver is already settling in my innards. We won't last long out here, even if we are snuggled beneath a gurrffa tent.

Something solid bumps against my back and nearly knocks me forward into the snow. Assuming Cay has returned from milking the gurrffa, I wheel about, ready to sock him for landing us in this fatal predicament.

I cry out. Instead of Cay, it's the flat-nosed face of a gurrffa staring at me. With its great gray orb of an eye, it looks me over, examining me with such earnestness, I could swear it's concerned for me.

That's when another line from Sal's episode bubbles up through the brain fog.

"PAD!" I shout. "I need you to talk to this gurrffa. Translate what I say into Tarrkan, and do it with the most spot-on Turf impression you've got."

The drone hovers into position. A flashing red light on his cylindrical body warns me that his battery could die any moment.

"We're in trouble," I tell the gurrffa, gazing intently into its eye. "We need your help. Please, carry us back to the city. If you don't, we'll die."

The gurrffa responds with low baying, shaking its shaggy head.

I hear the pitch of PAD's rotors dropping. A second later, his altitude does too. He's spent. Useless.

Please, please understand me. Please, save us. Without PAD, all I can do is project my thoughts at the gurrffa, this last hope of a savior. I pray that I unwittingly gained a knack for telepathy when I hit my head aboard the *Tantalus*.

The gurrffa snorts a plume of rank breath over my face. Then its forelegs bend, and it lowers itself onto its knees. The back legs follow, until its belly is resting upon the snow. It snorts again and tosses its head.

Did my telepathic plea work? I approach the gurrffa carefully. Near its shoulder, I lace my fingers through its tangles of ropy hair and give a gentle tug.

The gurrffa's only response is a nonchalant flick of its ear.

"Cay, let's go!" I cry.

He hasn't emerged yet from his milking mission. With all this wind and a forest of gurrffa yarn between us, I wonder whether he can hear me at all.

Pain shoots along my fingers and forearms as I try hauling myself up the gurrffa's side. Without any footholds to aid my climb, and bearing the added weight of two cameras, I don't make it far before I fall back into the snow.

I shout for Cay a second time. Again, he doesn't answer.

The gurrffa must be aware of my struggle, because it turns to check on me. Then it lowers its head onto the snow and gives another loud snort.

Climb up my face, I imagine it telling me.

So I do. The gurrffa grunts irritably as I clamber up the slope of its snout, between its eyes, and over the crown of its skull. I settle between its shoulder blades, then burrow into its fur until I'm nestled against its warm skin.

Maybe a gurrffa tent wouldn't be such a bad idea after all.

A minute later, Cay's voice rises above the wind. "Jer! Where'd you go?"

"Up here!" I raise my head so he can see me. "I think it wants to give us a ride. Remember what Sal said?"

"Never drink orange juice after brushing your teeth?"

"She said sometimes gurrffarr help lost travelers. I'd say we fit that description pretty damn well at the moment, wouldn't you? Besides, it's a helluva lot warmer in here."

"Can't argue with that," says Cay.

He lifts the milk pail—far from full, but apparently enough for our purposes—into my outstretched hand. Next comes PAD, who is much heavier than I would have guessed. I'm barely able to keep a grip on him as I drag him the rest of the way up the gurrffa's flank. Finally, according to my instructions, Cay scales the beast's snout.

"Oh! Comfy!" Cay says as he huddles beside me. "Do you think the Tarrkarr ever make them into beds? We *must* have one for our mechanical closet."

"Careful," I warn. "They understand more than you'd think."

Giving the fur clutched in my fists a quick but firm tug, I shout, "We're ready! Take us to the city."

Cay and I lurch between the gurrffa's shoulders as it pushes itself up from the snow. Invigorated with new purpose, the mighty gurrffa stands tall and trumpets toward the cloudless sky.

"Hang on tight," I advise Cay.

"How fast do you think one of these overgrown cows can move?" he asks. Still, he loops more fur around his clenched fist.

Good thing, too. Like an Olympic sprinter exploding off his marks, the gurrffa takes off. In great leaps and bounds, it flies across the wintry plateau, resembling a racehorse rather than Cay's "overgrown cow."

I lift my head from its fur just long enough to make certain we're pointed toward Tarrkan-Uffrra. Satisfied with our heading, and quite dissatisfied with the wind, I retreat again into the gurrffa's thick wool and nestle my frost-nipped face against its warm body.

Pressed into the flesh below my collarbone, Gram's good-luck diamond starts warming up too.

HOT SHOT HOTHOUSE

TURF IS BELLIED up to the bar, engaged in lively conversation with the only other hothouse denizen, when Cay storms up from the back-stabbing Tarrkan's blind side. Caught entirely off his guard, and undoubtedly stunned to see us alive, Turf hardly has the time to squeal a fearful protest before Cay slams him against the bar top.

Turf reaches for the sidearm at his waist, but Cay is quicker. He tears the weapon from its holster and tosses it to me.

I catch the unexpected weapon like it's a Theronian plasma knife, praying as I bobble it that I don't accidentally blow my own hand off. Once I have a firm grip on it, and not knowing what else to do, I aim the pistol's quivering barrel at Turf.

The other patron and bartender shout their objections to Cay's display of violence. I'm glad we came during Tarrkan-Uffrra's work hours, or else we'd be finding ourselves on the minority end of a drunken mob.

Cay ignores the angry Tarrkarr. He hurls Turf against the bar a second time. Seizing a fistful of the other's coat, Cay leans in close. In a tone unfittingly calm for the situation, he growls, "You left us out there to die. I want to know why."

PAD, who enjoyed a partial charge during our brief pitstop at the *Tantalus*, translates.

Turf doesn't say anything. He's too focused on the gun barrel pointed at his face.

"Jerricho's not gonna shoot you," Cay assures the frightened Tarrka. "Now, answer the question."

The withdrawn threat of death turns Turf into a braver Tarrka. "Eat my dung," he says.

Cay glances sideways at me. "Changed my mind. Shoot him."

"No! Please!" Turf squeaks. "Do not hurt me."

"Last chance," Cay says. "Why did you leave us?"

"After you hired me, another man offered me double to kill you," Turf admits.

"You should've used the gun," Cay replies with a smirk. "But you were too big a coward. Thought you'd leave it up to the gurrffarr."

"I am not a murderer," says Turf. "But I am poor, and my family has fallen upon hard times."

"Maybe that's because you waste all day drinking," Cay suggests. "But your family's problems aren't mine. This man who hired you—what did he look like?"

"He was tall. Even taller than your friend. But he was wearing a dark hood, so I could not distinguish his features."

Cay leans in closer. "Try."

"He was older, I think. I am not an expert on human aging, but he had gray hair. Maybe white. But, please, that is all I know!"

Cay releases Turf's shirt and backs off a step.

"Geiger," he says, spitting the name like it's a disease. "I should've known that butthole would try to poop on our party."

He approaches Turf again and rifles through the Tarrka's coat pockets. After finding only a handful of currents—a fraction of the amount Cay paid to hire him—he slips them into his own pocket.

"Cross me again," he threatens, "and Jer will shoot one of your balls off. Got it?"

"Yes!" Turf squeals.

Cay storms toward the exit. I follow, glad that I can lower the pistol at last.

As I slip out into the ever-twilit air, I wonder, *Do male Tarrkarr even have balls?*

THE *TANTALUS*

47 Days to Payment

I CERTAINLY HAVE BALLS. Currently, I'm thawing them in the hot sink-bath I promised myself would never happen. But after the events of the last week, and with few alternatives, I swallow my pride and take the plunge. My whole body doesn't fit, of course. Not even close. Still, it's enough to scratch an itch—and return feeling to one's manhood.

Cay is in the cockpit, warming up the old-fashioned way with a tumbler of whiskey, neat. He's also making use of the *Tantalus'* video monitor to call Cullan Jonas.

Instead of the behemoth Rouzh-man, it's Jaque Pinder's rodentlike face that appears on the vidcomm. When he recognizes Cay, the executive assistant's neutral expression changes at once to disappointment.

"What do you want?"

"A pleasure to see you too, Jaque," Cay responds. "Where's Jonas?"

"Occupied."

"That right? Well, maybe he'll un-occupy himself after you give him my message."

Jaque straightens his glasses. "And what message would that be?"

"That if I don't see him in the next two minutes, I'll sell my program to someone else."

It only takes twenty seconds. Cullan Jonas's broad head fills the monitor. His eyes are glassy and unfocused, his top two shirt buttons undone. Like Pinder, he's annoyed to see his newest food program host.

"Whaddayou want, Cantore?" he slurs. "I've go' company."

Offscreen, the hushed voice of a woman says something indistinguishable, leaving little uncertainty regarding the type of "company" Jonas is keeping.

"What a coincidence! I've got a naked friend here too," says Cay, jerking a thumb over his shoulder. "I'll show you mine if you show me yours."

"Don't even think about it, Cay," I holler.

Somehow, Cay's juvenile antics have a way of melting Jonas's otherwise icy demeanor. "So?" he asks. "How's progress? I imagine there's a reason you called."

"There is, in fact. Do you have any idea where Gustav Geiger is at the moment?"

"No, I don't. But as long as he finishes his work on time—which he always does—that prick can do whatever the hell he wants."

"Well, I *do* know where he is. As another coincidence would have it, Geiger is here on Tarrkanna-Rrui with me."

Jonas gives an indifferent shrug. "So? It's a free galaxy."

"But not so free that you can hire out someone's murder, I'm sure."

Jonas leans forward. "Are you tellin' me Gustav Geiger tried to kill you?"

"That's exactly what I'm telling you. He paid our Tarrkan guide to do it. Abandoned us in the freezing ice fields outside the city."

"Yet 'ere you are. Alive."

"We got lucky."

"And did this guide identify Geiger by name? Did you see 'im yourself?"

Cay's shoulders sag as he considers Jonas's questions. "Well, no, I didn't. But his description made it obvious. Said he was hired by a tall, aging human with gray hair."

"Look," says Jonas, "I did tell Geiger 'bout my arrangement 'th you. I'll admit to that. But I never shared any specifics 'bout your itinerary or th' episodes you're planning to shoot. Besides, when I told him what you were doing, he didn't have much reaction. Annoyed, maybe, but not angry or threatened."

"Geiger stands in front of a camera every day," Cay says. "Could it be that—oh, I don't know—he's just a good actor?"

"Maybe. But I've known 'im a long time. Geiger's a self-important ass, no doubts there. A killer, though? He doesn't have it in 'im. He barks plenty, but he dudn't have much bite."

More sultry murmuring draws Jonas's drunken attention offscreen. He grins at Cay and says, "Tha's all the time I got for you today. Other business to attend to. Glad t' see you alive."

He doesn't let Cay respond. The video connection ends, and the monitor goes dark.

Cay rises from his chair and enters the kitchen.

"Bath time's over, Jer," he says, opening the ice chest. "Dry off, then bleach the dickens outta that sink. We need it empty—and *sterile*—for filming."

GALACTIC EATS REHEATED
PRODUCTION SET

CAY LEANS OVER the Dutch oven, stirring gently as he looks ahead into my camera. A fully charged PAD hovers overhead, adding extra angles per my instructions. Later, I'll edit his B-roll into the finished product.

"Now that the boiled-down gurrffa milk has cooled," Cay tells our hypothetical audience, "we'll add that tiny bit of raw milk we set aside at the beginning. That's what contains the live bacteria required to turn the thickened milk into *mrrunkat,* that savory, yogurt-like substance we're going to use in our main dish."

Cay measures out a quarter teaspoon from the reserved raw milk and pours it into the Dutch oven. As he mixes it, he says, "Remember, it's important to let the cooked milk cool fully, or you risk killing the bacteria when you pour in your raw gurrffa milk. But you must never mix in more than that tiny quarter teaspoon. You'll be tempted to, because the yogurt-making process takes about ten days total, but uncooked gurrffa milk *is* toxic. While a quarter teaspoon isn't going to hurt you, adding extra could make you very, very sick."

Satisfied that the contents of his pot are sufficiently blended, Cay taps his wooden spoon on the rim.

"Now cover the pot and place it into your oven at one hundred fifteen degrees Celsius. It'll sit in there, untouched, for eight to ten hours. After that, all I'm going to do is ladle it into a glass container—*not* metal—where it'll continue to transform and set for the next nine to ten days. Leave your mrrunkat somewhere warm if you can, but you also want to make sure you're not scalding it. Next to a hot-water tank might be your best bet in most homes. Onboard the *Tantalus,* tucking it into a corner of the mechanical closet will do fine."

We pause. I reposition Cay so I can shoot from a different angle.

"Once the mrrunkat is finished, I'll demonstrate how you can use it to create a meat course that will even impress your most persnickety dinner guest."

And ... cut. I lower my camera.

"So we've got to wait a week and a half to finish the episode?" I ask.

"Of course not," Cay says with a wink. "Who's got time for that? I'll change clothes, then keep filming with the yogurt I bought two days ago."

"The yogurt you *bought?*"

"I had to start marinating the meat, didn't I?" says Cay. "It takes twelve hours!"

"Then why the hell did we risk our lives to get your precious milk from a live gurrffa?" I protest.

"Because it tastes better," Cay casually replies. "Like I told you before."

"But you're not even using it for the show!"

"Doesn't mean I won't use it at all. The best mrrunkat will be just for us. And think how much sweeter it'll taste after risking our lives for it!"

I'm too exhausted to push back any harder. "Whatever. I don't care. We're alive, so let's finish shooting. I wanna sleep."

"Excellent," says Cay. He's already unbuttoning his shirt.

Once his wardrobe change is complete, he removes a full jar of store-bought mrrunkat from the ice chest. After he tastes it for the camera and raves about its superior quality, he moves on to the next segment of his demonstration. While he whisks oil, salt, and pepper into the yogurt, he explains to the camera, "Since we're using gurrffa yogurt, we'll also use a big ol' hock of gurrffa shoulder as our meat headliner."

Another cut, another shot. Cay grunts as he heaves a meat hunk the size of my family's old pug from ice chest to countertop. He waves me in for a close-up of the untreated meat.

"Like shoulder cuts on many other animals, you'll see lots of connective tissue and fat," he says. He traces white lines in the meat with the index finger of his unmaimed hand. "If you try cooking a cut like this too quickly, you'll end up with a main course tougher than gurrffa leather. That's why we're going to give our shoulder meat the wedding night treatment. Low and slow, baby."

Definitely editing that part out.

From there, my body and mind slip into autopilot mode. As long as I hold the camera where it's needed, and instruct PAD to do the same, my attention doesn't matter much. The cutting floor is where every product truly takes shape anyway. I'll save my energy for that.

Using a smaller gurrffa hunk that has been swimming in its mrrunkat marinade for twelve hours, Cay performs a quick sear on all sides. As he does, he mentions something about a Maillard reaction— "A lot of science, but all you need to know is that protein, sugar, and heat make for a delicious, caramelly meat crust"—then sets the shoulder aside. Next, sliced onions take their turn sizzling in the pot. Once they're "gooey brown," Cay adds grated ginger, a healthy dose of molasses, freshly ground coriander, and both the zest and juice of a grapefruit. He lets the sauce thicken, then pours in gurrffa broth—also store-bought— until a third of the pot is filled with liquid. Finally, the seared meat returns to its "braising jacuzzi," and Cay slides the whole thing into the oven.

"Remember," Cay says, "we want low temperature, long cook time. I've set my oven to one hundred ten degrees Celsius, and I'm planning on a four- to five-hour braise. This should ensure that my meat is fully cooked, but also still juicy and melty tender."

Assuming we're done, I lower my camera.

"Camera up!" Cay says. "Not done yet, old chap."

I groan but do as he orders.

"While our gurrffa begins its braising journey, we're going to pull together a simple sauce to top our meat. Earlier, the mrrunkat went to work in the marinade, where it helped tenderize the gurrffa. Now, we'll put it to work again to add a note of freshness to our finished meat."

Cay places six ingredients in a line on the counter. He plops two heaping spoons of gurrffa yogurt into a ceramic bowl.

"Starting with the mrrunkat, we'll mix in a dash of sea salt ... a couple grinds of black peppercorn ... a palmful of sliced green onions ... a skosh more of our grapefruit zest ... and a sprinkling of fresh mint and basil, chopped or shredded, whichever is easier."

He tilts the bowl so I can have a good look inside.

"And there you have it, the perfect dipping sauce for your gurrffa. While our meat cooks, we'll let our sauce sit in the ice chest, where all our flavors can become better acquainted with each other."

Cay gazes straight into the camera. At long last, he says, "I'll see you in a few hours. Until then, eat well, friends!"

The camera drops to my side.

"Done?" I ask.

"For now," Cay answers. "Go ahead, get some sleep. Not that you should need it after your six-day nap."

TARRKAN–UFFRRA SPACEPORT

Section B, Stall 44

"WAKE UP, JERRICHO!"

I slip away from my unknown dreams, reluctant to return to the waking world. I'm already sitting up, and Cay is shaking my shoulders urgently. My first thought is that something must have gone wrong with his braising. It smells spectacular from where I'm sitting, but I suppose we'll have to do the shoot all over again.

"Where's the gun? The one we took from Turf?" Cay asks. Even in the dim light of the *Tantalus'* mechanical room, there's no mistaking the urgency in his expression.

I pause, gathering my thoughts from wherever sleep's haze has hidden them. "In my duffel, I think. Cabinet next to the sleeping bags. What's going on? Is it Geiger?"

Cay hurries into the *Tantalus'* main atrium and says, "Not sure. But it sounds like someone's in trouble."

Then I hear it too. It's muffled by the *Tantalus'* hull, but definitely there.

A female voice. Screaming for help.

"Tantalus," Cay tells the onboard computer, "disable the boarding ramp's automatic lights."

"Disabled," comes its mechanical reply.

"And dim the ship's interior lights too," Cay adds.

I follow him to the edge of the closed ramp. His finger hovers over the RAISE/LOWER toggle.

"Ready?" he asks.

I don't know what I'm supposed to be ready for. Regardless, I answer, "Yes."

The moment the ramp begins its descent, the distressed cries become clearer. Among them, I also hear the quieter grunts and spoken threats of whomever the woman is struggling against. Fortunately, the racket they're causing masks the sound of the *Tantalus'* boarding ramp.

Cay and I hurry down, unseen in Tarrkanna-Rrui's perennial pre-dawn murk. It doesn't take long to locate the source of the commotion. Where our individual spaceport stall joins the connecting walkway, three shadowy figures are writhing in struggle.

"Let me go! I'm not going back! Ever!"

In the pale light, I can barely distinguish a small woman. Her arms are outstretched, each locked in the grasp of the two larger beings. Like a prisoner being dragged to the gallows, she thrashes against them, desperately seeking to escape her fate.

Cay and I rush forward. He levels the sidearm, altering his aim back and forth between the two aggressors. "Let her go and back away," he barks. *"Now."*

One of them, a beefy human, raises his hands when he notices the pistol pointed at him. "You're making a huge mistake," he says, stepping away from the woman.

"I'm told that a lot," Cay replies. He shifts the pistol, aiming it at the other attacker, a musclebound Hekker. "You too."

More reluctant to obey, the snarling Hekker also does as told.

"Good boys," says Cay. "Now, run off, and don't let me see you again."

"No matter," the man says with a wicked grin. "You'll regret this soon enough."

"I'll take my chances. Go."

The two hurry away and disappear around a corner.

"Hey, look at that," Cay says, pointing bemusedly at the pistol in his hand. He flicks a small lever on its side. "Good thing they didn't notice I still had the safety on!"

I roll my eyes at Cay, then kneel beside the woman. She's hyperventilating, muttering incoherently between her deep gasps for air.

"You alright?" I ask. "Is there someplace safe we can take you?"

Her whispered plea is desperate. "Take me with you. Please."

Cay flashes me a helpless look. "We don't have enough ship to take on another passenger. But we can call the Tarrkan authorities for you."

Her eyes widen with fear. "No! Not them! They won't help me. Please, they'll be back soon. If you don't take me with you now, they'll kill me!"

Cay's hesitation lasts only a moment.

"Jer, help me get her to her feet."

"Thank you," she sobs. "Thank you."

Shouts arise from the twilight. It seems the two we let go are on their way back. With friends.

"You don't suppose they've come to apologize?" suggests Cay.

I'm in no mood for his fooling around. "Back to the ship! Hurry!"

Her assailants' imminent return puts some pep into the woman's step. In no time at all, we're back aboard the *Tantalus.* Cay slams a palm against the wall switch, and the boarding ramp begins to rise.

Just in time. Outside, Tarrkanna-Rrui's half-light becomes like Terran noon under a barrage of laser fire.

THE *TANTALUS'* COCKPIT

CAY WASTES NO time debating our next move. After lowering the woman to the floor, he hurries into the cockpit and hollers, "We ain't outta this yet, Jer!"

Before racing into the cockpit myself, I whisper, "Sit tight," to the young woman.

No, not *woman*. She's female, but she isn't human. Luatian, maybe, like Natania? Vandreek, perhaps?

There'll be time for answers later—at least, I hope there will. That might depend on our speed of takeoff. I already hear banging and angry shouts below the ramp, but have no clue how long it might take them to force their way in.

"Tantalus, prepare engines for immediate departure!" Cay yells.

"The ship's undercarriage is not presently clear for takeoff," the ship responds. "Other passengers are waiting to board."

"Don't care," Cay retorts. "Do what I say and prepare the engines."

A high-pitched purr, accompanied by a slight vibration, indicates that our ship obeyed its orders the second time. The shouts outside rise above the *Tantalus'* engines, more alarmed now than murderous. In my mind's eye, I imagine them stumbling over one another as they flee the ship's deadly thrusters.

"You might wanna find something to hold on to!" I shout at our new passenger. She's still on the floor, slumped in the fetal position.

"Tantalus, take us up and into orbit," Cay commands.

The ship responds at once. We ascend, first vertically, now at an angle into the atmosphere. Faster, faster, faster.

Then slower, slower, slower.

"What the—are we *stopping?*" I yell.

Not only do we decelerate to a stop. Moments later, the *Tantalus* is in reverse, coasting back toward the spaceport.

"Tantalus, I never told you to turn around," Cay says. "Keep heading into orbit."

No change.

"Let's go, Tantalus! Now!" Cay urges.

"I am unable to obey your instructions at this time," Tantalus casually informs us.

"And just why the hell not?" I reply.

"I am receiving an official transmission from spaceport authorities. We must return to the spaceport and remain grounded there until further notice," Tantalus says. "Because we are in Tarrkan-Uffrra's jurisdiction, my autopilot function must defer to their authority over yours."

I glance back to check on our young rescue. She's discovered one of the fold-down seats in the main cabin and harnessed herself in.

Who the hell is this chick? More importantly, who did we piss off?

"You know what this means, right?" Cay says. It may be the first time I've heard anything like resignation in his tone.

Prison? Torture? Execution? All sorts of dire potentials parade through my mind.

Cay answers his own question. "It's time to put all your video training to good use." Before I can inquire further into his intentions, Cay says, "Tantalus, disengage autopilot and switch to manual controls."

"Are you crazy?" I shout. "I watched videos for four hours! I can't take us into orbit!"

In response, Cay points at the drifting steering yoke.

Without anyone controlling it, the *Tantalus* lists from side to side. Fortunately, it seems the ship's auto-assist functions are still operating, because the stabilizers kick in and level us off each time.

You can do this, Jer, I tell myself. At the same time, a second, more truthful voice says, *Like hell you can.*

I close my eyes and breathe deep. It's okay. I can take two seconds to compose myself. Nobody is prying open our ramp, and the auto-assist features will keep us from plummeting to the frozen ground. We aren't in any immediate danger, which means I can take things slow, right?

Guess again.

"Looks like we've got some friends joining us," Cay informs me.

I open my eyes to see him jabbing a finger at the console's radar screen. A pair of triangular icons have entered our proximity. I'm only slightly relieved to note that they're Tarrkan peacekeeping vessels, not bloodthirsty, kidnapping criminals.

"Time's up!" Cay exclaims. Reaching across me, he punches the throttle into its all-the-way-forward position.

The force of acceleration stuns me, momentarily returning me to my critical disaster in the mechanical room. I recover quickly, seizing the yoke and obeying the pilot monitor's various assist prompts as best I can.

LOWER ANGLE OF ASCENT. WARNING! ANGLE OF ASCENT TOO GREAT! LOWER IMMEDIATELY! ADJUST THREE-POINT-TWO DEGREES STARBOARD FOR OPTIMAL ORBITAL ENTRY. WARNING! ORBITAL ENTRY TOO STEEP! ADJUST SIXTEEN-POINT-NINE DEGREES PORT!

"We losing 'em?" I ask Cay, not daring for a split second to tear my eyes away from the monitor and its instructions.

"More or less," he answers. "Less, I'd say."

"How close?"

"Hmmm ... twenty meters, maybe?"

"Twenty meters! Do they have guns?"

The police vessels answer for themselves as one sails into pole position in front of our windscreen.

Yep. They've got guns.

"Do *we* have guns?" I ask next.

"Just the one," Cay answers, flashing Turf's pistol. "Plus two more hidden under my shirtsleeves."

Tarrkan voices bark through the console speakers. Our ship translates. "Terran vessel 391005729965, call name *Tantalus,* please return at once to Tarrkan-Uffrra Spaceport, section B, stall forty-four. Occupants Cay Cantore and Jerricho Hatch stand charged with disturbing the peace."

"*We* disturbed the peace?" I echo.

I can't fathom how the Tarrkarr are holding *us* responsible for the incident at the spaceport. On Tarrkan-Uffrra, no good deed goes unpunished, I guess.

"I'm sorry, can you repeat that?" Cay asks calmly. "Disturbed the *piece* of what? Piece of cake? Piece of that Kit Kat bar?"

Like in the ice fields, Cay insists on playing his games.

"We have to give ourselves up," I plead with him. "Better than letting them blow us to smithereens!"

"I pick option three," he says. "PAD, unplug and get over here!"

"PAD? What's PAD gonna do?"

"Such a short memory," Cay chides with a condescending shake of his head.

PAD hovers between us. Cay slides aside to give the drone plenty of room.

"Get us out of this mess, PAD," Cay orders. "Full escape flight mode, if you please. Not *X-space*. *Es-cape*."

His overemphasis is understandable. We don't need a repeat of last week.

"I am sorry, but I am unable to fulfill your request at this time," PAD replies.

"Jeez," I mutter to Cay, "I knew *people* hated working with you, but you didn't say anything about machines. The blender incident is starting to make more sense now."

"Food processor," Cay corrects. "And what's *your* beef with me, PAD?"

"Like the *Tantalus*, my manufacturing regulations prohibit me from engaging in known illegal activities," the drone responds. "This includes adherence to all local municipalities on League member planets."

"Aren't you the perfect little boy scout," Cay growls. "Fine, then. I'll do it myself. As usual."

He simultaneously punches the throttle and twists the steering yoke to one side.

I shout, convinced we're going to plow straight through the lead police vessel. Instead, we shoot around its starboard flank, missing it by mere meters.

A burst of purple laser fire screams past us.

"What's the plan here?" I ask. "We'll never be able to plot our jump into X-space like this. We can't get away!"

"Incorrect," says PAD. "There is no need to make the jump into X-space at this time. These are municipal authorities, not planetary ones. The peacekeeping force of Tarrkan-Uffrra only has jurisdiction in the airspace around their city.

A second volley of laser fire sails safely past us and vanishes into a cloud.

"Legally, they will have no choice but to cease their pursuit in three ... two ..."

The *Tantalus* lurches violently. Cay drops altitude, thus evading a third attack from the police vessels.

" ... one."

Immediately, the laser fire stops. On the radar monitor, the distance begins to widen between the *Tantalus* and the green police blips. Seconds later, they've disappeared off the monitor entirely.

"The officials of Tarrkan-Uffrra must now contact planetary authorities if they wish to pursue further legal action," PAD informs us. "That, I presume, will take some time."

Ahead, the blue atmosphere is fading steadily to black. We'll be in low orbit soon.

"Let's not wait around to find out," Cay says. "Although I'm less concerned about the Tarrkarr and more worried about those thugs we fought off. The sooner we can jump into X-space, the better."

"It will be approximately thirteen minutes before we are liberated from Tarrkanna-Rrui's gravitational influence," PAD says. "We can then plot our X-space pathway."

With nothing else to do in the interim, Cay unclips his harness and returns to the *Tantalus'* main cabin. I assume he's going to check on our fugitive passenger. To make sure she's okay. Maybe even to soothe her if she's still frightened or in shock.

He doesn't. Instead, he makes a beeline for the oven.

"Gotta love cast iron," he says, adjusting the Dutch oven inside. "Lid stayed on the whole time. It's not even crooked!"

I roll my eyes. He needs to know how few shits a normal person gives about his dumb pot lid.

The young female isn't in her seat any longer. She's on the floor again, stretched out on her stomach. Her arms are crossed, creating a makeshift pillow beneath her head.

She's sound asleep. Right there on the cold floor of the *Tantalus*.

Now that the threats of brutality and death are behind me, my uncluttered mind can see that she is, indeed, Vandreek. This explains her humanoid features and slightly diminutive stature. Under the warm glow of the *Tantalus'* lights, it's clear that her skin bears a reddish hue, also an identifying Vandreek characteristic. Her hair is close-cropped, cut unevenly, like it was done by a monkey with a pair of dull scissors.

What draws my attention most, however, is the button-sized metal ring implanted in the side of her neck. If I were to roll her head to the other side, I would without doubt find a second ring there too.

I had a pit in my stomach before. Now it has opened to become an abyss.

Lost in silent thought, I retrieve my sleeping bag from the mechanical room and drape it over her.

Kneeling beside me, Cay says, "You know you'll have to wake her in a minute when we jump into X-space."

"I know. But a minute is a minute."

"Don't expect I'm gonna let you crawl into *my* sleeping bag later. I have boundaries, you know."

"I'm not worried about where I'll sleep." Pointing at the circlet in the peaceful Vandreek's neck, I add, "Because I'm a lot more worried we just stole someone's *castrata*."

"Ohhhhhhhhh balls."

A sharp *ding* startles me.

"Dinner's done!" Cay exclaims brightly. He looks at his watch. "And we've only got … nine minutes left to shoot the rest of the episode."

Reluctantly, I open the cabinet and retrieve my film gear.

But as I stand behind the camera, in every shot, I can't stop seeing our mystery Vandreek.

PETRA 7

- SAGITTARIUS -

THE *TANTALUS*

ALL FOUR YEARS of high school, I played linebacker for the Coral Sands Rattlers. I remember how, no matter how much physical conditioning I packed into the summer months, I'd be stiff as a day-old corpse the morning after our first game of the season.

So when I wake up after a long sleep in my pilot's chair, I swear for a moment I'm home in bed following a night on the gridiron. Between the business with the gurrffa herd and our spaceport fight-and-flight, it's like someone plastered me with wet cement and left me to dry. My neck and shoulders creak and crack, stubbornly resisting my brain's orders to look for the source of the voices that woke me up.

The Vandreek *castrata* is one of them. She's awake, sitting cross-legged on my sleeping bag with a plate in her lap, devouring gurrffa meat like a starved Grinnud.

Cay is kneeling beside her. He's speaking, but too softly for me to hear over the Vandreek's slurping and smacking. Every few seconds, she takes a break from demolishing her food to offer a brief word or two in response.

I coax my body out of the chair. Like the rest of me, my feet and ankles put forth their most agonizing protest as I approach Cay and our mystery passenger.

"How long have you been awake?" I ask, stretching some of the kinks in my upper body.

"Only long enough to share our names and favorite colors," Cay answers. "Mine's blue, by the way. In case you forgot."

To the Vandreek, he says, "Galena, this is Jerricho. My sidekick. His favorite color is green. Jer, meet Galena."

Her doe eyes, sparkling violet like an amethyst in the sun, lock with my own. I nearly melt to the floor.

"Nice to meet you, Galena," I say, offering a quick wave with my greeting.

The timid Vandreek wipes a dab of *mrrunkat* sauce from the corner of her mouth. "Hello," she says. "And thank you. If you hadn't saved me, they would've killed me."

"You're Vandreek, but you speak like a Terran," I observe. "How come?"

"I belong to a Terran businessman and his family," Galena answers. "Have since birth."

Since birth. As it is, the whole castrata system is an awful injustice. But the fact that someone can be born into it? Inherit slavery from their parents? Downright abominable.

"Your parents too?" says Cay.

Galena lowers her eyes. "Not anymore."

It's easy enough to deduce from her somber tone why her parents aren't castratae any longer.

"Those beings you were trying to escape—they were your ruling family?" I ask.

"They work for them."

"Why were they going to kill you?"

"I escaped two days earlier. Managed to steal the controller for my circlets."

Reaching inside her drab and tattered robe, she produces a palm-sized remote. I've never seen one—usually they're well-guarded by their owners—but I know immediately what it is.

"Each implant is paired to a controller like this," she explains. "They use it to track us. And ... punish us."

I know what she means by that last bit. I've seen it happen. RealityFeed Studios liked keeping a couple dozen castratae on hand. Why pay for grunt labor when you can have helpless souls do it for nothing? Once, when leaving for the night, I saw one writhing on the floor, shrieking and clawing at his neck. I ran to help, but the moment I reached him, he stopped. From thirty floors up, one of the studio bigwigs had been pressing a tiny button. Probably thought his private bathroom wasn't cleaned to executive standards or some bullshit like that.

"This isn't the first time I've run away," Galena admits. "I tried five years ago too. Only made it a few hours before the peacekeepers caught me. They brought me back, and my ruler beat me unconscious. When I woke up, he said he'd kill me if I ran again. He would, too."

"But that's illegal!" I cry.

"Yes," she says. "He'd be fined. Maybe jail time, but no more than sixty days. That's the maximum penalty for killing your own castrata. Besides, he'd just pay one of his lackeys to take the fall for him."

Cay points at the remote in Galena's hand. "How'd you manage to swipe it?" he asks.

The Vandreek's naturally red cheeks brighten. She glances away and, in a small voice, says, "There are things you have to do as a castrata to take care of yourself. Sometimes, things you hate. I found a way to make him … let his guard down."

I glance at my feet and frown. I don't know whether I should feel sick or angry.

Even Cay knows not to press. He switches topics. "Any port we enter, customs is gonna scan your circlet, and they'll know you're a runaway. Worse, they might think we stole you from your ruler. That leaves us with a bit of a problem."

"I can stay on the ship," Galena says, though she doesn't appear thrilled at the idea. "But some planets don't require you to immigrate through an authorized spaceport. Where are we going now?"

"Petra 7," I answer.

"Never heard of it," she says.

"Not many have," I say. "Only the insane or the suicidal would ever visit it. And us, of course."

"Why? What's wrong with it?" Galena wonders.

"I remember Sal's episode well enough to know its air isn't breathable," says Cay. "But beyond that, I don't know much."

I shoot him an annoyed glare. Then again, maybe I'm the idiot for thinking he might someday work through a plan before diving in. Hell, I'd settle for even sixty seconds of research.

Fortunately, Cay has me along.

"Before we jumped into X-space," I say, "I asked Tantalus about Petra 7. You're right. We can't breathe the air. Too much methane, not enough oxygen."

"A planet that smells like beer farts," Cay muses. "Looks like we're both using TARMs this time, buddy."

"There's also no sentient life there," I continue, "which means the League classifies it as Unprotected."

"And Unprotected means no spaceports or nosy patrol ships!" Cay chirps. "See, Galena? Your future is looking brighter already."

Every planet in the Milky Way falls into one of four classifications determined by the Galactic League. Some are *Member* planets, meaning they've achieved scientific advancements significant enough to become partners in the Galactic League.

Then there are *Protected* planets. Advanced sentient life exists on them, but they are not yet considered ready for belonging in the League. Any contact with a Protected planet is strictly forbidden. Until a hundred fifty years ago, Terra itself fell into this category. All that changed, of course, with Xavior Barclay's discovery of X-space travel.

Most planets in the Milky Way fall under the *Unprotected* banner, meaning they lack any meaningful sentient life. League beings are free to visit such planets at their leisure.

Finally, there is a small contingency of *Restricted* worlds. Usually for political or peacekeeping reasons, civilians aren't permitted to land on a Restricted planet.

Because Petra 7 falls into the *Unprotected* category, we don't have to worry about anyone checking Galena's credentials. But that doesn't mean all our problems are magically solved now.

"We have to return to a League world eventually, Cay," I remind him, hoping to temper some of his insensitive positivity. "We might not have to worry about it now, but we'll have to come up with a plan sooner or later."

Cay strokes his chin in mock thoughtfulness. "I choose later. For now, let's worry about our next episode. Your long nap put us *way* behind schedule, and there's only an hour left 'til we arrive at Petra. Plenty of time to watch another episode of *Galactic Eats.*"

"We're in X-space," I remind him. "We can't use Axon."

"How fortuitous, then, that I wisely downloaded the episode while we were on Tarrkanna-Rrui."

"And you didn't think to watch it *once* during those six days?"

"Jerricho," Cay says, feigning offense as he lays a hand over his heart, "I would never dream of watching without you. Come, then! To the monitor!"

As he bounds to the other side of the room, I offer a hand to help Galena off the floor.

She doesn't accept it. Leaning against the wall, and with an empty plate cradled in her lap, Galena is fast asleep once more.

GALACTIC EATS, EPISODE #131:

"Rock 'n Trollum"

OFFICIAL TRANSCRIPT.
EPISODE SEGMENT RETRIEVED FROM ARCHIVE BLOCK 32D, THIRD
PLANET ENTERTAINMENT, INC.

Deep gasps echo through the dark. Somebody is fighting for air. A flurry of motion, black shapes on a black backdrop, are accompanied by an animal cry of rage. There are screams, these ones human, panicked and terrified. Bouncing lights and labored breathing signify beings running scared. Another roar rends the air, followed by the visceral shrieks of prey caught by its predator.

Then all is still, but for a woman's punctuated gasps rattling through the darkness.

The screen brightens, depicting a desertscape of colorless boulders and matching dust beneath a mustard-colored sky. The only trees appear to have died long ago, leaving only twisted trunks behind.

Next, the lifeless planet is shown from high orbit. There are no clouds, only the slightly darker veins of mountains and dried-up ocean beds to texture the bright globe's monotony.

SAL
(narrating) Welcome to Petra 7.

The change to a low-orbit vantage point does nothing to improve the bleak planet's appearance.

SAL

(narrating) Many millennia ago, long before the Galactic League, this was a planet vibrant with life. Its inhabitants built cities, created culture and civilization, drank from its waters, loved and hated and everything in between.

The ruins of an ancient city appear. Its buildings have collapsed, and nothing moves along its wide lanes. Banks of dust cover everything.

SAL

(narrating) But, over time, Petra 7's atmosphere became toxic. Although nobody knows for certain why this happened, leading theories suggest that the people of Petra 7 mined too far underground. Deep pockets of methane were breached there, and the gas was released into their atmosphere. Whatever the reason, the results were catastrophic.

Ancient bones, half buried in dust and gravel, lie strewn upon the ground.

SAL

(narrating) Life on Petra 7 ... was choked out. Then again, maybe not *completely.*

The scene returns to the woman breathing heavily in the darkness. A beam of light catches a fleeting glimpse of a large creature pouncing at the camera. It has just begun letting out its angry roar when the scene abruptly changes again.

Sal Cantore stands in the *Eats Queen's* kitchen, wearing her coral-pink fedora. She addresses the camera directly.

SAL

(cheerily) Welcome, one and all, to my kitchen! And thank you for joining me on another episode of *Galactic Eats.* Now, my die-hard fans already know that we've done well over a hundred shows. But

I need to give all of you fair warning today—mostly because my producer is making me. This is, hands down, the most dangerous and deadly *Eats* feat we've ever attempted.

Sal is seen in front of the *Eats Queen's* large windscreen, surveying the land outside. A short distance beyond, a gaping hole leads into a barren hillside.

SAL

Inside lie the mines of Petra 7. Deep within them live the *trollums*, giant creatures unlike any other in our galaxy.

An artist's depiction of a trollum appears on-screen. The theoretical illustration portrays a bipedal rock monster with four powerful arms. A gaping hole occupies much of the trollum's head and is labeled *MOUTH*. The smaller stones inside it are *MASTICATORS*.

SAL

(*narrating*) You see, all other galactic life forms are either silicon-based or carbon-based—always one or the other—but the trollum is *both*. Which means, as my scientist friends tell me, they are composed of both organic *and* inorganic materials.

Sal stands again in front of the *Eats Queen's* viewscreen.

SAL

Over ninety-nine percent of a trollum belongs to the *inorganic* category. Its body is made of materials similar to rock and crystal, even precious metals, all of which are completely inedible to every member species in the Galactic League.

A new illustration fills the screen, a black and white sketch of a trollum's interior. The illustration's only color belongs to a tiny pair of objects deep in its abdomen.

SAL

(*narrating*) It's that less-than-one-percent portion of the trollum we're in search of today on *Galactic Eats*. Two fleshy organs called the *secretion heart* and the *oleum*.

Sal lounges on one of the *Eats Queen's* sofas, swirling a glass of wine.

SAL
Because trollums are mainly silicon-based creatures, they require oils to lubricate their moving parts, much like the combustible engines of yesteryear. The oleum, one of the two organs you saw in the diagram, is what manufactures a trollum's oil deposits.

Sal sets her wine glass aside. She rhythmically thumps her chest to mimic a beating heart.

SAL
Through a series of ducts and channels, the secretion heart then pumps those oils throughout the trollum's body.

Sal is now standing in her kitchen, surrounded by her cabinets and counters. Pots, pans, and other cookware hang from the ceiling.

SAL
Once we have tracked down and killed a trollum, my team and I will harvest its organs. When we're safely back here in my kitchen, we'll turn these into a simply succulent trollum stew.

The camera pans to the right. Four armed beings, three humans and a Hekker, stand at attention.

SAL
Here to assist us on this extra-dangerous mission is a team of qualified hunters. They'll help us track down, neutralize, and harvest one of Petra 7's trollums.

Sal approaches the leftmost soldier and lays a hand on his shoulder.

SAL
Meet Ryder, my number-one security guru. He's done no small amount of research to prepare for this particular episode.

In order, Sal introduces the other three. As she does, the camera gives each a close-up moment in the spotlight.

SAL

(off-camera) This is Yvonna. She's a seasoned veteran who has seen military action on both Yaveen and Pransk. Thank you for your service, Yvonna. Next, we have Dierdroff. Dierdroff has been with me from the beginning. He's spent the past hundred and thirty episodes either piloting the *Eats Queen,* fetching me ibuprofen after a few of the rougher episodes, or brewing my morning coffee. Today, he's helping me hunt a trollum—a task not for the fainthearted, I promise you. And, finally, there's Clurngsha the Hekker. He's told me the only thing he fears is dying of old age, which makes him perfect for the mission at hand.

The camera pans to the side, so that only Sal remains in the shot.

SAL

As you might imagine, hunting creatures with rock bodies poses a unique challenge. Standard weaponry is designed for use against carbon-based life forms. Our bodies are a web of interdependent systems and organs. Destroy one human organ, for example, and the whole person will likely die in short order. We also tend to be soft, fleshy things, which makes those organs easy to damage with, say, an Ultreen semiautomatic sidearm. For a silicon-based trollum? Things get a bit stickier.

Another illustrated diagram overtakes the screen, this time offering an aerial view of the trollum. An arrow points to the back of the creature's skull with the words *CONTROL CENTER / BRAIN* beside it.

SAL

(narrating) The easiest path to taking down a trollum is from *behind* it. In the back of its head is a clump of magnetic material similar to a computer hard drive. This is what serves as the trollum's control center, much like a brain does for most organic species. Destroy the control center, kill the trollum. Easy as pie, right? Not quite.

The diagram disappears, and Sal returns to the screen. Ryder stands beside her, smiling at the camera.

SAL

In order to explain our hunting strategy, let's turn to the expert.
Ryder, take it away.

RYDER

Happy to, Sal. Because a trollum does have those two organic
components—the oleum and the secretion heart—it requires
organic food to grow and maintain them. Typically, they find this
food in the form of the petra bats which also live in the mines, but
they also eat other organic material they might stumble upon. For
our purposes today, I've put together a mash of raw meat, fruits,
and vegetables, which we'll carry deep into the mine to use as
trollum bait. Once a trollum finds our bait and digs in, we'll attack
from behind with these.

Someone off-camera tosses Ryder a long-barreled gun.

RYDER

This beauty, crafted by Trillium Armorers, was designed for law
enforcement use against pirate vessels in troubled regions. That is,
in fact, its only legal use on League worlds. Since we're on an
uninhabited planet, however, there is no governance over our
using it today. If it's powerful enough to blow holes through a
pirate's hull, it should be powerful enough to blow a hole in the
back of a trollum's head.

SAL

Thank you, Ryder, for your explanation. It's also worth mentioning
that all four of our security personnel will be armed with Trillium
AA400s. No such thing as being over-armed down there!

Sal next grabs a Terran Atmospheric Replication Mask from the counter
and holds it up.

SAL

To make matters more complicated, we'll need to wear TARMs for
the full duration of our mining expedition. Earlier, I mentioned
Petra 7's toxic atmosphere, a high-methane, low-oxygen
composition. Silicon-based life forms respirate this well. Humans

do not. Without a TARM, none of us would last more than a couple minutes before passing out and dying.

The shot widens to include Sal with the full security team. Beaming her winning smile, she looks them over.

SAL
I suppose now's as good a time as ever. Ready, team?

RYDER
We're ready, boss.

SAL
Then, let the hunt begin!

The scene changes. Inside the mine's entrance, Sal marches into an ever-deepening shadow. In addition to the TARM sealed around her nose and mouth, a point-of-view camera is attached to her forehead via an elastic strap.

SAL
Due to the dangerous nature of this episode's food acquisition, I've only brought one camera crewmember with me. I have a second camera, which also serves as a headlamp, strapped to my forehead, and Ryder has a third strapped to his. Between the three of us, we should be able to capture enough footage to give you quite a show!

The next clips depict Sal and her security team journeying deeper into the mine. After this, in a scene illuminated only by headlamps, Sal stands against the tunnel's rough-hewn wall.

SAL
(whispering) **We've officially entered the zero-light portion of the mine—the trollums' domain. Here is where we set our bait and, with any luck, spring the trap!**

Under the beam of Sal's headlamp, she watches Clurngsha and Yvonna unseal the bait bucket. Both back away quickly, groaning and muttering their complaints regarding the organic mixture's potent odor.

SAL
(whispering) Too bad TARMs don't do much to filter out smell! Now we get into position and wait.

Sal next appears as a grainy, gray figure crouched against the tunnel wall. Quick shots also reveal the security team's other members in various positions around the tunnel. The camera returns to Sal.

SAL
(whispering) We can't use any visible light. That would give us away to whatever trollum happens by. So we have to use the camera's ultrasonic echo setting, which captures video by bouncing sound waves. Our security team has specialized goggles that do the same thing. This way, we'll be able to see the trollum in the dark.

More shots depict impatience among Sal and the security team, indicating the passage of time. Eventually, Ryder leaves his post to approach Sal.

RYDER
We might have to call it. My TARM's battery supply is dropping. We can try again tomorrow.

SAL
(with a deep sigh) Yes, I suppose you're—Wait! I've got movement!

At the tunnel's furthest detectable reaches, a grayish blob has appeared against the black background. It grows steadily.

RYDER
(turning around) I'll be damned. You're right, something's coming.

The gray blur approaches. Legs, arms, body, and head all take shape, becoming more defined by the second.

SAL
And it's coming *really* fast.

RYDER
(drawing a deep breath) Don't move a muscle. Don't breathe a
word.

The sprinting trollum, at least five meters tall, leaps at the barrel of organic slops. Its seismic landing is accompanied by a cascade of stones jolted loose from the tunnel walls. With one of its four hands, the trollum snatches up the entire slop bucket and crams it into its gaping mouth. A terrible sound, like gravel in a blender, echoes throughout the chamber, as the trollum's stony masticators crush both bucket and its contents into mush.

Almost as quickly as it arrived, the trollum retreats toward deeper caverns. It has just begun bounding away when a blast from Dierdroff's gun hurtles toward it. The laser fire sails harmlessly past the trollum's head.

At once, the trollum doubles back. A roar, half animal, half mechanical, erupts from its cavernous mouth. More lasers sizzle toward it. One connects, but it manages only to blast a small chunk off the trollum's shoulder. It does not slow the trollum's advance.

RYDER
Ah, shit!

In seconds, the trollum closes the remaining gap. With the speed of a striking cobra, it snatches up Dierdroff in all four hands. His shriek is cut short as the trollum tears him into quadrants and shoves the pieces, one after the other, into its meat-grinder mouth.

RYDER
Run, Sal! Get the hell outta here!

Ryder rushes toward the trollum's flank, shouting and unleashing a volley of laser fire. Surprised, the trollum swings a stony arm at him. The blow catches Ryder violently at the waist and sends him flying, helpless, into the darkness. After shoving the last piece of Dierdroff into its mouth, the trollum stalks away, sniffing loudly.

The camera now follows Sal, Yvonna, and Clurngsha as they race toward the shallower parts of the mine.

YVONNA
Too damn hard to see with these goggles. I'm turning on my headlamp. Damn thing already knows we're here anyway.

More running. An angry cry is followed by measured vibrations in the floor and walls around them, indicating that the trollum is in pursuit.

YVONNA
(indicating Sal and the cameraperson) **You two, run ahead. No, don't argue. Clurngsha and me—we'll stay here, try to slow this sonofabitch down. Go!**

Deep gasps echo through the dark. A clamor of gunfire and war cries follows. The sound of hurried footsteps is muffled by labored breathing. There is a flurry of motion, accompanied by an animal cry of rage.

SAL
(to cameraperson) **Get down and stay still!**

There are screams, these ones human. Another roar rends the air, followed by the visceral shrieks of prey caught by its predator. Then all is still, but for Sal's punctuated gasps rattling through the darkness. There is a sound of rustling, and visible light illuminates her face pressed against the rock.

SAL
(to cameraperson) **Your headlamp! Turn it off!**

An arm obscures the lens, fumbling about desperately. Then the beam of light lands—and freezes—on the trollum. It roars and springs at the camera.

But before the trollum reaches them, a volley of laser fire illuminates the darkness, catching the trollum in the back of its head. Deafening cries of agony reverberate through the cavern, and chunks of rock rain down around Sal. The trollum crashes to the ground. It skids, belly down, across the tunnel floor, and comes to rest mere inches from Sal's feet. The trollum does not move again.

A humanoid figure limps toward them, carrying a long-barreled firearm.

RYDER
(panting) Trollum down. You alright?

Sal's fearful expression disappears at once. She leaps up and stands victoriously over the dead trollum.

SAL
Ryder! You're alright! After you took that punch, I thought you were a goner.

RYDER
Takes more than that to kill me. Although an x-ray might be in order once we're off this planet.

SAL
Any sign of the others?

RYDER
Signs, yes, but not of life.

SAL
(facing the camera) At the cost of three brave souls, we've taken down the mighty trollum. Dierdroff, Clurngsha, Yvonna—we thank you all for your sacrifice.

Sal walks around the creature, searching intently. Her face brightens, and she points down at the trollum's torso. Here, four smooth plates of rock meet at a common corner.

SAL
Did you manage to hang on to your pry bar, Ryder?

RYDER
Sure did.

SAL
Good. Let's get to work, shall we?

The next few shots are of Ryder and Sal wrenching apart the trollum's back plates. Once these have been removed, Sal beckons the camera closer. Two brown, fleshy organs glisten within the cavity they've created.

SAL
There they are, the oleum and the secretion heart. Such little things, yet worth their weight in culinary gold.

Sal unsheathes a long knife strapped to her waist. Kneeling over the trollum's torso, she faces the camera once more.

SAL
Let's harvest what we came for, then haul ass outta here ... before an angry relative shows up!

END OF REQUESTED TRANSCRIPT.
DATE OF ORIGINAL AIRING: JANUARY 12, 2194 CE.

THE *TANTALUS*

46 Days to Payment

WE HAVEN'T EVEN landed on Petra 7, and my stomach is already doing backflips. I'm presently in the cockpit, taking orbital shots with my handheld ARRI, but my thoughts have flown to the planet's toxic surface and our hair-raising task which lies beneath it.

"So? What's the plan, Cay?" I ask. I look away from him. I don't want him to see the fear painted on my face.

Cay is sitting in the copilot's chair, feet propped up on the control console. Even he's been acting withdrawn since switching off the episode. "What do you mean?" he says. "We find a trollum, kill it, harvest the organs, and return to the ship."

I lower my camera and glare at him. "Just like that?" I say, snapping my fingers. "Did we watch the same episode? Did you see that thing? Sal had a trained security team along, and only one of them walked out of those mines alive! Why'd you decide to remake such a dangerous episode?"

Cay shrugs. "Danger sells. Also, I didn't know how *much* danger until now."

"What do you mean?"

"I never made it that far into the episode," Cay casually admits. "Couldn't get past the trollum stew bit. Downright offensive. Besides, I've got a security team of two. Plus PAD!"

"Don't make me go in there," pleads a small voice behind me.

It's Galena. We woke her so she could buckle in before we exited X-space. She's been sleeping in her seat ever since.

"I don't know what mines you're talking about," she continues, "but I'm extremely claustrophobic. Please, *please* let me stay with the ship."

"You're in luck," I answer. "We weren't counting on a third joining our party, so we only have the two TARMs."

Galena's shoulders relax. She breathes a sigh of relief. "Thank you."

"Even if we *could* all go," I say, directing my attention back to Cay, "how are you planning to take down a trollum? Did you bring a bunch of explosives I don't know about?"

"No," Cay answers, "but a few direct hits from Turf's gun oughta do the trick."

"Sal's team had anti-spacecraft rifles, Cay," I remind him, annoyed that I have to point out the obvious once again. "Whaddya think your peashooter's gonna do to a trollum?"

"First off, that was fifty years ago," Cay replies coolly. "Technology has been advancing at light speed since then. Even a 'peashooter' like this can shoot much bigger peas than one in Sal's era. Secondly, their anti-spacecraft rifles were all for show. They were adding to the drama and sense of dread."

"How do you know that?"

"Because when Ryder finally hit that trollum, he blew half its head off with a single shot. If its command center really is located in the back of its head, one precise shot, even from a peashooter, should kill it."

"Yeah? And when did you become such an expert marksman?"

"I'm not," Cay concedes. "But that's what target practice is for. Besides, a little time outdoors on Petra 7 will help me get used to my TARM."

THE MINES OF PETRA 7

"THIS TARM CAN suck a big one," Cay complains. "It's like someone's forcing a fart up my nose." He adjusts his facepiece for the twentieth time since leaving the *Tantalus*—which, if I turn to the side, I can still see a short distance beyond the tunnel's mouth.

If I followed my instincts and ran like hell, I'd be safe inside it in five minutes. Maybe ten. Sometimes I forget how much my CBS slows me down.

PAD hovers between us in the mine's deepening twilight. Besides carrying a second camera, he's also our bait. Dangling on a tether below him is an unsealed bucket of leftover gurrffa bits.

"It'll be the best meal a trollum's ever had," Cay boasted earlier when hanging it on PAD. "And hopefully its last."

Cay is pulling his weight too. He's carrying a small electric cooler inside his backpack, along with water and snacks in case we have to stay in the mine longer than planned. There's also some sort of plasma knife he thinks we can use to cut the trollum open once it's dead. And, holstered in a thick sock tied around his belt, is the pistol he swiped from Turf.

I have to hand it to Cay—he wasn't wrong about the gun. One shot apiece all but vaporized a pair of basketball-sized rocks outside the *Tantalus*. Of course, Cay's accuracy past a few meters was only marginally better than an inebriated chimpanzee's, but the demonstration of firepower provided me with a glimmer of hope that didn't exist prior.

"PAD, are you sure you can operate the camera *and* keep your sensors active for nearby life forms?" I ask.

I wonder how sensitive a trollum's hearing is. I'm afraid my thumping heart will give us away.

"Certainly," the drone answers. "I am far from exceeding my memory's capacity. There is no need to worry."

Like hell. I've got a few *massive* reasons to worry. First and foremost being that nightmarish meat-grinder mouth.

"Although," PAD continues after a moment's processing, "I do wonder how well my sensors will detect a trollum with such little organic material. I was not designed to detect non-carbon-based life forms."

Ahead, a swatch of light pours into the tunnel from overhead. Cay and I crane our necks upward as we approach it.

"It almost looks like a skylight," I comment. The wide hole above us is perfectly circular. "And look! There's another one further down the tunnel. I wonder what they're for."

Cay shrugs. "Probably so the Petrans could pull up miners in case of a cave-in. Or maybe for hauling equipment in and out."

We pass more of the strange skylights as we descend. Each one seems a little further from the sun—and the surface—than the last. Eventually, we find ourselves beneath the final pillar of light, staring ahead into the mine's soul-crushing darkness.

I don't try to hide the trembling in my words. "Are you sure you want to go deeper?"

"That's what she said," Cay remarks, echoing a joke so old, no one really knows when it began. Before I can strangle him, he follows it with an actual response to my question. "Trollums only live where it's pitch dark, so into the pitch dark we go!"

Each TARM is equipped with a pair of lights. We'll use them when the time is right. Since we don't want to attract attention until we're good and ready, we decide to travel by a pale violet light emitted by PAD.

Cay's pistol isn't in its sock holster anymore. It's clenched in his white-knuckled grip. At least, I'm assuming his knuckles are white. It's too dark to know for sure.

Using his lowest volume setting, PAD says, "The methane content is increasing as we continue deeper into the mine. I believe the theory that Petra 7's toxic atmosphere originated belowground is correct."

"I'll be sure to remember that next time I'm on *Jeopardy!,*" quips Cay.

Three hundred years that program has been on the air. But if we manage to survive a single five-episode season of our show, I'll consider us the luckiest sons of bitches ever.

We pass the black maws of tributary tunnels as we proceed deeper below the surface. I shudder to imagine what horrible things might live inside them. Things which might emerge to cut off any hope of escape.

"How much further, Cay? This has to be deep enough. Or do I need to remind you we're traveling with an open bucket of bait?"

"I thought we'd find ourselves a nice trollum cottage first," Cay says. "Knock on the door, invite ourselves in. Sit down and get to know each other over dinner. You know, see where the night takes us."

"Apologies for interrupting," says PAD, "but my sensors are picking up a life form approaching from the rear. Now a second and third as well."

I swallow my sudden urge to vomit. If I ruin my TARM, I'm dead.

A series of sharp squeals rends the darkness, like a hundred wet sneakers running over polished tile. I cover my ears, trying to block out the awful din, but it's no use. The high-frequency assault grows in a steady crescendo, drawing nearer and nearer.

"PAD, drop the bait!" Cay hisses. Aiming the pistol into the darkness, he backs toward the tunnel wall. "Do or die time, fellas! Get ready for trouble!"

No sooner is the last word out of his mouth than the trouble arrives. Something from the darkness slaps me across my right cheek. Before I have the chance to scream, something else whacks my forehead, then my neck, then my right cheek again.

And then ... it's over. The shrieks fade into the darkness before dying altogether.

"What the hell was that?" I ask, dabbing at a trickle of blood on my cheek.

"Petra bats," says Cay. "Sal said the trollums eat 'em. Those must've been the life forms PAD picked up."

"No, the petra bats are too small for my sensors," PAD replies.

There's that urge to puke again.

"Then ... something else is still coming?" asks Cay.

"Affirmative," PAD answers. "In addition to the three behind us, I'm detecting two more in the tunnel ahead."

Five. Five trollums.

We're dead.

"What about this way?"

Cay is pointing at the wall. I didn't see it before, but there appears to be a smaller tunnel branching off from the chief shaft we've been following.

"I detect nothing at the moment," says PAD. "The methane levels inside it are also slightly lower than those of the main tunnel ahead."

"Let's go, then," says Cay.

He stoops to grab the gurrffa bucket, but I swat his arms away.

"What're you doing?" he says. "We can't leave our bait here."

"We *are* the bait now. But if the trollums find this first, it might buy us a little more time."

Cay doesn't argue. Together, we hurry into the offshoot tunnel. Although narrower than the main mineshaft, it still seems plenty big for a trollum.

Which means we have nowhere to hide.

A minute later, that's exactly what I want and exactly what I don't have.

"Stop." PAD doesn't usually issue such abrupt orders. "Another life form is approaching."

"What about the ones in the main tunnel?" I ask.

"It seems the gurrffa distracted them, as you suggested," says PAD, "but only briefly. All five are approaching from the rear."

"If I didn't know better, I'd say they're hunting us," Cay whispers.

I remember how fast the trollum moved in Sal's program. We should be mincemeat in their bellies by now—or whatever it is they use to process food.

"They *are* hunting us," I say, chilled by the realization of it. "Sal had a giant vat of rotten food. The trollum probably smelled it a mile away. That's why it came running like it did. That's why it also didn't bother coming after Sal's team—not until Dierdroff shot at it, anyway. The stink was masking the rest of them. We don't smell that bad, but we do smell *some*. I think the trollums are tracking us. Like bloodhounds."

And, like bloodhounds, they have their quarry cornered.

"Whelp! Methinks one is better than five," Cay says. He brandishes the pistol like a brigadier leading the charge. "Forward, ho!"

I'm happy to let Cay lead the way. If I'm about to die, I at least want to know he went first.

"PAD, I need you to tell me how far the trollum is," Cay says. "Update me every five seconds."

"Over two hundred meters," PAD immediately responds.

Great. At least I have a countdown to my grisly death.

"One seventy-eight … one forty-four … one twelve …"

I'm sure that PAD is whirring away beside me, that my footsteps are grinding bits of stone beneath my boot soles, and that Cay's pants are *swishing* as he walks. Yet all I hear is my own blood pulsing through my ears.

At "fifty-three," Cay stops and orders PAD to turn off all exterior lights.

He does. The gloom collapses into a perfect black.

There's another sound to accompany my heartbeat. In the dark, a grinding. A *thud*. The scattering of stones. Another *thud*.

The trollum. It's coming.

Another noise, like someone sucking air through a straw. Then again. And again.

The trollum is smelling the air. Tasting it like a snake. Tasting *us*.

Nearer the trollum draws, and nearer still. Its steps rattle the soles of my prickling feet, creep up my leg, and set my heart to quaking. I want to run—*would* run—but know I would find five more the other direction.

The trollum is so close I can feel the air currents changing with its movement.

What are you waiting for, Cay? Shoot!

Maybe I *am* telepathic.

Cay illuminates the TARM's twin lights. They aren't terribly powerful, but after standing in the complete darkness, it's like being struck in the eyes with lightning. Unprepared, I recoil against the deluge of light.

So does the monster stalking us. The trollum barks its surprise and lurches backward.

Cay takes advantage—tries to, anyway. He aims his pistol and squeezes the trigger, but nothing happens.

"The safety!" I shout. "Turn off the damn safety!"

I hear a single, beautiful *click*. Just in time, too. The trollum, recovering from its initial surprise, is lunging forward.

Cay squeezes off a pair of shots, spears of bronze which streak into the monster's gaping mouth. The trollum, stunned, drops back another couple paces.

I hear the familiar, ghastly sound of its grinding mouth whirring to life. Cay didn't kill it. He just made it mad.

The trollum lunges forward. It snatches up Cay in two of its killer arms, pinning his gun hand uselessly to his side.

Game over.

Horrified, I watch the creature raise Cay to its mouth. In the cave behind me, I hear the cries of the other hunting party. I know exactly what it means.

I'm next.

But before the trollum can dispatch Cay, its rotating masticators grind to a halt with a godawful screech. The inside of its mouth seems to be seizing like a dry engine, and I smell burnt oil.

Cay's shot may not have killed the trollum, but he certainly disabled it.

The extra time is enough.

"Catch!" Cay shouts. His arm is still pinned, so he instead drops the gun into my waiting hands.

I take aim and fire. Not at the trollum's head, but at its shoulder.

The trollum shrieks and drops Cay.

"Keep shooting!" he bellows.

So I do. I shoot, and shoot, and shoot some more.

When I'm done, the trollum's body forms a lean-to together with the tunnel wall. It isn't moving. Since I didn't have a direct shot at the control center in the back of its head, I did the next best thing I could think of. I blasted away until its whole horrible head was gone.

I'm about to whoop a cry of victory when Cay says, "One down, five to go! Toss me the gun, Jer!"

I whirl about. My elation is squashed at once by the terror of imminent death. Cay's TARM has illuminated thirty writhing arms and legs, and they're approaching fast.

"Any bright ideas?" I shout, backpedaling toward the dead trollum.

"Besides letting them feed on you while I make my getaway? Nope."

Cay opens fire. His shots make contact, but it isn't enough to stop the roaring, raging horde. He's barely slowing them down.

We're toast. Or whatever it is trollums eat for breakfast.

Then, all at once, they halt. They huff low, coughing noises at each other, back and forth.

Are they ... talking? Perhaps discussing how best to eat us? Shish kebab over a fire, maybe? Boil and mash us?

One of the trollums shrieks. So does another.

I look down. The stones are rattling around my feet.

Another trollum barks at the others. Instead of continuing forward for their man meal, they scramble in retreat.

The trollums are *afraid*. Something bigger is coming.

It isn't only the pebbles clattering about. Some of the larger rocks join in too, jittering up and down and side to side like they've been drinking double espresso shots all morning.

A muffled *boom,* a thunderclap disembodied of its rain cloud, rumbles through the cavern. Something like a wave of rock passes underneath my feet, and I lurch forward.

"What's going on?" I shout, struggling to remain upright.

Cay seizes my wrist. His fingers are like molten metal to my diseased nerves as he yanks me toward the headless trollum. He shoves me into the narrow gap formed by the trollum's body as it leans against the wall. Rocks, boulders that could crush me like a bug, drop from the ceiling.

I squeeze my eyes shut, certain each moment will be my last.

The chaos goes on for a minute. Maybe more.

In the end, all is deathly quiet. And—adding another pearl to my string of miracles—I'm still alive.

Cay crawls out first. When I hear his groan, I'm not sure I want to follow.

I wriggle out anyway.

The reason for his despair is obvious. He's staring at a wall. One which was not previously there. Between us and our exit stands a floor-to-ceiling mound of rocks.

DEEP WITHIN THE MINES OF PETRA 7

"LOOK ON THE bright side," chirps Cay. "At least we aren't boiling in a trollum stew right now."

It's pretty bleak for a "bright side," but after surviving an encounter with six trollums, I'll take whatever I can get.

That seems to be the theme of my life lately.

Because someone has to counterbalance his gaslighting optimism, I say, "No, now we get to die slowly instead. These TARM power cells won't last forever, you know."

Behind me, a voice says, "You should both have over half your batteries remaining."

I spin, ready for another fight. Relief washes over me when I see a fog of glowing violet approaching us.

"You okay?" I ask PAD. Something seems akilter.

"I suffered a stress fracture in one of my rotor arms," he calmly replies.

Drones have no nerves, thus no pain. Lucky bastard.

"Did you get all that footage?" Cay asks. We're buried a mile below the surface of an uninhabited planet, but greed for his program prevails nonetheless.

"My camera is rolling as we speak," says PAD.

"Excellent! That footage will be pure Xilenian gold. Good boy, PAD, good boy!"

"He's not a dog, Cay," I remind him.

But Cay is already moving on to other things. He unzips his backpack and removes the plasma knife. Returning to the dead trollum, he says, "Might as well take what we came for."

"And I might as well take a leak."

Turns out, the plasma knife is far more efficient than Ryder's prybar. By the time I'm done zipping up my fly, Cay has sliced, scooped, and hacked his way down to the trollum's twin organs.

"Hold this open," he says, passing me the electric cooler.

As he plunks the slithery oleum into the cooler, trollum sludge splatters out, turning my fingers and forearms into the most disgusting Jackson Pollock ever. I've always had a weak stomach for guts and gore, and the grisly thought that I almost ended up inside one of these things isn't helping.

Don't puke in your TARM, Jerricho, I remind myself. *If you do, you're dead.*

I turn away when Cay also plops the slurping, squidgy secretion heart into the cooler. Mercifully, he takes it back from me, zips it, and returns it to his backpack.

"Now what?" I ask. "Tunnel's still caved in."

"Sal mentioned these mines were an elaborate network. There might be more than one way out. If there is, we're gonna find it."

"Or wander straight into trollum town square," I mutter.

"Then we can stock up on more oleums. Come on, let's get moving."

Our options are limited, so we tramp off the only way we can. We haven't been walking more than a few minutes before we find ourselves at an intersection of tunnels.

"You're wearing the lucky diamond," says Cay. "Which way, Magellan?"

Each tunnel looks no better or worse than the others. Each might lead us to freedom. Each might lead us into the arms of a troop of angry trollums. How can Cay possibly put the burden on me to make a life-or-death decision like this?

Then, a bolt of inspiration strikes.

"PAD, earlier you said there was less methane in this tunnel than the main one."

"That is correct."

"And was there less methane on the surface?" I ask.

"Yes. The surface atmosphere was partially composed of 3.9855% methane. Here, the air is 4.1585% methane."

"What about these other tunnels? Can you tell whether one has less methane than the others?"

PAD rotates, pauses, rotates, pauses, and rotates again.

"The tunnel to your left is only 4.133% methane, which is indeed less than the other two," PAD answers.

For fear of attracting unwanted guests, I suppress my happy dance. Besides, we aren't out of the woods—or, in this case, *mine*—yet.

"Lead the way, PAD," I say. "And whenever we come to a fork like this, keep following whichever path has the least methane."

We march on for what feels like ages. With my camera slung around my torso, my hands and wrists feel fine, but my feet are a different story. Each step is like walking barefoot onto a hill of pissed-off fire ants.

Can't be too much longer, I encourage myself. *There's got to be another entrance. There* has *to.*

Galena keeps visiting my thoughts as we wander the mine. She's not the typical girl I go after. I'm all about flash and—if I'm being honest—a bit of self-absorption. The girls who lead high-paced lives. Who take a hundred pictures of themselves every day, even on the mundane ones. But Galena is nothing like them. She's demure. Softspoken. Has restless eyes that are always on the lookout for danger.

She's afraid, I think. Can't blame her, really. Not after the tidbits she's shared about her life.

I wonder what she'll do if we never come back. Will she be able to fly the *Tantalus* without us? And how would she ever use X-space without PAD there to supply a second set of coordinates? In the end, her fate might be even bleaker than ours.

"Methane at 3.992%," PAD informs us. "Only marginally greater than at the surface."

Hope flutters again in my breast, like a kaleidoscope of monarchs winging toward the sky.

And then it comes crashing down into the pit of my stomach. Dead. Just like we are.

"Well," muses Cay, "that's less than ideal."

Ahead, strangling the last prospect of our salvation, is another cave-in.

NOT SO DEEP WITHIN THE MINES

OF PETRA 7

I SIT WITH A HUFF on one of the very boulders blocking our escape. "You got a bright side for me this time, Cay?"

"Ummm ... I brought snacks!" he cheerfully announces.

A minute later, we're sitting next to each other, rhythmically raising our TARMs to take quick bites, then securing them again around nose and mouth so we won't asphyxiate. Whatever packaged bar he brought tastes like horse food, but to me, it may as well be a steak dinner.

Once I've washed down my last bite with a swig of water, I ask, "So? What now, Cay?"

"Sorry, Jer, but you caught me in a rare idea-less moment. We *could* pass the time debating whether we'd rather suffocate to death or be eaten by trollums."

I lace my fingers behind my head and lean back, as if looking to heaven for a solution. The mine ceiling staring back at me is unsurprisingly silent.

But that doesn't mean it has nothing to say.

I sit up abruptly. "PAD, shut off your exterior lights," I order.

"What's going on? More trollums?" Cay asks, pistol ready in his hand.

"Look up there. I think I see ... little lights?"

"You're imagining—Wait! I see 'em too!"

"What do you think they are? They're only in that one little part of the ceiling."

"I don't know. Petran glowworms?"

"It's weird. The cave ceiling is *green* there. That's more color than I've seen on this whole godforsaken planet."

Cay leaps to his feet. "Those aren't glowworms, Jer, they're *stars!* We must be beneath one of those skylight things, like we saw by the other entrance, only it's nighttime now."

Holiest of craps! He's right!

And yet, it does us no good. We have no way up and out of the hole.

But *someone* here does.

"PAD, fly up and see if you fit through," I say.

No kiss from a pretty woman could elate my heart more than hearing PAD, far above us, say, "It is tight, but I do fit."

"If we can hang on to your tether, can you carry us up?"

"Doubtful," PAD answers, gently sinking toward us from the ceiling. "My maximum carrying capacity at Terran gravity is eighty kilograms. Petra 7's gravity isn't as strong, which means I can carry close to one hundred kilograms at full working capacity."

"I'm less than that," says Cay. "Beam me up, PADDY!"

I can't believe it. We're going to survive this nightmare!

"Unfortunately, the stress fracture I suffered during the cave-in has debilitated me. I can, at most, carry only sixty kilograms of additional weight."

"Then you'll have to go back to the *Tantalus* and get Galena," I reply.

"Like humans, Vandreeki are unable to breathe such high methane content," says PAD. "She will require the use of a TARM."

Cay and I share an uncomfortable glance. We know exactly what that means.

I sigh, slip off my mask, and hand it to PAD.

"Be quick about it," Cays says, before passing me his TARM so I can take a breath.

PAD doesn't need to be told twice. He hovers up and out of the hole and disappears.

Back and forth, back and forth we go, breathing, then passing the TARM to the other. Minutes go by, each one an hour, as Cay and I await the appearance of our saviors.

More light seeps through the hole in the ceiling. The former forest green has become more of an emerald.

We've officially survived our first night on Petra 7. And, with any luck, our last.

"Did you hear that?" Cay whispers. He sits up sharply, alert.

I shake my head and draw a slow breath from the TARM. Listening.

My ears perk up. A harsh bark, still distant, bounces along the tunnel walls.

"*Please* be those bat things," Cay pleads aloud.

If it comes to fighting even one trollum, we're more screwed than a five-current hooker. We can't put up a stand while passing a TARM back and forth.

"I thought trollums stayed where there wasn't any light," I say. "What would they be doing way up here?"

"Maybe Sal was wrong," Cay suggests. "Or maybe they're out for revenge." He pats his backpack, which presently holds one of their friends' organic remains in a cooler.

We hear something like a howl, deep and grating.

"That's no petra bat," I mutter. Breathe. Hand over the mask. "What're we gonna do, Cay?"

When I notice his wide grin behind the TARM, I assume he has finally lost his mind. Then I follow his eyes up to the ceiling.

PAD is back. He's hovering toward us through the skylight. And, against the faint green backdrop, I see the silhouette of a young Vandreek female a dozen meters above me.

"No time to waste, PAD," says Cay. He casts a worried glance toward the other end of the tunnel. "More trollums incoming."

PAD deposits the end of his cable into Cay's hands, then floats away.

When Cay tries passing the tether off to me, I shake my head. "You go first."

I wish I could say it was nobility prompting my generous offer. Really, it's pure practicality.

Cay gives me a skeptical look but doesn't say anything. He doesn't want to waste air while I'm still wearing the TARM.

"I've got forty pounds on you at least," I explain. "I'll need you up top to help pull me out."

Cay is plainly aggravated by this, mostly because he knows I'm right. He tugs on the tether. It's taut. He loops the cable around his wrist and forearm, then does the same with his boot.

I take three deep breaths from the TARM. Once I've filled my lungs until they're ready to pop, I shove the mask against Cay's face and slip the elastic band around his neck.

"Pull me up!" he shouts to our rescuers above.

The trollums, not so distant as before, react to his voice with voices of their own.

Jerky inch by jerky inch, Cay rises toward the skylight. Toward safety.

Below him, holding my breath, I'm surprised how fast my lungs start to burn. During the glory days of my high-school football career, when I conditioned daily, I could have held my breath for two minutes, no problem. But the years—and my illness—have softened that guy. I used to be a statue of bronze. Now I'm a teddy bear with a slight paunch.

The trollums aren't far. I hear that same straw-sucking sound the one we killed was making before Cay shot it. They're sniffing out our trail. Soon, they'll follow the scent to me.

If I'm not out of this hole by then? Curtains.

Hurry up, hurry up, hurry up!

Cay is halfway to the top, sliding steadily upward.

Movement at the other end of the tunnel seizes my attention—and my heart. One ... two ... three trollums. They're sniffing the ground, crawling on their six limbs like giant insects. Fortunately, sight must not be a primary sense for them. If it were, I'd already be dead.

Above me, Cay snaps his fingers to get my attention. He's dangling the TARM by its strap, ready to drop it.

"No butterfingers!" he whispers before letting go.

I may have played linebacker, but I was also my conference's interceptions leader. Plus, my lungs are about to explode, so I'm highly motivated. As soon as the dropped—and caught—TARM is safe in my hands, I jam it against my face and suck in the sweetest breath of my life.

But the sweetest breath is also the loudest. All three trollums raise their heads, alerted to the presence of their quarry.

They're done snuffling. The lead trollum lets out a terrific roar, and all three break into a run.

"Shit! Grab the cable, Jer!" Cay screams.

I've been so fixated on the trollums, I failed to notice the tether dangling in front of me. With every bit of my feeble strength, I lock my hands around the cable. Since there's no time to form a better foothold, I yell, "Pull me up!"

Cay and Galena must be sweating adrenaline. I'm yanked upward so hard and fast, my hands slip an inch down the tether. Add burning skin to my burning joints and muscles.

Nearer draws the light of day, and nearer yet. I can't believe it—I'm actually going to make it!

Then I jerk to a stop.

"No!" I cry, glancing down.

One of the trollums has caught the bottom of the tether. It seems confused, uncertain what to do with the long, dangly thing it found.

The moment of hesitation is what saves me. Cay appears overhead, brandishing the pistol.

"Sorry if I shoot you!" he cries, and he squeezes the trigger.

I hear a bellow of rage below me but don't dare to look down. I don't dare to look at anything. I can't. My every focus is now on my fingers. My palms. My wrists. My forearms. They're on fire. Burning, shaky, weak.

I'm sliding upward again, I think. It's hard to be certain of anything at the moment. Anything, other than the knowledge that my strength is gone. That my fingers are slipping off the tether—*have* slipped—and that I am holding nothing. That I will fall for one second, maybe two, and then will be ripped apart and consumed by the trollums.

Something seizes my wrist like a vise. I shriek against the agony of it.

But I'm not falling. Not yet, anyway.

I dare to open my eyelids a sliver.

Cay's face, purple and drenched in sweat, stares down at me. His hands are clamped around my wrist and forearm.

Then PAD appears too. A pair of his retractable appendages lock together under my armpit. Together with Cay, he hauls me up from the hole.

When I collapse onto the rocky ground, Cay dives at me. Only moments after rescuing me, his outstretched fingers appear ready to strangle me.

He rips the TARM off my mouth and crams it over his own.

After a few breaths, the purple in his face subsides to an angry pink. Between those great gasps, he makes a single comment. "Those ... trollum giblets ... better make ... some outstanding ... tartare."

GALACTIC EATS REHEATED

PRODUCTION SET

45 Days to Payment

"GREAT. NOW KEEP the angle but zoom in. And don't be afraid to move your arms closer too."

"Like this?" Galena asks, shoving the camera *way* too close to Cay's plated trollum tartare.

"That's perfect," I answer with a grin. "You make a great third camera!"

She doesn't. But she's trying hard to be useful. I don't want to crush her spirit.

Besides, I have to admit that she's sort of adorable. Unsure of herself and nervous about everything she touches, but always kind and eager to help however she can. Maybe those traits have become ingrained due to a lifetime of service in the castrata class. Whatever the case, I find her presence soothing, even tranquilizing, especially in the midst of the Cay cyclone tearing through my life.

Cay. Who is presently beaming at the camera like we weren't almost killed a few hours ago. Though to be fair, the half-bottle of tequila we drank to calm our nerves may have something to do with his bubbly demeanor.

"It's the rich, fatty quality of these organs which lends itself so nicely to making the perfect tartare," he reminds his hypothetical audience. With the edge of his fork, he slices a hunk off the mound of mixed meat, herbs, and garlic.

I almost puke when he slides it into his mouth. Once you've seen those organs raw, and considered how close you were to becoming part of them, it's impossible *not* to feel a little queasy.

Unless you're Cay, apparently, who moans and says, "The Armagnac, together with the drizzle of balsamic glaze on top, does a beautiful job of cutting that richness and balancing everything with a divine touch of sweetness. Mwah!"

Cay gives his work the chef's kiss, then turns to Galena's camera. "That's it for today's episode. If you ever find yourself hankering for tartare, I'd skip the trip to Petra 7 and opt for a duck liver instead. Not quite as exotic, but at least your duck won't get together with its friends and try to murder you. And if you absolutely *have* to have your trollum craving fixed, do be sure to bring a bigger gun."

Facing me, he says, "On the next episode of *Galactic Eats Reheated*, we're heading to the uninhabited planet Nabishna. There we'll be seeking a somewhat less dangerous quarry, the prized Encelas mushrooms, so bring your appetites! Until then, eat well, friends."

I stop rolling and instruct Galena and PAD to do the same.

Immediately, Cay keels over and power-vomits into the wastebasket. The stench of tequila-basted trollum hits me like a jab to the nose, and I back away, choking down vomit of my own.

"Not so great?" I ask with a smirk.

"Disgusting," he says, wiping his mouth. "But after watching us, who in their right mind would possibly try to prove me wrong?"

"I don't know. Maybe one day *your* grandkid will be stupid enough to come to Petra 7."

"Pardon my interruption," says PAD, floating beside us. "While filming, I also took the initiative to conduct a background analysis of the cave-ins at the mine. After cross-referencing my memory with Axon's analytical bots, I can say, with over ninety percent diagnostic certainty, that the cave-ins were caused by a pair of charged explosions set at the mine's two chief entry points."

"What exactly are you saying?" I ask. But it isn't hard to read between the lines.

"Someone knew you went inside," PAD answers, "and didn't want you coming out."

"Did you see anything?" Cay asks Galena.

Still holding her camera in the ready position, she shakes her head and points at the windscreen. "No. We aren't facing the entrance, and I don't know how to use any of the ship's instruments. I do remember the ship rocking at one point, but I assumed it was just the wind."

Cay scowls. "Geiger. I'd bet my life on it. Didn't quite snuff us on Tarrkanna-Rrui, so he came after us here. Question is, how's he following us?"

"You gonna call up Jonas again?" I ask. "See if he can make Geiger back off?"

"Nah. Jonas won't ruffle his number-one star's feathers. Besides, I've got a better idea."

Cay grins and starts for the cockpit. Almost as quickly, he reverses course. "But first, I brush my teeth."

THE *TANTALUS'* COCKPIT

CAY PLUCKS SOMETHING small and rectangular off the control console. It's about the size of the old postage stamps I remember from my history textbooks. I think at first that he broke some knob or instrument. Then I remember what our last visitor on Terra handed him before she left.

"Ameliana?" I ask skeptically, sitting in the other chair. "You think she'd rat out her own grandpa?"

"A grandpa she obviously hates," Cay reminds me. He inserts Ameliana's contact card into the vidcomm's data port. As he initiates the brief information transfer, he adds, "Besides, you heard her say she wants to take over Geiger's empire someday. This might be her chance."

He presses the green *CONNECT* button on the monitor. Seconds later, Ameliana's confused face fills the screen. In the metal wall behind her, a star-studded viewport makes plain that she is presently traveling through space—presumably with her grandfather.

When she realizes it's Cay who has come calling, she recoils in genuine surprise.

"Uh—hello!" she exclaims, recovering quickly. "You have only been gone a couple weeks. I didn't expect to hear from you until you were back on Terra." She raises an eyebrow. "You're not finished already, are you?"

"Not yet," Cay answers. "We've had a few setbacks."

"Setbacks? What kind?"

"The kind I think your lovely grandfather is behind. First, on Tarrkanna-Rrui, someone hired our guide to abandon us in the ice fields. Then on Petra 7—"

"You went to *Petra 7?*" Ameliana interrupts, incredulous. "Do you have a death wish?"

"No, but *somebody* is wishing my death. When we were down in the mines, someone blew the exits and trapped us underground with some *very* hungry trollums."

Ameliana absorbs the information, then says, "I wouldn't put it past him. My grandfather hates anyone he sees as a potential rival."

"Enough to kill them?"

Ameliana nods. She leans in close and lowers her voice. "He has done it before. Never himself, of course. He hires the jobs out, like he did with your guide. But he's quite experienced in making people ... disappear. Honestly, I wouldn't be surprised if he even had a hand in Sal's disappearance."

At this she grows visibly uncomfortable. Her cheeks burn with the shame of some secret.

"What is it?" Cay asks.

"He also took steps to keep your dad out of the picture. You know all those 'business partners' who kept cheating him? They did it under Grandfather's direction. He knew Marq was the more talented chef, so he beat him into submission."

Cay sinks back in the chair, his expression blank. He's always thought less of Marq for his lack of business chops. Turns out the deck was stacked against him the whole time.

"Sorry," Ameliana mutters.

Cay shakes his head. "Not your fault. You're not responsible for what your grandpa did."

"Sins of the family. Anyway, I wish I could help more. But I shouldn't talk much longer. I'm on Grandfather's ship, and there are too many listening ears nearby."

"Understood. Thanks for the help. And tell your grandpappy 'thank you' too. If it weren't for those perfectly timed explosions scaring away the trollums, we'd be dead for sure."

"Where are you headed next?" Ameliana appears immediately regretful for asking the question. "You don't have to tell me if you don't want. Me being a Geiger, I would understand completely."

"Nabishna," Cay answers without another moment's hesitation.

"Never heard of it," says Ameliana.

"Way out in Centaurus," Cay explains, indicating the arm of the Milky Way which houses the planet. "It'll take us almost three days in X-space to get there. Not a League planet, thank Cosmos."

"Why does that matter?" Ameliana asks.

"We may have run afoul of the peacekeepers on Tarrkanna-Rrui. Disturbing the peace, or something like that. We managed to escape the municipal authorities, but we have no idea whether there might be a League-issued warrant out for our arrest. So that complicates things."

"Grandfather Geiger has some powerful connections. I'll look into it for you," Ameliana promises.

Cay beams at her. "You're a rose among thorns."

"Do you always lay it on this thick with the ladies?" she says, blushing. "Be safe, Cay. I hope you have better luck on Nabishna. I will send you a message if I hear Grandfather making any plans to visit that part of the galaxy."

"Thanks again. Bye, Ameliana."

She waves and winks, and her face disappears from the monitor.

Cay looks at me. Sweeping an arm toward the windscreen and the bleak landscape beyond, he says, "Ready to get off this rock?"

"Even more than Tarrkanna-Rrui."

As Cay prepares the engines, I step up into the *Tantalus'* primary cabin. PAD, anticipating our upcoming takeoff, is securing himself into his preferred docking corner.

Our other passenger, however, is missing.

"Galena?" I call out.

I expect a response from the lavatory. It's the mechanical closet she emerges from instead.

"Why were you hiding in there?" I ask, looking at her quizzically.

"I didn't want to be in the background of the video," Galena answers shyly, "in case the authorities are monitoring communications for me."

"Good thinking. We'll be more careful here on out, okay?"

Galena forces a grin and nods.

"We're taking off in a few minutes," I inform her, "so you might want to strap in somewhere."

I already know where. Same seat she always uses, closest one to the exit. Doesn't matter that it's the least comfortable chair onboard. She's setting herself in the best position to make a break for it if ever she has need of a quick escape.

I return to the cockpit. My ass has barely grazed the seat when a warning light flashes on the control monitor.

"Tantalus, what's the alert for?" I ask.

"The fuel rod is at less than ten percent capacity," the ship replies. "It is highly recommended that you replace it prior to X-space travel."

"Do we have enough left to bring us into orbit?" Cay asks.

"Yes," Tantalus responds.

"Then engage autopilot and take us up," Cay orders. "We'll deal with it then."

THE *TANTALUS'* MECHANICAL CLOSET

GROWING UP IN a lower-middle-class family with five siblings, the word *thrifty* more or less defined my life. Almost all my clothes were secondhand. By the time they'd worked their way down the brotherly line, they were fifth hand. Dinners were made from scratch, the chicken to beef ratio roughly ten to one. Vacation didn't mean exotic trips to interstellar locales. No, we camped, or perhaps spent a few days with Gram.

Before this adventure, I thought I knew the meaning of *cheap*. Turns out, broke Cay is redefining the word every day.

"First the spare nav cartridge, and now this?" I say in disbelief, staring down at the silver rod in my hands. It's a lot heavier than it looks. "What antique store did you buy these from?"

"My good friend Slyce Cobb knows a guy who sells 'em cheap," Cay answers. "Manufactures them himself, right in his own basement."

"That's illegal, Cay. Is the kitchen the only thing you spent decent money on?"

"That and the booze, yes. And if you keep talking to me like that, I'm going to cut your bonus."

I set the fuel rod on top of the others. Piled in the storage cabinet is a modest mountain of cheap-ass, homemade tungsten cylinders. Each is filled with deuterium and topped with a two-pronged cap that connects it to the engine's power centers. Admittedly, I haven't spent much time in the guts of many vehicles—My gearhead cousin tried, and failed, to educate me when I was in high school—but even I know these suck.

With reckless abandon for my bonus, I say, "They're worse than the ones your grandma would have used!"

That's saying something, too. I was only eight or nine years old, but I remember the headlines. After all, it was huge news. A group of galactic physicists announced a discovery they called the Veridonian Principle. I never understood the ins and outs of it, but the upshot was a massive leap forward in fuel efficiency.

"You think I don't know that?" Cay replies. He's fiddling with the spent fuel rod, trying to figure out how to unlock and remove it. "This crappy rod was apparently the one included in the ship's purchase price. When Slyce brought the *Tantalus* to Gram's, he tried selling me an upgrade that's a thousand times more efficient."

"And you didn't buy it? Why? Just one would've lasted this entire trip!"

"Because it also *costs* a thousand times more, and you don't have that kind of money. Besides, I'm not keeping the *Tantalus* when we get home. Why buy a fuel rod that'll still be ninety-nine percent full?"

"How 'bout so we don't run out of juice in the middle of an X-space flight? We could end up stranded anywhere!"

"A risk I was financially obligated to take."

"I'm glad you're so comfortable rolling the dice with our lives."

Cay grins and points at my neck. "Isn't that what lucky crystals are for?"

He tugs at the used fuel rod lodged in its housing. It doesn't budge, so he punches it a couple times. Still, nothing.

"Stupid thing won't come out anyway," he grumbles. "Do we have a sledgehammer onboard?"

"You aren't doing it right," I say, nudging Cay aside. "You can't *beat* it out of there."

"Better leave this to our resident X-space expert, then," Cay says, stepping back. "I'm incredible at nearly everything, but these mechanical nuances are lost on me."

He leaves. Without Cay distracting me, it takes thirty seconds to figure out how to unlock the used fuel rod. The actual removal of the thing is no picnic though, especially for someone with CBS. The rod fits snugly in its port—I suppose you don't want nuclear fuel jiggling around while you're in X-space—but after considerable wrestling, I manage to slide it free. Inserting the fresh rod takes a lot less effort. Once I've given it a half turn to lock it in place, I return to the cockpit.

"Tantalus, set course for Nabishna," I order, massaging my arms.

"Our X-space path to Nabishna requires a layover," Tantalus replies.

"Layover?" I ask. "What the hell's a 'layover'?"

"I had to do this between Terra and Uilik once," says Cay. "Never asked why, though."

PAD, who is preparing the secondary coordinates and path, provides an answer. "X-space layovers are necessary whenever an HMO—a high-mass object—interferes with a direct path to your destination."

"Wait—what?" I say. "HMO? High-mass object?"

"Objects such as a neutron star or a black hole," PAD replies. "Certain star clusters, perhaps. Due to their density and mass, they interact negatively with X-space pathways, making them unstable and highly dangerous. They also cause significant interference to the normal flow of time. Many beings find such time dilation off-putting, as the rest of the universe seems to pass them by at an accelerated rate."

"So we have to go around?" asks Cay.

"*Around* is not the scientific term," says PAD. "But, essentially, yes. We travel first to a different point in space, from which the final jump can be made safely."

I think I understand. You can't pass through brick walls, so you take the sidewalk *around* the building. Makes sense.

"Whatever," Cay says, throwing up his hands. "I don't care *how* you get us there. Just get us there."

"Affirmative," PAD and Tantalus reply in unison.

NABISHNA

– OUTER CENTAURUS –

GALACTIC EATS, EPISODE #148:

"Not Mushroom for Error"

OFFICIAL TRANSCRIPT.
EPISODE SEGMENT RETRIEVED FROM ARCHIVE BLOCK 32D, THIRD
PLANET ENTERTAINMENT, INC.

The *Eats Queen* floats in space. Occupying the right half of the monitor is a globe of rich emerald, adorned with the sapphire veins of rivers and lakes.

> SAL
>
> *(narrating)* Flung far from the galactic core, at the extreme end of Centaurus's mighty tentacle, you'll find lonely, and lovely, Nabishna.

Scenes change rapidly, depicting the various biomes, geographical features, and wildlife samplings as they are mentioned.

> SAL
>
> *(narrating)* The only planet to orbit its star, Nabishna is a world of lush forests and sweeping grasslands, rushing streams and cerulean lakes. Here, all sorts of creatures flourish, ranging from the tiny nervils in their underground burrows, to the mighty Encelas oxen stampeding across the plains.

An orbital view displays the gemlike Nabishna once more, this time without the *Eats Queen* in the picture.

SAL

(narrating) **Nabishna truly is a slice of paradise ...**

In a moment, the vivacious planet transforms into a world engulfed in flames.

SAL

(narrating) **... but only for five days, until the entire planet turns into a hellish firescape.**

A computer-animated model of Nabishna with its star, labeled NAB-15, overtakes the screen. A football-shaped white line denotes the planet's elliptical path of orbit.

SAL

(narrating) **Nabishna's parent sun is what's known as a K-type star. These lower-mass bodies are smaller and cooler than most other stars in our galaxy. This means a planet's orbit may also take it closer to its star than most others. But because of Nabishna's extreme elliptical path around NAB-15, whenever it approaches its minor axis—approximately once every six Terran days—the star's heat becomes too intense, and the planet is set ablaze.**

Sal walks alongside a broad viewscreen, overlooking Nabishna.

SAL

You might think it impossible for such an inhospitable planet to support life. But, as we've so often discovered here on *Galactic Eats*, life overcomes.

Now Sal is walking through a lush rainforest. Flowers open around her in real time, blooming in moments from green buds into magenta blossoms.

SAL

Nabishna has overcome by evolving an incredibly rapid life cycle, one which plays on a hundred-hour loop in rhythm with its waltz around NAB-15. Flowers bud, bloom, wilt, and die within a matter

of minutes. A creature is born in the morning, a reproducing adult by lunch.

Another animation is displayed, this one of a subsection of the planet. A high, grassy plain overlooks a deep and forested valley.

SAL
(narrating) **Our *Galactic Eats* mission today will see us landing on an open grassland called the Encelas Mesa.**

A golden X marks a location on the lip of the mesa, right at the cusp of the valley.

SAL
(narrating) **From there, my camera crew and I will navigate our way down to the heavily forested Encelas Valley. Here, I'll introduce you to a hidden delicacy known only to very few ... until now.**

A mushroom materializes on the forest floor, growing up from nothing in a matter of seconds. The camera zooms out, so that the first mushroom is now seen surrounded by hundreds more. All of them rest in the shadow of a tree with broad, aquamarine leaves.

SAL
(narrating) **Each cycle, Encelas mushrooms grow up under the shade of the forest's blue-leafed bolero tree. Keeping in mind the abbreviated lives of everything on the planet, we will only have a thirty-minute window during which we can harvest this rare and prized fungus.**

Sal is standing again in front of the *Eats Queen's* large viewscreen.

SAL
Because the mushrooms bloom near the end of Nabishna's life cycle, as soon as we find and harvest them, we'll have to hurry back to the *Eats Queen* before we're fried, literally, by NAB-15.

Sal places her signature fedora on her head. She winks at the camera and tips her hat playfully.

SAL
But that's just another day in the world of *Galactic Eats*.

The scene changes to an on-planet location. Sal strolls through a field of lush grass swaying with the wind. She tucks errant locks of long brown hair behind her ears to keep them from blowing into her eyes and mouth.

SAL
Because of Nabishna's lack of visitors, our only competition for these delicious mushrooms will be—

END OF REQUESTED TRANSCRIPT.
DATE OF ORIGINAL AIRING: APRIL 7, 2194 CE.

THE *TANTALUS*

42 Days to Payment

"WHAT HAPPENED?" I ask. "Where'd Sal go?"

Cay, Galena, and I are staring at a monitor that has gone suddenly dark. In the screen's center, a small gray box offers an undetailed explanation: AXON FEED DISRUPTED.

"You've never been to fringe territory, have you," Galena says knowingly.

Stuck in close quarters with us the last three days, she has begun, inch by inch, emerging from her shell. Now that we've all had a hand in rescuing one another, a mutual trust has formed. She's quicker to offer an opinion without first being asked. Yesterday, she even cracked a joke at Cay's expense.

Little steps, but steps all the same.

Now, after seeing our blank stares, Galena goes on to explain, "Out here, near the edge of the galaxy, Axon is pretty inconsistent. Data feeds, communications, programs, other things like that—they don't always work the way you need them to."

Cay shrugs. He motions toward the blank monitor and says, "I'm not worried about it. I don't remember the whole episode, but I *do* remember Sal making a very subpar cream of mushroom soup."

"So what are *you* planning to make?" I ask, more out of boredom than genuine curiosity. Three days is a long time to be stuck on a ship.

"Cream of mushroom soup, duh," Cay answers. "But mine'll be *over* par."

"Have you ever golfed before?" I contend. "You *want* to be below par, Cay."

"Whatever. Point is, if you want to highlight the flavor of a good mushroom, you can't beat cream of mushroom soup."

He approaches the cockpit and stares out the windscreen. Looming before us, and looking like the husk of a giant cantaloupe, is Nabishna.

"Thanks to your extended hospital stay on Tarrkanna-Rrui, we're behind schedule," Cay says. "If we arrived at the point of orbit I think we did, the Encelas mushrooms won't bloom for another three days. Which, as it turns out, is only a few hours before the entire planet lights on fire."

"Sal said there weren't many visitors here," says Galena. "Does that mean there's no sentient life? No spaceports, no peacekeepers?"

Cay chuckles. "After Sal's episode, things started heating up here— pun very much intended. So many beings came to harvest the mushrooms, they started murdering each other. That's how valuable they became. Eventually, the League decided to close off Nabishna. They put armed patrols around it to keep mushroom hunters out."

"Then how do we get in?" I ask.

"They called off their patrols two years ago," Cay answers. "The mushrooms are lab grown now—at least, some version of them. They must've figured a lack of demand meant the violence here would stop. Technically, Nabishna is still a Restricted planet, but nobody's keeping track anymore."

"If the mushrooms are grown in labs, why the hell are we risking our lives for 'em?" I ask with a tone of challenge. I'm not a cat. Who knows how many lives I've got left?

Cay answers my question with one of his own. "Have you ever eaten lab-grown beef?"

"Yeah. So?"

"And have you ever had a ribeye cut right off the cow?"

"Well, yes, I—"

"I know you did, because I made you one a couple weeks ago. So you should understand exactly why I need the real deal."

I'm about to grumble a comeback when I notice Galena. She's standing in the cockpit, staring a thousand miles down at Nabishna. I step past Cay to join her. Her Vandreek eyes are wide, not with fear as I've seen them in the past, but with wonder.

"Instead of staying up here, could we wait for the mushrooms down on the planet?" she asks timidly. After living a life of self-denial, it must feel foreign to ask for something she wants. "I'm tired of being stuck on the ship. And since there's no sentient life, it'll be safe for me. Nobody's looking for an escaped castrata down there."

Behind us, Cay answers, "I don't see why not. The atmosphere is similar to Terra's—at least, Sal seemed to be breathing it fine. There's liquid water and edible plants, so it's also a chance to restock supplies."

He skirts past us to his copilot's chair. "Tantalus, do a planetary scan to find a good landing place on the Encelas Mesa, as close as possible to the valley rim."

Cay glances over his shoulder at me and Galena. "Buckle up, you two. Safety always comes first on *Galactic Eats Reheated.*"

ENCELAS MESA

WHEN I WAS nine years old, the Hatch family adopted a dog. It was some kind of pug, white with rust-colored spots and missing half an ear. A truly ugly beast, if I'm being honest. The old boy had been impounded from an abusive older couple and brought to the humane society in Proctor, the suburb next to Coral Sands.

For months, seven-year-old Josephina had been begging my parents for a puppy. She finally got her wish that Christmas. The next day, we all rode to the humane society so she could pick out her perfect canine companion.

When I saw the ugly pug cowering in the corner of his kennel, I turned up my nose in disgust and moved on. But not Josephina. She took one look at him and, for some crazy reason, fell in love. Right there, even before someone came to open the kennel door for a proper meet and greet, Josephina named him Frederick.

A terrible name, I thought, *for a terrible dog.*

During the tram ride home, Frederick lay on the floor, curled up and shaking. He wouldn't make eye contact with any of us. When we arrived home, we brought him to our fenced-in backyard. It didn't matter that it was winter—Josephina wasted no time trying to teach him to fetch. But Frederick had no interest in such games. Not yet. An icy breeze was blowing in from the west, and all Frederick wanted to do was breathe it in. Eyes closed and nostrils flaring, he calmly, contentedly, pointed his nose into the wind and inhaled his own freedom, like he was breathing for the very first time.

Standing beside me, so close the tiny hairs on our arms are tickling each other, Galena reminds me of that old dog. She's much prettier, of course, and has both ears intact. But as she closes her eyes and sucks in Nabishna's fragrant air, I remember that she too is experiencing her first real whiffs of freedom. No overbearing ruler grunting orders. No *Tantalus* walls to confine her. No TARM with its ionized, metallic undertones.

Just ... air. Fresh air. Fresh air she is free to breathe for as long as she wants.

"Don't get too used to it," Cay tells her, dispelling my unspoken thoughts. "We've only got four days here."

We're standing in a line on the mesa's edge, gazing down into what appears to be a massive, ancient crater. The afternoon breeze sweeping up from the deep valley is warm and humid but not uncomfortable. The slope to the bottom isn't sheer, but it is steep. It'll take plenty of time and effort to find a path down when the mushroom hunt arrives.

But that's tomorrow's problem. Today, we're happy to escape the confines of the *Tantalus*. Even PAD with his cracked rotor seems a bit more buoyant out here.

"Hard to believe mushrooms will be popping up in a rainforest anytime soon," Cay comments.

He isn't wrong. Apart from a scattered handful of tiny, sage-colored succulents, Nabishna is devoid of life.

"Or that we'll be able to stock up on supplies," I add. I expected we would find little life this early in the planetary cycle, but I'm perplexed at the lack of water. How can anything grow without it?

"The days here seem to move a lot faster than on Terra," I note. We're already encroaching on early evening. Like a vast army on the march, dark shadows creep across the valley floor. "PAD, how many Nabishnan days equal one on Terra?"

"I am not presently receiving any Axon signal," the drone answers, "but will insert your question into my task queue."

"Can you tell how long until dark?" Galena asks, breaking free from her trance to join the conversation.

PAD swivels his "head"—the upper portion of his central cylinder— and trains his primary optical sensor on the wide disk of NAB-15, now low over the horizon. After a lengthy pause, he says, "There are approximately eighty-eight minutes until sunset. I cannot estimate how long twilight will linger afterward."

Galena thanks him sweetly, then jumps and cries out, "Look at that!"

She's pointing at the ground between us and the *Tantalus*. At first all

I see is fire-baked dirt. Then I spot them. Thousands of spindly hairs are poking up from the ground, approaching us like a tiny green wave crashing down from the mesa's higher slopes.

"It's grass!" I exclaim. "There must be moisture trapped underground. Or maybe this kind of grass doesn't need anything more than humid air."

A second wave follows the first, this one the color of midsummer lilacs. Cup-shaped flowers, no bigger than pips on a domino, are growing up around our feet.

I laugh. Galena giggles.

From the corner of my eye, I catch Cay raising an unamused eyebrow. "Aren't you two a couple peas," he says, his tone frosted with a thick layer of sarcasm.

Before I can reply, Galena points excitedly at some other phenomenon she's noticed. "See that? Something's coming out of the ground!"

Enthralled, she cavorts up the hill, where a dozen low mounds have formed in the earth. Like bubbles trying to break through a thick stew, they pulse, rising faint millimeters higher with each upward thrust. The top crumbles off one mound in a tiny shower of dirt, revealing the lumpy pink head of some wrinkly, needle-beaked critter.

"Awww," coos Cay. "Itty-bitty scroties."

Within moments, there are twelve peeping chicks—at least, they sort of look like baby birds—all writhing together in a tight ball as they clean dirt off each other.

"They must lay their eggs deep underground," I posit. "Maybe they escape the worst of the heat there, then dig their way out once things cool off."

Galena kneels. She extends a hand to one. It sniffs at her, then nips at the nearest finger. She laughs and jerks her hand away. Seconds later, she tries again. This time, the pink prune lets her stroke its naked body.

Except it isn't naked anymore. Fuzzy white hairs have sprouted to cover it entirely. Within the minute, twelve overstuffed cotton balls are skittering around our feet, chasing and playing and roughhousing like over-sugared children.

"Life overcomes," mutters Cay, echoing a line from Sal's episode. "I'm going back to the *Tantalus*. Jer, we should record those voiceovers so you can edit them into the video."

This may be the first time ever that Cay wants to work while I'd rather play. But there's still plenty to do before we can tie a bow on

Petra 7, and I'd rather not fall behind. All this risking of our lives will be pointless if the episodes aren't cut by the time we return home.

The mental image of the Hekkra ripping off my arms puts an extra spring in my step as I follow Cay toward the boarding ramp. At the bottom, I pause and look back at Galena. Her avian friends have moved on. A dozen platinum specks now swoop over the valley.

And Galena herself is a portrait of serenity. Sitting in the blossom-studded grass, chin tilted toward the sky. Eyes shut. Strands of hair dancing on her forehead, as life blooms around her, and she with it.

THE *TANTALUS*

CAY IS FINISHED recording his voiceovers, and I've barely begun today's wave of editing, when Galena hurries up the *Tantalus'* entrance ramp.

"You might want to look outside," she tells us. "I think there's a storm on the way. A bad one."

Her announcement is perfectly timed. A dark shadow falls over the ship's windscreen, and the *Tantalus* trembles. Its landing gear creaks as a steady stream of wind pummels the ship.

"Holy cannoli," Cay mutters. "You aren't kidding."

"I've never seen clouds move so fast. They looked like a wave rolling across the sky."

Cay slides into the pilot's chair. "Let's get back into orbit. No sense taking unnecessary chances. Tantalus, bring us—"

He never finishes the command. A bomb has just detonated on our roof.

We're under attack.

That was my first thought, anyway. Through the windscreen, I see what's really going on. Hailstones, big as bowling balls, are transforming the flowering lawn outside into a crater field.

I think I'd prefer being under attack.

"Tantalus, get us the hell outta here!" I shout, securing my harness. "Galena, strap in! Hurry!"

A waterfall thunders against our roof. It cascades down the windscreen, washing out our visibility.

That's when Tantalus delivers its dismal response. "Due to the storm's ferocity, as well as my safety precautions, the ship is unable to take off at this time. Any attempt would result in instantaneous failure and a high likelihood of death for all onboard."

I can hardly hear Cay over the storm's uproar, as he says, "I hope you brought your rainboots. Looks like we're waiting it out."

Another bomb, worse than the first, sends a shockwave through the *Tantalus*. Moments later, the ship's power flickers, then dies altogether, leaving us in a ghastly darkness.

ENCELAS MESA

41 Days to Payment

"WHAT A MESS. Look what you've gotten us into *this* time, Jerricho Hatch."

Cay and I are squelching our way around the *Tantalus*, surveying the aftermath of the cyclone. The torrent must have first eroded the clay beneath our landing gear, then replaced it with washed-out soil from the higher slopes. The result? All six of our landing legs are buried a meter deep in rapidly drying muck.

The reason for the quick dry-up is obvious. New plants are sucking in the moisture with a conquistadorian greed. And it isn't only grass and tiny flowers this time. A handful of scattered saplings, no more than knee-high shoots when we first stepped outside, have grown as tall as the *Tantalus*. Broad shrubs with swaying fronds have likewise material-ized around us, climbing up through the barren ground like Koosh balls come alive, freeing themselves one rubbery filament at a time.

PAD, wrapping up a survey of the *Tantalus'* roof, returns with distressing news. Adopting a sympathetic tone, he says, "My prognosis is quite negative. The thermal release valve, which ejects the ship's heat waste, was pulverized during the storm. This subsequently allowed rainwater to flood the primary electrical compartment. The *Tantalus'* main transformer is ruined."

"Which means?" I ask impatiently.

"The ship has no electricity, and its hull is critically compromised. The cabin would experience an immediate pressure loss if subjected to space travel."

"So you're telling me we have no power to take off, no way to survive even if we could reach orbit, and three days to figure out the problem before Nabishna burns us alive?" Cay asks.

"That is an accurate summary."

"Is there any way we can send out an SOS? Or any kind of communication?" I inquire.

"Only if there were another ship within range of this planetary system," PAD answers. "I could use my own power supply to tap into the communications console and give it a charge. But because we receive no Axon signal here, I can only send out short-range messages, such as a distress *ping*. If any ship is in range, its onboard communications system would automatically alert me to its presence and alert its crew of our trouble."

Cay sighs. "Do it. Then come back outside. We'll need your help."

As PAD flies off to do his job, Galena calls to us from the canyon rim. Despite the terrible misfortune we've suffered, she sounds as wonderstruck as ever in her newfound liberty. "Cay! Jerricho! You *have* to see this!"

"Better be something cooler than naked birds popping outta the ground," Cay grumbles.

It is.

The valley below, which yesterday was drier than a cynical skeleton, is teeming with life from crater wall to crater wall. A lush forest, brought to life by the storm's drainage, carpets the vast basin floor in richest green. Among these adolescent trees run rivers and brooks, all fed by a hundred waterfalls cascading down the canyon walls. And, at the center of it all, shimmering like an aquamarine gemstone cut by the gods, are the tranquil waters of a newborn lake.

The scene is so breathtaking, I forget I only have seventy-two hours to live.

When our gawking is done, we return wordlessly to the *Tantalus*. Not even Cay can conjure up a snide remark or sarcastic quip for what we've seen.

PAD exits the ship to meet us. His news hurls us back down to *terra firma*.

"I am sorry. My distress signal was not returned to me. I found no other communications devices in our vicinity."

"We're on our own?" I ask, though I already know the answer.

"Yes. We are alone."

Cay absorbs the news with a deep sigh, then points at my chest and smirks. "Now might be a good time."

"Good time for what?"

"To break open the *good* bourbon. And for you to start praying to that crystal hanging around your neck."

ENCELAS MESA

"TURN THAT FROWN upside down!" Cay calls from across the field. "Pouting never once helped you, Jer. Why do you think I'm your only friend?"

I'm sulking in the shade of the *Tantalus,* trying in vain to escape the midday heat. I turn away and try to ignore him. But our relationship is that of a dog with a bone. He's the dog. I'm the bone. And he doesn't know the meaning of the phrase "leave it alone."

"Ah found a stream over yonder," he says, doing his best cowboy impression—which is pretty terrible. "What say ya fetch yerself a pail an' help me an' brother PAD haul water fer the well."

"You don't put water *in* a well, dumbass, you take it out," I retort with a scowl. "Besides, what does it matter? It'll all be vaporized in a couple days. Along with us."

Cay points at two creatures nearby. They look like tiny dogs with long, slender fingers. One has mounted itself on top of the other, and they're in the midst of a vigorous copulation.

"They'll be vay-poh-rized too, but that don't stop them fine critters from humpin' each other's brains out," Cay argues, still using the cowboy voice. "Them're makin' the most o' their short time, an' we should too. 'Sides, PAD kin use his solar chargers to keep up his power supply, which means he kin keep sendin' out the distress signal. Ah'd sure hate to die o' thirst afore the rescue team arrives!"

I raise my hands in surrender. "Okay, okay. As long as you promise to knock off the stupid western thing."

By the time I've taken a pair of trips to and from the stream—Cay continuing to speak like a cowboy the whole time—I have to admit that doing something is better than nothing. I busy myself with more tasks, hoping they might fool me into believing life will go on after Nabishna. Using a mop handle and sturdy bit of shrapnel, I create a makeshift pick-axe to dig the *Tantalus'* landing gear free. Under PAD's oversight, we also repurpose an interior panel from the lavatory wall, using it to fashion a temporary seal over the mangled pressure relief valve.

Before I know it, night is falling. As I suspected, Nabishnan days are considerably shorter than Terra's. If I were working my regular shift at RealityFeed Studios, I'd still be burping up lunch.

I'm about to head up the *Tantalus'* ramp when I notice Galena in the dying light. She's back at the crater rim, sitting and staring out over the valley. A twilight breeze tugs at the edges of her robe. Nothing better than Cay awaits me at the top of the ramp, so I instead wander between the scattered trees to Galena.

"You like it here, don't you," I say, easing myself onto the ground beside her.

Galena nods. "This is the first time in my life I haven't felt trapped."

Ironic, considering we're stuck here. But Galena doesn't seem bothered by our impending doom.

"Did you see other places as beautiful as this? When you'd travel with your ruling family?" As soon as I ask it, I sense Galena's tension.

"Yes," she answers after a short pause, "but never on my terms. It wasn't a choice, just another chore. Not like this. I can walk where I want, sit where I want, eat when I want, do what I want. These have been the best hours of my life."

My heart sinks. I'll never truly understand how miserable her existence has been, but it sounds like something I wouldn't wish on my worst enemy.

"Who are they? Your ruling family?"

Galena lowers her chin and frowns. "I'd rather not talk about them."

"Whatever happens—*if* we somehow manage to get off this planet —I'll protect you from them. I promise."

She gives me a wistful grin. "That's sweet of you. And stupid. There are only two roads for me, a lonely one and a captive one. If I'm going to be free, I can never return to civilization. Anywhere I go in the Galactic League, I'll be recognized for the castrata I am. Which means I can only live in the remotest places of the galaxy."

"Can we at least bring you somewhere safe?" I ask. "Somewhere no one will find you?"

"That's the deal, yes."

"What do you mean? What deal?" I ask quizzically.

"The one I made with Cay. He never told you?"

I shake my head, brow furrowed.

"That first day after you rescued me, when you were still sleeping, Cay told me if I helped with the rest of his project, he'd bring me anywhere I want."

Of course he did. I should have known Cay would use her like that. He's more than happy to help out—no problem!—but only if he's getting something in return. Does any decency live in him? Is there *room* for any decency alongside his ego? His selfishness?

Galena shudders. She pulls her knees up to her chest. According to PAD's calculations, Nabishna is at its zenith, its furthest point from NAB-15, which technically means we're outside in the middle of winter. Now that night is falling, Galena's breath plumes in the chilly air.

She gazes up at the sky. So do I. The stars are conquering it rapidly, one by one, as the last lingering forces of daylight retreat behind their sun king. Each star might hold a world, beautiful like this one, but gentler, where Galena could start her life, alone but anew.

"I wish I could stay here forever," she whispers. Faint tears glimmer in the starlight. "You want to protect me, Jerricho? Then freeze this night forever and let me live beneath these stars."

Dear Cosmos, does she ever look beautiful. Always, yes, but especially in this moment. In this magical, deadly place, under this star-spangled sky.

I don't realize I'm doing it until I'm doing it. Like the *Tantalus'* autopilot reacting to its external stimuli and data sensors, my hyper-romantic brain can't help but move in for a kiss.

Idiot.

Galena stops me cold. She plants her palm firmly against my chest.

"No, Jerricho," she whispers. "I'm a fourth generation castrata. I can't imagine why my great-grandmother ever had a child, or my grandmother, or my mom. But I will never—*never*—pass this life on to another."

"I—Galena—I'm sorry," I stutter. "That was ... that was stupid."

But my apology is unnecessary. It appears Galena has already moved on from the awkward moment. She's staring up again. The Milky Way has become a luminescent tapestry smoldering from one end of the heavens to the other.

"It looks so much different here than on Terra," I remark.

This is the same Milky Way I've always seen, but from a new angle, it's a completely changed galaxy.

Galena's voice also seems changed, and very small, as she says, "How can such a beautiful place be home to so much ugliness?" She sighs. "But I suppose I have my own ugly parts too."

"You? Ugly? Nah," I respond, hoping to inject some levity into her sudden melancholy.

"All of us," she says matter-of-factly. "You. Cay. Even me. *Especially* me."

I dig deep for a response but come up empty. Fortunately, Galena saves me from my own awkwardness. "We should go back to the *Tantalus*," she says. "Who knows what sort of creatures might come out at night?"

She stands and ambles off ahead of me. As I watch her silhouette against the tapestry of the Milky Way, growing smaller with every step, I wonder whether she might keep walking, walking, walking, until she becomes lost among the stars altogether.

THE *TANTALUS*

40 Days to Payment

I WAKE SOMETIME in the middle of the next day. When you're used to a Terran sleep schedule, it's damn disorienting trying to adjust to another planet's cycle, especially one whose clock spins as fast as Nabishna's.

A quick glance around the cabin tells me Cay and Galena already began their day. I mosey down the boarding ramp, expecting to find them outside, but they're nowhere to be seen. Only PAD is present, nestled in the long grass with his retractable solar panels angled up toward NAB-15. He absorbs the warm rays like a surfer taking a rest from the waves.

"Where'd Cay and Galena go?" I ask the drone.

He doesn't answer. Doesn't acknowledge my presence at all.

I snap my fingers and yell, "Hey! PAD! Where are the others?"

This time his optical sensor rotates to face me. "Would you please repeat yourself? I didn't understand clearly."

I'm near enough now to shout into his audio receiver. "Where are Cay and Galena?"

He points a titanium appendage at the crater rim. "They left ninety-four minutes ago, hoping to find an easy route to the valley floor."

"Thanks," I mutter. Because I even feel rotten for yelling at a robot, I say, "When's the last time someone serviced you? Cleaned you out?"

"I am unsure," PAD replies. "I must be switched off before someone services me, so I am usually unaware when it happens."

"When's the last time you were turned off?"

"The same day I was transferred into Cay's care."

"Maybe you need a cleaning. Come with me."

Back aboard the *Tantalus,* I retrieve a small sack of tools from one of my camera bags. After shutting down PAD, I go to work, systematically removing the proper screws and other hardware necessary to pop his head panels free. I've never worked on a drone before, but I've done enough camera maintenance to feel comfortable around most midsized electronics. PAD may be on the larger end, but he probably isn't much more complicated than a high-end studio camera.

Once I've freed his head panels, I lay them carefully on the floor beside me. I scan his innards for dirt, corrosion, and loose wiring. Other than a little dust, probably from our adventure in the mines, I don't find any issues, so I replace the panels and move on to PAD's longer "body" capsule.

I've removed a single panel when I find the problem. A black hemisphere, about the size of a chopped-in-half golf ball, has been fastened to the panel's interior wall next to PAD's audio receiver. My weakened fingers are barely strong enough to pop the black thing free. After turning it over in my palm, I lower my face for a close-up investigation of its flat surface.

"Rubber cement?" I say aloud. "What kind of shit manufacturer uses rubber cement in a drone?"

Without replacing the panel, I switch PAD on and hold the black half-ball up to his "eye."

"Do you know what this is?" I ask. "I found it stuck inside one of your panels."

PAD takes it from me. After scanning it from a few different angles, he says, "It's a tracking device."

"Are you normally outfitted with one?" I wonder.

"Yes," he answers.

I sigh, but the relief is short-lived.

"Though not with one as powerful as this," he continues. "Many personal assistance drones are manufactured with a standard tracking device in them. Mine, for example, is located in my posterior capsule. However, it is much smaller than this one, with only a planetary range that allows my owner to locate me if I am lost or stolen."

"What about the one you're holding?"

"This is a long-range tracking device, used to locate objects across the galaxy. They are highly illegal for civilians. Their use is mostly restricted to covert military or peacekeeping operations overseen by the Galactic League."

"What about the adhesive? It looks like rubber cement to me. Who would use that in a drone?"

"Perhaps somebody inexperienced with electronics. Perhaps somebody in a hurry."

Or perhaps both. It doesn't take long to do the math.

The sound of footsteps on the boarding ramp diverts my attention. Cay parades in, wearing his toothiest smile.

As soon as Galena enters behind him, I remember what happened last night and lower my eyes, embarrassed. Good thing I'm not a White guy, or I'd be glowing redder than a sunburned cherry.

"Look who's finally awake!" Cay exclaims. "I hope you enjoyed your sleep." Noticing our drone in his partially disassembled state, he asks, "What'd you do to PAD? Was he mouthing off to you? Because that's *my* job."

In reply, I toss Cay the black hemisphere.

"What's this?" he asks, turning it over as he examines it.

"I found it inside PAD. He was having hearing problems again. Thought maybe he needed a cleaning. That was glued inside the panel by his audio receiver. PAD tells me it's a long-range tracking device. Its signal must have been interfering with his audio comprehension."

"Geiger," Cay growls. "He bugged PAD, then sent Ameliana to deliver him."

More confused than concerned, Galena mutters, "But why would he—?"

"That's how he found us on Tarrkanna-Rrui," Cay continues, cutting her off. "That's how he found us on Petra 7. And that might be how he *saves* us on Nabishna."

"Saves us?" Galena and I ask in unison.

Cay explains. "If he followed us to Tarrkanna-Rrui and Petra 7, why wouldn't he follow us here too? He'll know we made it out of the mines when his tracker suddenly shot to the other side of the galaxy."

"But if his ship hears our SOS signal, couldn't he just wait it out? Let NAB-15 do his dirty work for him?" I argue.

"His ship hasn't heard it," Cay confidently replies. "PAD's *ping* hasn't bounced off anything yet. Right, PAD?"

"That is correct."

"So ... what? We wait for him to land and hope we can outsmart him?"

"No. We'll be *ready* to outsmart him."

"Ameliana?" says Galena. She seems to be tracking him better than me.

"Exactly!" Cay throws an arm around her shoulders and hugs her to his side. "Looks like our time together was beneficial in more ways than one. I must be rubbing off on you, you clever, *clever* girl."

Galena rolls her eyes. I must be rubbing off on her too.

"PAD," says Cay, "are you able to send out a generic ping? *Without* an SOS?"

"I can, although any communications system will still recognize and record the event."

"And could you send a message to a specific contact nearby? If you have their contact codes?"

"I can."

Cay points at the lifeless comm console. "Then do it. Just the anonymous ping for now. Let's see if there's anyone nearby."

The half-naked drone shamelessly floats off to do as directed.

For my part, I'm beginning to catch up to Cay's train of thought. "So, if Geiger comes with Ameliana onboard ..."

Cay finishes my sentence. "We message her, and she figures out a way to rescue us."

Something isn't sitting right with me, but I can't put my finger on what. It's a thousand-piece jigsaw puzzle, and nine hundred ninety-nine pieces are right where they need to be. But there's one piece, obscure but important to the overall picture, still out of place.

"And in the meantime—what, we sit here and wait?" I ask.

"In the meantime," Cay replies, "we move forward with the plan."

"We're two days away from incineration, and you're still thinking about mushrooms?" I'm not really as surprised as I sound. Cay has never demonstrated a high capacity for the sane perspective.

"What else would we do?" he says. "I can't make the *Tantalus* fly again. Can you?"

Galena must sense the mounting tension between us. She interjects to say, "We found a path to the valley floor. That's what we were doing this morning."

"About the first thing that's gone right since we landed," Cay adds. He glances at his wristwatch. "Approximately nineteen hours from now, that mushroom will bloom. We might as well be there when it happens. If we're gonna make it off this rock, let's at least get what we came for."

From his station plugged into the communications console, PAD calls out, with as much enthusiasm as I've ever heard in a robot, "My signal bounced back! Based on response time, I believe there is a ship in orbit around Nabishna."

Normally I hate it when Cay's right. This time, I'll make an exception. Extra crispy is great when it comes to fried chicken or potato wedges, but I'd prefer if I didn't have to use that description for myself.

Cay doesn't gloat in his victory, though I imagine I'll hear about it later. Instead, he takes Ameliana's contact card from his pants pocket and hands it to PAD. On a torn scrap of parchment paper, he scribbles a brief message. This, too, he gives to PAD.

"Send that exact message," Cay instructs him. "When Ameliana responds, make sure she knows our planetary coordinates. She'll take care of the rest. I *know* she will."

He whirls around to face me and Galena. His unkillable confidence is shining brighter than NAB-15 as he says, "Do or die time, boys and girls. Grab your cameras, and let's find ourselves the rarest mushroom in the galaxy."

ENCELAS VALLEY

CAY AND GALENA'S morning wasn't wasted. I had been dreading a hike down the crater's steep slopes, especially with the added weight of a camera, but my two companions discovered a gentler route requiring minimal acrobatics. There was still *some* scrambling over boulders—to be expected, given our task—but it was minimal. Within an hour after leaving the *Tantalus'* shadow, we stepped foot on the valley floor.

The going isn't so easy anymore. The forest is thick and caught in a state of constant change. The uneven ground is covered in a layer of thick underbrush, whose sticky fingers seem to grab at our boots, trying to trip us with each step.

We can't see more than twenty meters ahead at any given point, so PAD takes up the role of navigation. He floats above and ahead of us, our Star of Bethlehem guiding us along the clearest paths he can find toward the lake at the valley's center.

Three hours into the hike, dusk is already settling over us. Another short Nabishnan day comes to its end as we hunker down among the exposed roots of a sprawling tree.

Pointing up at it, I say, "Those leaves are shaped like my Gram's Christmas-tree cookies."

"I had a cookie once," Galena wistfully replies. "I stole it when we were cleaning up after a party. Mother gave me a good slap when she found out. Told me if our ruler caught me doing something like that, he'd give me far worse."

"Well," says Cay, opening his backpack, "I don't have any cookies, but I do have an extra-nutritious, manufactured-with-love ration bar."

After our meager dinner, we make ourselves as cozy as we can and shut our eyes. I was worried the night would be too cold to sleep, but

Nabishna is warming quickly as it approaches its "summer" season. Wearing my down jacket, and with nothing but a springy clump of moss for a pillow, I discover I'm quite comfortable.

Especially with Galena beside me.

Exhausted from the hike, I fall into a deep, hard sleep.

At some point during the planet's darkest hour, I awaken to find Galena curled against me. Her head is resting on my shoulder, and her rhythmic breathing mingles with the peaceful sounds of the Nabishnan night.

And one not-so-peaceful sound. A harsh snuffling, somewhere in the dark. It reminds me of Dad clearing his sinuses whenever he's got a cold. But where Dad might snort a couple times and be done, this one keeps at it. Every ten or fifteen seconds it pauses, but only for a moment before going at it again.

Whatever-it-is hangs around for a while. At one point I think I hear footsteps—or hoofsteps, or pawsteps—but they don't sound terribly close to our camp. Before too long, the nocturnal critter moves on, melting away into the forest's darkness along with its odd snuffling.

I don't sleep the rest of the night. While the others dream away, I watch the sky grow steadily lighter. I know I should wake them so we can be on our way, but that would spell an end to snuggle time with Galena. Given the choice, I'd rather burn with Nabishna than disrupt the status quo.

NAB-15 is just peeking through the trees when Cay awakens. I didn't have the heart to disturb Galena, but Cay finds no problem doing so himself.

"Wakey wakey, eggs 'n bacey!" he hollers, jabbing her shoulder with the toe of his boot. "Long day ahead of us, young lady."

Cay also wakes PAD from his low-power mode and asks, "How much further to the lake?"

"Approximately two-point-eight kilometers, as the crow flies," PAD answers. "Adjusting for deviations and obstacles, perhaps four kilometers of travel on foot."

"A good morning's stretch," says Cay, tossing us each another dull meal bar.

We hike through the morning. With every passing minute, Nabishna seems to warm another degree. By the time NAB-15 is hanging directly overhead, I'm drenched in sweat and sipping constantly from my aquabottle. If things keep up at this rate, I'll be dead from dehydration long before the vengeful star cremates me and my friends.

At last, we break through the trees onto the open shoreline of the valley's great lake. Without consulting the others, I drop my camera and backpack, remove my boots and socks, and wade into the water. The fire in my toes, my feet, my ankles—and now, I realize with a new gut-punch, my lower calves—subsides, but not much. With every new adventure I undertake, the Clarion-Burgess residing within me is growing stronger. Part of me was hoping this crazy trip with Cay would take my mind off it, yet every day seems to be a reckoning with my own mortality.

"Did you see the trees we passed a minute ago?" Cay calls from the shore.

"No. What about 'em?" I shout back.

"They had blue leaves! Beautiful, perfect blue," says Cay. "Well, more like a teal, if we're splitting hairs. Still, I'd bet anything it was that blue-leafed bolero from Sal's video." He glances at his watch. "In a couple hours, the Encelas mushrooms will be blooming a hundred meters behind us."

I'm sloshing back onto shore when Galena asks, "Do you ... think I could go for a swim?"

Cay shrugs and says, "I forgot to bring the water wings, so stay shallow."

As Galena shamelessly begins peeling off her outer layer of clothing, I can't help but keep her in the corner of my eye. I'm being creepy—I know I am—but I'm powerless to wrestle my gaze away from her entirely.

Of all things, it's Cay who does the wrestling for me.

"Come on, lover boy," he says, low enough that Galena can't hear him. "Let the slave belong to no one but herself for a while. Besides, I've got a couple things I want to narrate by the bolero trees while it's still light."

"Yeah. You're right," I concede, and force myself to turn away before my eyes can steal anything more from Galena.

ENCELAS VALLEY

39 Days to Payment

EVEN WITH THE lakeshore breeze rolling over us, the night is uncomfortably sticky when Cay's alarm sounds.

"Rise and shine!" he calls to us in the darkness. "Those mushrooms ain't gonna wait 'til daylight!"

We've only been sleeping a couple hours, but I feel instantly alert and refreshed. My circadian rhythm must be adjusting to Nabishna's brief cycle of night and day. Too bad I won't have longer to finish that acclimatization. One way or another, it's about to come to an end.

As PAD awakens from sleep mode, he illuminates our lakeside bivouac. We don't have much by way of supplies. Within a couple minutes, we're loaded up and ready to go.

PAD leads us by memory to the grove of blue-leafed boleros Cay and I filmed earlier. Everything is much the same as we left it, but with one glaring exception.

Scattered among the gnarled trunks are hundreds of mushrooms. They're easy to spot—probably even more so than in the daytime— because each mushroom radiates a faint glow.

"Jer, Galena, start rolling your cameras," Cay orders. "PAD, turn off your lights. I want our audience to see this the way we are."

Once cameras are ready and operating, Cay kneels onto the leaf-strewn ground and says, "Our patience on Nabishna has finally paid off. Here, in the heart of the Encelas Valley, flaunting their bioluminescence in the dead of night, are the rarest mushrooms in the galaxy." With the back of his arm, he wipes away the sweat beading on his forehead. "And not a moment too soon! In a few hours, Nabishna will approach the minor axis of its revolution around NAB-15. When it does, it'll cook everything—and every*one*—on this planet."

Cay removes a pair of gunnysacks from his backpack. As he begins collecting mushrooms, he holds one up to Galena's camera and grins. "I wonder if they'll make my poop glow." He pops the mushroom into his mouth. As he chews, he moans and says, "Can't beat that! Good Cosmos, that is outstanding. Absolutely beautiful."

After the first sack is filled to bursting, he proceeds with the second, saying, "We'll want as many mushrooms as possible for what I've got planned. Since Nabishna is getting warmer by the moment, I'll transport the mushrooms in these specialized cold-storage bags. You can't tell from your program monitor, but the interior fibers are radiating cold air. So, even as Nabishna starts cooking, our mushrooms should remain fresh and tasty."

PAD, operating the third camera overhead, drops altitude suddenly. "Pardon my interruption," he says, "but I am counting eleven life forms approaching the area."

"What kind of life form? People?" I ask hopefully. Perhaps Ameliana has arrived with rescue.

"No. They are too large to be humanoid beings," says PAD.

"We got what we came for," Cay says. "It's time to go anyway."

The words have hardly left his mouth when a cacophony of ghoulish shrieks pierces the night. They're coming from the direction of the lake, which means they can't be far.

"Ooooh, willikers," murmurs Cay. "I just remembered part of Sal's episode."

"*Now* you remember?" I cry.

"There may not be many mushroom hunters that come from *off*-planet anymore. But there are some big, violent ones that live *on* the planet. And they don't care much for competition."

The strange snuffling sounds I heard last night revisit my ears. Not coming from one creature this time, but from many. Seconds later, their snuffles are accompanied by crackling leaves and snapping twigs. Through the thick undergrowth, the mushroom hunters streak toward us.

PAD beams his brightest lights in the direction of the commotion. The creatures, thrown into confusion by the sudden presence of flood-lights, rear back with squeals and snorts of surprise. Their hesitation is brief, but it's long enough to see what we're dealing with. Yellow, slitted eyes burn in the darkness. Ivory tusks, scimitars, gird the creatures' long faces, two on each side. A prehensile snout, about a meter long and as thick as my forearm, dances in front of each creature like it has a mind of its own, sniffing the forest floor for edible treasures.

Treasures like our mushrooms.

They don't seem particularly murderous—not yet, anyway. But something tells me their ambivalence might change when they realize we're running off with their mushrooms.

"Let's get outta here," Cay whispers. "PAD, lead the way!" Cradling both gunnysacks in his arms, he crashes off through the brush behind the fleeing drone.

Galena and I hurry after him. We've hardly left the bolero grove when we hear the enraged cries of the jealous beasts. Our thievery has been discovered, and they sound dead set on making the guilty party pay.

First Petra 7, now Nabishna. Why are we always running for our lives in the *dark?*

PAD does his best to illuminate the forest for us, but there are simply too many obstacles. Tree branches act like whips, cutting into my forehead and cheeks. Vines and creepers snatch at my frantic limbs, nearly managing at one point to hijack the camera hanging at my side.

Despite our desperate efforts, the creatures are gaining on us. And *fast.*

A few feet ahead of me, Cay halts and spins around. He draws the sidearm at his hip and squeezes off a trio of shots. A hellish squeal suggests that at least one of the lasers hit its mark. But after hearing the ensuing war cries, I wonder whether Cay did more harm than good. At once, the panic created by the gunshots is swallowed up in a pursuit more bloodthirsty than before.

I've only got one idea that might save our asses: give them what they want.

Cay's not going to like this.

I throw myself onto the ground in front of him, hoping he won't accidentally shoot me. He doesn't, though I'm sure he'll soon wish he did. Seizing one of the mushroom-loaded gunnysacks, I yank it from the crook of his arm.

"What're you doing?" he cries, lowering the pistol as he tries snatching the bag back from me. "We need those!"

"Sorry, Cay. It'll have to be appetizer portions for this show."

Fighting through the pain of it, I shotput the gunnysack into the night. It lands in front of the giant hoglike creatures and bursts open. Mushroom shrapnel flies from my gunnysack grenade, littering the ground in their pale glow.

My plan works. The mushroom-crazed creatures stop to gobble up as many of our sacrificed morsels as they can. One wears the gunnysack like a feedbag, greedily searching for mushroom residue inside it.

"Hurry," I say, pulling Cay off the ground. "They're distracted, but won't be for long. Let's get outta here before they realize we have a second bag."

We run. Once we're confident that the Encelas boars—Cay even remembers their name now—have abandoned any further pursuit, we slow to a brisk march.

Daylight is returning. With it, a brutal heat. The trek's physical toll on my diseased body was already crippling. Now that Nabishna's oven has been set to *BAKE*, I'm afraid I won't make it back to the *Tantalus* to learn whether rescue ever came.

When NAB-15 rises over the crest of the crater rim, my shock is twofold. First, I can't believe how much of the sky it now fills. Second, I can't believe we aren't already on fire.

Cay checks his watch. So casually I want to strangle him for it, he says, "We might have less time than I thought. Better pick up the pace."

I scoff. I don't have any "pick up" left.

By the time we reach the slope leading up to the *Tantalus,* the temperature must be damn near forty-five Celsius. For a moment I'm convinced I'm melting, but a glance at my fingers only reveals streamlets of sweat dribbling off them.

We're partway up the slope when I glance across the valley. A haze of thick, dark smoke is rising on the far horizon, stretching from one end of the world to the other. Thousands of flying creatures, whether birds or otherwise, flock ahead of the smoke, trying in vain desperation to outrun their fate.

Like us, they're as good as dead. Nabishna's *BAKE* is finishing at a *BROIL*.

That's when my legs give out at last. I yelp as I fall to my knees.

Ahead, Cay hears me and turns around. Shuffling back to me, he says, "Jer! You alright? Come on, we're almost there."

He helps me to my feet, but I only manage a couple steps before I stumble again. This time, I collapse all the way onto my elbows.

"You two ... go on," I wheeze. "All ... dying here ... anyway."

Cay and Galena exchange exhausted looks of concern. Without speaking a word to each other, she extends her arms, and he hands over the gunnysack.

Grunting, Cay bellies underneath my prone form. I feel his back and shoulders pressing against my chest as he raises me, millimeter by agonizing millimeter, off the path.

"What ... the hell ... are you doing?" I say. "You can't ... get us both ... to the top."

"You know those stories? The ones about moms who lift scabbs off their trapped children?"

"Yeah?"

He plants a loud smooch on my sweaty forehead. "Call me mommy."

"You crazy motherfu—"

"Close enough!"

A loud groan explodes through Cay's lips as he straightens his legs to stand upright. All two-hundred-plus-a-camera pounds of Yours Truly are draped over his shoulders like a rich woman's overstuffed boa.

"Holy balls, you're friggin' *huge*," Cay says. "You comfortable up there, ya giant sonuvabitch?"

"No," I moan. Red dots are swarming my vision.

"Me either. Let's go."

With each step he takes, another jolt of pain arcs through my bouncing ragdoll body. I could pass out any moment, but I'm not sure whether it'll happen due to the heat or to sheer agony.

"Almost to the top, sweetie," he mutters. "Hold on a little longer for Mummy."

This time, I don't have enough energy to tell him off.

We arrive at the rim. My vision clears just enough to make out the *Tantalus* some fifty meters up the slope. Like someone duped by a desert mirage, my heat-baked brain must be inventing things that are not there.

Our ship isn't alone on the mesa. It's sitting beneath the shadow of a much, *much* larger vessel.

That's when the world fades to black, and my consciousness soars away to distant—and more temperate—worlds.

GALACTIC SPACE
– OUTER CENTAURUS –

ABOARD THE *ROYAL AUSTRIAN*

38 Days to Payment

FOR THE SECOND time in as many weeks, I wake up surrounded by medical tubing and monitors. My bed, however, is exactly one shitload more comfortable than the plank the healers of Tarrkanna-Rrui gave me. It's also a good deal warmer.

I'm not dead. How am I not dead?

My head is pounding, tongue so dry I'm worried it might be permanently welded to the roof of my mouth. Some of Nabishna's fire must have settled in my upper joints too, because every time I move even a single millimeter, I'm punished with a deep burning sensation.

It takes a good mental pep talk—*Come on, Jer, you can do it, big fella!*—but I eventually sit up to take in my surroundings. The room doesn't look like it belongs in an infirmary. Rather, it appears as if medical equipment was moved into a regular cabin to accommodate me.

There's one thing I'm quite certain of: I'm not onboard the *Tantalus*. I follow the breadcrumbs of memory until I arrive at the logical conclusion.

I must be onboard that ship. The giant one I assumed I was hallucinating.

Geiger's ship. It *has* to be.

But that makes no sense. He tried to kill us on Tarrkanna-Rrui and Petra 7. Nabishna was ready to finish us off. Why rescue us now?

I slide off the bed and onto wobbly legs. Once I've steadied myself, I totter to the cabin door like a giant baby taking its first steps. I hope to find answers on the other side—and a couple gallons of water.

Instead, as the door *whooshes* aside, I find a familiar face staring back at me.

"Gyahrmasheez!" I shout, inventing a new word as I tip backward.

"Sorry!" Ameliana says. She grabs my elbow to steady me. "I was coming to see if you were awake yet. Your friends are in the dining hall. My grandfather has prepared a meal for everyone."

"So we're—"

"Alive," she finishes. "Alive and onboard the *Royal Austrian*. You and Cay must be the luckiest people I know."

"What about the *Tantalus?*" I ask. I'm afraid to hear her answer.

To my surprise—and relief—she chuckles and says, "Also lucky. The *Austrian* was just large enough to tow it into orbit."

I follow Ameliana into the hallway. I'm surprised by what I find there. My whole life, my idea of space vessels has been cold and stark. Titanium alloy plating over everything. Little or no decorations. All function, no form. But the *Royal Austrian* is nothing like my utilitarian concepts. Instead, I feel almost like I'm back at the funeral parlor where we held Marq's memorial service—emphasis on the *almost*. Here, the exposed wood and flower-patterned wallpaper work together to create an ambience that's both warm and elegant. The mulberry carpet running down the center of the marble floor creates an atmosphere of importance. Or, considering the name of the ship, perhaps *royalty* would be the better word for it.

As we walk, I speak in low tones to Ameliana. "It wasn't luck, you know."

She stops. Glancing both ways down the hallway to make sure no one is within earshot, she asks, "What wasn't luck?"

"Your grandpa coming to Nabishna. He put a homing device in the PAD unit you delivered. It's how he followed us to Tarrkanna-Rrui and Petra 7 too."

Ameliana frowns. "That tracks. The moment he heard what Cay was up to, Grandfather has been obsessed with taking him out. Just like every other threat to his status."

"So why'd he rescue us now? I'm trying to do the math, and it doesn't add up."

Ameliana flashes an impish grin. "You can thank me for that. I convinced him Cay could give him something he wanted."

"The Trees of Eden," I speak confidently.

"They're the *only* thing he has wanted," Ameliana confirms, "since long before I was born."

We continue down the hallway, then take a sharp right to find ourselves at a spiral staircase. The din of chatter and clinking tableware floats down from above.

"Listen," Ameliana says, grabbing my forearm. There's no mistaking her tone of urgency. "Other than sending me to deliver that PAD unit, my grandfather doesn't know anything about my contact with you and Cay. Let's keep it that way. If he's in the dark, I can keep him in check."

I give a brisk nod. "Not a word from me. But Cay's got a big mouth. Can't make any promises there."

Ameliana laughs. "Good enough for me. Now, we'd better get upstairs, or my grandfather will start wondering what we're up to."

GUSTAV GEIGER'S DINING HALL

"WELCOME TO MY TABLE, Jerricho Hatch," greets the gray-haired man standing at the head of the elegant hardwood table. Surrounding it are seven chairs. Two are occupied by Cay and Galena, and in front of each seat is a covered, silver serving dish.

"Please, take a chair beside your castrata friend," Geiger continues, motioning toward Galena. "And to my granddaughter, of course, goes the foot of the table."

Like the other areas I've seen of the *Royal Austrian*, this room isn't at all what I would expect. Rather than exposed metal and cold diode lighting, polished stone walls and a hardwood floor call to mind the dining hall some aristocrat of old might have built in his mansion.

I sit as directed, and Geiger moves on to introductions. Gesturing toward a serpentine Lai'oshan sitting across from Cay, he says, "This is Wenlyn o' gla Myrn. She has worked as my head videographer, producer, and frequent writer and director for over thirty years. A couple seasons ago, she even won an award for our episode on galactic caviars."

Wenlyn o' Whatever-the-Hell-Her-Name-Is stares at me with unblinking orange eyes. I imagine her unhinging her lower jaw like a Terran snake to swallow me whole, and wonder how many crew members were last seen in her company. Human eyes are as inadept at distinguishing between Lai'oshans as we are one bluegill from another, but I'd wager good money this is the same one I saw at Marq Cantore's funeral.

"And this is our newest member, Drummond Paetski," says Geiger.

A beefy man, not much older than me and built as sturdy as a tank, offers an almost imperceptible nod. "Call me Drum," he says.

I'm not sure what captures my attention most about him. It's a three-way tossup between his white-blond hair, glacial-blue eyes, and thread-popping muscles. I can't imagine where I might have met him before, yet there is something undeniably familiar about him.

"Drum is my new head of security," Geiger explains. "He recently returned from two tours in the Ryhonites, squashing insurgents there until the Galactic League discharged him from service for his war crimes."

Drum snorts. "What they call war crimes, I call gettin' the job done."

"Exactly the sort of attitude that will take you to the moon, so long as you stick with me," Geiger replies with a light chuckle.

Cay, who has remained impossibly silent until now, snaps his fingers. Wagging one at Drum, he says, "I remember you! You lived on mine and Jer's floor at Sol 3 U. You were a couple years older than us."

Drum sneers and says, "I remember you too. You're the crazy asshole who tried burnin' down the dorm."

"Guilty as charged!" Cay looks him up and down—the parts visible over the tabletop, anyway—and whistles. "You got ... *bigger*. Someone's been eating his spinach!"

"Among other things."

Interrupting them, Geiger says, "Ameliana likewise remembered him from school. She's the one who convinced him to apply for the opening."

"And I'm very thankful for it," Drum says, giving her a courteous grin and nod.

Geiger takes his chair at the head of the table. "Forgive me. All this talk, while our food grows cold! Please, everyone, enjoy the meal I have prepared for you."

He claps his hands twice, and the door behind him opens. Through it comes the same female castrata I've seen accompanying Geiger before. The doleful Vandreek approaches the table and lifts the silver lid off Geiger's serving tray. He inhales deeply, then instructs the rest of us to uncover our trays also.

I hate to admit it, but the food both looks and smells divine.

"Here we have pan-fried balladuck breast, fresh from the Karthon system, topped with a sweet-and-savory cherry caper sauce. For sides, there are butter-seared and roasted potato medallions, along with a salad of mixed galactic greens." Geiger casts a nasty glare at his castrata. "I do apologize for the impropriety of serving the salad alongside the hot foods. *Someone* has forgotten her fine-dining etiquette."

From inside his pocket, Geiger removes a black object. He presses a button on it, and the castrata doubles over with a yelp of pain.

Galena tenses beside me. Her fork quivers in her clenched fist.

As Geiger returns the controller to his pocket, he tells the castrata, "You may leave until called for."

She leaves, but Galena doesn't relax.

Cay takes a bite of the balladuck breast. He makes a show of difficulty in swallowing, then says, "Needs salt."

"I'm sure it does," Geiger replies with a good-natured chuckle. "I have an unfortunate family history of heart problems and am under the doctor's orders to tread lightly with the sodium." In a gesture of apparent goodwill, he slides a pewter salt cellar across the table to Cay. "For those of you without high blood pressure, there is flaky sea salt. *Bon appetite.*"

Cay isn't convulsing or foaming at the mouth yet, so I figure Geiger isn't trying to poison us. Besides, why would he save our butts on Nabishna, only to murder us on the *Royal Austrian?*

I take a bite of potatoes. They melt in my mouth like the butter saturating them.

"I must admit," Cay says between bites, "it's awfully nice of you to slave away in your kitchen, making a meal for prisoners like us."

"Prisoners?" Geiger replies. "You are mistaken, my boy. You are no prisoners of mine. You are guests. My *rescued* guests."

"What luck that you happened by Nabishna when you did," says Cay. "A more suspicious person would say it's a mighty big galaxy for such an astounding coincidence."

"I often harvest the mushrooms of Encelas," Geiger replies with casual nonchalance. "You of all people should know how superior they are to those lab-grown monstrosities. Speaking of which, I've kept yours safe in my own icebox. You'll have them back, of course."

"How gallant of you."

"Anyway," Geiger continues, ignoring Cay's derision, "when the *Royal Austrian's* comm system received the distress ping sent by your drone, I guessed it meant trouble."

He seems to have no idea we discovered his tracking device in PAD. Cay hasn't mentioned it either, which means he must have some plan to take advantage of Geiger's ignorance.

Laying his fork sideways on the platter of half-eaten food, Cay asks, "Why help us? You clearly wanted us dead on Tarrkanna-Rrui and Petra 7. Failed, of course, like this miserable attempt at dinner. Why not let Nabishna finish what you couldn't?"

Geiger swallows a sip of wine and says, "I am terribly sorry for whatever misfortunes you have had. But I assure you, I was not the one behind them. From the rumors I have heard, Cay Cantore has no shortage of enemies in this galaxy."

"And you're, what, just a good Samaritan doing his charitable deed for the day?"

Geiger shakes his head. "No, I'm afraid not. Altruism and I don't belong in the same solar system, let alone the same sentence."

"What, then?" Cay demands.

"I saved you because I believe we can help each other. We both have a goal—the *same* goal—and I suggest we work together to achieve it. Nobody has found the Trees of Eden in hundreds of years. We both stand a much greater chance of success if we work together. Wouldn't you agree?"

"And you're planning to hold us hostage until I do? 'Cause I won't."

Geiger sighs. He takes another sip of wine. "I will do no such thing. It is an open offer, one unaccompanied by threats."

"So we can leave?" Cay asks. He seems shocked by Geiger's unexpected affability.

The Food Fürst struggles to hide his disappointment as he says, "My mechanics have already finished repairing the *Tantalus*—free of charge, if you're wondering. You may leave whenever you wish."

"Excellent," Cay exclaims, jumping to his feet. "In that case, I wish to leave at once. I'm *starving*. I need to find myself a decent meal somewhere."

THE *TANTALUS*

BACK ABOARD OUR ship, we begin an immediate hunt for signs of sabotage. So far, it appears Geiger was true to his word about fixing the *Tantalus* and letting us leave hassle free. Even PAD's radio scans are coming up empty. And why not? Geiger still thinks his tracker is glued inside the drone. He lets us do the heavy lifting, we figure out how to get to the Trees of Eden, and he follows us.

This time, though, we're a step ahead of him.

We're battening down the hatches, preparing to sever our connection with the *Royal Austrian*, when we hear the airlock elevator activate. I exchange a worried glance with Cay. The airlock is also our docking point, connecting the *Tantalus* to Geiger's ship. Maybe he isn't letting us off so easy after all.

When the airlock door opens, Ameliana rushes through.

"Hey!" Cay greets her cheerfully. "Did you decide to ditch that old fartface and join the cool-kid party instead?"

Ameliana is in no mood for banter. "I don't have much time," she says. From underneath her sweater, she reveals a rolled-up length of paper. She unfurls it and lays it flat across the kitchen counter.

"Whatcha got there?" Cay asks.

"A map of Outer Centaurus. When Jerricho informed me of my grandfather's tracking device, it gave me an idea."

She points at one of the map's thousands of black dots. "We're here, in outer orbit around NAB-15." She then jabs at a different dot. "And this is Theronia. It's the nearest League planet. By X-space, it's only a couple hours from here. It also happens to be the ship-building capital of the galaxy."

"So? Why do we want to go there?" asks Cay.

It's clear he isn't following, but I can't blame him. Neither am I.

"If you ditch the tracker on one of the outgoing vessels, it'll send my grandfather on a wild-goose chase," Ameliana explains. "It won't keep him off you forever, but it'll at least buy you some time."

"That's brilliant," says Cay. "One problem. We still don't know if League authorities are on the prowl for us after the Tarrkanna-Rrui incident."

Ameliana's face brightens. "Oh! Right! I looked into that for you, like I said. There was a report with a warrant, but you were only charged with a misdemeanor. Something about a disturbance at a bar? Anyway, all they wanted was a small fine. I settled it for you."

"Jerricho will pay you back when this is all over," Cay assures her.

Tenderly, Ameliana lays her hand on his and gives it a squeeze. "Don't worry about it. Pay me back by making me dinner sometime."

"If you're lucky, I'll make you breakfast too."

Ameliana chuckles. "If you're half the cook you think you are, luck won't have anything to do with it."

Not daring to arouse suspicions by lingering, Ameliana hurries to the airlock and steps inside.

"You forgot your map!" Cay calls after her.

"Keep it," she replies with a saucy wink. "You can return it to me whenever we have that breakfast together."

ORBITER EATERY

37 Days to Payment

FROM A THOUSAND miles away, through the diner window, the entire planet of Theronia looks like a factory. Everything I see of the ship-building world reminds me of a pile of ancient gray bones.

Cay and I are sitting in a booth, "sharing" a gritty vitamin milkshake. He insisted we split one. To cut costs.

Cheap bastard.

Galena isn't with us for obvious reasons. A tiny diner like the Orbiter Eatery isn't required to perform a full ID scan of every ship that docks with it—that would be highly impractical—but any surveillance system connected to Axon performs an automatic scan of every being it registers. An escaped castrata is bound to raise a red flag.

Sitting in the booth behind me, a gang of orange-eyed Mirillian pirates is celebrating their most recent prize with a round of drinks. Their guttural voices aren't naturally disposed toward Commonspeak, which means their boisterous conversation in a non-native tongue must be a flex move. They're letting everyone in earshot know exactly who they are and what they've been up to.

Cay slurps the last of "our" vitamin shake through his straw—the bendy kind, like kids usually use, as per his insistence. When he's finished, he leans forward conspiratorially. Hiding his mouth behind his fingers to throw off any lurking lip readers, he whispers, "Does this milkshake taste like sweaty underwear to you too?"

I pound my palm against the tabletop. "Dammit, Cay, what's the plan here? We've been sitting in this booth for an hour. Last time our waitress came by, I'm pretty sure she gave us the finger—or whatever it is Squimmos give."

Cay pats the duffel bag next to him. The tracking device I removed from PAD is inside, ready for a new host. I just don't know what we're waiting for.

"Don't look," says Cay, "but there's a trio of League soldiers at the back end of the diner. They must be waiting here for a pickup transport, 'cause they've got all their gear with them."

He leans in even closer. I'm pretty sure I can feel his lips brushing my ear as he whispers his idiotic plan. Before I can object, he's out of the booth and on his way to the far side of the Orbiter Eatery, duffel in hand. I groan and hurry after him.

"Good evening, good sirs," heralds Cay. He offers the soldiers, one human and a pair of tri-horned Yurans, what I'm sure is a sloppy and disrespectful salute. This he follows with a patronizing chuckle. "Or is it morning? Or noon? This is my first time away from Terra, so I can't really tell."

The grizzly human soldier, who appears as annoyed as he is bearded, raises a hand to shut Cay up. "Look, man, we're trying to enjoy a quiet dinner here between shuttles. Leave us alone, would ya?"

Cay feigns hurt. He takes a step back and says, "Absolutely, absolutely. But my dearly departed dad, he was a soldier like you. I wanted to thank you for your service, that's all."

The soldier rolls his eyes. "Whatever. You're welcome."

"*And* I wanted to let you know those Mirillians in the booth behind us—well, they've been bragging about a sizeable cache of shimmer they've got on their ship."

The soldiers look at each other and chuckle.

"Yeah, the entire diner's been hearing about it for the last hour," the human soldier says. "But we aren't peacekeepers, and we don't have a warrant, which means there ain't shit we can do about it. So, like I said before, would ya leave us alone? Please?"

At this Cay drops his chin and pinches the bridge of his nose. If I didn't know him better, I'd swear he's about to cry.

"Look, I didn't want to bring this up," he says with choked voice. "It's just ... *so* disrespectful toward heroes like you. But they were also arguing about which of you was the ugliest. In the end, I think they agreed it was you." He nods at the Yuran closest to the wall. "They said your mother made you join the military so a mine might explode in your face, that it could only improve your chances of finding a wife. And another one—

oh, I can't go on!—he said not even a Malvudian would be desperate enough to jump in the sack with you."

The three soldiers, agitated at last, share a nonverbal conversation. The next moment, they've left their seats—and their bags—behind, intent on giving the Mirillians a piece of their mind.

Before the soldiers can think twice about the confrontation, Cay unzips one of their bags. He stuffs the tracker deep inside, then zips it shut again.

"Let's get outta here," he mutters, "before they join forces with the pirates to beat *us* to death."

But on our way out, an illuminated display case grabs my attention. Its shelves are piled high with all kinds of baked goods. Remembering a certain castrata who has only eaten a single cookie in her life—and a stolen one at that—I stop.

This is one injustice Jerricho Hatch has the power to rectify. A dozen ought to make up for my pathetic attempt at a kiss on Nabishna.

"How much for that package of chocolate cookies?" I ask the cashier.

Amid the shouts of an escalating confrontation behind us, Cay chirps, "Dessert! How thoughtful, Jerricho!"

"Don't even think about it, Cay," I reply. "Those're all for Galena."

"I won't touch 'em," Cay promises, "as long as you buy me that stunning loaf of sourdough in the case next to them."

I sigh and nod at the cashier to do as Cay said. Five currents isn't worth the argument. Besides, things are getting physical on the other end of the diner. Lingering any longer seems imprudent.

GALACTIC EATS REHEATED
PRODUCTION SET

"A LOT OF PEOPLE don't like mushrooms because of the texture," Cay tells Galena's camera. "That's what makes cream of mushroom soup the perfect flavor-delivery system for everyone, both the mushroom lovers and haters alike."

We're back aboard the *Tantalus,* still in Theronian airspace, shooting the third episode of *Galactic Eats Reheated.* When I asked Cay why we weren't using X-space time for filming, he told me not to question his methods, then proceeded to destem and slice the mushrooms we harvested on Nabishna.

Cay now directs my camera toward those mushroom stems. Sliding them off his cutting board into a small Dutch oven of boiling water, he says, "When Sal made cream of mushroom soup fifty years ago, she discarded the stems. Lots of chefs do that because the stems are so woody. They're fibrous and tough. But we're putting them to good work, turning them into mushroom stock that we'll use a little later in the soup-crafting process. For now, I'll move the pot to the hot plate on the other end of my counter. There's lots more to do, and I prefer working without a face full of steam."

After setting the Dutch oven aside, he hoists a heftier one onto the hot stove and plops a couple tablespoons of butter into it. As he walks through the steps, he narrates for the cameras.

"Once the butter is bubbling gently at the bottom of the pot, we add half our sliced mushrooms and sauté them for ten to fifteen minutes, until caramelized. *Don't add salt yet.* Mushrooms have a lot of water in them. Adding salt too early in the process will wick a lot of that water out of the mushrooms and into the bottom of your pot. When that happens, they get rubbery and don't brown well. So, as tough as it might be for all you salt lovers, stay away from it. For *now*. In the meantime, as the mushrooms caramelize, you'll have other work to do, mincing your shallots and garlic."

PAD, Galena, and I continue filming Cay and his work-in-progress from different angles. Each time he stirs, or chops, or rips thyme leaves from their stem, we're there. Without B-roll footage like this, most programs would be entirely unwatchable. The supplemental video, secondary to the main arc, helps maintain a pleasing pace, folding in smooth transitions and "down time" for the viewer's brain. Plus, it's a great opportunity to add a bit of eye candy without disrupting the flow of the storytelling.

When Cay is satisfied with the caramelization, he mixes in the remainder of the sliced mushrooms. "I'm not sautéing these as long as the others, because I want them to maintain a fresher quality. It's all about adding *layers* of flavor into the finished soup."

He gives the mushrooms two more minutes, then says, "Now we'll add our minced shallots and garlic, our chopped thyme, a healthy pinch of salt, and a few grinds of pepper, and continue letting it sizzle on medium-low heat until soft."

More minutes pass. Cay removes some of the larger mushrooms from the mixture. He sets them aside—"texture for later"—before uncorking a bottle of pinot grigio.

"A lot of people use cheap wine for cooking," he says. "If you happen to have some in the pantry because Uncle Scrooge and Aunt Cheapskate gifted it to you last Christmas, be my guest. Good chefs hate waste, and cheap wine has to end up somewhere. Given the choice, however, get yourself a nice bottle." Cay takes a swig. "After all, half the reason for cooking with wine is so you can drink a glass on the side."

He splashes wine straight from the bottle into his Dutch oven, and a plume of fragrant steam bathes his face. Using his wooden spoon, he scrapes the bottom of the pot and says, "Once we've deglazed our Dutch oven, we'll let everything simmer another couple minutes to reduce the liquid.

"While it's simmering, let me introduce you to my sourdough loaf. You may think this bread is for serving later with the soup, and we certainly will do that. But I'm also going to slice a hunk off the loaf right now and cut it into cubes. I'm eyeballing it, but you'll want about two cups' worth. Set it aside, we'll use it in a minute."

Cay returns to the original Dutch oven on its hot plate.

"Normally I'd let the stock simmer about an hour to fully extract flavors. Today, for time's sake, I'm cutting corners, removing it from the heat after only half an hour. I'll live. Take about a quart of this mushroom broth—you can always add more later, if needed—and pour it into the main pot.

"Back to the sourdough cubes. I'm going to do something Grandma Sal would never have thought to do, even on her best day. We're throwing our bread straight into the pot with everything else. Adding the sourdough accomplishes three things: it provides acidity, deepens the flavor profile, and gives extra body to the soup. Now we'll let everything simmer together on low heat for about ten more minutes."

He slides over to a section of the adjacent counter. Here, more ingredients are waiting.

"While the soup is simmering," he says, "soften a couple ounces of cream cheese in a separate bowl. Add a dollop of Dijon mustard and a half-cup of our soup, then mix it all together with a fork until you have a smooth, creamy consistency."

Cay takes a short break—and a few long pulls from the wine bottle— before adding the cream cheese mixture to the rest of the soup.

"Time to use one of my favorite kitchen tools," he exclaims, plugging in a cylindrical gadget. "The immersion blender! You *could* use a normal blender for this, but it's clunky, creates a lot more dirty dishes, and often results in burns. Spend the money on a good immersion blender. You'll save yourself a lot of headache in the end."

Cay blends the contents of the Dutch oven until he's satisfied with its silky texture. He tastes a spoonful, adds a pinch of salt, then mixes in a cup of cream and the mushroom bits he set aside earlier.

"Finally," he says, "we'll season the soup with a couple gratings of nutmeg—Don't overdo it, nutmeg is powerful stuff!—and a splash or two of balsamic vinegar, to taste."

He tries another spoonful and smacks his lips. "Perfection. At this point, if you'd like, you can turn out the lights to see whether cream of Encelas mushroom soup does indeed glow. I'll assume it does and skip that part."

Cay dishes the soup into bowls, garnishing them with sprigs of thyme. Galena and I take a couple shots of him enjoying the soup, then I reposition Cay so that he's standing in front of the *Tantalus'* windscreen. Time to tie a bow on this session.

"Thanks for joining me on this episode of *Galactic Eats Reheated*," he says. "On our next episode, I'll take you to the primitive world of Kili'a'an. You may know it as the location of my grandmother's final episode. It's also the location of a rare egg. An egg that is truly out of this world. Until then, eat well, friends."

PAD, Galena, and I cut our cameras.

"Nice work," says Cay, with a hearty tone of congratulations.

"Thanks," I mumble, a bit surprised. Cay Cantore rarely praises someone other than Cay Cantore.

"I was talking to myself," he says.

Expectation met.

"Off to Kili'a'an, then?" I ask. Compared to trollums and routinely combusting planets, I'm almost looking forward to primitive tribes-people and poisoned darts.

"Not quite," Cay answers.

"What else do we have to do here?" I ask.

"Have you seen the state of our pantry?" Cay replies. "There's a supermarket station orbiting nearby. Unless you're planning to eat PAD, we need to reload our supplies before the next leg."

"As I am utterly indigestible to humans," says PAD, "I do not recommend the former course of action."

KILI'A'AN

– NORMA –

THE *TANTALUS*

35 Days to Payment

CAY POWERS OFF the monitor a moment after hearing his infant father's cries. For education's sake, we decided to rewatch Sal's "Narrow Egg-scape" episode prior to landing on Kili'a'an. In typical Cay Cantore fashion, he has ended it before Sal can step foot in her kitchen and—to borrow his words—offend his imagination's taste buds.

I'd be bawling my eyes out if our roles were reversed. Cay, however, seems utterly unmoved by hearing his recently deceased father bawling as a baby.

Fixed only on the next leg of his goal, he says, "This should be no problem. We find a clear place to land in the Needles, track down a *vulva-fool*—or whatever that bird was called—steal a couple eggs, dodge a poison dart here and there, and be on our way to the Trees of Eden by this time tomorrow. It'll be easier than making crème brûlée!" He chuckles at himself. "Just kidding. Nothing is easier than that. Which is why I'll take those eggs and make *oeufs à la neige.*"

"And can you give us the non-douchey version?" I retort.

"Eggs on snow," he says. "Fluffy egg-white meringues, afloat on a sea of *crème anglaise.*"

"I thought I asked for the non-douchey version."

"It's a custard sauce, Jer. Don't be such a philistine. Still a dessert, but I'll highlight the *whole* egg, not just part of it."

Beyond the *Tantalus'* windscreen is an azure-and-emerald marble. Complete with two ice caps at its poles, the approaching planet so closely resembles Terra, I'm homesick just looking at it.

How long has it been since we left? A month? It feels much longer. I used to talk with my parents almost every day, but between zipping through X-space, near-death experiences, Axon dead zones, and an annoying reliance on Cay's tel, we've hardly exchanged a dozen messages since I left.

Soon, I remind myself. *You'll be home soon.*

Between now and then, I worry about the amount of dying there might be. Moved by that fear, I ask, "How can we avoid any encounters with the Ni'aruti? You know, the locals?"

"What fun would that be?" Cay retorts. "It's the danger that makes for such great programming!"

"We *could* attempt a night landing," PAD suggests. After a few weeks together, even the robot has trained itself to ignore Cay's inane comments. "Because of our propulsion systems, the *Tantalus* cannot entirely subdue every form of visible light emission, but it *can* switch off all electronic sources. We may thus be able to avoid attracting any unwanted attention."

"Yes, but landing at night, in a mountainous jungle region, without using any lights sounds a little—oh, I don't know—*crashy* to me," Cay retorts.

"Pardon me for saying it, but my trust in the ship's autonav system dwarfs my trust in your piloting abilities," PAD replies. I could almost swear there's a cheeky edge to his tone. "When we arrive in lower orbit, I would suggest five or six passes over the Kalumma region. The *Tantalus* will then be able to scan and map Kili'a'an's surface with detailed accuracy. With enough information, the autonav could execute a stealth landing even if everyone onboard were asleep."

"How long would those scans take?" Galena asks.

"Roughly one Terran day."

"No way," says Cay, shaking his head definitively. "We can't waste that time. After Kili'a'an, we still have to find Mei-Li Tan and the Trees of Eden, and we have no clue how long that'll take. I know it might seem like we have plenty of time, but I need Jonas's money transferred into my account by the Malvudians' payday, or else I'm dead meat. The schedule's way too tight."

"I hope I'm not out of place saying so, but we should take our time to do it right," Galena argues. "If the Ni'aruti catch us, it'll be a lot longer than a one-day delay."

Cay waves her off. "We'll work fast. We already have an onboard map showing where all the major villages are. We'll make sure we steer clear when we're finding a place to land in the Needles—Kalumma—whatever they're called."

"What if we can't find a nest right away?" I argue. "What then, Cay?"

"How could that happen?" he fires back. "We have a lucky *crystal*, remember?"

I'm getting angry again. In Cay's mind, he's always as right as a ninety-degree angle. Anyone who disagrees is being obtuse.

He doesn't wait for me to respond to his crystal comment. Taking matters into his own hands, he heads toward the cockpit and says, "Tantalus, get ready to bring us to the surface. But don't take us down quite yet."

"Got something else to do?" I ask. I know better than to hope Cay has changed his mind.

"It's been a few days since I tried contacting Mei-Li Tan," he answers. "I'm gonna leave her another message before we land. If somebody as well-connected as Geiger can't find the Trees of Eden, what chance do *we* have? Mei-Li—she's the key!"

He stops in his tracks to flash us a self-satisfied grin. "And—wouldn't you know it?—*I* am a poet!"

KALUMMA

"The Needles"

"GAWKING IS FOR the Grand Canyon," Cay scolds in a hushed voice, "and Mrs. Peasel when she's doing hot yoga."

It's impossible not to gawk. We're hiking through the most entrancing landscape I've ever seen.

"Who the hell's Mrs. Peasel?" I ask, lowering my camera. I hate myself for taking his bait.

"She lived across the street when I was twelve. Single mom, had a daughter my age who I was friends with. Didn't care much for Lilian, but she was a means to an end, so I put up with her."

Who *isn't* a means to an end for Cay?

"You can lust over the footage all you want, just like I did with Mrs. Peasel," he says. "But do it later. Right now, we've gotta find those eggs and hurry back to the *Tantalus* before some Ni'aruti hunting party turns us into human pincushions." Remembering we're in mixed company, he oh-so-politely adds, "Or Vandreekian."

"It's *Vandreejan*," Galena corrects him dryly, "but I appreciate your inclusivity."

Through the lens of my ARRI, I soak in our surroundings. We're wandering among a maze of high spires. Weatherworn and ancient, they look as if they might crumble around us at any moment. Between these austere peaks, providing a canopy to shield us from the daytime heat, is a jungle of broad-leafed greenery. Although here, the "greenery" seems to make use of whatever colors it damn well pleases. Some foliage is deep purple and flecked with green spots like the tree in Sal's episode. Others have burgundy branches with leaves of bright gold, or drape-like fronds which brush against the earth and remind me of the kelp that washed up onshore during my family's beach vacation. If this place weren't already known as the Needles, I'd toss "Kaleidoscope Jungle" or "Rainbow Woods" into the naming hat.

We aren't far from the *Tantalus* when a bank of gray clouds rolls in. With them, a light but steady rain begins to fall.

Can't say I care much for that. I was already uneasy, wondering whose unwelcome eyes might be watching. Now there are ten thousand raindrops spattering the leaves to conceal any approaching footsteps.

"Are you waterproof, PAD?" Cay wonders with a sideways glance at the drone.

I don't hear the answer. Beside me, Galena yelps in surprise.

Or, rather, in pain. With my non-camera hand, I grab her upper arm to steady her, then help lower her to the ground.

"What happened?" I ask. I look her over for a protruding dart or some other projectile.

"I slipped on that rock," she answers with a wince. "Twisted my ankle."

Cay kneels beside us. "Can you walk on it?"

"Probably," says Galena.

"Good. Then we should keep going."

"No, we should take her back to the *Tantalus*, Cay," I protest. "Then you and I can come back and find your stupid bird."

Cay shakes his head. "She'll be alright. We have to keep going. There might be a nest in any one of these cliffs."

"Dammit, Cay, Galena's not your slave," I tell him through gritted teeth. I know right away I've crossed a line.

Since PAD has been tracking our path through the jungle maze, I turn to him and say, "Take us back to the *Tantalus*."

"Don't listen to that order, PAD," says Cay. "You'll stay with me. With *all* of us."

"I am sorry, Jerricho," PAD tells me, "but I was transferred primarily into Cay Cantore's employ. I'm afraid I must follow his orders over yours."

"It's the right move, Jer," Cay assures me. He offers Galena a hand. "Trust me."

She takes his hand, and he helps her to her feet.

"Feel alright? Can you put any weight on it?" he asks.

Galena tests it and nods. "I'll be fine."

"See, Jer!" he says. "Right as—well—rain!"

She's *not* fine. I can see it the second she starts hobbling after him. But her life as a castrata has conditioned her to disregard her own needs and do as she's told. Whether the orders are coming from her ruling family or from Cay.

"Can I carry your camera, at least?" I ask her.

She frowns. Shakes her head. "No. I'm alright. Thank you."

We wander the labyrinthine Kalumma for another hour before we finally find what we're looking for. PAD is the first to spot the nest, about three meters off the ground in a cliffside crag.

This might be our lucky day after all. Sal and Mei-Li had to wait for their vivi-fa'ool to leave its nest, but we've discovered one left unattended. For the moment, at least, we don't have a defensive, razor-clawed mama bird to deal with.

"PAD, float up there and check for eggs," says Cay.

A few moments later, the drone reports back. "There are two eggs in the nest. However, my appendages are not delicate enough to retrieve them safely. One of you will have to extract them."

"That's okay," Cay replies. "You worry about channeling your inner Jerricho to film the big moment. You too, Galena."

I assume I'll also be channeling my "inner Jerricho," but Cay has a different idea. "Time to put those football muscles to good use, macho man. I need you to give me a boost."

A few years ago, I could have tossed Cay into the air, dropped to the ground for a dozen pushups, and been back on my feet in time to catch him. But things have changed since then. I have a hard time holding my camera for more than a few minutes without a break. Giving Cay a lift may be beyond present-Jerricho's disabilities.

But I've kept my secret to this point, and my foolish pride wants to keep that cat suffocating in the bag. So, with a groan, I lay my camera on the ground and interlace my fingers to create a foothold for Cay. As soon as he steps into my locked hands, it's like our Hekkra friends are already ripping my arms off. Inch by agonizing inch, I struggle to hoist him up the rock face toward the vivi-fa'ool nest.

"Higher, Jer!" he yells down at me. "Let's go!"

PAD whirs above us, taking close-up footage as Cay's face comes level with the nest. I glance up to see him reaching cautiously for the eggs inside it.

"Check. These. Out!" he exclaims, looking into PAD's camera. "Oh, sweet Cosmos, they look like something spawned from a giant oyster's one-night stand with the Easter bunny. Big, pink, shimmering pearls, swirling with those lovely pastels. I almost feel bad we'll be cracking these beauties open when we return to the *Tantalus*."

My fingers. Shit. Shitshitshit. Between the sweat, rain, and my generally weakening state, they're starting to slip apart. I groan, trying to cinch them together again, but in vain. The gap widens. Then a little more.

"Let's tuck these into my basket," Cay says. "I used one of my shirts to provide a little extra cushioning between the two—*Yearghjerwhatthe!*"

The rest of my strength gives out. Cay comes crashing down on top of me. For the briefest moment, we remain upright, his knees clenched around my torso like some bizarre circus performance gone wrong. Then we both topple over and onto the ground.

Amidst the commotion, I hear the awful sound. One after the other, a pair of *splats* on the stubbly grass behind me.

"Nice, Jer!" Cay shouts. His face is contorted in annoyance. "Those eggs will be *delicious*. I love 'em with a good sprinkling of dirt."

"You stayed up there too long, going on about their color," I retort. "If you woulda just grabbed 'em and come down, we wouldn't've had a problem!"

Glaring at me, Cay says, "You couldn't hold the tether on Petra 7. You couldn't keep up with us on Nabishna. And now you take a giant crap all over our afternoon by dropping me and smashing our eggs! Jer, what the *hell* is going on with you?"

"What the hell's going on with *me?*" I yell, kicking him violently off me. "What about *you?* When were you planning to tell me how dangerous all this shit would be? I've almost died *four times* already. I don't care if this is your dream. I don't care if those Hekkra rip you into a hundred thousand pieces. You aren't worth my life, and you aren't worth Galena's."

I brush the dirt off my arms and neck, then pick up my camera. Thank Cosmos, it isn't broken. When we fell, I nearly landed on top of it.

The angry words burst through my lips before I have time to give them a second thought. "I'm *done*, Cay. You can have whatever film I've edited so far—I don't care—but I'm done. Drop me and Galena off on the nearest League planet, and I'll figure out how to get us home from there."

"That's a very generous offer," says Cay. He's raising his hands above his head, though I have no idea why.

That's when I realize he isn't looking *at* me. He's looking *past* me.

"Unfortunately," he goes on, "you'll have to ask someone else's permission for that."

Fear grips my heart. I turn around slowly.

Forming a half-moon around us, with enough arrows nocked, darts loaded, and knives drawn to leave all three of us looking like deceased hedgehogs, is a party of Ni'aruti.

Their faces are distinctly feline—think "black panther" more than "housecat"—but instead of fur, their skin is bare and appears almost waxy. Their colors range from burgundy to black, even to burnt orange, but all of them have a dark pigmentation. By contrast, their wide eyes are vivid shades of green, gold, or brown, all of which seem to burn a hole through my mortal flesh as they stare into the well of my soul.

At once, a coffee-colored panther, presumably the leader, steps forward. He issues hasty instructions to the rest. I don't understand anything he's saying, but I am surprised how similar his vocal tones and cadence sound to my own. If he were using Commonspeak instead of cat-ese, I wonder whether I'd be able to differentiate at all between his speech and a human's.

First, Cay is disarmed, his pistol handed to the leader. Next, two Ni'aruti wrench my hands behind my back. Whatever twine they use to bind my wrists bites into my skin, giving me the sense that if I tried to wriggle free, I would only succeed in sawing off my own hands.

Next to me, Galena whimpers, afraid, as her wrists are also bound. My heart sinks with the realization that, as a castrata, she has probably suffered this sort of treatment before.

PAD is hovering in circles above us. His circuits must not be cut out for this sort of situation, because he seems uncertain how to handle himself.

One of the Ni'aruti aims a thick, barbed arrow at the drone but does not fire.

The leader steps in front of me. Using words I can plainly understand, he says, "Command your machine to come down, or we will have no choice but to destroy it."

My mouth hangs open in shock. Isn't this supposed to be a primitive people? They have no spaceports. They shoot darts, not lasers. How, then, am I hearing Commonspeak from his lips?

"You better come down here, PAD," Cay orders. He does, after all, have authority over the drone.

PAD does as directed. The moment he is within reach, a shorter Ni'arut, one of the few wearing an upper-body garment, seizes him. She confiscates PAD's camera and hands it off to a fellow Ni'arut. I'm surprised to see how delicately they treat both the camera and PAD himself. I'm further surprised when the uncivilized being locates the drone's power switch, as if she has been dealing with advanced machinery her entire life.

Another important-looking Ni'arut draws my attention away from PAD. This one wears a thin, silver wreath on his head, decorated with a rainbow of jungle flowers and leaves. He kneels where the vivi-fa'ool eggs lie, shattered and splattered upon the earth. From his waistband, he removes a metal tool. Other than its serrated edges, it looks much like a garden spade. With it, he cuts a circle in the rocky soil around the two eggs. He pries up the round section of ground, broken eggs on top, and lifts it into his arms.

Over the eggy, soily mess, he begins to sing the most hauntingly beautiful song I've ever heard. Even when the chieftain barks more orders, and my sight is stolen away by the rough fabric of a blindfold, the lullaby continues its haunting, bewitching and beguiling me as nothing else has before.

The spell is broken only when I feel something sharp in my back. It's accompanied by a single word from the chief.

"March."

NI'ARUTI VILLAGE

WHEN THE BLINDFOLDS come off, evening is settling over Kili'a'an. A quartet of moons arc across the darkening half of the sky, each in a different lunar phase.

We're standing at the edge of a village. The homes before us are constructed from unrefined materials—wood, stones, mud, and the like—yet they appear sturdy and elegant, designed by highly skilled hands.

A great commotion is rising among the villagers. They shout to each other, calling friends and family to gather around us. All of them wear curious expressions. Seeing our bound hands, they must wonder what crimes we aliens have committed in their land.

Behind me, the Ni'arut chieftain fires off a volley of orders. A few of their war party's younger-looking members scurry off. Along with the rest of the mob that has formed around us, we start moving again, deeper into the organized grid of buildings.

"What do you suppose is going on up there?" Cay asks in a low voice.

Ahead is another gathering of bustling Ni'aruti. Some are unloading bundles of wood, while others assemble the logs into an organized pile.

My heart seizes.

"They're building a bonfire, Cay. A *bonfire*. Oh, shit. Shitshitshit."

"You don't suppose they brought us over to roast marshmallows, do you? I'll start thinking up a good ghost story, just in case," Cay says. "Also, you should think about cleaning up that potty mouth of yours."

The bonfire ring is at least five meters across. There must be some kind of flammable substance underneath it all, because when an aged Ni'arut strikes two stones together and sends a shower of sparks over it, the whole lot bursts into flame.

At least I don't see a roasting spit.

The chief leads us to a massive boulder. The side facing the bonfire is flat and has a dozen bronze shackles embedded into the rock. He cuts the sharp twine binding our wrists, but only so his muscular henchmen can transfer us directly into the metal shackles.

At least they're more comfortable. Small consolation, but I'll take it.

When the chief cuts Galena's bindings, I expect he'll shackle her next to Cay. He doesn't.

"Stand here," he instructs her. "Do not try to run, and you may remain free."

He addresses us next. "Now shall your crime be judged."

"I don't suppose we're allowed to call a lawyer," Cay replies hopefully.

The chief ignores his comment. Facing the villagers, he raises his arms. They fall into immediate silence. In a booming voice, he explains our crimes to them. I don't need to speak their language to know that's the case, because the crowd reacts with a mixture of weeping and snarling. During his lengthy speech, other Ni'aruti interject their own comments or questions.

Finally, the chief addresses us again.

"With the input of my people, I, Sar'un of the Ni'aruti, of the village of Rau'ihan, have cast judgment upon your guilt. This night, the sky pirates shall be purified of their crime."

The chief—Sar'un—has hardly finished speaking when more Ni'aruti arrive. They, too, carry armloads of wood for the fire.

"Ironic," Cay murmurs. "Usually I'm *doing* the cooking."

My head snaps toward him. "We're about to die, and you're still making jokes?"

"Oh, lighten up, would you?" Nodding toward the rising flames he adds, "Because you're about to anyway."

Sar'un unlocks our shackles. He leads us to the edge of the crackling bonfire.

The Ni'arut who earlier collected the broken vivi-fa'ool eggs approaches us. He's holding a polished stone platter. On it is the clump of earth he cut from the ground. The liquid portion of the eggs has since soaked into the dirt, but the shards of their pearly shells sit atop the small mound. Stopping in front of Cay, the Ni'arut extends the platter toward him. He motions with his head toward the bonfire.

"Do you want me to carry them in? I think I'll pass," Cay says.

"This is Qapar," Sar'un explains. "He is our *yi'im*, high priest of Rau'ihan. They were your hands which destroyed the eggs of vivi-fa'ool, and so your hands must offer them into the fire."

A Ni'arut standing beside me thrusts a long pole into my hands. The wide, flat surface at the end makes the whole thing look like a comically giant spatula.

"Cool pizza peel," Cay comments.

"It is called a *huimpul*," says Sar'un. "You will use it to place the *stoon'a* into the fire. There, the flames will release vivi-fa'ool's offspring from their terrestrial prison, so that they may enjoy the flight you denied them."

Cay looks at me, shrugs, and places the platter onto the huimpul's flat end.

I groan. It's heavier than I was expecting. As I extend it toward the fire, I strain to keep the whole thing from tipping forward. The last thing I want is to further piss off these Ni'aruti with an unceremonious dumping of their dead bird babies.

Sar'un stops me. "No. Not you." The chief points at Cay. "Him."

Cay doesn't argue. Without realizing the instant relief it causes me, he takes the huimpul out of my hands. When the stoon'a breaches the outer flames, Qapar starts singing the same mournful tune as when we were first captured. The rest of the Ni'aruti join in, every eye fixated on the mound of dirt holding the eggs' remains.

Gently, Cay lowers the huimpul's flat end until it rests in the center of the bonfire. He jerks it out from beneath the stoon'a, leaving the platter and its contents veiled behind the dancing flames.

At once, the singing stops. Raising his arms, Qapar grunts a few short syllables. The gathered Ni'aruti reply in unison.

All falls silent.

"That's it, then? Purification complete?" Cay asks Sar'un.

"No," the stone-faced chief replies. "That is yet to come."

Sar'un barks at the Ni'aruti guarding us. At once, they seize me and Cay by our outstretched arms.

I shout, certain they're about to toss us into the fire too. Appease the gods of the vivi-fa'ool with a twofold human offering.

They don't. Instead, they march us away from the fire, toward the closest of the modest homes. Going ahead of us, Sar'un opens a door. Warm lamplight spills out into the darkness.

"This is my *yurrat*—my home," he says. "You may move about freely inside it. The doors and windows will be guarded. Do not attempt to leave."

Our Ni'aruti escorts lead us past Sar'un and deposit us inside.

I turn, expecting to find Galena following us. She isn't. She's nowhere to be seen.

Before I can raise my voice in protest, the door is slammed shut, leaving me shaking with dread over Galena's fate.

THE CHIEF'S *YURRAT*

TRYING TO DISTRACT myself from my copious worries, I explore Sar'un's yurrat. The home is well-built and graceful, yet in a way which seems to thrive on simplicity. Its smooth walls are bare, devoid of even the most rudimentary decorations. Glass orbs, aglow with spritely tongues of flame, dangle from a ceiling of straight, uniform logs.

The yurrat is composed of three separate rooms. The largest contains a dining space, kitchen, and gathering area. A squat, six-sided table, surrounded by thin seating pads, provides a place for Sar'un's meals. The kitchen is composed of a wood-burning clay stove, a few no-frills cabinets, and—to my surprise—a sink whose faucet runs with a constant stream of water. The gathering area at the furthest end of the room houses a wall-to-wall rug of plush animal skins. Arranged upon it are lounging cushions of varying sizes.

A doorway beyond the gathering area leads into a bedroom. In one corner is a raised bed, large enough for two adult Ni'aruti. A pair of smaller beds, placed end to end, occupy the opposite wall.

Finally, accessible from both the bedroom and the gathering area, is a washroom. Here I find another sink and, lower to the floor, a stone basin. Like the sink in the kitchen, a perpetual flow of water runs through both.

I kneel in front of the basin. Amazed, I mutter, "It's a toilet."

I wonder if they have two-ply on Kili'a'an. It's been a while since I took a proper—

The opening of a door, followed by more Ni'aruti voices, breaks my train of thought. I hurry back into the yurrat's main room. I can't contain my gasp of relief when I see the guards ushering Galena inside, unharmed but for the slight limp caused by her sprained ankle.

PAD, still powered down, arrives in the arms of another Ni'arut, who deposits him gently onto the floor.

"You're alright!" I cry, looking Galena over. "What'd they do to you?"

"Nothing," she says, taking a seat at the table across from Cay. "Sar'un wanted to talk to me. He asked whether I was with you against my will. I told him no and explained how you rescued me. He asked if I'd be more comfortable staying in a separate house or here with you. I chose here."

"Anything else?" asks Cay. "Any hint of what they're planning to do to us?"

Galena shakes her head. "No. Sorry."

After this, there's nothing but waiting. My heated exchange with Cay this afternoon hasn't been forgotten. Now that there's a lull in the day's otherwise constant action, an awkward tension hangs in the air, one punctuated by our silence. Eventually, Cay selects a couch-sized cushion in the gathering area and falls into one of his blithe, instant sleeps.

I'm tired too. Sitting on the animal-skin carpet, my back against a cushion, I close my eyes. When I hear Galena's approaching footsteps, I crack an eyelid to see her settling beside me. To my surprise, she leans her head on my shoulder.

"Thank you," she whispers.

"For what?"

"For worrying about me. Besides my mother, you might be the first person who has."

Emboldened by her decision to sit with me, I grab her hand and squeeze it. Even I can sense when it's best to say nothing at all, so I keep my mouth shut. I want to preserve the moment untainted.

Soon Galena's rhythmic breathing tells me she has fallen asleep. My mind likewise begins wandering the worlds that exist between waking and sleeping. I've almost nodded off entirely when the door opens again, jolting me back into full consciousness.

Sar'un's stoic form stands against the darkness outside. "Join me at the table," he orders, closing the door behind himself.

As we force ourselves back onto weary feet, Cay asks, "How do you know Commonspeak? I didn't think Kili'a'an was a member of the Galactic League."

"We do not consider ourselves as such," Sar'un answers, "though we once did. That is why I know your tongue. Yet not I alone. Many Ni'aruti speak it, as do other tribespeople among the Na'umata. You will not hear many using it, however, for most do not like how it sounds on their tongues."

"I thought a planet had to achieve interstellar travel before being invited into the League," I say.

Sar'un scoffs. "We are not the ignorant animals you might think we are. Did you never wonder why Kili'a'an is not classified as a Protected planet?"

Cay and I exchange guilty glances. He answers for us both, saying, "Everything we knew about you seemed so ... primitive. You know, loin cloths and arrows. Uncivilized stuff like that."

"If we went around blasting one another's heads off and bowing to slimy politicians, would that seem more 'civilized' to you?" Sar'un challenges. He shakes his head with disappointment. "Perhaps the Na'umata seem primitive to such advanced beings as yourself, yet we achieved star travel long before Terrans or Vandreeki ever dreamed of it."

"Then why don't we see Na'umata anywhere else in the galaxy?" Galena wonders. "Why do you stay here?"

Sar'un leans back. He looks around, deep in thought, before answering, "Because this is what we chose for ourselves. When Kili'a'an first achieved interstellar travel, we believed fortune and greatness would be found among the stars. Over time, we realized how wrong we were. Our people were changing, but not for the better. Anxiousness and fear replaced contentedness and simple joys. The bonds of community became swallowed up in the unending struggle of individual ambition. So, our people made a decision. We abandoned the stars to return to our ancestral roots."

"And you've managed to stay in isolation this whole time?" Cay asks.

Sar'un laughs bitterly. "The League does not cede its jurisdiction so easily. Technically, we are still bound to galactic law, yet we follow only those we choose. It is why we have not scanned your credentials, nor given you any formal admission into Kili'a'an." His gaze falls upon Galena. "It is also why no one was alerted that you traveled here with an escaped castrata."

The Ni'aruti chief leans forward. His voice is low and dangerous as he says, "But that is enough of your questions. I did not come here to be interrogated, but to do the interrogating."

I gulp. I'd rather not learn what a full-blown Ni'aruti interrogation entails. I'm prepared to tell him anything he wants.

"Why did you come here seeking the silverbird's offspring?" Sar'un asks plainly.

"We're making a program," I reply quickly, giving Cay no opportunity to weave a lie.

"A program," Sar'un echoes. "Expound."

Entertainment programs didn't exist in the galaxy until humanity became involved in the League, long after Kili'a'an's self-imposed return to tribalism. Remembering this bit of history, I say, "It's hard to explain. A program is a ... a moving picture we watch on—"

Sar'un waves me along. "I know what a program *is*. As I said, we maintain some League contact. I want to know what *your* program is and why you've brought it to my jungle."

"It's a ... food thing," says Cay. "We've been finding exotic foods around the galaxy to use in our cooking. A long time ago, my grand-mother became famous doing the same thing. But I'm a much better chef than her. I wanted to show our audience more sophisticated ways to use those foods."

Sar'un processes Cay's explanation, then asks, "And what are you seeking through this ... *food* program?"

With a nod toward Cay, I say, "He owes a lot of money to a couple Malvudians."

"That is all? Money?" Sar'un shakes his head. "I do not believe it. Surely there are simpler paths toward attaining such hollow ends."

"Then ... admiration, maybe," Cay admits. "Appreciation for my gift."

"The admiration of others?" Sar'un asks. "Or your own?"

He doesn't wait for a response. Standing, he motions for me and Cay to do the same. Galena begins following suit, but Sar'un raises a hand to stop her.

"No. You will remain here to discourage any escape attempts. I do not know what honor humans possess, but I sense they would not leave you behind."

"Where are we going?" Cay asks.

Sar'un strides purposefully toward the door. It's clear he expects us to follow.

"Into the night," he says.

KALUMMA

34 Days to Payment

WITH FOUR MOONS adrift above us, reflecting the light of a star we cannot see, night on Kili'a'an isn't much darker than evening. It's the *quality* of the light that's so different. It's gentler, and with an infusion of liquid platinum that settles like morning dew over the polychromatic jungle.

I'm capturing it all on film, of course. Sar'un insisted. Outside the yurrat's front door, one of our guards handed me my camera at the chief's instruction.

When Sar'un saw my confusion, he said, "If your program is as important as you say it is, perhaps some good will come of this after all."

Now the three of us—me, Cay, and Sar'un—creep wordlessly through the Aruti Jungle among Kalumma's weathered stone sentinels. Once in a while, some creature of the night will screech a warning, then go crashing off through the underbrush. Other than those few disruptions, the night is still and silent.

Until it isn't. At first, the ghoulish wail is so distant, I'm only able to hear it in the dead space between our footsteps. But it isn't long before the drawn-out cry is as present and constant as the moons overhead. Something about it strikes me as eerily familiar.

I lower my camera suddenly. I realize what it is we're hearing.

It's the song. Only this time, the *yi'im* Qapar isn't the one raising the lament to the stars. It is no Ni'arut at all.

Sar'un stops. Like Sal did in a program she made fifty years ago, the chief pushes a purple branch aside so we can see into the clearing beyond. Even in the moonlight, I recognize where he has brought us. After all, only a few hours have passed since we were last here.

Sar'un points across the clearing to the craggy rock face. At the bird, whose silvery feathers have been electrified by the kindred moonlight.

"Is your machine recording this? For your program?" Sar'un asks, his somber voice hushed.

I nod. I'm ashamed to look him in the eye, so I stare through my camera's eyepiece instead.

"In her lifetime," Sar'un says, "the female vivi-fa'ool bears but a single clutch of eggs."

"But Sal—my grandma—said they lay eggs once every three years," Cay protests.

"She was wrong," is Sar'un's blunt reply. "You robbed the silverbird of everything when you robbed her nest. Tonight, she mourns the loss of her children, the loss of a motherhood which will never be. I brought you here so that you could capture her song of sorrow. The song of her heartbreak. For your *entertainment* program."

Cay has no response. No glib comeback, no crass comment.

He just stares, and blinks, and breathes.

After a minute, Sar'un eases the tree branch back into place. "We have intruded long enough upon the bereaved mother," he says. "Come. Let us return to Rau'ihan."

THE CHIEF'S *YURRAT*

SLANTED RAYS OF sunlight awaken me the next morning. I sit and look around the room, wondering where I am and how I got there. Like a storm on Nabishna, the events of the past day come flooding back. With them comes an anxious nausea, as I wonder what fate will befall us here in the Ni'aruti village of Rau'ihan.

I stumble into the living area but find only Cay there, sitting at the table. "Where's Galena?" I ask.

He doesn't respond. His bloodshot eyes gaze down at his hands, folded on the table in front of him. Cay Cantore isn't someone who spends much time lost in thought, but that's certainly how he appears at the moment.

I snap my fingers. "Yo. Cay. Galena. Where is she?"

"Don't know," he says with a shrug. "She was gone when I woke up."

The Ni'aruti seem to hold Galena in higher standing, so I decide not to worry. Wishing to avoid any interaction with Cay beyond what's necessary, I turn my attention to PAD. The drone is still powered off. Although the Ni'aruti handled him as gently as could be expected, he's filthy from our romp through the Aruti Jungle.

I find a rag in one of the kitchen cupboards. After wetting it in the sink's flowing water, I set to work cleaning PAD. His rotors are in special need of attention, having collected all kinds of jungle debris. The crack in his damaged arm is likewise packed with dirt. Using my pinky nail, I dig out what I can.

I'm about to move on to his dusty sensors when Sar'un enters the yurrat with Galena. Behind them are two Ni'aruti, each bearing a large platter of food.

"You must be hungry," Sar'un states. "I neglected to feed you last night. It was an oversight on my part."

The Ni'aruti deposit their platters on the table and leave without a word.

It's difficult to describe the meal I sit down to. One platter holds an assortment of native fruits and vegetables, but the other contains a sampling of hot foods that don't resemble anything I've ever seen on Terra—nor the other planets we've visited these past weeks.

Cay bites into a foamy orange cylinder spewing steam from a hole in its center. At once his eyes widen. "This," he says, chewing rapidly, "is unreal! I've never tasted anything like it! I feel like a caveman who just discovered pizza."

Sar'un gives him a scornful sort of laugh. "Of course you have not. The Na'umata have lived in isolation for thousands of years. What else could it taste like *but* something unique and of our own? Or are Terrans so arrogant as to believe they were the first to invent tasty food?"

"Not Terrans," I chime in. "Just Cay."

Sar'un backs toward the door, saying, "Eat quickly. When I return, we will conclude our business."

With that ominous note, he departs the yurrat.

I join Cay, and Galena sits beside me. She must have eaten already, because she doesn't take part in the meal.

"Where'd you go? When you woke up this morning?" I ask between bites.

"I was wandering the village," she answers. "The guards don't seem to mind letting me come and go."

I guess there's at least *one* advantage to being a castrata in our galaxy.

She stares longingly out the window at the homes beyond. "It really is lovely here," she says. "Everyone is free. They share everything with each other and live in true community. Even though they have different roles to carry out, no one acts like they're more important than anybody else."

It's exactly what Galena has been searching for her entire life.

I open my mouth to speak, but the words catch in my throat. I know what I should tell her. I should tell her to stay here, hidden among a people who have forsaken the stars in exchange for a home. I should tell her to live out her days on Kili'a'an, in peace and freedom, far away from any who would enslave her. Manipulate her.

But what I *should* say never comes. And I know why.

I don't want Galena to stay on Kili'a'an. I want her with me.

To my shock—and annoyance—it's Cay who makes the offer I cannot. Softly, he says, "You should stay with them. They'll hide you here. Protect you. I don't know *how* I know it ... but they will."

Galena lowers her eyes in thought, then says, "No. We made a bargain, and I'll see it out."

"You've helped enough," Cay says. "We'd be dead on Petra 7 if you hadn't been there. You don't owe us anything."

Galena sighs. She shakes her head. "The Ni'aruti are lovely beings, but they could never relate to me at the deepest levels. They've been free all their lives. I won't stay here, haunting them with my demons."

Infant tears well in her eyes. She stands abruptly and, with no further word, hurries into the washroom.

Cay and I eat in silence. Strangely, his magnanimous offer has thawed the icy wall of my anger, only to erect a different wall of resentment. After everything that's happened, how could *he* be the one to make her that offer of freedom? It should have been me, and I'm sure I would have worked up the nerve if I'd been given another minute. But Cay had to swoop in. Be the hero. Leave me feeling like just another of the selfish, manipulative assholes who have made Galena's existence all about themselves.

I continue stewing in silence, even when Sar'un enters the yurrat once more. With him are four beefy Ni'aruti. One is holding a trio of blindfolds.

"The time has come, sky pirates," Sar'un announces.

"If this is the end for us," Cay says, standing in compliance, "I couldn't have asked for a better last meal. Not even if I made it myself."

KALUMMA

"WE ARE HERE," Sar'un announces. A moment later, our blindfolds come off.

I'm staring at the *Tantalus*.

"That's it?" says Cay. "You brought us back to our ship? What happened to our purification?"

"I pray you received it last night," Sar'un replies. "Though if you prefer a purification of pain rather than rebuke, I would have no trouble arranging such a thing."

The pair of Ni'aruti carrying PAD set him on the long grass beside Galena.

"You're letting us go," Cays says. He sounds skeptical. "Just like that."

"Every life has value," says Sar'un. "Even that of a murdering sky pirate."

Defensively, Cay says, "I think 'murder' might be a bit of an overstatement."

Sar'un crosses his arms and looks down at his clawed feet. "Many years ago, another human invaded the Kalumma to harvest vivi-fa'ool's children. She, too, brought cameras to record her unholy deed. I can only imagine she was the grandmother you spoke of last night."

"She was," Cay admits. His cheeks burn with shame, a rare malady for him.

"I was there," Sar'un says quietly. "I was a very young Ni'arut then. When her security team opened fire, my grandfather was killed in the attack. Our lives meant as little to her as any animal's."

"I'm sorry about that," says Cay, "but your people *did* shoot first. They tried killing her with those poisoned darts, and I've got the video evidence to prove it."

Sar'un gives a bitter chuckle. Pulling one such dart from his belt pouch, he says, "Did it look like this? They are not poisoned. They contain an anesthetic, a plant extract which would have put her to sleep for a few minutes. We wanted to protect the eggs. Nothing more."

From a satchel at his waist, Sar'un removes a silvery object. The pistol. For a split second, I wonder whether he's about to shoot Cay and fulfill some longstanding oath of vengeance.

He doesn't. Instead, he turns the weapon over to Cay.

"Perhaps you will think better of your destructive decisions in the future," Sar'un says. "They do not only impact *you*. They also impact everything—and every*one*—around you." He motions to the Ni'aruti guarding us, and they step away. "If such a day should ever come, return here, and you will find my friendship awaiting you."

With those final words, Sar'un and his entourage turn and march off into the jungle.

Cay watches after them until they have disappeared from sight. He's wearing a curious expression. I'm not sure whether he's still pondering Sar'un's words, or if he's simply waiting until the Ni'aruti are far enough away to launch a second expedition for his coveted eggs.

Then, perpetuating what might be the longest silent streak of his life, Cay heaves the dormant PAD off the ground and carries him up the *Tantalus'* boarding ramp.

THE *TANTALUS*

BACK ABOARD OUR trusty ship, I unload my camera equipment into its designated storage compartment. Behind me, Cay connects PAD to the *Tantalus'* power supply. Moments later, I hear the drone's rotors spinning to life.

"What now?" I bark over my shoulder at Cay. At this point I'm not bothering to mask my resentment.

"I'm ... not sure," Cay answers quietly. "We can't go back to Terra. Not with Galena, anyway."

"What, then? We just float around the stars 'til we die of old age?" I retort.

"Nah. Only until the Malvudians come for us," Cay says.

"Even better," I mutter, shaking my head at his cavalier attitude.

In an attempt to defuse the bomb ticking between me and Cay, Galena looks herself up and down and says, "I'm a mess after all that hiking around the jungle. What I wouldn't give for a bath right now!"

"Can't do much about that, sister," Cay says. "We're still short on showers around here. Though Jer's found that the sink works well in a pinch."

"I was thinking," says Galena, "maybe while we're figuring out the next step, we could do it on an Unprotected planet nearby. One with fresh water."

Galena is still speaking when I march into the lavatory. Before we left Terra, Cay converted the shower into a makeshift pantry. But all the proper plumbing is still there, which means the only thing standing between Galena and her shower is the shelving he installed.

I get to work at once. A minute later, I've dismantled the obstacle.

Cay's stupid shelves, and all the dry goods they held, lie scattered on the floor outside the lav.

"Don't forget a towel," I tell Galena, pointing at the checkered one hanging beside the kitchen sink. "They're small, but two or three does the job alright."

Once Galena is shut inside the bathroom, Cay kneels among the pantry wreckage. With a sideways glance my direction, he says, "You could at least help me pick it up."

I do. Together we relocate the damaged shelves to the mechanical closet. Despite helping Cay tidy up my mess, I know we're still far from good. In fact, during our silent tidying, I've been wondering whether we'll ever be good again. Since we first met each other at Sol 3 University, I've kept my deepest feelings about Cay buried where no one could see them. Sure, I'd bicker with him, but it was more like what you'd hear spending an afternoon with an old married couple. A sniping shot here and there, but I never let anything serious slip out.

Until now. Now, everything has changed. *I've* changed, anyway. Cay is the same smug, selfish prick he always has been.

"Look," I finally say. I'm surprised how calm my own words sound. "I'll help you finish what we started. But after that, I'm done with you. Done with this—this—*friendship*, if you can even call it that. All you do is use me. Is use everyone around you. And I'm finished with it."

A silence falls over us. Galena must be enjoying her shower, because I hear her singing softly. Or maybe talking to herself? It's hard to tell over the running water.

"That's probably true," Cay admits, though his challenging stare tells me he's far from a wholesale acceptance of my assessment. "But before you overplay your martyr card, I wonder whether *you* haven't done some using of your own."

"The hell's that supposed to mean?" I fire back.

Answering my question with one of his own, he says, "Why didn't *you* tell Galena to stay in Rau'ihan? She would have been happy there, safe in a place she'd obviously fallen in love with."

"You're using that against me? Something I *didn't* say?"

"Yes, but something you *should* have said, and you know it. We've been best friends for almost a decade. You think I can't read your mind, Jer? Even a little?"

I'm searching for my comeback when—and, thank the stars, 'cause I've got nothing—PAD interrupts us. Plugging him into the *Tantalus'* power supply also connects him to its many systems, including the communications console. He must have detected an alert after powering up, because he says, "The *Tantalus* received a transmission while we were away. Judging from its timestamp, it arrived yesterday, shortly after our departure into the jungle."

"Who's it from?" Cay asks. "Ameliana?"

"Unknown," PAD answers. "The contact data is both unregistered and encrypted, which most likely indicates an illegal transmission."

I give Cay my angriest glare, the kind that says "this ain't over yet," and follow him into the cockpit. A blinking light on the comm monitor reveals that our mystery caller left us a message.

Cay hits the button to play it, and a woman's aging face fills the screen. I recognize her at once. She was one of the guests at Marq Cantore's funeral. She had been sitting on the other side of the aisle next to a younger woman. When her eyes had met Gustav Geiger's, there was no mistaking her hatred for him.

Now, from Cosmos-knows-where, those same dark, discerning eyes stare at us, accentuating her already stern expression.

"Cay Cantore," she begins, "I'm Mei-Li Tan. I understand you've been trying to reach me these past few weeks, and I apologize for the delay in my response. I've been traveling through fringe territory the past four months, working on a documentary with Zinn Teal. During the majority of our time there, we were cut off from communications."

I raise my eyebrows, impressed. Perhaps even a bit starstruck. Zinn Teal's name is plastered all over the Sunset City Rescue Zoo. He might be the most famous zoologist in the history of the Milky Way.

Mei-Li's recorded message continues. "Currently, I'm at my home in the Eagle Archipelago. I'd be happy to visit with you here and share what I know about the Trees of Eden. And there's no need to worry about your castrata friend. I'll pull whatever strings are necessary to ensure you can bypass the normal security checks. If you couldn't tell by my unregistered transmission, I'm a woman who knows how to work ... *around* the law. Send me a message when you're on your way. And do hurry. I'll only be here a few days before leaving on another assignment."

The video ends, and Mei-Li Tan disappears.

"Tantalus, how long from Kili'a'an to the Eagle Archipelago?" Cay asks.

"Approximately fifty-four Terran hours," the ship's mechanical voice answers.

Cay whistles. To me, he says, "We better boogie on outta here before she disappears again. You help your lady towel off, and I'll let Mei-Li know we're on our way."

THE *TANTALUS*

32 Days to Payment

THE LAST TWO days have consisted of four activities: eating, sleeping, editing, and finishing the last of our booze stash. Make that five, if you also count *ignoring Cay* as an "activity." Other than our necessary interactions for his voiceover narrations, I've hardly said a word to him. Any time he has tried breaking the ice with a nostalgic comment or lighthearted joke, I've responded with unimpressed grunts and continued about my work.

We don't have much longer in X-space, and I want to catch a few hours' sleep before we arrive at the Eagle Archipelago. Presently, we're shooting a wrap scene for our vivi-fa'ool episode. Standing in the kitchen with a clean whisk and empty bowl, Cay explains how we escaped our scrape with the Ni'aruti.

"They say in order to make *oeufs à la neige*, you've got to break a few eggs," Cay says to the camera. "Unfortunately, we don't even have the broken ones to show for our trip to Kili'a'an. But the lessons we learned there, along with a renewed sense of gratitude for life, are well worth the trade-off. Thanks for joining me on *Galactic Eats Reheated*. Next time I see you, I'll show you something that will blow you all the way to the Andromeda Galaxy. Until then, eat well, friends."

I stop rolling. As if the camera were bursting into flame, I set it hurriedly on the counter. I've been holding it for over an hour—take after take—and my forearms, wrists, and fingers feel worse than if they actually *were* on fire.

Galena has taken up long, quiet stretches sitting in her corner again. On the floor. Knees drawn to her chest. A glazed sort of look in her eyes. She really does hate being stuck on this ship. For the first half day after leaving Kili'a'an, she seemed interested in the work I was doing. I taught her about short takes and long takes and how they were important in creating a varied pace. I explained the difference between point-of-view, high-angle, and over-the-shoulder shots—among many others.

But it wasn't long before she started withdrawing into herself. After our time on Nabishna and Kili'a'an, she must be downright depressed being boxed in by the *Tantalus*' stainless-steel walls.

The caged bird, once it tastes freedom, will never be happy in its cage again.

"You need anything?" I ask. I approach her cautiously, like I would a wounded animal.

Galena doesn't speak, just shakes her head and turns away. After stretching out on my sleeping mat, she lays her head on her crossed arms.

I sigh and return to my editing. When I glance back at Galena, she has already slipped away into the realm of sleep.

The only reliable place she has ever found freedom in her life.

EAGLE ARCHIPELAGO

– SAGITTARIUS –

THE *TANTALUS*

31 Days to Payment

"WE'VE ARRIVED AT the Archipelago," Cay speaks into the comm console. "According to our autonav, we'll be landing in approximately forty galactic intervals—or fifteen Terran minutes, if that's still your thing."

Immediately after dropping out of X-space, we received a message from Mei-Li telling us to land at the Bellamina District. Even my Terran-raised ass has heard of Bellamina. It's one of the most coveted pieces of real estate in the galaxy. I'm not sure I'm rich enough to even *look* at the place, and a glance out the *Tantalus'* windscreen tells me why.

The Pillars of Creation loom before us. They're among the most breathtaking sights in all the Milky Way. Like stalagmites rising from a cave floor, these "pillars" of the Eagle Nebula, composed of hydrogen and stellar dust, pulse with the glow of the infant stars they're giving birth to. In reality, the Pillars are a few light-years away, yet they feel incredibly close, like I could reach out and grab them if only the windscreen weren't in the way.

Galena brushes against me. Her violet eyes bulge with wonder at the scene in front of us. It's the first excitement she's shown in two days.

"What are those?" she asks. She's pointing not at the dazzling spectacle, but at a funnel-shaped collection of massive space rocks which seem to be aimed at the Pillars.

PAD takes it upon himself to respond. "Those are the asteroids that make up the Eagle Archipelago."

"Which one are we going to?" Cay asks.

"The Bellamina District resides upon the foremost asteroid, also known as H-1. Bellamina provides the best unobstructed views of the

Pillars of Creation. It is also home to some of the galaxy's wealthiest beings."

"Uh, Cay?" I say. At least one of us can see obvious problems when they're right in front of us. "How are we going to leave the *Tantalus?* We don't have pressurized suits."

Again, PAD interjects his answer. "There is no need for specialized equipment on H-1. The asteroid is one of four in the Eagle Archipelago that have artificial atmospheres, allowing residents to move about freely without any need for pressurized gear. While H-1's atmospheric makeup differs slightly from Terra's, you should have no trouble functioning in it."

One question answered, I go for another. "What's happening on that huge asteroid? The one closest to us?"

The hunk of space rock appears alive, or perhaps unstable. As I lean toward the windscreen and focus, I notice scores of large ships coming and going.

"That is H-12," says PAD, "also known as Spice Rock. It has no external atmosphere, though the large tunnels and caverns within it have been sealed and pressurized. It serves as a hub for hundreds of spice combines, vessels which harvest stellar dust near the base of the Pillars. They then return to H-12, where processing plants sift a spice called *stardust* from the rest of the raw materials."

"Stardust? Never heard of it," I reply.

"Of course you haven't," says Cay. His eyes are like saucers. "It's the rarest spice in the galaxy, worth more than its weight in pure rhodium. Even I've never tasted it—never even *seen* it. With a sprinkling of it, I could buy a whole restaurant."

"Let's worry about paying back your Malvudian friends first," I say, hoping to ward off any foolhardy ideas.

The *Tantalus* cruises along the outer edge of the asteroid funnel. Soon, H-1 comes into view. Unlike the others, much of the rock is carpeted in lush green. A city, quite large for such a small asteroid, spreads like a thick web from a brightly lit central hub located in the asteroid's umbra, the dark half facing away from the Pillars. Even here, on the asteroid's backside, massive villas dot its surface, uplit by powerful spotlights so that their owners can show off to passing ships.

If that's how impressive the homes on the "poor" side of town are, I can't imagine what we would find on the other half—the prime real estate facing the nebula.

"For a program producer," Cay says, his tone bordering on suspicious, "it seems Mei-Li has done quite well for herself."

"What are you getting at?" I ask.

"She worked with Sal a long time," he says. "Call me paranoid, but I can't help wondering how much of her savings account *should* belong to me."

Ahead, I see the spaceport, Port Bellamina, situated near the edge of the city's dense center. The *Tantalus* decelerates for its descent and landing.

"Buckle up, everybody," Cay mutters. "Things might get bumpy."

PORT BELLAMINA
Landing Platform 33

"MEI-LI! IT'S GREAT to finally meet you." Cay extends his hand as he strides boldly down the *Tantalus'* boarding ramp.

The woman waiting at the bottom carries an elegant air about her. Sharp, shining eyes, unsuited to her advanced age, dart among us, judging, deciding then and there whether she will like us or not. She's also tiny. Like, the top of her head doesn't reach my armpits tiny.

That's why it's so surprising—and delightful—when she slams a rock-hard fist into Cay's gut. With a rush of escaping air, he doubles over, clutching his stomach.

"Nothing personal," she says, straight-faced, as she grabs his upper arm to steady him. "But I was never able to do that to Sal. It's been almost fifty years, and I still haven't gotten over that bitch abandoning me."

Mei-Li offers a crisp nod apiece to me and Galena. She turns and strolls toward a four-seater land jet hovering nearby.

"Come along," she calls back to us. "I'll take you to my home."

MEI-LI TAN'S GREAT ROOM

"HOLY FRIGGIN' CRAP," Cay says. His mouth is agape, his eyes bulging. "This is where you *live?*"

For someone with Cay's self-proclaimed finer tastes, Mei-Li's mansion is a dream. We're standing in the great room, a cavernous expanse topped with a duraglass dome. Its lights have been dimmed to accentuate the mystical glory above us, as the Pillars of Creation look down through the transparent ceiling.

Noting our amazement, Mei-Li says, "Some beings wonder why anyone would spend such a fortune to live on an asteroid. But if they ever visit Bellamina, they stop wondering. Wealthy Terrans build mansions in the mountains or along the seacoast, and our galactic neighborhoods do likewise—when conditions allow it. Inside Bellamina's artificial atmosphere, we maintain just enough cosmic radiation to stay warm, yet not so much that we start growing extra limbs."

Cay runs his fingers along a decorative table carved from a solid piece of otherworldly blue hardwood. Knickknacks—if you can call million-current sculptures *knickknacks*—are arranged on top of it.

"No offense," he says, "but how do you afford all this? I know successful producers do alright for themselves, but ..." He trails off, leaving the rest to Mei-Li's imagination.

She finishes his thought. "But you want to know whether this rightly belongs to you. Whether I siphoned some of Sal's fortune into my own bank accounts. Cheated my own godson."

Cay shrugs. "Jer was wondering."

Liar. Pathological to the end.

"You have to admit," he continues, "it would make sense."

Mei-Li's stoic lips crack a tiny grin. "I've done well in my producing career. Working with your grandmother set me on a path to lifelong success. For that, I owe her much. But I owe much more to the fact that I married an Arnaux."

"An Arnaux?" I exclaim, unable to stop myself. "An of-the-richest-family-on-Terra Arnaux?"

Mei-Li nods. "Podrique Arnaux, to be specific."

"Seriously? We had no idea! Is he here now?" I ask.

Mei-Li shakes her head. "Dead. For twenty-three years, actually."

In a feeble attempt to recover from my bout of foot-in-mouth syndrome, I mutter, "Sorry for your loss."

"Don't be," Mei-Li says. "The Arnauxs are assholes, every one of them. By the time I realized just how *big* an asshole Podrique was, he was already dying. I figured I'd ride things out until widowhood, then keep the fortune. And the homes."

I turn my attention to a young woman entering the great room. Her wavy blond hair triggers my memory at once. She was sitting with Mei-Li at Marq's funeral.

"Kora, please meet our guests," says Mei-Li. "This one—Galena, was it?—might have lots in common to discuss with you."

It's then that I catch a glimpse of something I didn't notice at the funeral. Behind Kora's coils of thick hair, embedded on both sides of her neck, are two silver circlets.

"You own a castrata?" I ask, scowling at Mei-Li. Anyone who enslaves another being will never be a friend of mine.

Noting my irritation, Mei-Li smirks and replies, "Kora spent much of her life as a castrata—nineteen years, was it?—before I bought her. And *liberated* her."

I relax at once, loosening the fists I didn't realize I was clenching.

"It's a dreadful system, the castrata," Mei-Li continues. "We may have gained the stars when we joined the Galactic League, but we traded away our humanity for it."

"Why do you still have your circlets?" I ask Kora.

Now it's Kora's turn to smirk. "To remember," she answers. "Both what I *had,* and what I *have.* I keep my circlets because they remind me each day of Mei-Li's gift. A gift few like me ever receive."

"Even if they do gain their freedom," says Mei-Li, "most castratae have nowhere to go. If they still have family, they usually don't know where. They have little education beyond whatever is required to serve their rulers. So, once I liberated Kora, I gave her a choice: pursue a path of her own making, or stay with me."

Mei-Li motions toward a nearby doorway. Beyond is a room with ample furniture, whose colors are muted by soft lighting. "You've had a long journey. What say we settle in with a drink?"

MEI-LI TAN'S PARLOR

SHEETS OF BLACK stone, flecked with glinting minerals, panel the parlor walls. They're so polished, I can see myself and everything around me reflected in sharp, monochromatic detail—including Galena, with whom I'm sharing the plush leather loveseat.

Working behind the parlor's abridged bar, cocktail shaker in hand, Mei-Li appears to be in her element. "I was a bartender before becoming a producer on *Galactic Eats*," she informs us. "Of course, that was a lifetime ago. I've had fifty-plus years and unlimited funds to improve my mixology since then."

Mei-Li pours the shaker's contents into two wide-rimmed cocktail glasses. One she hands to Kora, the other she keeps for herself.

Apparently "guests first" isn't a social norm when you're a multi-billionaire.

"What will you three have?" Mei-Li asks.

Cay, sitting on one of the barstools, grins. "Make me something I've never had before."

Unimpressed by his swagger, Mei-Li turns to me and Galena. "And for you?"

Galena lowers her eyes. "Nothing for me, thank you."

Given alcohol's tendency to turn otherwise demure people into unruly hooligans, most rulers don't allow their castratae even a drop of it. Offering Galena a drink is a little like offering Moses a BLT for lunch.

"To the rest of the galaxy, you may be a castrata," Mei-Li says, "but to the people in this room, you are an equal being. What will you have?"

Galena looks to me for tacit reassurance, then says, "I'll have whatever Jerricho's having."

"Do you have any scotch?" I ask.

Waving at the sagging shelves behind her, Mei-Li answers, "Yes. Thirteen kinds."

"They'll have whichever's most expensive," Cay interjects. "Two fingers apiece."

When everyone is seated, drinks in hand, our conversation resumes where it left off in the great room.

"Kora has become a daughter to me," Mei-Li says, swirling her cherry-tinted cocktail. "Sometimes she even fights with me like one!"

"Only when you're being unreasonable," Kora counters.

"But your grandmother," Mei-Li goes on, ignoring Kora's comment, "was like a sister to me. At first we were collaborators, each seeking our own ends. But over time, we became more. She became my best friend." A dark shadow passes over her face. She gazes at her glass, diving deep into the pools of memory. "Then Sal abandoned me. Left me behind so she could make the journey to Eden alone. Worst thing she could have done to me—that *anyone's* ever done to me."

"Do you know how to get there?" Cay asks bluntly. Mei-Li's mention of Eden has put everything else far from his mind.

Mei-Li stares at him. "The Galactic League called it a suicide journey. They banned Eden's coordinates thousands of years ago and made it illegal for anyone to share them. To *own* them."

"You didn't answer my question," Cay says, holding her gaze. "Do. You. Know?"

A flicker of mischief tints Mei-Li's otherwise stony appearance. She stands and approaches an intricate woodcarving hung on the wall. It is, I realize, an artist's depiction of the Trees of Eden, etched expertly into a thick sheet of wood.

"It took Sal and I two years to track down Eden's coordinates. Of course, when she disappeared, she took the nav cartridge with her. Didn't even have the courtesy to make me a copy. Bitch move, like I said. After I married Podrique and became a woman of means, I spent years on Axon's black markets before I found those coordinates again. Podrique was dead by then, but I had gained somebody else in my life—Kora—and my priorities changed. I always imagined I would attempt a journey to Eden when I was older, but at some point, I crossed into the realm of *too* old."

Mei-Li grabs a corner of the woodcut hanging on the wall. She pulls it toward herself, and the woodcut swings outward, revealing a safe hidden behind it. After providing a numeric code, fingerprint, and retinal scan, the safe unlocks. From within, Mei-Li produces four silvery navigation cartridges. She leaves the safe open and sets the cartridges side by side on the coffee table in front of me and Galena. Two look like standard nav cartridges, but the others are different. They're darker, less polished than the others.

"These," she says, pointing at the standard cartridges, "provide the landing coordinates for your first and third jumps."

"First and third? There's more than one?" Cay asks, leaving his bar-stool to join us.

"In theory, yes. Two there, two back."

"Jer's had one-night stands more complicated than that!" Cay exclaims, ever the cavalier.

But I detect the nuance in Mei-Li's eyes.

"The other two cartridges are QRDs—Quick-Read Drives," she explains. "They're highly illegal."

"Illegal? Why?" I ask.

"Because they bypass the Galactic League's protocol on X-space jumps. Normally you need two independent sources whose X-space coordinates are in complete alignment. This way, we don't wind up with all sorts of vessels landing in the middle of stars or getting lost forever along incomplete quantum pathways. But these QRDs override the need for coordinate redundancy. All you have to do is jam one into your ship's cartridge port, and it'll alter your course in a hurry, sending you immediately back into X-space. Pirates love them, which is probably another reason the League criminalized them."

I swallow hard. Jerricho Hatch already ran afoul of the law on Tarrkanna-Rrui. I certainly don't relish the thought of being caught with one of these QRDs in our possession.

"But why do we need two of them?" Cay asks. He picks one up for a closer look.

"The first gets you there, the second brings you home," Mei-Li answers. "Though I suspect you'll only ever use one. Or neither."

Nope. *Definitely* don't like the sound of that.

A wooden desk sits against one of the parlor walls. On top of it is a data processing monitor. It's here that Mei-Li brings both the QRDs and the standard cartridges. She opens a tall drawer in the desk. From it, she removes a pair of standard nav cartridges. Then, returning to the open safe, she produces two more QRDs. She places them on the desk beside the rest, bringing the total to eight.

Speaking to the monitor, she says, "Disconnect all access to and from Axon. Do not reconnect until I give full, coded authorization."

"What are you doing?" I ask, perhaps a bit suspiciously. "Why are you disconnecting Axon?"

"I'm duplicating illegal information from illegal devices onto more illegal devices," Mei-Li responds. "I'd say privacy is rather prudent, wouldn't you?"

From another drawer, she removes a tangle of wires. These she uses to connect the four standard cartridges and four Quick-Read Drives to the monitor. Mei-Li spends a few minutes giving various commands. A progress bar appears on the screen, indicating the beginning of a data transfer.

"This will take a few hours," Mei-Li says, turning away from the monitor.

"That long?" Cay replies. "It only takes a few seconds to download coordinates and an X-space path from Axon."

"That's because Axon works thousands of times faster than an old-fashioned hardwire transfer. We're copying an entire map to navigate quantum roads. *Complicated* doesn't begin to describe it."

Neither I nor anyone else needs to ask why Mei-Li is making copies rather than handing over the originals. She still hopes to take her own trip to Eden someday. A final itch to scratch.

A new voice floats into the room behind us, low and gravelly. "Pardon my interruption, ma'am."

We turn as one toward the parlor door. Here, a large being—Rouzh, I assume—fills the space inside the doorframe.

"Your dinner is ready," the Rouzh announces.

"Wonderful. Thank you, Nissim," Mei-Li replies. To the rest of us, she says, "Let's continue our conversation over dinner. I may have the coordinates you need, but that doesn't mean a journey to Eden is as simple as plugging them in."

She shakes her head and frowns. "Far from it, I'm afraid."

MEI-LI TAN'S DINING HALL

FORKS AND KNIVES tinkle against our dinnerware, iridescent plates fashioned from mother-of-pearl—or some other galactic equivalent. In addition to a salad of sweet greens imported from Twahal, we've each received a generous filet of seared *carabbi* and a pile of roasted pink tubers, both of which Chef Nissim says come from her home planet of Rouz.

Cay is plainly unimpressed with the food. I, however, am impressed he's keeping his mouth shut about it.

Regardless, Mei-Li reads his halfhearted reception of the meal and asks, "Have you ever seasoned food with stardust?"

That gets his attention. Cay perks up instantly, eyes wide with hopeful wonder. "Stardust is one of the most expensive substances in the galaxy. So, no, I've never tried it."

Mei-Li slides a small pewter bowl across the polished tabletop. Cay catches it and opens the lid. Inside is a powdery gray substance.

Stardust.

"Don't overdo it," cautions Kora, seated next to her adopted mother. There's an impish grin playing on her lips.

Cay's expression is downright orgasmic as he sprinkles a pinch onto his fish and potatoes. He slices off a hunk of *carabbi* and holds it up on his fork, gazing at the stardust-sprinkled morsel like someone beholding a deity face to face.

He places the bite in his mouth. Chews. Swallows.

And scowls.

"Tastes like salt!" he exclaims.

Mei-Li laughs. "Stardust's chemical composition is slightly different from Terran table salt, but, yes, that's essentially what it is."

"Then why's it so flapjacking expensive?"

"Because its image is so exotic," answers Mei-Li. "A good salesperson can make people believe they need just about anything, and that they should spend just about anything to have it. Did you know people used to bottle water and sell it on Terra?"

Everyone, even Galena, snickers at this remark.

Mei-Li's expression becomes drawn and serious again. She says, "Sal was one of the best saleswomen I ever knew, and the product she sold was herself. The quality of her cooking didn't matter so much, not when the swashbuckling, fedora-wearing Sal Cantore was the woman making it." Mei-Li pauses. "But with the Trees of Eden, it was different. She wanted to give her audience something incredible. Something they'd never seen before, and never would again. In doing so, she would seal her own immortality among the stars."

Mei-Li grunts with dry amusement. "Funny. When she never came back, she found her immortality anyway. Sal Cantore. The woman. The legend."

"What do you think happened?" Cay asks, drawn in by Mei-Li's rapturous view of his grandmother.

"Rationally?" Mei-Li replies. "That she was either ripped to pieces or vaporized."

"Why? How?"

"According to our information, stolen from the League's archives, you have to make a double X-space jump to go to Eden. That's because it orbits a black hole near the center of the Milky Way. Unfortunately, the planet is blocked from a direct X-space shot by some sort of bowl-shaped galactic hurricane. It's a unique interstellar entity, an anomaly of energy unlike anything else we know. Whatever it is, it interacts with X-space too much to find a direct path through it. Eden, then, is pinned between the two—the black hole on one side, and the strange galactic storm on the other.

"The only way to get there is by jumping dangerously close to the black hole, then angling back toward Eden inside the bowl of the hurricane. It's that second jump which is so critical. You must make it immediately, before the black hole's tidal forces rip your ship—and you—to pieces."

"How much time is there to make the second jump?" I ask.

"It's hard to know," Mei-Li says. "I'm not sure how many others have tried making the journey, but it's been thousands of Terran years since anyone returned. Based on my best research, and depending on the spaceworthiness of your vessel, I would assume you only have seconds to make the jump. Ten, fifteen tops."

"No room for error," I mutter. I haven't eaten much, but my appetite has vanished regardless.

"Not even a split second's delay," Mei-Li confirms. "This, of course, was before the discovery of the Veridonian Principle. As you might imagine, escaping a black hole's gravity requires a lot of extra energy. With the quality of fuel rods available to us back then, it not only meant inserting the QRD, but also changing out the fuel rod in those same precious seconds. The journey to Eden was no less than a two-person job, yet Sal abandoned me and the rest of our crew to do it herself. We were a family. Then ... she cut us out."

Cay wears a vacant expression. Staring at nothing, or perhaps everything, he says, "Maybe Sal didn't want you dying for her crazy dream."

Mei-Li scoffs. "Sal wasn't that selfless. I think she couldn't bear the thought of scrubbing the adventure, but she still needed someone around to take care of Marq. He was so little then. Sal's parents could have done it, but neither was in the best of health."

"Dad never talked about who raised him," Cay says. "It was you, wasn't it."

"I did. Marq was only a few months old when I took responsibility for him."

"What happened between you?"

"We had a falling out," Mei-Li answers with a sigh. "Over your mother, actually. I hated that whore. Still do, wherever she is. She was the first of many to take advantage of him, and I saw right through her. Marq didn't. I tried to protect him, but in the end, I had to let him make his own mistake."

"Given the choice between you and Sal, it sounds like Dad ended up with the better mom."

Mei-Li glances sideways at the young woman next to her. "The only one with any right to judge that statement is Kora." Giving her adopted daughter a lightning-quick wink, she adds, "Don't worry, sweetheart, I won't put you on the spot."

We eat in silence, processing everything Mei-Li revealed.

A minute later, Cay asks, "Do you think it's real? Eden? I mean, if no one's come back for thousands of years, maybe it's nothing more than a myth."

Mei-Li looks again at Kora. "*She's* the Eden expert here. I'll let her answer."

Kora swallows her bite of tubers and clears her throat. "I don't know if I'd call myself an *expert*. But, yes, Eden lore is a hobby of mine."

"Bordering on obsession," Mei-Li chirps.

Kora waves off the comment. "There are so many ancient records of Eden, it must have existed once upon a time. There are even rumors that all life in our galaxy began at Eden. But, given its position between the hurricane's destructive forces and the black hole, it also seems likely Eden's luck would run out sooner or later. Whether that's happened already, your guess is as good as mine."

"So you think I'm chasing someone who's not even there," Cay says, more statement of fact than question.

"Again," Mei-Li responds, "from a *rational* standpoint, I don't see how she'd be alive after all this time. And if she *had* survived, she would have come back. Still, this is Sal Cantore we're talking about. Luck seemed to worship her. She was a legend for a reason, Indiana Jones with boobs and a cutting board. If anyone could have pulled it off, it was Sal."

"Let's hope I inherited some of her legend," Cay remarks.

At this, Mei-Li sets down her silverware and leans toward him. Looking more solemn than a Gothic gargoyle, she says, "Turn back, Cay. There's too much at stake. Don't go risking it all on a myth."

As she says that last bit, her eyes flit toward me and Galena.

Grave admonition administered, Mei-Li perks up at once and says, "Can I interest anyone in dessert? Nissim will serve it back in the parlor. We'll be more comfortable there."

MEI-LI TAN'S PARLOR

DESSERT PLATES, EMPTY but for a few crumbs, sit with dirty forks on the parlor coffee table. I'm unsure what I just ate, but even Cay seemed satisfied with it.

"Nissim's forte in the kitchen is as a pastry chef," Mei-Li comments from behind the bar. She's fixing the room another round of drinks. "A galactically respected one, at that. I chose her to be my personal chef because of Kora's long sweet tooth."

"My sweet *tusk*, she usually calls it," Kora adds.

"It really was delicious," says Galena. The lifelong castrata seems nervous offering an opinion in front of so many people, and she shows it by rocking in her seat.

"I'm glad you enjoyed it," Mei-Li congenially replies.

"I'm sorry, but would you mind if I used your washroom?" Galena asks. She stands suddenly, looking pale. "I'm ... not used to the alcohol, I think."

"Of course," says Mei-Li. "Kora, would you mind showing Galena to her guest suite? You may use the attached washroom there."

They leave, and Mei-Li brings me and Cay a pair of drinks garnished with orange peel.

"Nothing too fancy," she says, "but I usually enjoy a negroni after my evening meal."

She sits in a luxurious chair beside Cay's. After taking a sip, she smacks her lips satisfactorily. "Supposedly good for digestion, too. As if anybody needed another reason to drink one."

We sit in an uncomfortable silence. I've imbibed my fair share of booze during the last month, but even with the tolerance I've built, my mind feels like someone wrapped it in a fuzzy cloth. I guess five stiff drinks will do that to a guy.

"You know," Mei-Li says, staring at Cay over the rim of her glass, "I figured you were coming here to ask for money."

"Why's that?" Cay replies.

"I was at Marq's funeral," she says. "I saw the Hekkra. Of course, I wondered why you weren't there. With my resources, it didn't take too much digging to figure out why. I suppose that's also the reason you're taking on the Trees of Eden."

Cay nods. "One of the reasons, yes."

Mei-Li swirls her drink. Takes another sip. Gazes into the bottom of her glass. Finally, she asks, "How much?"

"How much what?"

"How much do you owe your Malvudian friends?"

Even in the parlor's low lighting, I notice Cay's cheeks flush pink, and not just from the alcohol.

"Two million," he sheepishly replies.

Mei-Li nearly performs a spit take. After swallowing the mouthful of negroni, she says, "Two *million?* That must have been a hell of a restaurant you put together."

Cay grins. "Malvudian interest rates are a touch above industry standards. Besides, it would've been the finest dining in the galaxy if I could've convinced the kitchen staff to stick around."

Mei-Li shakes her head. "Perhaps you didn't inherit as much of Sal's magnetism as I thought."

"Magnets repel things too, you know," I interject.

"Maybe I've spent too much time watching you with women," Cay shoots back.

I scowl but can't come up with a second barb. Damn booze is dulling my brain.

"Two million. That's a lot of bacon," says Mei-Li, setting down her drink, "for *most* beings. But for Podrique Arnaux's widow? Two million is hardly a drop in the bucket. I've got paintings in this parlor worth more than that."

"What are you saying?" I ask. My heart thumps with anticipation.

"I'm saying I'll give it to you," she says.

Cay and I exchange shocked glances. His eyes might be even bigger than mine.

"I've been angry at Sal for fifty years," Mei-Li continues, "but she still took me along for the best ride of my life. She gave me my big break. Turned me into an industry name. I don't owe you boys a thing, but I *do* owe her."

"Two million?" I respond. I can't believe what I'm hearing. "You're just ... giving it to us? No strings attached?"

"Not everyone's a selfish asshole," Mei-Li says, flashing an accusatory glance at Cay. Maybe intended for him, maybe for his grandmother. "But there is *one* string."

"What?" Cay and I ask in unison.

"You only get the money if you call off this trip to Eden. Consider it a buyout. Leave here without those QRDs, and I'll shim the funds into your account the second you're off my doorstep. Pay back the Malvudians and move on with your lives."

"If you don't want me going to Eden," Cay asks, "why offer the coordinates at all?"

"Because you're Sal's offspring. You'd get there one way or another," Mei-Li answers. "Besides, there's always been that burning question inside me. The one that wonders, every day since Sal left, whether she might have made it. Whether she might still be out there somewhere. Alive. Better you risk your lives than me risk mine trying to answer it."

"So much for not being a selfish asshole," Cay retorts.

Mei-Li chuckles. "Nobody's perfect."

Kora returns to the parlor without Galena. I straighten in my chair, alarmed at the omission.

Noticing my reaction, Kora says, "Your friend asked for privacy. She said her stomach didn't feel right."

I relax. We aren't in a Petran mine or stuck on Gustav Geiger's ship. We're among friends—at least, I think we are. Still, the past weeks have left me with frayed nerves and a few trust issues. I might have some things to iron out with a therapist once we're back on Terra. Which, I'm happy to note, could happen as early as tomorrow.

"Can I have some time to think about your offer?" Cay asks Mei-Li.

That's when the switch flips inside me. I shoot up to my feet.

"Time?" I yell. "What *time* do you need, Cay? We've got the money!"

"It's about more than—"

"More?" I repeat. "You want *more,* you selfish dick? Look, you don't have to pay me a single pip of that two million. Hell, I'll even sign your dad's restaurant and apartment over to you, if *more* is what you need."

Cay raises his hands into a defensive posture. "You don't understand—"

"I don't understand? Don't understand *what?*" The booze has put my inhibitions into *SLEEP* mode and awakened my tongue. "All I need to understand is that I don't wanna die. And I don't want Galena dying either."

"That's not—"

But I'm past listening. I throw up my hands and half stumble, half storm to the parlor door.

"Kiss my ass, Cay," I holler. Then, realizing how little of Mei-Li's mansion I've become acquainted with, I add, "And can someone, for the love of the Cosmos, please show me to a bedroom?"

MEI-LI TAN'S GUEST ROOM

30 Days to Payment

DURING MY FIRST three years of high school, long before I ever heard of Clarion-Burgess Syndrome, I suffered from severe insomnia. It arrived the night before freshman football tryouts and took up residence through the end of my junior year. But it didn't affect me in the ways you might expect. I didn't spend every day staggering through some zombie-esque haze. In classes, extracurriculars, and especially on the football field, my mind streamed with such an intense volume of activity, I sometimes thought my head might pop.

But on the weekends, and during longer breaks? That's when I would collapse, dragging for days and days. After many promises—and threats—from my mother, I finally cooperated to see a therapist the summer after my junior year.

It only took two sessions with Dr. Conrad to dig to the root problem. The insomnia was merely a symptom, grown from my crippling anxiety. For many people, anxiety causes them to shut down and hide away. In my case, it drove me to be the best, both in the classroom and on the gridiron. Every night, when I should have been asleep, I was mulling over history facts, math equations, tackling form. My mind simply wouldn't shut off.

When I started sleeping through the night again, I figured I'd beaten my anxiety. At worst, I had trimmed it to a manageable level. Dr. Conrad's sessions had fixed me, I decided, so I stopped seeing him.

But tonight, I'd give just about anything for five minutes on his couch.

After my outburst in the parlor, Kora showed me to my cavernous bedroom. I fell asleep well enough—the ample booze made sure of that.

It also made sure I woke up two hours later to use the toilet in my private bathroom.

That's where the streaming questions and intemperate worries started crowding my mind. It doesn't matter that my climate-controlled bed is like lying on an oversized pancake. Anxiety's ripping, tunneling claws are tearing into me like a starved Grinnud into a porterhouse.

When Cay and I left Terra on our self-appointed mission, I had little confidence we might actually discover a way to long-lost Eden. Certainly I had no clue how rife with dangers the journey there would be. Now that we do know, how can Cay possibly consider pressing forward? Mei-Li described it as a suicide journey, and that's exactly what it is. It would be one thing if we were choosing between a black hole or a Hekker ripping us apart. But with Mei-Li dropping two million currents in our laps, how could Cay go on risking his life in pursuit of Eden? And offering up me and Galena as a side bet?

Twenty minutes later, sleep is nowhere on the horizon. Just an expansive field of questions and an endless forest of potential conversations, scenarios, and dilemmas for my mind to trek through.

I've only realized one thing for certain: I'm crazy thirsty.

Careful to keep quiet, I tiptoe out my bedroom door. The nearest drinking glasses I've seen are in the parlor, so I set course for the opposite end of the great room. With only the empyrean Pillars of Creation watching from overhead, I slink through the silent mansion.

MEI-LI TAN'S PARLOR

THE GLOW OF the data monitor illuminates my murky path as I make for the parlor sink. Behind the bar, I down a glass of water, then follow it with a second. I'm about to fill my cup a third time when my eyes fall on the desktop.

Earlier, before I stormed off to bed, eight devices had been plugged into the monitor: four standard nav cartridges and four Quick-Read Drives. Now there are only half as many. Mei-Li must have returned the originals to the safe.

But when I glance over at the Trees of Eden woodcut, something seems off. It's tough to tell in the shadows cast by the data monitor, but it looks like the safe is ajar.

If Mei-Li returned the ultra-precious cartridges, wouldn't she also lock and hide the safe again?

I set my glass beside the sink. I'm about to investigate when a noise outside the parlor diverts my attention. Not daring to breathe, I alter my course and make for the door. Peering around it, I scan the great room, looking for the source of the disturbance in this otherwise sleeping home.

I locate the intruder at once. Entering through the front foyer, a small, furtive shadow slinks along the far wall.

Then the shadow steps into the glow emanating down through the duraglass dome.

The intruder is Galena.

MEI-LI TAN'S GREAT ROOM

"GALENA!" I WHISPER across the vaultlike room.

She stifles a cry and spins to face me.

"What are you doing?" I ask, hurrying toward her. "Why were you outside?"

Galena sniffles. "I wanted to take a walk before I'm stuck on the *Tantalus* again."

Even in the faint light, I see she's been crying. Without thinking, I wrap her in my arms. I half expect she'll push me away again, like that night on Nabishna, but she doesn't. This time she leans into me, returning my embrace with her own as she sobs against my chest.

I don't bother asking what's wrong. Our future is murky, perhaps for her more than anyone. Either she embarks on a deadly trip to Eden, or we take the money and our adventure comes to an end, leaving her a fugitive castrata evading capture wherever she goes.

"I'll do whatever I can to help you," I assure her. "You know that, right?"

Galena nods. Her face is pressed against Gram's crystal hanging on its chain. The gem is biting into my left pec, but I don't care. Let her drive it all the way into my heart, just as long as I can hold her like this.

The Azazule diamond must also be cutting into Galena's cheek, because she pulls away and asks, "Why do you wear it? The necklace?"

Removing the diamond from beneath my shirt, I lay it in my palm and say, "It's supposed to bring you good luck. My Gram gave it to me before we left. Lent it, really. I thought it was a bunch of old-fashioned hocus-pocus at first, but it's tough to argue with the good luck we've had on this trip. I was sure we were goners a couple times, but here we are!"

Acting on impulse, I remove the necklace and loop the chain over Galena's head. I step back to admire her.

"Jerricho, I can't—"

"Yes, you can," I insist. "I've had more luck than one man deserves. If nothing else, maybe this silly crystal caused me to meet you. If it has any power at all, you deserve it more than anyone. It's time for Galena to catch a break."

"What about your Gram? Won't she want it back?"

"She might be a little upset, but she'll get over it."

Galena lowers her eyes and whispers, "Thank you. Thank you for helping me. But you're wrong. I don't deserve it. I don't deserve anything from you." She looks up again and smiles. "But I'll take it anyway. Cosmos knows I could use a bit of luck."

One rejection is usually enough for me to turn my sights elsewhere. But Galena is different, and Nabishna feels like it was ages ago. Perhaps it's the Pillars of Creation blessing me from overhead, or maybe she has turned me into a big enough fool to risk a second rejection. I don't know. But before I can think better of it, I tilt her chin toward mine and lean in to kiss her.

This time, she doesn't stop me. If anything, she's leaning in too. Wanting it to happen. Maybe even *willing* it to happen.

I guess I don't need Gram's crystal changing my luck.

It's like a movie. Too much like a movie, actually. Just as our lips are about to meet, a door shuts somewhere in the house, spoiling the moment.

Maybe I need the diamond after all.

Still holding each other, Galena and I hurry into the dark hallway leading to the bedrooms. We flatten ourselves against the wall, glancing this way and that for the source of the noise.

Emerging from the corridor that leads to Mei-Li's dining room, a dark figure strides confidently into the great room.

It's Cay. He makes straight for the parlor.

What the hell is he doing? Getting a drink, like me? And why is he wearing his backpack?

Cay disappears into the darkness beyond the parlor door. Galena and I watch, breathless, our fingers intertwined. Our hearts beat in syncopated rhythm with one another.

A minute passes—not even—before Cay exits the parlor. Like a man on a mission, he marches to the foyer door and throws it open. Here he hesitates, but only for a second as he glances back into the mansion's darkness. Then he cinches his backpack tight against his shoulders and leaves, closing the door behind him with a quiet *click*.

Galena looks up at me, concerned. With a sinking sensation, I realize the moment for our kiss has, like Cay, departed.

"What's he doing?" she mouths.

I shake my head, then point at the parlor. Whatever answer Cay left us, I'm certain we'll find it there.

MEI-LI TAN'S PARLOR

THE PARLOR DESK, still illuminated by the data processing monitor, has undergone an obvious change in the last five minutes. When I was getting my drink, four nav cartridges were wired into the computer. Now zero remain, and they've all been replaced by a single sheet of paper.

I pick it up. Cay's handwriting. No surprises there. It reads:

My Dearest Grandgodmother,

I'll most likely be a spaghettified version of myself by the time you read this, courtesy of one black hole. If you're too senile to notice it on your own, I've taken your nav cartridges and the QRDs with Eden's coordinates.

You were right. In the end, this really wasn't about the Malvudians. They just gave me a push out the door. It was about the adventure and the immortality that will belong to me when I pull this off.

I guess the asshole doesn't fall far from the tree.

I hope you'll consider giving the two million currents to Jerricho, regardless of my decision. When I go missing, I'm worried my creditors will hold him accountable. None of this is his fault. It's mine. He shouldn't have to pay for my many mistakes.

If I do find Sal, I'll say 'hello' from you. I'll also pass on that sucker punch you gave me at the spaceport. Sounds like the bitch has it coming.

A thousand hugs and kisses,
Cay

When I'm done reading, I pass the note to Galena. She skims it and says, "We have to go after him."

I bite the inside of my lip. "Do we?"

"What do you mean?" she says, glaring. "We can't let him do it alone!"

"Why not?" I retort. "If 'alone' is what he wants, why shouldn't we let him have that? We'll pay back his debt, and I'll take you somewhere safe. Somewhere you'll be free. Why should we go to Eden and risk dying for Cay's stupid dream?"

"If we aren't with him, he *will* die, remember?" Galena counters. "He can't switch out those cheap fuel rods *and* the nav cartridge at the same time."

"He can use PAD," I argue.

Galena shakes her head. "PAD doesn't fit in the mechanical room, and he can't use the QRD."

"Why not?"

"He can't do anything illegal, remember? It goes against his programming." Making for the parlor door, she says, "Do what you want. I'm going after Cay."

Caught in the tension between my longing for Galena and my fear of death, I remain rooted to the floor. I'm a coward and I know it. Yet, like every other coward who knows it, I lack the ability to do or be otherwise.

Ashamed, I crumple Cay's note in my fist.

In that act of crushing the paper, I see the tattoo on my forearm.

Wings spread. Mid-flight. Soaring into an imagined sky.

The monarch. *My* monarch. An everlasting emblem inked into my flesh. A sign of who I want to be. A crushing reminder of who I am not.

The monarch's great migration is filled with countless dangers, both by air and by land. It risks everything to make a thousand-mile journey, so that it might arrive in a land it knows nothing about, all because of a dream embedded in the collective consciousness of its species.

Although it will never return home, the monarch goes. Not because it is forced, but because it *must*. Will I really be outdone by a butterfly?

To hell with that. Time to bury the old Jerricho Hatch, so that a newer version might arise and take flight.

Before I know what my diseased feet are doing, I'm stealing back through Mei-Li's mansion. In the guest room, I lace up my boots and retrieve my backpack. Then I hurry out into the asteroid's artificial atmosphere, praying I can catch my friends before it's too late.

PORT BELLAMINA
Landing Platform 33

VIA MEI-LI TAN'S land jet, the trip to her home from Port Bellamina took only a few minutes. It's a different story going back on foot. Nearly an hour after closing Mei-Li's front door, and forty minutes after catching up to Galena, we arrive at the spaceport.

My dogs are barking. And biting. Six rushed kilometers in these boots, coupled with the CBS, has me presently welcoming the idea of an amputation. The moment I'm onboard the *Tantalus*, I'm ditching the shoes. Maybe forever.

But first things first.

"Cay!" I yell, as Galena and I scale the final steps onto Landing Platform 33.

The lone figure making his way up the *Tantalus'* entry ramp whirls about, surprised to hear his name. He frowns when he spots us.

"What are you doing here?" Cay calls back. "I was supposed to be halfway to Eden by the time you woke up."

"And halfway to dead," I reply. "How were you planning to do two jobs at once? You can't switch the fuel rod *and* the QRD."

Cay shrugs. "I'll figure something out. I *am* Sal's grandson."

"And—what—you thought you'd sneak off without us? Strand us in this hellhole?"

"If a mansion with three daily meals prepared by a private chef is your idea of the word *hellhole*, then yes," Cay answers. He strikes a rare serious tone. "I can't let you come with me, Jerricho. Or you, Galena. It wouldn't be right."

"Aw, screw you," I tell him. "Now's not the time for turning all selfless and noble. Maybe in a couple weeks, but not today."

Cay chuckles. "Don't be so naïve, Jer. I wrote a note for Mei-Li, asking her to give you the two million so you can pay off my debt. Then, after I come back from Eden, we'll take the full payout from Jonas for ourselves! It's a win for everyone!"

"Except Mei-Li," Galena points out.

"Did you see that mansion? Mei-Li's done enough winning for one lifetime."

"How exactly were you planning to finish the last episode without me behind the camera?" I challenge. "You don't know squat about videography."

"But PAD does," Cay replies. "Everything you know, he's learned. Whenever we come home, you can upload his footage—or download, I forget which is which—and finish the episodes. Another win for everyone! It's a win-win-win-win-win situation."

"You know, Cay, you're a shit friend sometimes," I say, shaking my head, "but you're an even shittier liar."

"Jeez, enough with the 'shits' already."

"Ever since Kili'a'an," I continue, ignoring his interruption, "you haven't been your full-blown Cay Cantore self. For once, maybe in your entire life, you're thinking about somebody other than you."

"It's a bad look on me, isn't it," he says, grimacing with disgust. "Let's hope it's just a phase. Anyway, congrats on catching me here, but you still can't come. Sorry."

"Like hell I can't." Facing the ship's open interior at the top of the boarding ramp, I yell, "Tantalus, don't obey any orders Cay gives you. Not until I say otherwise."

From deep inside, I hear the ship's faint voice acknowledging the command.

"Tantalus," Cay hollers, "disregard Jerricho's order. He's lost his mind."

"Request denied," Tantalus answers. "Master Jerricho's authority supersedes yours. I must await his permission."

For once, it's Cay who is flustered while I wear the cocksure grin.

"PAD might have to obey you," I say, "but the *Tantalus* was purchased in my name with my loan, remember? That makes me top dog. At the end of the day, you're *my* sidekick."

Cay's irritation melts in an instant. "You know you're gonna die, right?"

"Everybody has to sometime," I reply with a cavalier shrug. "Might as well be in the midst of a beautiful flight. Besides, after this we'll finally be even."

"What do you mean?"

"I'm paying you back for rescuing me from the fire."

"The fire *I* started."

"A trivial detail."

As the three of us make our way up the ramp, Cay says, "If I'm going to spend eternity snuggling with someone in a black hole's singularity, I'm glad it'll be you, Jerricho Hatch."

THE *TANTALUS*

"CAN WE RUN over the 'plan' once more?" I ask. When I say the word *plan,* I put air quotes around it. To me, it sounds less like a plan and more like a network of loose ideas, a spiderweb on the back end of a hurricane.

The Pillars of Creation loom beyond the *Tantalus'* windscreen. Every time I look at the celestial masterpiece, I promise myself I'll buy a place on Bellamina too. Apparently all I have to do is marry into old money.

"There's no sweating anything right now," Cay says. "For our first jump, we'll use the nav cartridge as normal. The only difference is that the onboard nav system doesn't know where we're going, so it can't upload coordinates from Axon. PAD will have to serve as our secondary."

"Yes, and may I strongly object once again to this entire maneuver?" the drone chimes in.

"You may object," Cay replies. "And may *I* once again suggest that you shut your piehole?"

PAD is presently connected to the nav cartridge, making a copy of the X-space information. As at Mei-Li's residence, the information transfer from cartridge to drone is painstaking. PAD claims he's able to download the data faster, but doing so would risk anomalies in the code. I'm guessing an anomaly isn't a problem we want to run into while navigating the quantum realm of X-space.

In front of us, a star chart illuminates the navigation monitor. It represents only a fractional subsection of the outer Galactic Bulge, but even in this tiny slice of the cosmos, a thousand points of light wink back at us.

And, in the midst of them, is one gaping dark sphere.

Galena points at the inky blotch. "That's the black hole, right? Gemini 2-X?"

Cay nods. "That's it. That's where Mei-Li's coordinates are taking us. I hope."

"So when we drop out of X-space next to this black hole," I say, "I'm supposed to unbuckle myself, run into the mechanical closet, and switch out our fuel rod? In fifteen seconds or less, before we turn into spaghetti? It's not possible, Cay. Not a chance."

"Who said anything about running *into* the mechanical room?" Cay replies. "In my version of things, you're already there."

I shake my head furiously. "No way. I remember what happened last time. Cracked ribs, punctured lung, and a concussion. I lost six days of my life, Cay. *Six days!* I'm not doing that again."

"Don't be such a fuddy-duddy," chides Cay. "We'll use a couple tethers, strap you in good and tight. The moment we drop out of X-space, you use those hunky football muscles to switch the rods. Once you're done, I shove the QRD into the cartridge dock. We jump into X-space and arrive shortly thereafter at Eden. Clean and easy!"

"Clean as pissin' into the wind," I grumble.

Scowling, I leave the cockpit. My heart has climbed so far into my throat, I'm afraid I'll choke on it. I remember how much effort it took to replace the fuel rod the first time around. It's a tight fit by necessity, and they're heavier than they look. What if my muscles just ... quit? Like on Petra 7, when Cay and Galena were hauling me away from the trollums? Or when I dropped Cay on Kili'a'an?

Until now, I've kept my secret hidden. I didn't want Cay knowing anything about my disease. I can't stand the thought of people pitying me, looking at me like some stray, three-legged dog rooting around a trash bin. For as long as possible, I want to be the same Jerricho Hatch that my coworkers, my friends, and Cay have always known.

I glance back at the others, and my gaze settles on Galena. There's a new power at work against me now. One even stronger than all the crushing force of a black hole.

"Hey, Cay?" I say, before I can second-guess my decision. "Can you come with me to the mechanical closet? I want to make sure I know what I'm doing."

Once we're inside, I shut the door.

"What's going on?" Cay says. "I don't know anything—"

"Can we trade jobs?" I ask. I'm unable to meet his eyes.

"You understand this technical crap way better than me," he replies.

"I can jam something into a hole along with the best of 'em. But quick-changing a fuel rod? That's a little more complicated."

I sigh. "You don't understand. There's something I need to tell you. Something I haven't been open about."

Mocking my somber demeanor, he caresses my cheek and whispers, "You can tell me anything, Jer."

"You know, you don't *always* have to be an asshole," I say, swatting away his hand. "I have ... a problem. It's called Clarion-Burgess."

"What is that, like, a diarrhea thing? So, hit the head before we make the jump."

"Worse than that, actually. It's a disease. I won't get into all the details, but it's made me pretty weak, especially my hands and feet. It makes for a good amount of pain too."

Cay takes a moment to mull over my big reveal. "That's why you fell on Petra 7, isn't it," he says. "Why you couldn't keep going on Nabishna, why you dropped me on Kili'a'an. It's why you're always achy after a long day working the camera. Yeah, I've noticed. But why didn't you tell me before now?"

"I guess ... I didn't want you treating me different," I answer.

"What do you mean? I treat you like crap! You yourself have pointed that out a hundred times this trip. *Different* could only be an improvement."

"You know what I mean. I didn't want you to think I was helpless. A cripple."

Cay doesn't say anything. He edges past me toward the stash of fuel rods and heaves one off the floor. He holds it out with both hands, studying it.

"Alright," he says, "you're gonna have to show me how to do this, like, a hundred times to make sure I don't blow us all up."

I grin. "Thanks, Cay."

After I take him through the steps—press and hold the release lever, twist rod to the left, press and hold second release until the rod pops free, slide it out, insert new rod, twist to the right to lock into place—Cay practices the motions himself.

During his third practice run, I say, "Remember, you'll be in here without a proper harness. That means you might get roughed up when we come out of X-space. Whatever happens, you have to fight through it."

Without warning, I shove Cay's head against the wall.

"Dick!" he cries. "What'd you do that for?"

I answer by pointing at the fuel rods. "Go! Fast as you can!"

He does. I'm using a very inaccurate stopwatch—my head—but I clock him at nine seconds after his initial hesitation.

"Whaddya think?" he says. "Fast enough to keep the *Tantalus* from breaking apart?"

"Let's hope Mei-Li's fifteen-second estimate holds water. But, yeah, if you do it that fast when it counts, I think we'll be alright."

"Good. Because all this rod-and-insertion stuff is getting a bit hot for me. I need a cold shower before we leave."

"You're in luck. I recently unconverted the pantry into one."

"Noted. Now, hobble your crippled heinie back to the cockpit before I change my mind," Cay says.

Together, we return to the cockpit. I buckle myself next to Galena.

With a knowing smile, she asks, "Did you two figure everything out?"

"Yeah," I answer, looking sideways at Cay. "I think we finally understand things."

Cay's sincerity tank must have run dry. He ignores Galena's question and instead asks PAD, "How's the download coming? We ready to go, or what?"

"I have completed the download," PAD answers. "Whether we're truly *ready* for this undertaking is an entirely different matter."

"Good enough for me," Cay replies.

"Tantalus," I say, "prepare us for an X-space jump according to the coordinates and mapping provided by PAD and the nav cartridge."

"Preparing," says Tantalus. "Designated coordinates do not appear on official Galactic League registers. Continuing with this course may be detrimental to this ship's functionality and hazardous to the health of all onboard. Do you wish to proceed?"

I look at Cay. He returns my uncertainty with his cocky grin and a reassuring wink.

"Yes," I tell Tantalus. "We wish to proceed."

"X-space travel to inputted coordinates has an estimated relative duration of thirty-four hours and seven minutes," Tantalus informs us. "When you are ready to make the jump, please initiate the sequence by speaking the word *jump*."

I exhale a deep breath and close my eyes. Once I give the command, we'll take off.

There will be no turning back. It will either end in death or at Eden.

Beside me, Galena must be thinking the same thing. She grips my forearm until her nails dig into my flesh.

Twice the words form and die on my lips. On the third attempt, I manage to utter them out loud.

"Jump, Tantalus."

"Initiating jump sequence," the ship acknowledges.

But before it has finished speaking, Cay points excitedly out the windscreen. Off our starboard flank, a much larger vessel has coasted into view.

"That's the *Royal Austrian!*" Cay cries, astonished. "How the devil's food did Geiger find us here?"

The Pillars of Creation, along with everything else in our windscreen, begin to fade and warp. Cay's perplexity likewise transforms into an exultant smile as he exclaims, "Doesn't matter anymore! Let's see that dillweed follow us now."

The *Tantalus* gives a violent lurch forward, and the galaxy disappears.

We're on our way.

THE *TANTALUS*
28 Days to Payment

NO MATTER HOW many times I see it, the kaleidoscope of X-space never fails to mesmerize me. Moving along the quantum foam of constant inconstancy, we somehow both fill the universe and cease being part of it, all at the same time.

The Cosmos, and our place in it, truly are a boggling, beautiful mystery.

Cay and Galena are stretched out on the sleeping mats, PAD is resting at his charging station, and I'm quietly editing video at the kitchen counter. I wear only one earbud as I work. We're fourteen hours from our X-space destination, but I'm keeping my other ear unoccupied. Ten minutes before we drop out of X-space, the *Tantalus* will sound a warning alarm. In theory, this should wake any sleepers and allow them plenty of time to buckle in. But, given the seriousness of our situation, we decided one of us should remain awake at all times.

If there's one alarm I definitely *don't* want to sleep through, this is it.

I reach a good point to pause my editing and take a leak. When I exit the lavatory, Galena is awake, sitting on the stool at my counter workstation. Somehow, her unkempt hair and sleep lines make her even lovelier to me.

"You didn't sleep long," I comment. "Everything alright?"

Galena grunts and says, "Yeah. After all the build-up on Bellamina, I didn't expect I'd be so bored again. Dead, maybe, but not bored."

"It'll be plenty exciting soon enough," I reply.

Galena fiddles absentmindedly with Gram's necklace. There's a faraway look in her eyes.

"I sure hope its luck holds out," I say, pointing at the Azazule diamond between her fingers.

"You told me it's lucky," Galena replies, "but you never told me why."

I chuckle. I know how stupid the legend sounds, especially in this age of practically infinite scientific achievement. Still, there's something comforting in the superstition. I've repeatedly caught myself taking solace in it during this whole harrowing trip.

"They say the crystal interacts with a parallel universe," I explain. "Specifically, a universe where everything goes right. Then—I dunno—some of that universe's good juju bleeds into ours, or something. It's silly, but my grandpa was a pilot, and the one day he forgot to bring it with him, there was a horrible accident that killed him. Coincidence, I'm sure, but that stuff sticks with you."

Galena loses herself in thought again, then says, "If there *is* a universe where everything goes right, it's the furthest one from ours."

I frown and grab her hand. She doesn't pull it away.

"I know you were dealt some tough cards," I say, "but it's not *all* bad in our own universe."

"I know. *You're* not."

I look away. Her vote of confidence has dredged a buried nugget of guilt to the surface. If we're about to die, I'd rather fess up and do so with a clean conscience.

"Maybe not entirely bad," I concede, "but I'm also not entirely *good*. Galena, I ... made a mistake. Back on Kili'a'an. I saw how happy you were there. I should've told you to stay with them." I hang my head with regret. "But I wanted you with me."

Galena lowers her eyes. She, too, looks ashamed. "Everyone acts on their selfishness sometimes. Even castratae like me."

"After the life you've had, you deserve a bit of selfish," I say. "Any idea yet where you want to end up when this is over?"

She shakes her head. "Not really. Not a black hole, that's for sure. But ... somewhere no one will ever find me."

"Even me?" I ask in a small voice.

"*Especially* you."

I take her other hand. "Even if it's just the two of us forever, I want to be with you, Galena."

"You say that now," she says, "but you'd change your mind. Separated from everything you know and love? Forever? It's a long time." She squeezes my hands. Her pitying stare makes me want to find my own lonely corner of the universe. "I like you, Jerricho. I do. But don't get attached. This doesn't end with us together."

A different voice—not Galena's—startles me. "Is it just me, or does it feel a little awkward in here?" Cay says. He's digging sleep crust from his left eye with his pinky nail.

Galena backs away from me. Her red Vandreejan cheeks are an especially bright shade of ruby.

"I'm hungry," Cay goes on, without missing a beat. "Anyone else hungry? Thought I might whip something up. Call it a last meal, if you want."

"I could eat," I mumble.

Cay opens a cabinet and places a bottle of bourbon emphatically on the countertop.

"Where'd that come from?" I ask. I'm quite certain we drank the last of our booze after Kili'a'an.

"Nabbed it from Mei-Li's bar on my way out," Cay admits. "I also nabbed some of the nicest steaks I've ever seen from her kitchen. She's so loaded, she'll never even notice they're missing."

I crack a smile. So *that's* why we saw him sneaking out of the dining hall.

Galena seems to have forgotten her embarrassment. She beams a contented grin and says, "A last meal with my two favorite men in the galaxy? It sounds *splendid.*"

And that's exactly what it is. Splendid. Around Cay's fancy marble countertops—Or are they granite? I forget how to tell the difference—we stand and feast like royalty. We eat aged ribeyes, medium rare, and guzzle whiskey like there will be no tomorrow. We laugh, because there's nothing else we *can* do in such a tense hour as this. We regale each other with the story our adventure has been so far, as only those who have experienced a true adventure together are able to do. We retrace our star-tracks from Tarrkanna-Rrui to Bellamina—the ups, the downs, the insane and inane—and laugh some more, until six eyes are shining with the tears of mirth.

Most importantly, in our revelry, I push all thoughts of black holes, tidal forces, galactic hurricanes, and, most distressing of all, Galena's resolute rejection far from my mind.

THE *TANTALUS*

27 Days to Payment

"DO OR DIE TIME, boys and girls," Cay announces. "First time I've ever been able to say that."

"Are you kidding me, Cay?" I object, glancing up from my datapad's editing dashboard. "You've literally said that a hundred times on this trip."

"Yeah. But this time I really, *really* mean it."

I'm trying to keep my composure. The *Tantalus'* warning alarm sounded a couple seconds ago. Ten minutes until we ascend up from X-space, which means there's a legitimate possibility I'll be dead in eleven.

If that is indeed the direction we're headed, I won't even have time to send my family a goodbye message once we drop out of X-space. I tried recording one before leaving the Eagle Archipelago, but nothing sounded right. In the end, I deleted them all from the queue. If I never come home, Mei-Li knows enough to tell them how it happened.

"Put your equipment away, Spielberg," Cay says, referencing one of my favorite film pioneers. "Or would you prefer Spike Lee, since you're Black?"

"They're both dead, Cay," I reply. "I'd prefer not being associated with *either* of them right now."

"Fair enough. Either way, shut it down and lock it up. It'd be a shame if all our work was destroyed the moment we come out of X-space."

I return the various pieces of equipment to their respective cases. As I carry the gear to its storage cubby, my eyes briefly meet Galena's.

She looks away. Ever since our "last meal," a frost has been building between us. Even if we manage to survive the upcoming maneuver, I doubt things will return to normal. Our last conversation had an unmistakable tone of finality to it. One I still refuse to accept, and one she resents imposing.

As I stow my equipment, she asks, "What do you want me to do, Cay?"

"Sit next to Jer in the cockpit," he answers. "You're his backup. If he passes out or fumbles things, you have to get that cartridge home."

Three minutes later, Cay is making a fine racket as he secures himself in the mechanical closet, and Galena and I are sitting in the cockpit. Although we're beside each other—sharing the pilot's chair, even—she maintains as much separation as she can. Earlier, she had no problem with our arms, shoulders, and hips brushing against each other. Sometimes, I could have even sworn she was leaning into me.

Now her arms are crossed. Her shoulders are curved out and away from me, and she has slid as far toward the seat's edge as her harness allows. Not only has she slammed the door on any possibility of being with me, but she's also creating literal distance between us.

The QRD, our only hope of survival, passes back and forth between my shaking hands. I'm not sure if I'm sick because I'm on the cusp of death, or whether it's Galena's rejection. Either way, I find myself wishing I had a wastebasket beside me.

I glance at the countdown clock. Two minutes.

Past the windscreen's thick layer of duraglass, X-space froths and melts in its rainbow of colors. As beautiful and mesmerizing as ever, it's hard to imagine this quantum landscape serving as gateway to the hell we'll soon find ourselves in.

"Hey," Galena says, laying her fingertips on the restless QRD. "We only have one of those. Why don't you be *my* backup instead?"

Clutching the cartridge, I shake my head. "No. I got this. I'm fine."

"You're not," she asserts. She grabs the QRD firmly and stares at me. "I don't know exactly what's wrong with you. Whatever it is, I'm guessing it's why Cay is in the mechanical room and you're out here. But I'm not letting you kill yourself and the rest of us because of some misguided sense of male pride. Give me the cartridge. When we drop out of X-space, you yank the other one out of the port, and I'll put this one in. If anything happens to me, then you take over the QRD too."

"And if anything happens to *you*," says PAD, floating down beside me, "I will do my best to finish the job."

I can't help but crack a grin as I say, "I thought you couldn't participate in anything illegal?"

"Preservation of life is my highest priority," he replies. "It may even, at times, supersede a strict adherence to League legislation."

"Then I guess it's settled," I concede. "Galena, Jerricho, PAD. Between the three of us, *someone* will get the job done, right?"

I'm still reluctant, but I turn over the QRD anyway.

"All set back here!" Cay calls from the mechanical closet. "Give me a countdown before we ascend, would you?"

"Sure. I'll give you ten seconds," I holler back.

"Better make it twenty, that way I can finish peeing my pants."

"You're not scared, are you?" I taunt.

"'Course not. But if I'm about to die in the cold of space, I want my crotch nice and warm when I go."

Jokes. Always jokes, even at the end. Somehow, in this moment, I find it comforting.

One minute.

Realizing I may be running out of time for words, I say, "Galena, even if I can't be with you, I want you to know something. I wouldn't have traded these weeks with you for anything. Not for all the fruit on all the Trees of Eden."

I'm surprised to feel the warmth of her cheek against my shoulder. "I'm glad I met you, Jerricho," she whispers, and a single tear dribbles down her cheek.

Then the moment ends. She sits up straight.

Thirty-eight seconds.

The faces of my parents, my siblings, Gram, my old football teammates—even Dirk Plath—materialize in the X-space bubbles outside. But they seem distorted. Faint. I try to remember the colors of their eyes, the shape of their wrinkles, their moles, their smiles, but the harder I try, the less clear they become. Every one of them feels so far away, as if a lifetime were separating us rather than a couple days in X-space.

How long ago it all seems. Have I aged a year since then? Five? Twenty? Will they recognize me when I come home? *If* I come home?

I realize then that it is I, not they, who have changed. A part of me swells with immense pride to know that the Jerricho who left Terra will never return to it, and that a new Jerricho might—but only if the new Jerricho is a much luckier bastard than the old.

My eyes pop open.

"Twenty seconds!" I shout back to Cay.

I wish I had shared some parting words with him. But, on second thought, no. Sap and sentimentality never were our thing. Why start now?

"Nineteen ... eighteen ..."

I look at Galena. She looks back and nods, brimming with far more confidence than what I'm feeling.

"Eleven ... ten ... nine ..."

We face the windscreen. The countdown clock on the monitor. The infinity of X-space. Which, I notice, itself seems changed. Thin and stretched, like a bite of taffy on a warm day.

"Four ... three ... two ... *one!*"

An intense pressure slams against my chest as we ascend out of X-space. That particular sensation is nothing new. It happens every time, which is why we wear a harness. What *is* new is the accompanying impression that something powerful is trying to pop my head off my shoulders *and* yank my feet through the floor at the same time.

A fiery orange halo outlines the windscreen, as it captures refracted light from a source beyond my line of sight. But the rest is black. A darkness so brutal, so complete, it would send trollums shrieking for a nightlight.

Right away, I know what it is. I'm staring into the obsidian eye of our black hole.

Behind me, I hear a terrible crash and clattering of metal on metal.

"Holy shiitake!" Cay yells. Then: "Got one!"

I don't have time to respond. I have my own job to take care of.

Reaching forward, I lock both hands around the nav cartridge lodged in the console port. I expect it to pop out easily—until it doesn't. All this time, we've been using the *Tantalus'* onboard system for our primary X-space mapping, and PAD as our second. I never considered I might have to do more to remove it than pull.

"Shit!" I scream. My fingers are talons, curved and locked around the cartridge.

Galena yells something too. At first I think it's an expletive like mine, until I realize she's pointing. At what, though?

Without another thought, she unbuckles her harness and lurches forward.

PAD beats her to the punch. He presses a button next to the cartridge port, a release mechanism I failed to notice in my panic. The cartridge, which I've been yanking on with all my might, shoots out and smashes against the bridge of my nose. An awful crunching sound accompanies the impact. I assume it's my nose cartilage breaking.

Then I realize it's something far worse.

It's the *Tantalus*. I see the chaos reflected in the windscreen as lightbulbs shatter, one by one, sending showers of sparks raining down from the cabin ceiling.

"Cay!" I scream. It feels like ages since I heard him in the mechanical room. In reality, only six seconds have passed.

"Go! Now!" he screams in reply.

Something—maybe the whole ship—is creaking like an old scabb in an industrial compactor. A godawful shudder accompanies it, as if we're a Christmas present Gemini 2-X is shaking to figure out what's wrapped up inside.

Galena, still free of her harness and with no time to redo it, jams the QRD into the nav port. The *Tantalus* twists violently. A fiery line flashes from one end of the windscreen to the other. Then the ship surges for its descent into X-space.

I'm unsure which part of Galena's body smashes into my head as she hurtles past me. Whatever it is, I'm convinced it's the last thing I'll ever see.

EDEN
– GALACTIC BULGE –

THE *TANTALUS*

I'M FLOATING THROUGH X-space. Again. The foam is warm, relaxing. I wonder whether this is what a baby feels like inside its mother's womb. Yes, that must be where I am. I'm a fetus, and this is my incubation period. There's something attached to my forehead. It's sticky. Umbilical cord? No, it's too cold to be an umbilical cord. I reach up to peel it away. It's rough, sort of bumpy, like a starfish. How'd a starfish find me out here?

Then the Being of X-space speaks. It sounds a lot like Galena. "Leave it there. It'll help you heal faster."

Come to think of it, my head does hurt. I don't see anything among the quantum foam I could have conked it against. Then again, who knows what else might be out here? There *are* starfish, after all.

Speaking of, I'd better pry it off my head before it gets too attached.

"Stop, Jerricho," the Galena-voiced Being says. "Leave the poxxy bandage where it is."

In an instant, my floating-through-X-space hallucination disappears. I'm flat on my back on the *Tantalus'* heated floor, staring up where the ceiling would be if only two faces weren't blocking my view.

"I think you need to watch the X-space safety video again," Cay says. He reaches beneath my shoulders to assist me into a seated position. "You and all objects should be securely fastened whenever you jump. Girlfriends included."

Galena's lips turn downward with momentary displeasure, but she otherwise ignores Cay's comment. She herself didn't walk away unscathed from the X-space jump. Her war badge comes in the form of a laceration running from left temple to earlobe. Rather than a poxxy bandage like mine, her cut is held together by some sort of clear glue.

"What ... happened?" I ask, my vision swimming. "Are we dead? Inside the black hole?"

"No," Galena answers. "Not yet, anyway. When I inserted the QRD, we jumped immediately, like Mei-Li said. I wasn't strapped in and went flying backward. Hit you pretty hard on my way."

"*And* ruined my beautiful sink," Cay adds.

I look at the kitchen. The faucet has snapped clean off.

"I'm lucky to be alive," Galena says. "We all are."

"What about PAD?" I ask. "He was with us too."

"He's fine," Galena answers. "His sensors auto-adjusted him, like normal. He's charging at his docking station."

I don't know why, but hearing that the drone is alright fills me with relief. He's become more than a tool for capturing video footage. Along the way, PAD has turned into a full-fledged member of this ragtag team.

The X-space alarm sounds, startling me and setting off a second alarm inside my chest. I swear, if I ever make it back to Terra, I'm never going interstellar again.

"Oh! Time to take our seats," Cay chirps. "This time, be sure to buckle up."

I do, but instead of going to the cockpit, I crawl to one of the fold-down seats in the rear of the cabin. Galena, my fellow casualty, doesn't join me. She opts instead for a place in the cockpit with Cay.

Can't say *that* doesn't hurt. Then I remember the last words she spoke before the chaos began, the tear sliding down her face, and I feel better. Not much, but a little. That'll have to be enough for now.

I close my eyes, flirting with sleep, until I feel the lurch of the *Tantalus* ascending from X-space. The pit returns to my stomach when I remember what it means.

We're here. Eden. At least, where Eden is supposed to be.

When I glance out the windscreen, I see nothing but stars and space. Could be that when we exited X-space, we did so angled away from the planet. If that's the case, Tantalus will have to perform gravity scans until we lock onto a planetary mass. *If* Eden is here at all.

"Uhhh, Jer?" Cay calls back. "Be a dear and bring your camera, would you? Our audience might want to see this."

Sitting in the cockpit, Cay has a wider field of vision than I do in the back of the cabin. I'm not sure what he sees, but I do as directed. After undoing my harness, I retrieve my camera from storage and hurry into the cockpit.

Galena's unblinking eyes gape straight ahead. Her hand covers her open mouth. Whatever Cay spotted certainly has her attention too.

I set my camera for a wide-angle shot. I want to capture as much of the windscreen as possible. But when I look through my lens at the starfield beyond, I see only more of the same. A black backdrop swirling with a million dots of starlight. Apparently, my knock to the head was worse than I thought, because my vision is still swimming. That must be why I can't spot whatever has so captivated Cay and Galena.

No. Wait. There's nothing wrong with my vision at all. When I look around the cockpit, everything is normal. Galena's face, Cay's face—they're both steady as stones.

A bright flash catches the corner of my eye. When I look back into the starfield, it's gone. Maybe it was never there to begin with.

That's when the question hits me: *Where's the storm?*

Mei-Li mentioned some sort of galactic hurricane. I expected to find a swirling, turbulent mass here, a deadly mouth ready to clamp down on lonely Eden and swallow it whole. But there's nothing of the sort. It's something entirely different. Empty space itself seems to bubble, warping the starfield as if I'm looking at it through a pot of boiling water. It isn't unlike the frothing of X-space—minus the trippy colors, of course.

I cry out. So does Galena. A violet arc of some unknown energy streaks from one end of the windscreen to the other, where it disappears like a snake down its hole. A second arc, crimson, follows the first but in the opposite direction.

"Wake up, PAD," Cay calls back to the drone. "We could use your expert analysis here."

But after a few minutes of observation, which includes a triple demonstration of the violet-crimson arc war, PAD is as much at a loss as the rest of us. "The Anomaly is unlike anything I know of. I am sorry, Cay, but I cannot be of any help in solving this mystery."

"Thanks anyway," Cay mumbles, transfixed.

Another burst of violet branches across the starfield. This time, its flight is interrupted by the silhouette of a dark circle in the foreground. I squint, focusing on the swatch of space where the circle appeared. Now, without anything backlighting it, I can't discern a thing.

"Tantalus," I say, "turn off all lights, interior and exterior."

The lights we have left, anyway, I mentally add, remembering how many shattered during the twelve seconds between X-space jumps.

The ship obeys my command. With no ambient light saturating our eyes, the hidden object emerges from the darkness.

Cay's single, whispered word sounds almost worshipful.

"Eden."

In the hollow of the great boiling bowl, it hangs, a dark sphere against an even darker starscape. The half facing us is illuminated dimly by the black hole's molten halo. It is a lonely and featureless boulder, caught in the last gasps of twilight.

"Tantalus, can you take a scan of the planet? See if there's anything you can learn about it?" I ask.

A minute later, Tantalus shares its findings. "The planet toward which we are heading is unmapped on any League charts. Besides starlight, it seems the unknown planet is illuminated only by the light shed from the black hole's accretion disk. My initial scans indicate that the amount of visible light at the near pole is approximately one-point-two percent of Sol's luminosity on Terra. This percentage diminishes the further one travels from the pole. Nearer to its equator, there also appear to be smaller pockets of light emanating from the planet itself."

Light? Coming *from* the planet, rather than beaming down on it? In my limited experience, that can only mean one thing: there must be people there, creating it.

PAD speaks up next. "I suggest we make a low-orbit lap around the planet. My own sensors will work better at a closer range, and Tantalus will also gather important data."

Nobody objects. I'm nervous we'll pass too close to the hurricane as we sail around the planet's backside, but PAD seems to think we're safe, so we must be.

As we draw nearer to the far pole, Galena says, "If I didn't know better, I'd think Eden was another black hole from this angle."

She's right. Without Gemini's dim light, the back half of Eden is steeped in total darkness. If anything *is* living on the surface, I don't think we'll find it here.

Galena gasps and points. "Oh! Look at that!"

Like club-goers loaded with shimmer, dazzling auroras dance in rings around Eden's pole. Frenetic eddies of blue, bronze, and fuchsia put on a brilliant performance, entertaining what may be their first audience in a thousand years.

"But how can they exist?" I wonder aloud. "Aren't auroras caused by solar particles? There isn't any star here!"

"Yes, but my face is utterly resplendent," Cay says. "I like to think all planets would react this way when I fly by."

"The Anomaly is emitting a strange energy," PAD informs us. "Massive quantities of heat and radiation, not unlike what our own Sol emits."

"But ... *how?*" Galena asks.

"That, I'm afraid, is a mystery I cannot answer," says PAD. "I do believe, based both on my readings and the intensity of those auroras, it is highly unlikely that this side of the planet is able to harbor life. If it does, it would have to be silicon-based rather than biological. Even that would be unlikely."

I gulp. I remember the last time I encountered silicon life forms. It's an experience I don't wish to repeat.

"How big is it? The planet?" Cay asks.

Tantalus answers this question. "The unknown planet is slightly larger than Terra's Moon."

"What about its composition? Its atmosphere?" I inquire.

"Atmospheric readings suggest a mixture of gases breathable for both Terran and Vandreejan beings," says Tantalus. "I have not yet completed enough scans to provide an accurate composition of the unknown planet's surface."

"What's the temperature like?" asks Galena.

"It is a curious thing, especially with all the energy from the Anomaly," says PAD, "but the temperature seems relatively stable at twenty-one degrees Celsius, perfectly safe for most beings within the Galactic League."

"Even without a star?" I reply. Nothing about this makes sense. So little sense, in fact, that even PAD doesn't bother trying to explain things further.

After rounding Eden's far pole, we curve back toward the black hole. From this distance, the collapsed star looks harmless, an obsidian marble ringed with fire. It seems almost silly to think it nearly killed us a couple hours ago.

Now it's Cay's turn to point excitedly. "Are you seeing that? Up that way. There's some kind of bluish light."

"PAD, are you able to scan for biological life from this distance?" I ask.

"I am," the drone replies, "and it is tremendous. The whole upper hemisphere seems to be a blanket of life. But the greatest cluster of biological material is overwhelmingly concentrated around the blue light."

"And if there's life on Eden ..." I begin.

"... it means Sal could be on Eden," Cay finishes.

The blue light, at first a distant haze, becomes brighter and more distinct as we orbit toward it. From this height, we still can't determine the source of the light, but whatever it is covers an area twelve kilometers in diameter—according to Tantalus' readings, anyway. Like one of Terra's large cities, the pinpricks of light are faint and scattered near the fringe. Closer to its brilliant center, they increase in density and radiance.

"Tantalus, are all the exterior lights still off?" Cay asks.

"Affirmative," the ship replies.

"Good. Keep it that way. And keep scanning as you find us a safe place to land. *Outside* the perimeter of the lights, please."

"In the dark?" I ask uncertainly.

Cay nods. "You're finally getting that stealth landing you always wanted."

EDEN

"GOT YOUR CAMERAS READY?"

We're standing at the bottom of the boarding ramp in near darkness. Eden's springy turf is fresh beneath my bootheels, and a bouquet of earthy perfumery cascades into and out of my nostrils. Over the past weeks, I've introduced myself to a half-dozen new worlds, yet none struck me as so alien, so truly otherworldly as the one greeting me now. I'm caught in such a state of sheer mystification, I hardly register—and entirely ignore—Cay's question when he first asks it.

"Hey!" says Cay, snapping his fingers. "Drool over it later. Get your cameras ready."

We do. I position Galena for a secondary angle closer to Cay, then tell PAD to do his thing taking all the aerial shots he can. With Cay standing in front of the illuminated ramp, in stark contrast to the environing darkness, I hit *RECORD* and call, "Action!"

Cay begins. "Our search for the galaxy's most exotic foods has led us to some dangerous but extraordinary places. We tussled with frostbite and betrayal on Tarrkanna-Rrui. We dove deep into the deadly mines of Petra 7, where we nearly became trollum chow. We harvested the exquisite Encelas mushrooms of Nabishna and experienced the heartbreak of losing our vivi-fa'ool eggs, while gaining instead a handful of important life lessons. But no program series bearing the words *Galactic Eats* would truly be complete without an attempt on the mother of them all, the holy grail, the El Dorado of culinary conquistadors across the galaxy. I'm speaking, of course, about the fruit of the Trees of Eden."

I pause Cay, telling him to take slow steps toward me when he continues. I likewise instruct Galena to move fluidly in step with him. Then I give Cay the nod, and he goes on.

"Some fifty Terran years ago, my grandmother, Sal Cantore, disappeared in search of Eden. If the myths are true, perhaps she discovered the fruit but became so entranced by it, she decided she could never be parted from it again. Or, as seems more likely, she perished on her daring quest. Today, we're about to learn the answer to one of the galaxy's most high-profile disappearances ... and one of its greatest mysteries."

Cay spreads his arms, like he's embracing the gloom that surrounds him. "Because that's where we are now: Eden. Following a set of ancient coordinates provided by an anonymous source, we have just landed on the fabled world, a planet shrouded in enigma and legend for thousands of years. Will we find my grandmother here? And will we find the Trees of Eden? Or will we discover that both are now nothing more than legends of their own?" He clasps his hands together, as if pleading with his viewers to accept his gracious invitation. "Join me for the adventure of a lifetime on our season finale of *Galactic Eats Reheated.*"

And ... cut. Damn, he's good. Even I have goosebumps after hearing that.

"What now, boss?" I ask.

Cay checks his hip, making certain the pistol he swiped from Turf is still there, as he says, "We find the Trees, of course." Loud enough for PAD to hear from overhead, he adds, "I want cameras rolling nonstop. My eye in the sky doesn't blink, got it, PAD? Anything could happen here on out, and I don't want to miss a *second* of it."

Even though it's dark as night and we're treading unfamiliar terrain, there's no question which direction we need to travel. The blue glow beckons us forward like moths to a bug zapper—though I do hope this light leads to a happier outcome. Dark, brushy plants, as tall as a full-blooded Rouzh, obscure our view of whatever lies ahead. Of course, we could ask PAD to share what he sees as he hovers above us, but no one does. For once, we three landbound beings are of the same mind. Like teenagers on a date, teetering on the cusp of their first kiss, we don't want anyone *describing* the moment to us. We want to discover it for ourselves. We want our own eyes, our own senses, to bathe in each thrilling moment of our adventure's climax. Whether for better, or for worse.

"What are those?" Galena asks, breaking the silence of our enchantment.

On the ground, not far ahead, are filaments of light. *Blue* light, not much wider than a human hair. Like vines, they creep along the ground, luminous capillaries reaching toward us from the denser region of light ahead.

I film Cay as he kneels to examine the glowing tendrils. He squeezes one between his thumb and forefinger. It offers only slight resistance as he pulls it up from the ground. With it come more attached tendrils, so that he looks like someone holding a segment of glowing spiderweb.

"I think they're tiny roots," he tells the camera. "Like those on the very bottom of a weed you've just pulled from your garden."

Gently, he lays the fragile strands back on the mossy soil. As we continue onward, weaving among the bushes, the network of glowing roots becomes denser, and many of them thicker. By some strange impulse, I avoid walking on them, like I'm playing a near-impossible game of "Don't Step on the Crack." I've never cared about hurting roots before, but for some reason, stepping on these feels akin to dancing on grave markers. There's a sacred aura about them, even if they are nothing more than roots.

The further we go, the thinner the brush forest becomes. After an hour hiking through the foliage labyrinth, we at last break free of its confines.

Cay, in the lead, inhales a deep breath and does not let it out. Galena and I do the same. We're petrified with seraphic awe.

They remind me of stately willows. Willows enhanced by an angel's brushstrokes, painted with a celestial incandescence. Running from top to bottom along their trunks are thick bands of pulsing blue. The trees' drooping branches are dappled with glowing teardrops of the same color, studded among feathery leaves of silver. The trees nearest to the grove's perimeter are the smallest, about the size of a modest backyard willow. Further in, the trees look taller, older, their skin ridged and knotty.

"There they are," Cay says, his voice hardly a whisper. He speaks not as a showman for a camera, but as someone so in awe, he must convince himself what he's seeing is real. "The Trees of Eden."

"All the light we saw from above ... is coming from the *trees*," Galena gasps, overcome with amazement.

We set course for the nearest of them, but before we reach those first outliers, Cay stops. Facing the camera, he crinkles his nose and asks, "Anyone else smell that?"

I take another step forward, inhaling deeply through my nose. At once, I regret doing so.

"What *is* that?" I ask, recoiling. "Smells like something died."

Galena raises her arm, pointing ahead. "I think it's coming from there."

Against the greater radiance of the trees behind it, we didn't see the tiny sapling at first. It's only a few paces away, growing atop a low, misshapen mound, where it shimmers with the faintest of light.

Cay steps cautiously toward it. Before he reaches the sapling, he stops abruptly and says, "Jerricho wins the guessing game."

"What do you mean?" I ask, lowering my camera.

"It's a corpse," he says. "Not human, based on the size of it. But someone died here, and this tree is taking advantage of the body's nutrients."

"What kind of people don't bury their dead?" Galena asks. Her intense Vandreejan eyes remain locked upon the heap of rotting flesh.

"Not sure," Cay answers, "but I'm guessing we'll find out before this is over."

Choosing a wide berth around the sapling and its fertilizer, Cay continues toward the grove. "Let's keep moving. There's no fruit on this little guy, and all this talk of corpse-eating trees is making me hungry."

THE OUTER GROVE

THE NEXT TREE we come to isn't much taller than my parents' scabb. Although it is undeniably breathtaking, a quick glance at its branches reveals it to be a fruitless beauty.

My heart sinks. "What if the fruit isn't in season?" I wonder aloud. We never considered the possibility that the Trees of Eden might bear fruit intermittently, like those across most of the galaxy. How stupid are we?

"One empty tree doesn't mean much," Cay answers. "Besides, this one's shrimpy compared to the others further in. Maybe it's too young to bear fruit."

The next few trees aren't much bigger but are just as barren. With each empty one we find, I feel a little sicker.

Cay remains optimistic. "Eden doesn't orbit a star, which means it might not have regular growing seasons like Terra. We'll find some fruit, don't worry. We came too far *not* to."

The further we delve into the grove, the closer to one another the trees grow. But they aren't the only things rising from the ground here. Scattered among them are squat, boxy objects not much taller than me. Wisps of smoke drift skyward from some of them.

"They're huts!" Cay whispers excitedly to the camera. "Not only have we discovered the Trees of Eden, but we've also found proof of civilization, some sort of community here on the lost planet."

Even though Cay doesn't say it outright, I decipher what he's thinking from his tone. If there's a community here, it means his grandmother might be here too.

Despite this discovery, the forest is eerie with silence. The huts' residents must all be indoors, because there isn't a soul milling about the area.

All for the best. We can knock on doors looking for Sal later. Our first priority is the fruit. Furtively, we snake our way through the hushed trees and huts, diving deeper into the grove.

At last, we strike gold. A tree, twice as tall as those before it, whose supple branches are heavy with pear-shaped fruits the size of small plums. Like the leaves, the fruit's outer skin is silver, interlaced with dainty filaments of bioluminescent cobalt.

Further along, I see that the trees grow larger still. But there's no need to go on. This one has what we came for. Half, anyway.

"Film me finding and eating the fruit," Cay says. "Then we'll look for Sal."

Glancing around, I still don't see anybody else. Strange, considering how many huts we've passed. I would have guessed at least one restless soul might be wandering the grove.

It all seems too easy. I'm sure there's something more going on, some hidden piece we aren't seeing.

Heart racing, I position Galena, then roll my own camera.

Cay speaks. "We've finally found a mature tree, one absolutely loaded with fruit, and I've gotta say—just look at how exquisite they are!" He holds up a heavy branch to give his viewers a close-range peek at Eden's ripe fruit. "These silver beauties are rumored to be so intoxicating, anyone who tastes even a single bite will never willingly be parted from them again."

With little effort, he plucks one from the tree and displays it on his open palm.

"I'm about to learn once and for all whether the legend is fact or fiction."

His fingers close around the fruit. He raises it to his nose. Shuts his eyes. Inhales an overdrawn whiff of its fragrance. Looks at it again. Turns it in his hands. Opens his mouth.

In that moment, I realize I don't want him to eat it. I don't know why, but this feels wrong. Cheap and degrading. Like pissing in a gold toilet or mixing century-old Lagavulin with soda.

Yet we've come so far. Endured so much. There's no way I can stop him now. Not after everything we've done to arrive at this moment. The biggest moment of his—and, if I'm being honest, my—life.

I can't stop him. But someone else can.

"Don't," a commanding voice calls out.

Cay lowers the fruit. Together with me and Galena, he turns sideways, alarmed.

A crowd of beings, perhaps two dozen in number, has emerged from the forest to surround us. All are dressed in simple, dark robes—if dressed at all—and wear braided wreaths of silver twigs on their heads. None of them seem particularly threatening or hostile. Still, it's clear from their stony expressions that they mean business.

A male alien, Luatian like my most recent girlfriend Natania, steps toward us. He's older, with feathery, graying hair and ample wrinkles around his eyes.

"Who are you? Why have you come?" he asks, eyeing up my camera.

"This is Jerricho," Cay says, jerking a thumb at me, "and she's Galena."

"And you?" the Luatian says.

"My name is Cay Cantore. I came for the Trees of Eden."

A hushed murmur breaks out among the crowd. They're surprised, and I can't blame them. It must not be an everyday occurrence that they receive visitors to their planet.

The Luatian raises a hand to quiet them, and they shut up at once. He extends the same hand, palm up, toward Cay. "Give me the Eden apple," he says. "No arguments."

Cay frowns. Reluctantly, he hands over his prized fruit.

"Your cooperation is appreciated," the Luatian tells him. "Now, come with me."

With those words, the rest of the mob closes in around us, leaving us no choice but to accompany them deeper into the grove.

THE EMPRESS GROVE
26 Days to Payment

"WHERE ARE YOU taking us?" Cay demands after the first minute of our forced march.

"Patience, Cay Cantore," the Luatian replies. "It is simpler to show you than to tell you."

"Can you at least tell us your name?" Cay asks.

"I am Wessel, one of the elders of the Children of Eden."

As we hike deeper into the grove, I rest my camera on my shoulder. Cay gave strict orders to film everything, and for once, I'm inclined to listen. There isn't a moment of this magical place I ever want to forget.

In case something happens to my camera, it's reassuring to know I'm not the only one filming. PAD must have hidden himself when he detected the approaching posse, because he's nowhere in sight.

Good robot. Use the trees as cover and keep filming.

Unlike Nabishna or Kili'a'an, with their thick undergrowth and tangling vines, the going is fairly effortless here. Aside from a few exposed roots, whose lambent glow makes them plenty easy to avoid, it's as painless as walking through the Coral Sands Butterfly Oasis.

It's obvious as we go that we're entering older layers of the forest. The trees are ever taller, some two or three times the diameter of those on the grove's outer edges. Their trunks are scarred and gnarled, thick husks made rugged with the abandonment of their youth. The light they cast is different too. They glow more silver than blue, dripping with the soft radiance of a nonexistent moon.

"This is the Empress Grove," Wessel informs us. "The oldest trees on all of Eden grow here."

"How old are they?" Galena asks. Her voice is hushed with reverence for the wizened trees.

"Nobody knows. Some say as old as the Universe itself."

"That's impossible," Cay scoffs.

"Yes. But the Universe is an impossible place," Wessel replies without missing a beat.

Ahead, there is an abrupt break in the trees.

"Is that the end of the forest?" I ask.

Our guide shakes his head. "No. Up there is the beginning."

"The beginning of what?" Galena inquires.

"Of *everything*."

I flash Cay a look of concern. He returns it with a goofy "hell-if-I-know" look of his own.

It seems with each step we take on this lost planet, we discover a deeper layer of amazement than the step before. From glowing root tendrils to glowing trees, from Eden apples to the Empress Grove, we're awash in a sea of magnificence, drowning in wave after wave of unrivaled splendor.

When we arrive at the forest clearing, we stop.

I'm speechless, choking on another wave of Eden's marvels.

"Oh ... *my*," Galena gasps. Her Vandreejan eyes sparkle like amethysts.

Wessel smiles. "We call her the Matriarch."

In the center of the clearing, draped from crown to root in supple branches, is a monolithic tree which dwarfs all those behind us. Unlike the silvery blue fruits of its younger siblings, those adorning the Matriarch are burnished fists of blazing amber.

Near the tree's base, nestled among a mammoth tangle of exposed roots, is another hut. In its doorway stands a woman, the first human we've encountered on this mystical planet. She approaches us at once. Her piercing green eyes jump from me, to Cay, to Galena, as she examines the three strangers to her grove. There are a few gray streaks in her otherwise loam-brown hair, and the beginnings of crow's feet have begun creeping toward her temples. But I would bet both my kidneys the woman walking our way isn't a day over forty.

Still, there isn't a trace of doubt in my mind who she is. After all, I've analyzed her work via the *Tantalus'* program monitor many times over the past weeks. On the fabled planet Eden, alive and well—and still dazzlingly beautiful, I might add—is Sal Cantore.

THE COURTYARD OF THE MATRIARCH

"I CAN'T BELIEVE I'm saying this," I whisper aside to Cay, "but—damn!—your grandma's still got it."

"Dude, now you know how I feel about *your* grandma," Cay whispers back.

I scowl at him. "Don't you get it, Cay? That's the most gorgeous *eighty*-year-old I've ever seen!"

"Cantores age well," Cay says. He flourishes a hand at himself. "I give you Exhibit A."

"Enough of all the whispering," Sal says, eyeing us suspiciously. "Who are you? And how did you come here?"

Cay must be as shocked as I am to hear her voice, the same one he's heard on old *Galactic Eats* episodes his whole life, because he stammers out an uncharacteristically befuddled response. "I—uh—we came here on our ship."

Sal crosses her arms and glares at him. "A ship? You don't say! What I mean is, *how* did you find this place?"

"With a lot of luck," Cay coyly answers.

Sal frowns. "Fine. Don't tell me. At least give me your names."

Cay gestures at me and says, "This is Jerricho. He's my sidekick."

"Cameraman," I correct. "And director, and producer."

Ignoring me, Cay continues. "And this is our castrata friend, Galena."

Galena gives Sal a reverent nod. I wouldn't have picked her for the starstruck sort, but she seems awed standing in the presence of a galactic celebrity.

Cay steps forward. He lays a hand on his chest and looks his long-lost grandmother straight in the eye.

"And my name is Cay. Cay ... Cantore."

Sal's jaw drops. "What did you say?" she whispers.

"Cay Cantore," he repeats. "Surprise, Grandma!"

It's Sal's turn to stutter with shock. "You're—you're Marq's—"

"*Was*, unfortunately," Cay says. "Marq died a few weeks ago. Cancer."

"Liver disease," I remind him.

"Right. Liver disease."

Sal raises a hand to her mouth. She gasps back the tears forming in her emerald eyes. "My baby is dead? Oh, that seems ... impossible! He was so tiny when I left."

"He got bigger," Cay says. "If it makes you feel any better, he loved food too, like you. Ran his own restaurant, right up to the day he died. You would've been proud of him."

Sal sighs, regaining her composure. "I always wondered whether I might see him again. Now I have an answer." Looking again at Cay, she gives him the same million-dollar smile that won over so many adoring fans. "But if he's left me such a handsome grandson, it must mean he at least found happiness in his life."

I'm glad Cay doesn't correct her.

"And seeing you," Sal says, wrapping her arms around Cay, "has brought happiness to mine."

Sal holds him close for a long moment. When she breaks their embrace, she turns to address the surrounding crowd. "It's okay. He isn't a threat. This is my grandson!"

"When he spoke his name, I imagined you two might be connected somehow," Wessel says. "May I leave him here in your keeping?"

"Of course," says Sal. "We have plenty of catching up to do. *Decades'* worth, I should think."

The Luatian elder nods and motions to the crowd. At once, the black-robed beings amble away and disappear among the trees.

Sal sets course for her hut.

"Please, join me for a cup of tea," she calls over her shoulder. "And keep those cameras rolling. It'll feel nice being on film again."

SAL CANTORE'S HOME

SAL IS BENT OVER a shallow counter, dispensing dried leaves into four polished stone mugs. On the wood-burning stove beside her, a tin kettle sends up tendrils of steam.

Cay, Galena, and I are on the floor of the one-room hut, sitting cross-legged around a low table.

"Technically, this isn't tea," Sal informs us. "It's night rose, a plant that grows out in the wildlands. Personally, I think it's much better than tea."

As someone who has never acquired much taste for tea, I'm glad to hear it.

Sal pours a measure of scalding water from the kettle into four cups. After she sets them on the table, she lowers herself onto the floor to sit beside Galena.

"Sorry for asking," I say, unable to contain my curiosity any longer, "but how can you still be so—you know—*young?*"

Sal places her hands on her hips and shimmies seductively. "That's the miracle of time-shift," she says with a laugh.

"Time *what?*" says Cay.

"Time-shift," repeats Sal. "Though I suppose the technical term is *time dilation*. Time isn't constant everywhere. It flows differently, especially near high-mass objects."

"High-mass objects," Galena mutters, putting the pieces together more quickly than me and Cay. "Like a black hole."

"Exactly," Sal confirms. "Because of Eden's location orbiting the black hole, time moves slower here. Relative to the rest of the galaxy, anyway."

I feel queasy. PAD mentioned time dilation when he explained the reasoning behind X-space layovers. At the time, I had no intention of coming within kissing distance of a black hole, so I dismissed and forgot the information.

Now I wish I had paid more attention.

Cay and I exchange morbid glances—and gulps—over the unfortunate implications of Sal's revelation. We thought we had twenty days and change remaining until the Malvudians' deadline. But we just executed a U-turn dangerously close to Gemini 2-X. Even now, we're living in slow motion while the rest of the galaxy zooms onward. For anyone in populated space, Axon automatically adjusts clocks to keep a galactic standard time. But way out here? Who knows how many ticks remain on our countdown.

"Don't worry," says Sal, noting our pained expressions. "You'll lose a few weeks—maybe a month—but you'll be back home before too much of the galaxy has passed you by."

"I'm afraid it's a teaspoon more complicated than that," says Cay. "We have a bit of a deadline."

"Deadline? Does it have anything to do with those cameras?" Sal asks.

"You know what they say about good ideas," Cay replies. "They just get better with age! Meet the production crew of *Galactic Eats Reheated.*"

Sal grins. "Clever. Very clever. And ballsy, bringing the show all the way here. You didn't eat any Eden apples yet, did you?"

"No," Cay answers, shaking his head. "Your mob stopped me before I could take a bite."

Sal's relief is evident. "Good. That means I still have a chance to share my story with the galaxy." Staring across the table at her grandson, she takes a sip of her night rose non-tea. "But let's hear *your* story first."

SAL CANTORE'S HOME

Unknown Days to Payment

"THAT'S QUITE THE TALE," Sal says. She doesn't sound impressed. "You should know better than to slip into bed with the Malvudians. Although, to be fair, I've slipped beneath the covers with a few unsavory characters too. Metaphorically *and* literally."

Cay, who just finished recounting the abridged version of our story, scrunches his face in disgust. "Dad never knew who his father was. I don't have any Malvudian in my family tree, do I?"

Sal chuckles and says, "No, nothing like that. Though in hindsight, there are one or two I'd happily replace with a Malvudian."

Four cups, emptied of their night rose, sit cold in front of us. It was damn delicious, and I'd kill for a second round, but Sal seems too engrossed in catching up with her grandson.

"So?" Cay says after a moment's silence. "Aren't you going to tell us *your* story?"

Sal nods at me. I understand at once that she wants me to fire up my camera. I do, and her demeanor changes at once. She's not just Sal Cantore anymore. She's the Eats Queen, whose on-camera personality created a legend long before she became lost to the stars.

"Like Mei-Li told you, I made the journey to Eden alone. I was kicking my own chance of survival square in the taint, but I couldn't endanger my crew. My *family*."

She speaks with the same easy, crude manner Cay uses. Like grandma, like grandson.

"If it was so risky, why come at all?" Cay asks. "Why leave your baby behind, knowing you might never see him again?"

"I put it off for a while, convinced myself Marq and my show were enough." Sal sighs like she's reliving the struggle all over again. "In the end, I knew I couldn't leave such an epic stone unturned. Couldn't bear not knowing whether Eden and these trees were real. So I made the terrible decision to make the trip myself. Alone."

"But how did you do it?" Cay wonders aloud. "Switching the fuel rod *and* the nav cartridge at the same time was a job that took all three of us. Even then, we were only seconds away from becoming black hole food. How'd you manage all on your own?"

"I didn't."

"You didn't? Then, how did you get here at all?"

"When I ascended up from X-space, I only switched the nav cartridge. I knew I'd run out of fuel before reaching Eden and pop back out of X-space again. I just hoped it wouldn't happen in the middle of a star or the accretion disk. *Or* still too close to the black hole itself. When I did eventually run out of fuel and was forced out of X-space, I simply changed the fuel rod and kept going."

"But how?" I ask. I know I'm the cameraman. It's improper for me to butt in like this. But her story makes no sense, and I need an answer. "Traveling through X-space only works from a specific entry point to a specific exit. Wherever you popped out, you'd need a whole new system map to reenter X-space. Axon doesn't reach these parts of the galaxy, though, so how'd you do it?"

Sal gives me the same lopsided grin I've seen a thousand times on Cay's face. With a playful gleam in her virid eyes, she says, "That might've been my most ingenious idea of all. I figured the ship's onboard computer could detect an anomaly as large and powerful as the supposed hurricane, and I was right. From there, I simply traveled at light speed. I figured if the only way to round the corner and double back toward Eden's backside was by stopping *that* close to a black hole, Eden itself couldn't be terribly far. It only took me a couple days at light speed to reach it, even less than I expected. I admit, I was damn proud of myself when I arrived here with more than enough fuel for the return journey."

"Then why did you stay?" Cay asks. Suddenly, he both looks and sounds agitated. "Why didn't you come back?"

Sal raises an eyebrow. "Excuse me?"

"Why didn't you come back?" Cay asks again. "Even if the Eden apple was better than all the galaxy's most delicious food rolled into one giant piece of cosmic sushi, you still had a baby waiting at home for you. *My dad* was waiting for you, not to mention Mei-Li and your crew. Why. Didn't. You. Come. Back?"

Sal's gaze drops to the table. For a moment, I'm convinced she's fighting back tears. Then she stares gently at Cay and says, "There's more to the story."

At once, she stands. "Come outside with me."

THE MATRIARCH

Unknown Days to Payment

"WHEN I ARRIVED on Eden," Sal says, "I made for this tree right away. The Matriarch."

She rests her fingers delicately on the aged tree's hoary hide. Inside the curtain of its fruit-laden boughs, we're immersed in light and history as old as the galaxy.

"I spotted her during my orbital scans," Sal goes on to explain. "There was something obviously different about her, something I had to have, and I wouldn't settle for any of the lesser trees."

She strides from the trunk to the Matriarch's drooping branches and plucks one of its fruits. The Eden apple glows in her fist like the coal of a crackling bonfire broken loose from its brothers. She raises it to her nose, appraising it with a strange blend of adoration and hate.

Sal speaks like someone detached from her present self, as she retreads regretted memories. "The she-Andalyte who lived here warned me not to eat, but I didn't pay attention. So close to my dream, I was far beyond listening to anybody."

Casually, Sal bites into the Eden apple. She chews it. Swallows it. Scowls, and callously tosses the rest aside.

"When I was finished eating—and filming the bit, of course—I made for my ship again. But I hadn't even reached the edge of this clearing when the spasms started ripping through my stomach. That's when I learned why no one ever leaves after they've eaten the fruit of Eden. Because they *can't*."

"What do you mean, 'they can't'?" Galena, unblinking, asks in a hushed voice.

"The trees don't let you," Sal explains, simply but cryptically. "Once you've eaten, they have an everlasting claim over you. You see, when a person eats the fruit, its microscopic seeds disperse throughout the eater. Far smaller than those of any other fruit, the seeds flow through your blood. Embed themselves in your muscles, your organs. Anywhere they can find. And every one of those seeds maintains a bond with its parent tree. Like a mother who doesn't want her children straying too far from her watchful eye, who will even kill someone that tries stealing them away, the Trees of Eden do the same with their seeds. Anyone who eats the fruit and leaves the proximity of their parent tree will be killed by the seeds within them. They activate, growing like weeds in double time as they feed on their host and devour them."

"Is that what happened to the dead guy we passed on our way here?" I ask.

Sal frowns and shakes her head. "No. That was probably Perri. He was a lovely Xilenian and a good friend. The seeds also sprout whenever a host dies. We move them beyond the edge of the grove so we don't have to watch new trees grow from their decomposing bodies."

I've noticed that Cay has become pensive. Morose, even. He has remained silent, letting Galena and I ask the questions.

Now he speaks, measured and thoughtful, like a man deliberating whether to cut off his right leg or his left. "If I eat the fruit, I can never leave," he calmly asserts. "I'd have to stay here forever too."

"You wondered why I never came home to your dad," Sal says. "This is why. This ... *damned* fruit is the reason why. And because of the galactic storm on one side of Eden and the black hole on the other, I couldn't export a transmission either. I was never able to share my story with the galaxy. Was never able to tell my little Marq I loved him. Was never able to explain why I'd never be coming home. Since that day, I haven't left this clearing. The younger trees allow their eaters a bit more freedom, but this old bitch likes to keep her offspring uncomfortably close."

"I'm ... so sorry," Galena says. Her eyes are glassy.

"It's my own fault," Sal says with a shrug. "When you fly too close to the sun, you shouldn't be surprised when your wings melt away."

"You've been here, all on your own since then?" I ask.

"Not on my own," Sal answers. "The Matriarch is something of a place of worship for the Children of Eden. A place of reverence, anyway. Many come here daily. As the Keeper, I always have company. It's not so bad a place to live, either. Eden is always the same temperature, and there's never bad weather. Between the trees' fruit and the local wildlife—more than you'd imagine, if you can believe it—there's plenty of food for everyone. All in all, once you get used to it, it's not a bad life. Peaceful. Uncomplicated. In a way, it's what everyone's looking for, isn't it?"

I can't help noticing Galena's eyes as Sal describes life on Eden. They look exactly as they did during our first days on Nabishna, when she was finally free of the *Tantalus*.

"So," says Cay, "in order to eat the rarest food in the galaxy, I'll have to stay here forever. Or I can leave, be free, but live out my days never knowing the taste of an Eden apple."

Sal shakes her head. "It's not like that at all, actually. The Eden apple—it's not what everyone thinks it is. You're as mistaken as I used to be."

If Sal was planning to go on, she doesn't get the chance. At that moment, an electric tremble fills the air, paired with the unmistakable whine of spacecraft engines.

Four heads snap to attention, scanning the perpetually dark sky for the source of the noise. It doesn't take long to spot it. A sleek, quicksilver vessel, illuminated partly by its own exterior lighting and partly by the Trees of Eden, descends toward the planet's surface at breakneck speed.

Each more spiteful than the other, Cay and I speak the same hated name together.

"Geiger!"

EDEN

Unknown Days to Payment

WE STREAK THROUGH the grove, Cay leading me and Galena in a footrace toward the *Royal Austrian*. As we come to the outskirts of the forest, we see Gustav Geiger's massive vessel. It has sacrificed at least one of Eden's smaller trees and a handful of huts in its landing. We're just in time to watch two of the ship's boarding ramps drop to the earth.

"How'd he find us?" Cay wonders aloud.

"Must've had a second tracking device," I suggest. Somehow, though, I know that isn't the answer.

"Or he got to Mei-Li," says Cay. "There *was* only one set of nav cartridges when I swiped them that night. Plus, we saw the *Royal Austrian* hanging out in Eagle Archipelago airspace."

Chaos is the only apt description for what happens next. A platoon of armed beings, twenty strong, races down the ramps and into the frantic crowd of Eden's residents. The soldier in charge alternates between shouting orders to his own underlings and shouting them at the villagers.

I recognize him at once. The white-blond hair is a dead giveaway.

Drum Paetski. Didn't like him when we met onboard the *Royal Austrian*. Certainly don't like him now.

A few lasers sizzle upward through the atmosphere. Warning shots, probably, but their effect is immediate. The Children of Eden closest to the soldiers give themselves up at once, raising their hands, paws, flippers—and whatever other appendages they might have—in surrender.

Even as some of Eden's luckier citizens flee past us into the forest, we run toward Geiger's army.

I'm surprised to realize I'm unafraid. Perhaps after surviving lethal temperatures, murderous trollums, and a black hole, there's little I'll be afraid of ever again.

Drum Paetski notices us approaching and sneers. He raises his firearm, a long-barreled rifle, and aims it at Cay.

"Look who survived Gemini!" he shouts. "You just lost me a hefty bet. Unless I shoot ya and bury ya before—"

"Well done, Mr. Paetski," an unctuous voice calls down from the *Royal Austrian's* boarding ramp.

Glancing over his shoulder, Drum growls, "Too late. Lucky you."

Gustav Geiger is wearing ornate show robes of emerald green, frilled with embroidered gold leaves. A victorious smile plastered across his smug face, he strides down the ramp. His producer, Wenlyn o' gla Myrn, flanks him with a quartet of camerapeople. She's already barking orders, pointing in every which direction as she stations them for the appropriate shots.

A few steps behind them, carrying a leather satchel and looking like she wished she'd stayed on the ship, is Ameliana. Scanning the confusion, she spots us and casts a worried grin at Cay.

From among the captive Children of Eden, a familiar voice says, "What is the meaning of this?"

It's Wessel, the Luatian who led us to Sal.

"Perhaps I should ask you the same question," Geiger replies. He sweeps an arm toward the luminescent trees. "What is the meaning of *this?* Of hiding such treasures? Keeping them all to yourselves?"

Wessel spits at Geiger's feet. "We do not hide them. Eden hides herself. Only the very fortunate—or *un*fortunate—ever look upon her."

"Be that as it may," says Geiger, "I do require your assistance. Show me to the tree, the one I saw before we landed."

"Why should I, or anyone here, assist a destroyer like you? Find the tree yourself."

Geiger sighs wearily. "I had hoped we might avoid these sorts of unpleasantries. Truly, it isn't my style. Alas, sometimes blood must be shed."

With a sideways glance at Drum, Geiger gives a lazy flick of his wrist.

One burst of laser fire later, Wessel is flat on his back. His limbs are splayed at awkward angles, and a fresh hole sizzles in his forehead.

"Geiger!" Cay cries. He rushes forward amid the terrified cries of the other hostages. "What do you think you're doing?"

"Ah, Mr. Cantore!" Geiger exclaims, clasping his hands together. "I guessed it was your ship we passed over during our descent. How comforting to know you also survived your journey here."

Geiger motions again, and Cay stops in his tracks. He's staring down the barrel of Drum's rifle.

"How the hell did you find us here?" Cay demands. "We got rid of your tracking device after Nabishna. Even if you put another one on our ship, it shouldn't have worked to lead you all the way out here."

Geiger chuckles, shaking his head in disbelief. "Tracking device? Who would use such a thing? They're far too unreliable. Besides, you're right, this is far outside Axon's transmitting range."

His gaze shifts away from Cay. At first, I think he's looking at me. Then I realize he's looking at the person *next* to me.

"I find that people are much more reliable than tracking devices," Geiger says, "just so long as you're using the right tool. And, I must say, well done, Galena."

One invisible fist slams into my gut, while another seizes my heart. My fingers, hand, and forearm lose what feeble strength they had left, and my camera drops to the hard ground with a sickening crunch and tinkling of shattered glass.

I turn to face Galena. I'm hardly able to muster the words I speak. "It was *you?*"

Galena doesn't acknowledge me. Her eyes are locked upon Gustav Geiger, her ruler, as she strides forward to kneel at his feet.

"I live to serve," she says, her once lively voice replaced by a cultish monotone.

Cay directs his rage at Geiger. "We rescued her from *you* on Tarrkanna-Rrui?"

"Oh, I don't know if *rescued* is the proper word," says Geiger. "*Obtained* would be more accurate. After Jonas's assistant let it slip that you were first going to Tarrkanna-Rrui, I went there ahead of you and bribed a customs official to tip me off whenever you arrived. Then I staged Galena outside your ship with a couple members of my security team and ordered them to create a scene until you came to her aid. All she had to do was sell the ruse, and it seems she did a beautiful job of it."

"You still couldn't have tracked her all the way here," says Cay. "Even Nabishna would have been a stretch. It's at the edge of Axon's range."

Geiger taps his chin like someone deep in thought. "If only there had been some way she could remain in communication with me. Then she would be able to share your exact moves, even before you made them ...”

“The circlet controller,” I mumble miserably, speaking more to Galena than Geiger. “You told us you stole it. But your ruler had it the whole time, didn’t he? What you showed us was a communicator designed to *look like* a controller.”

“Bravo, Mr. Hatch, bravo!” Geiger exclaims. “Yes, Galena told me you were headed to Nabishna. I hoped once I rescued you there, my act of goodwill might convince you to play nice. Yet you spurned my attempts to work together. To your own detriment in the end, I’m afraid. Eventually, I acquired what I needed at Bellamina.”

“That’s why you left Mei-Li’s,” I whisper. “You told me you wanted to take a walk. But you were selling us out.”

Galena stands and faces me. Still devoid of emotion, she nods stiffly and says, “Yes. That’s right.”

I see, hanging at her throat, the Azazule diamond I gave her that very night, and the betrayal burrows deeper into my burning chest.

“So,” Geiger declares triumphantly, “I finally had the coordinates to Eden. And, as they say, the rest is history. Though, I must admit, I am surprised to see *you* here. I sent Galena back to destroy Mei-Li’s original nav cartridges.”

Galena looks pleadingly at Geiger, a serf daring to elicit her lord’s mercy. “I thought I successfully wiped them clean,” she says, “but there must have been some kind of protection against deleting their information. By the time I realized my error, it was too late.”

She’s lying, of course. She never touched the nav cartridges after returning to Mei-Li’s.

I caught her before she could finish the job.

“There will be penance for your mistake, of course,” Geiger assures her with a sneer. “All in due time. For now, I have more pressing business to deal with.”

Drum steps forward. He levels his rifle barrel against the bridge of Cay’s nose.

Behind her grandfather, Ameliana stiffens.

“I saw you coming from the grove,” Geiger says. “If you value your life and the lives of everyone else here, you’ll take me to the tree.”

“She’s called the Matriarch,” Cay growls. “And I’ll take you. But leave everybody else alone. They have nothing to do with this.”

"Bad idea," Drum advises Geiger. "A bartering chip's worth its weight in gold, and we've got a few dozen here. I say we hold 'em hostage. Leave most o' your soldiers here to guard 'em. I'll pick a couple to come with me, and we'll escort you and your new friends to the tree. Best to travel light."

"A fine idea, Mr. Paetski," Geiger agrees. Glancing over his shoulder at Ameliana, he barks, "Did you bring my show cutlery like I asked?"

His granddaughter clutches the leather satchel at her side and nods. "Right here, sir."

"Good," he says. There is an insatiably wicked gleam in his eyes as he looks again at Cay. "Lead the way, Mr. Cantore."

A snarling Hekker shoves the barrel of his firearm into my back, and I lunge forward. With Cay beside me and Geiger's entourage behind—Galena included—we set off for the grove.

I cast a doleful glance back at the dead Luatian, wondering whether we will all share his fate before this is over.

Already rising from Wessel's abdomen, uncurling its infant fingers as it reaches for Eden's obsidian heaven, is a tiny sapling.

With his death, new life begins.

THE COURTYARD OF THE MATRIARCH

Unknown Days to Payment

"MY! SHE *IS* BREATHTAKING." Gustav Geiger's breathless voice corroborates his statement as he stares, wonderstruck, at the ancient tree across the clearing.

Tall, lithe Wenlyn arranges a pair of camerapeople. With the Matriarch in the background, Geiger says a few words to his hypothetical audience about the incredible discovery he has spent his life pursuing.

"You still have the pistol?" I whisper sideways to Cay.

He nods. "Tucked inside my waistband."

"That's enough whispering outta you two," Drum's threatening voice growls behind us. "Either shut your food hatch, or I'll give you a second one in the back o' your head."

"Me or him?" Cay asks innocently.

"Both o' ya. Now *shut it.*"

Geiger finishes his brief monologue, and we proceed across the clearing.

Again and again, I catch myself glancing at Galena. The fact of her betrayal makes sense well enough, but there are certain details that don't make any at all. If she were nothing more than Geiger's loyal servant, why was she crying when she returned to Mei-Li's? It's not like she was expecting me to catch her sneaking around. And why the insistence that we go with Cay? Shouldn't she rather have insisted we stay behind so she could eliminate any competition from Geiger's field of play? Why risk her life tussling with a black hole, and all of it for two people she was actively working against?

They're answers I realize I might never have. Presently, I'm struggling to see how we ever leave Eden alive—or dead, for that matter.

We're nearing the Matriarch's outer veil of branches when a lone figure emerges through them. Sal Cantore, wearing purest loathing on her face, is coming out to greet her old nemesis.

"Oh!" Geiger gasps. "Is it really you? The famous Sal Cantore, in the flesh!" Looking her up and down, he says, "In the *beautiful* flesh, I might add. You have hardly aged a day!"

"Like I explained to Cay, it's the time-shift," Sal explains. Then, icily, she asks, "What are you doing here, Gustav?"

Geiger shakes his head, still unconvinced the woman standing in front of him isn't a figment of his imagination. "All this time," he muses, "almost fifty years, everybody has assumed you were dead. Yet here you've been, hiding away your culinary incompetence from the rest of the galaxy. I can't say we haven't been better off for it."

"How dare you come to this sacred place with your filthy stooges? *And* with captives?" Sal rebukes him sternly. Calmly, she walks past Geiger to stand beside Cay. "Leave my grandson alone. Your quarrel isn't with him. It's with me. It's *always* been with me."

"That isn't quite accurate, I'm afraid," Geiger replies. "Once upon a time, it may have been true enough. However, your dear grandson recently thrust himself dead center into the field of competition. That presents me with a terrible problem, you see."

Casually, almost lazily, Geiger reaches inside his dress robes. When his hand emerges, it's clutching a polished silver pistol. I assume he's going to fulfill some longstanding fantasy and shoot Sal. Instead, he turns the weapon on Cay.

"Gustav! What the hell do you think you're doing?" Sal cries. Like a bolt of lightning, she jumps in front of her grandson.

"Isn't it obvious? I'm killing him," Geiger answers matter-of-factly. "I'm about to shock the entire galaxy by revealing the legendary Trees of Eden. Certainly you don't expect me to share my spotlight by letting your grandson produce a rival program." He shakes his head in pity, then tells Cay, "You should have accepted my offering of peace aboard the *Royal Austrian*. But that starship, as they say, has now sailed."

"It's how you've always gotten ahead, isn't it," Cay taunts. "You can't do it on talent alone, so you use intimidation. Force."

Geiger grins. "I use what works."

"Please, Gustav, don't kill him," begs Sal, raising her hands in a desperate plea. There is something almost flirty in her tone as she adds, "For old times' sake?"

The corner of Geiger's lip twitches. "We did have a fun night on Kember, didn't we? It was the wine's fault, I'm sure. Still, we made a memory I'll never forget."

"That's not all we made that night," Sal says softly, red with sudden shame.

Geiger raises his eyebrows in surprise. The pistol barrel drops an inch.

Sal sighs and says, "It's true. My little Marq ... he was *your* son."

"Impossible," Geiger replies in disbelief. "Marq wasn't born until a full year after. I did the math, just to be certain."

"Time-shift is a bitch, isn't it?" says Sal. "I was bouncing all over the galaxy back then, and Gemini 2-X isn't the first black hole I've seen. It might've seemed like a year to you, but I assure you, it was nine months for me."

Standing behind her grandfather, Ameliana's eyes widen. Her shock is followed by a flush of shame as she realizes the implications of Sal's revelation. The man she has shared more than a few flirtatious moments with is her own cousin.

"Look," says Sal, striking a tone of reason, "you don't need to kill Cay. If you're so worried about the competition, then disable or even destroy his ship. He'll be stuck here, and you can go on your way. Thanks once again to time-shift, even if he *did* leave Eden someday, it would be long after you showed off the trees to the galaxy. You still get your shining moment, and you don't have to kill your grandson in the process."

Geiger lowers the gun. "It makes sense, I suppose. He certainly didn't get his talent from *you*. Very well, I'll be sporting about it. For old times' sake, as you say."

Sal exhales a deep sigh of relief. "Thank you, Gustav."

"By way of our newfound courtesy," Geiger says, "I must insist that you and your grandson join me beneath the Matriarch. You'll be my special guests, honored to witness my triumph firsthand."

Sneering at both Cay and Sal, he adds, "After this, the Cantore name will be as forgettable as your finest cooking. You'll both die here, and I will be immortalized forever."

With Geiger in the lead, Sal and Cay beside me, and a trio of lethal firearms in our backs, we pass through the Matriarch's curtain of fruiting branches.

THE MATRIARCH
Unknown Days to Payment

NEAR THE MATRIARCH'S TRUNK, Wenlyn o' gla Myrn arranges the four camera-beings while Geiger mutters through some practiced lines. Ameliana stands awkwardly beside her grandfather, casting furtive glances at both Cay and Drummond Paetski behind him.

Galena waits off to the side, expressionless. In all the excitement, I didn't register the fact that she's still in possession of my second camera.

Geiger notices too. He approaches Galena and says, "You may return Mr. Hatch's camera to him. I would very much like for him to film this moment."

Galena refuses to meet my gaze as she hands me the unbroken camera. That she won't let me look into those exquisite violet eyes is a twisting of the knife even more painful than her betrayal.

"Turn it on, please," Geiger orders me. "I'd like to leave all of you with a memento of this historic occasion."

Scowling, I do as he says. Some battles aren't worth the limited energy I have these days.

Sal steps forward—a risky move with a gun in her back—and says, "You don't know what you're doing, Gustav."

Geiger scowls at her. "I know damn well what I'm doing."

"No, you're a fool," Sal says. "The Children of Eden won't stand for this. Nobody but the Keeper is allowed to eat from the Matriarch. They revere this tree like a god, Gustav."

"This tree's fruit is clearly superior to those in the rest in the forest," Geiger replies. "And, unlike your viewers, I will not settle for second rate."

"It's not that simple."

"Enough!" Geiger shouts. "You will not derail my greatest achievement by appealing to the religious whims of this uncivilized cult."

He spins on his heels and gives Wenlyn a stiff nod to tell her he's ready. She positions him in front of the Matriarch's silver trunk for the ideal shot, and he turns on his most gleaming grin for her camera. After a deep breath, he launches into his rehearsed monologue.

"As you know, my many decades have been rife with culinary accolades, awards, and achievements. Yet for all those years, the crown jewel has eluded me. Today, she eludes me no longer."

Geiger angles toward the Matriarch's nearest interior branch, glowing with its evenly spaced fruits. At Wenlyn's direction, one of the camera-beings—a blue-skinned Skruut, I think—comes in close to give Geiger's audience a front-row view of the emberlike Eden apples.

"They say," Geiger continues, "that the fabled fruit of the Trees of Eden is so utterly captivating, anybody who eats of it will never freely part from it again."

He plucks an apple from the branch, then motions for the cameras to cut. Turning to his granddaughter, he extends a hand and barks, "My paring knife, Ameliana. The one with the jade handle. I want to give my followers a good look inside the fruit."

Ameliana unclasps the cutlery satchel and fumbles about inside it.

One more time, Sal makes her desperate appeal. "Gustav, I'm warning you. This isn't what you think it is."

Geiger takes a menacing step our direction. "Interrupt me again," he snarls, "and I will rescind our deal. Grandson or not."

Seething, he whirls around to retake his position, shouting, "The knife, Ameliana, the knife!"

And a knife is what he gets. Not the jade-handled paring knife he ordered, but something rather larger. Something large enough, in fact, that when buried all the way to its hilt in Geiger's chest, the final few inches of its gory blade protrude out the old man's back.

Gustav Geiger gasps. Stumbles backward. Grabs the butcher knife's handle and tries to pull it out. But it hardly moves. He's too weak. Life is leaving him, and quickly.

Wenlyn o' gla Myrn, his decades-long producer, shrieks with rage. Whether she's jumping to Geiger's aid or to attack the person who stabbed him, I never find out. She reaches neither. A single laser, fired from one of the guns behind us, slams into her chest and throws her backward.

She's dead when she hits the ground.

Three of the camera-beings flee. The fourth holds her ground, watching the scene knowingly. At once, the runners are dispatched by another rapid burst of laser fire. Their lifeless bodies join Wenlyn on Eden's cold ground.

Geiger stumbles forward and collapses against Ameliana. Against the very granddaughter who thrust the knife into his chest. The slender fingers of one hand clutch her shirt, even as he goes on holding his prized Eden apple in the other.

No longer pompous or confident, his voice is fragile, trembling, as he rasps, "Ameliana? Why?"

"I'm done waiting around for you to die," she answers coldly. "Your time is up, old man."

Cruel steel flashes in the perennial twilight. Ameliana's closed fist flies upward, catching her grandfather in the neck.

Gustav Geiger makes a terrible gurgling sound. In horror, I realize he's choking on his own blood. A moment later, it cascades over his lower lip and down his chin, like fondue from a chocolate fountain.

Ameliana plants a bootheel in his stomach and shoves him backward.

The Food Fürst, eyes open but unseeing, crashes spread-eagle onto the ground, the jade handle of his favorite paring knife protruding up from his blood-soaked throat.

And the Eden apple, Gustav Geiger's elusive crown jewel, slips free and tumbles away from his lifeless fingers.

THE MATRIARCH

Unknown Days to Payment

I'M STARING IN SHOCK at the grisly scene, unsure whether I should be repulsed or relieved, when Cay tells Ameliana, "I know you're my cousin and all, but I might kiss you anyway."

He takes a step toward her. Just as quickly, he halts.

Once more, he's staring down the barrel of a pistol. Geiger's pistol, in fact. Only this time, Ameliana is the one holding it.

Keeping the gun trained on Cay, she kneels to pick up her grandfather's fallen Eden apple. To the lone remaining cameraperson, the blue Skruut who didn't run like the others, Ameliana says, "Get ready to reshoot. Make sure the old man's body isn't in the shot." She pauses. "On second thought, make sure it *is*."

Cay stands, hands raised and still as a stone. His brow is wrinkled with confusion as he struggles to connect the dots. It doesn't take long before the light of realization dawns over him.

"It was *you*," he says. "All the way back on Tarrkanna-Rrui, it was *you*. Geiger really didn't have a clue about Turf double-crossing us. The cave-ins on Petra 7, the explosions … that was all you, wasn't it?"

"Figure that out all by yourself?" Ameliana replies.

"*And* you're the one who put the tracker in PAD," Cay says with a wry chuckle. "Genius."

"Not really," says Ameliana. "You're so self-absorbed, you never stopped to consider someone might be *faking* interest in you. Even if that 'someone' was Gustav Geiger's own granddaughter."

"But what about the gray-haired man who paid off Turf?" Cay asks, perplexed once more. "That couldn't possibly have been you."

"Not her," replies the gruff voice of Drummond Paetski. "And not gray, either. More of a light blond."

"Of course!" says Cay, smacking his own forehead. "Gustav Geiger's new hire for security chief, headhunted by none other than Ameliana herself. Doing *her* dirty work the whole time. I suppose you were the one who followed us to Petra 7 and blew up the entrance to the mine."

"Guilty as charged," Drum admits with a self-satisfied grin. Indicating the two soldiers he brought along to the Matriarch, he says, "I had help, of course. It wasn't hard to convince Geiger I needed to add a few more to his team. Beings I could trust. Too bad *he* couldn't."

"Of course, Nabishna would have finally been the end for you if Grandfather hadn't received Galena's distress call," Ameliana says.

"But how could she send one?" I wonder, casting an accusatory glance at our ex-companion. "There was no Axon at all on the planet."

"True," says Galena, entering the conversation. She doesn't seem particularly perturbed by her ruler's demise. "But those communicators also send out shortwave radio transmissions, and Geiger was already in orbit above Nabishna. I told him where we were going, and he followed us there."

"That's why you were hiding in the mechanical closet when Cay contacted Ameliana on the vidcomm," I say. "You told us you were worried your face would be flagged by League authorities. Really, you thought Ameliana would recognize you and blow your cover. Geiger didn't want her to know about you, did he."

Galena nods coldly.

"I had no idea he had inserted his own spy," Ameliana admits. "Bad luck for me. Of course, when I saw her with you onboard the *Royal Austrian,* I realized I could gain even more of your trust by telling you to ditch the tracker. From that point on, I knew Grandfather would do the work for me, following you around the galaxy wherever you went."

"When you acted like you didn't know me on the *Tantalus,*" says Galena, "I realized you must be up to something, otherwise you would have blown my cover."

"And I knew you couldn't out me to Cay without revealing yourself to be Grandfather's spy," says Ameliana. "I couldn't have planned it better myself! Of course, I did wonder why you never told Grandfather I was helping a Cantore. Naughty castrata, you!"

"Isn't it obvious?" says Galena. Angry tears well in her eyes. "I hated him. After everything he did to me, who wouldn't? So I was more than happy to keep quiet and let you scheme against him." Indicating Geiger's body, she adds, "It worked out for both of us in the end."

"It did," Ameliana agrees. "Grandfather is finally out of my way, I hold Cay Cantore hostage, *and* I have the Trees of Eden! The three ingredients in my recipe for glory."

"But why bother with me at all?" Cay asks. "Why not just kill Geiger and take over his empire? Enjoy all the fortune and glory he'd built over his lifetime?"

"Two reasons," says Ameliana. "First and most important is that I hate you. You must be the most arrogant bastard I have ever met. And second ... because I know you're better than me. Quite simply, if I am going to be number one, I need you out of the way. Always have, even when we were at University together." With a sadistic sneer, she raises her right hand and waggles her fingers.

"The food processor? That was you too?"

Ameliana gives a casual shrug. "I thought if I pureed your hand, I would finally be at an advantage. Unlucky me—it was only your middle finger still in the blender when I reactivated the power strip."

"It's a pity I didn't inherit the Geiger family's evil genius gene," laments Cay. "Then I'd be truly unstoppable."

"But that's enough of my diabolical reveal—for now, anyway," says Ameliana. She looks at me. "Camera up, Jerricho. I want multiple angles when I shoot my debut moment, and I'm a few camerapeople short."

"Like I'd help *you,*" I scoff.

"Oh, do play nice," she says. "Help me document the most historic moment in the galaxy of food programming, and I may let you live out your days on Eden with your best friend. It's a far better offer than I gave Grandfather dearest."

I scowl but raise my camera anyway. Once more, it's a situation where it doesn't pay to fight.

Ameliana looks into my lens and begins. I get a good shot of the bronze Eden apple as she raises it high and says, "Here I hold the most legendary fruit in all the galaxy. This, friends, is the Eden apple. Hundreds of beings have been lost in their pursuit of it. Undoubtedly, most have died." Her lower lip trembles, and a strain fills her voice as she goes on. "A list that now includes my dear grandfather. Gustav Geiger, whom you know better as the Food Fürst, is the most recent casualty in that quest, murdered here by the crazy cultists who call themselves the Children of Eden." A steely resolve fills her gaze. She looks confidently at the camera once more. "But they have been dealt with. In honor of my grandfather's incredible legacy—and his life's greatest dream—I have taken it upon myself to finish what he started."

Like Cay did earlier, Ameliana opens wide to take a bite of the Eden apple. Also like Cay, someone stops her before it reaches her lips.

"Don't, Ameliana," orders Sal.

Ameliana pauses and glares at her.

"If you eat the Eden apple, this tree will own you. I know this to be true, because it owns *me*. It will plant its tiny seeds inside you, and you will never be able to leave this grove. Not unless you're willing to pay for it with your life."

"She *lies!*" Galena hisses. She steps in front of Sal, a wild look in her eyes. "She just wants her grandson to be the first. She wants him to win fame and glory for their whole rotten family. He's already finished film- ing what he needs. All he has to do is get home alive and share it. They concocted this story—this *lie*—the moment they heard the *Royal Aus- trian* approaching."

Sal can't hide her surprise at Galena's brazen tale. She stammers to find a rebuttal, looking very much indeed like someone perpetuating a lie, as per Galena's accusations.

"I—we—the Children of Eden, we're all trapped here by those trees," Sal implores. "There's a reason none of us have left, a reason we haven't gone home to our families, our friends, our lives. Surely you must recog- nize that."

"More lies," insists Galena. "These cultists simply don't want to share their treasures. True, everyone who comes to this planet lets their ships rust and rot. Why do you think that is? It's because they'll never leave these divine fruits again."

"She's baiting you, Ameliana. She's not—"

"Shut up!" Ameliana snarls at Sal. With a murderous expression, she looks at me and says, "Keep filming."

I swallow the lump in my throat and hit *RECORD* on my camera.

Showing off the Eden apple once more—though with a bit less poise than before—Ameliana says, "In memory of my late grandfather, I take this bite of history."

And she does. Her teeth snap off a crisp hunk of the glowing fruit. She chews it. Swallows it. Moans, and makes a face like she's having the galaxy's best-ever orgasm.

"Oh, sweet Cosmos," she says, allowing a bit of juice to dribble from the corner of her mouth. "It's ... indescribable! I knew it would be delicious, but I was absolutely unprepared for this—this—*symphony* of flavor. I understand why nobody wants to leave Eden after eating this. I, for one, know that the Eden apple will haunt me for the rest of my life. This is a moment I will cherish—will *treasure*—until the day I die. I hope I have done my grandfather proud, and I am so pleased I got to share this beautiful moment with all of you."

She motions at me and the Skruut to cut our cameras. The moment we do, she scowls. Like it's crawling with worms, she glares in disgust at the remainder of the Eden apple.

"It tastes like ... nothing!" she exclaims. "Maybe slightly bitter, even. It certainly wasn't worth all this trouble." She grunts bemusedly at Geiger's corpse. "You're lucky I killed you, old man. Dying from this disappointment would have been far worse."

With an apathetic shrug, she tosses the rest of the Eden apple over her shoulder. "No matter. My viewers won't know the difference. As far as they're concerned, I just ate a bite of heaven."

Ameliana points at the cutlery satchel resting beside Geiger's body and says, "Galena, gather the knives. The ones I buried in him too. My audience will eat up the nostalgia factor whenever I use them on my show."

Galena frowns but begins the grisly business. Geiger's death doesn't mean she's free, only that she now belongs to his psychopathic heir.

Ameliana approaches me and grabs my camera. "Thanks for the footage. You played nice, so I'll play nice too. Stay here until I'm gone, and no one else will get hurt. I will take the rest of the crew and leave." She winces at Cay with a false display of regret. "I *will* have to destroy the *Tantalus* before I go. Sorry, but I can't have you spoiling things by telling everyone how I knocked off my own grandfather. I'm sure you understand."

"Now that I know you're my supervillain cousin," Cay replies, "I might be more attracted to you than ever. Maybe it's one of those 'forbidden fruit' things. Whaddya say? Take me with you so we can find out together?"

Ameliana pats him lightly on the cheek and gives him a patronizing smile. "Not my type. Sorry. I do wish you a wonderful life here, enjoying all the Eden apples you can eat!"

Cackling at her own dark humor, she and the rest of her troupe march off victoriously.

As they disappear beyond the Matriarch's veil, I notice Galena hanging a few steps behind them. Just before passing beyond the branches and out of sight, she removes one of Geiger's long knives from the cutlery satchel.

Then, in a single motion, she conceals the blade again, this time beneath the folds of her tattered castrata robe.

THE COURTYARD OF THE MATRIARCH

Unknown Days to Payment

THERE'S NO POINT in staying with the tree, so we follow Galena beyond the veil. Back in the open space separating the Matriarch from the rest of the grove, I watch as she hurries to catch up with the rest of Ameliana's company.

Like the sapling that sprouted from Wessel's stomach, a new concern grows within me. I ask Sal, "Are you sure she can't leave? That she's trapped here?"

"Positive," Sal says. "And that terrifies me."

"Me too."

"What do you mean? Why?" Cay asks.

"I mean, what's that crazy bitch gonna do when she figures that out?" Sal replies.

I swallow hard. With everything happening at warp speed, I hadn't thought that far ahead. Now my imagination is running amok in a hundred different directions.

They're approaching the tree line when a scream, shrill with agony, rings out across the clearing. Ameliana, marching confidently at the head of her company, drops suddenly to her knees and clutches her stomach.

"Hey! You alright?" Drum asks, offering her a hand.

"Yes," Ameliana answers. "Just a cramp or something."

Even from this distance, I detect the concern in her tone.

She takes another step and screams again, louder and longer this time.

"Back!" she shouts, panicked. "Take me back! Back toward the tree!"

Drum grabs her beneath the armpits and drags her backward into the middle of the clearing. When her anguished cries die down, he lowers her onto the ground.

Ameliana glares up at Galena.

"You!" she hisses. "You tricked me into eating it. You *and* your mother will pay dearly for this."

In a glance, Cay and I exchange a single word: *Mother?*

"I'll torture her in front of you, then kill you both," Ameliana declares. She pushes herself onto her feet and snatches the cutlery bag from Galena. "The rest of my castratae will remember you for a long time once I'm finished with you. I'll teach them what happens to the disobedient *and* their loved ones."

Seething, Ameliana turns to face the tree, the Matriarch now holding her in bondage.

"So, it won't let me leave, will it?" she shouts, marching toward us. "We'll see how much hold she has over me once I'm through with her. Drum, did you bring any explosives along?"

The security chief pats the hefty rucksack on his back. "Always do. Fission-88s. Same type I blew those mines on Petra 7 with. Should be plenty to take out a tree. Even a big bastard like that."

"Good. Set them around the Matriarch."

As Ameliana walks by her, Sal grabs her arm. "Don't do this!" she pleads.

"That tree might be a billion years old," Cay adds. "You can't just blow it up!"

Ameliana stops, but only to bellow more orders at her team. "Bring these three with us," she says. "I'm done with unexpected delays. If they love the tree so much, they can have the honor of dying with it."

Her promise of death is the catalyst Cay needs to spring into action. His chef's hand, quick and precise, withdraws the pistol hidden in his waistband. He raises it, takes aim at Ameliana's unprotected back, and squeezes the trigger.

Nothing happens.

A split second later, Drummond Paetski shows us he's worthy of bearing the title "Security Chief." With a single, fluid movement, he sends an amber beam directly from his rifle into Cay's pistol.

The smoldering wreckage of our stolen sidearm careens uselessly onto the grass.

Cay howls, doubling over in obvious agony. "Son of a buttermilk biscuit!" he screams, clutching one hand with the other. "Are you friggin' kidding me? *Another* finger?"

Sure enough, next to the stump of his middle finger is a second char-red nub, cauterized by the same laser blast that created it. A strong aroma of burnt meat lingers in the air, and his index finger is nowhere to be seen. Vaporized, probably.

"You civilians and your safeties," Drum says. He's shaking his head, disappointed. "They always make you a half-second too slow."

Ameliana seizes Cay's wrist. She examines his twice-damaged hand with a satisfied smirk. "It's still not what I hoped to accomplish with the blender—"

"Food processor," Cay groans.

"—but it'll do, I suppose. Now, to the tree, all of you. I have spent too much time already on this godforsaken planet."

THE MATRIARCH

Unknown Days to Payment

"WE GOT NOTHIN'" to tie 'em up with," Drum remarks.

Together with Cay, Sal, and Galena, I'm on my knees, fingers laced behind my head. As a bonus, I'm the lucky boy who scored the spot next to Gustav Geiger's blood-drenched corpse.

"After you set the explosives, drag them to the base of the tree and shoot their kneecaps off," Ameliana replies. She sounds as casual about cold-blooded murder as someone reciting the next step of a recipe.

I gulp. The body count beneath the Matriarch is about to double.

Squatting in front of his open rucksack, Drum removes a dull metal cube. He looks it over with admiration, like a proud father examining his newborn baby.

"Buddy o' mine invented these," he brags. "They pack a helluva punch. Four oughta do the trick. Eight, if you want to make good and certain."

"Use eight," says Ameliana. "A little overkill can't hurt."

Easy for her to say.

Ameliana and the unnamed human soldier assist Drum in setting the charges. After the first few, they move around the tree's mammoth trunk and out of sight, leaving the Hekker to guard us. The Skruut cameraperson stands nearby, keeping a nervous eye on the explosives planted at the base of the tree. She is also armed with a small pistol, though she appears as capable of using it as Cay.

We're kneeling on the ground, awaiting the fate Ameliana has planned for us, when I hear a familiar noise. A steady buzz behind me, as if a hive full of bees were busy at work nearby.

PAD. He's stayed out of sight since our initial encounter with the Children of Eden.

Escape flight, indeed.

The question is, what's he up to?

I glance sideways at Cay. It's plain from his expression that he also hears PAD.

More importantly, so does the Hekker guarding us. When he hears the drone hovering behind him, he turns fully, grunting with surprise.

Galena seizes the opportunity. In a flash, the knife she hid under her robes is in her hand. Springing up at the distracted Hekker, she rams the broad-bladed knife through his throat. Other than a muffled, Geiger-esque gurgling, the only sound he makes in death is that of his body crumpling to the ground. As he collapses, Galena snatches the rifle from his lifeless claws and lobs a fatal shot into the surprised camera-Skruut's torso.

Stabbing the Hekker didn't raise an alarm, but the laser blast certainly does. Angry shouts erupt from the other side of the Matriarch.

"To my house!" cries Sal, wrestling both the pistol and camera from the dead Skruut. "Go!"

We're streaking toward the Matriarch's branch curtain when the first bursts of laser fire careen past us. Some are so dangerously close, I can taste singed air.

Sal and Galena return errant shots of their own to cover our retreat. A high-pitched shriek, definitely male and human, tells me at least one shot wasn't so errant after all.

One down. Hope swells within me. Maybe we'll survive this scrape yet.

But a second scream bursts that bubble of hope. I turn to see Sal bellyflopping to the ground. The pistol she nabbed from the Skruut flies from her grip and clatters out of sight among a thick tangle of roots.

Galena pivots. She drops to one knee and fires in the direction of the Matriarch's trunk, forcing Ameliana and Drum to take cover.

With so much adrenaline pumping through my system, I've hardly noticed how much pain I'm in—that is, until Cay and I hunker beside Sal and throw her arms over our shoulders. We hoist her off the ground.

"Leave me," she moans. "What are you idiots doing? Save yourselves."

Cay shakes his head. "I already buried my dad—"

"*I* buried your dad," I remind him.

"—and I didn't come all this way to bury my Nana too. Now move those legs!"

She does. With her cooperation, it doesn't take long to gain the cover of the thick branch curtain. Moments behind us, Galena bursts through as well.

The Matriarch's branches shield us from sight, but not from gunfire. Lasers rip wildly through them, showering us in silver leaves and twigs and bronze Eden apples.

Fortunately, Sal's hut is close. PAD leads us through the open doorway, and we tumble in after him.

We're alive.

But who knows for how much longer?

SAL CANTORE'S HOME

Unknown Days to Payment

CAY AND I HAUL Sal to her bed. I take the Skruut's camera from her, and we lay her gently on her stomach.

"You ... damn ... idiots," she pants. "Coulda been ... killed."

"Compared to what most people call me, 'damn idiot' is basically a compliment," Cay says. "You'll call me something way worse when I do *this*."

He pulls the bottom hem of her black robe up past her undergarment, exposing her lower back. There's a dark circle of charred meat indicating where the laser passed through her. It looks hideous and smells worse, but it's also low and off to the side, just above her hip bone.

"I'm no doctor, and I'm even less of a gambler, but I'd wager they didn't hit anything vital," says Cay. "You are one lucky granny."

"I'll call myself ... lucky if ... we last another ... five minutes," Sal replies.

"Maybe they'll just blow the tree and leave," Cay says hopefully.

Sal shakes her head. "They won't. I made sure of it. That's why I ... grabbed the camera. Ameliana won't leave ... without her footage." Noting Cay's indignant expression, she adds, "That tree is ... worth more than ... all our lives. I couldn't let her ... destroy it."

"They're about to destroy it *and* us," says Galena, kneeling beside me. "We need a plan."

I know she betrayed us and all, but the sight of Galena carrying that huge rifle is making me fall for her all over again.

Our moment of peace doesn't last. Sal's entire home shudders as gunfire slams into the far wall. Plaster and dust rain down on us.

A plan. *We need a plan.* But with one gun, little training, and no protected place to take a clear shot, what plan could possibly work?

The bombardment outside stops abruptly. Ameliana's venom-sweet voice calls out in singsong fashion, "Oh, Caa-aay! I need my caaameras!"

Shuffling to the door, Cay opens it a crack and sings back, "Oh, Ameliaaanaaa! Kiss my hairy aaa-aaass!"

I hear voices outside, low and indistinguishable. Our final two opponents know they have us over a barrel. They're taking their time, strategizing the best way to eliminate us without destroying the cameras—and their valuable footage.

My eyes dart about Sal's tiny home like caffeinated pinballs. I'm looking for something—*anything*—that might help us. Dishware, cleaning rags, night rose leaves, bedsheets, table, PAD, a book …

PAD. The drone is hovering over the low table we sat around hardly an hour ago.

The inkling of an idea takes root. Soon, it's a full-grown plan.

"Do you still have your tether?" I ask PAD. "The one you used to save me and Cay on Petra 7?"

"Affirmative," is PAD's simple response.

"How is *that* supposed to help us?" asks Cay.

"Because I think he can kill Ameliana."

"I'm afraid not," says PAD. "My programming prohibits me from intentionally harming a living being."

What about un*intentionally?*

PAD is new to the party. He doesn't know anything Sal told us about the seeds killing their host.

"Then maybe you could give Ameliana a ride," I say to the drone. "You know, wrap her up in your tether and provide a … *lift* back to the *Royal Austrian.*"

"Due to my damaged rotor arm, my carrying capacity is still limited to sixty kilograms," PAD reminds me.

"Well?" I challenge him. "You're a flying computer, aren't you? Can you carry Ameliana or not?"

PAD processes the question before answering. "It will be close, but I imagine so. Depending on the weight of her clothing and other accessories, she may be on the upper end of the margin."

"Then *drag* her lousy ass if you have to!" shouts Cay. He has caught on to my plan and seems enthusiastically on board.

"They'll be shooting at you the moment you're out the door," I warn PAD. "It's finally time to put all your escape flight training to good use!"

PAD doesn't say anything. He's a robot, a few dozen pounds of metal packed with gadgets and pre-programmed information, yet he appears attuned to the gravity of the danger ahead.

"I'll lay some cover for you," Galena says. She clutches the rifle like an action heroine, a far cry from the demure castrata Cay and I "rescued" a few weeks ago.

"Thank you," PAD says quietly.

Galena offers him a tight smile. She edges toward the door and grabs the handle.

"Ready when you are," she says.

PAD doesn't hesitate. "I am ready now."

Galena throws open the door and jumps back, allowing PAD plenty of room to zip past her. The moment he's outside, she follows as far as the doorway. There she drops to her knees and begins sending a hail of gunfire Ameliana and Drum's direction.

I don't witness what happens next. Too bad CBS isn't a disease that lets you see through walls. What I *do* know is that the next seven seconds feel eternal, and each moment of it like a single camera frame that might record our salvation ... or our ruin.

Then I hear the beautiful words from Galena's beautiful lips: "He's got her! PAD's got Ameliana!"

I cheer and pump my fist.

But the moment of triumph is short-lived.

Galena's face falls, ashen.

"She shot him," Galena croaks, before squeezing off another barrage of gunfire.

I hurry to her side in the doorway. I need to see for myself.

One of PAD's four rotors is completely disabled. It dangles uselessly, connected by a couple wires and nothing more. Bit by bit, PAD is losing altitude, his other three rotors working overtime to ensure a softer landing for the human hanging below him.

Damn protective programming ...

In only a few seconds, Ameliana will be on the ground again. They'll be two guns to our one—and a shitload of explosives to our none.

Whatever comes over me, I don't know. I've always been safe Jerricho. Timid Jerricho. Eat-your-peas-'cause-your-mother-said-so

Jerricho. Which is why I surprise even myself when I sprint past Galena, out the door, and away from the safety of Sal's hut.

I run, faster than hell on a rocket, toward the middle of the clearing. To the position where, as best I can calculate, PAD is about to land.

When he does, it will be with a very angry Ameliana in tow.

THE COURTYARD OF THE MATRIARCH
Unknown Days to Payment

I MIGHT HAVE expected Drummond Paetski to notice my frenzied race toward his boss. I'm barely out the door when I find myself swear-dancing around the lasers that are screaming past my ankles. If it weren't for Galena's cover fire throwing Drum off-kilter, even a cat would've lost all nine of its lives by now.

My muscles scream, rebelling against the hell I'm putting them through. Still, I press on, undeterred.

Ameliana is so focused on her safe landing, she doesn't notice me advancing from behind. Good for me. At this point, the element of surprise might be the only element working in my favor.

She's about twenty meters ahead of me when she hits the ground. Curling into a ball, she tumbles over the turf. The moment she stops tumbling, she frantically sheds the tether's coils, swearing heartily as she does. Then she stands tall, pistol raised, and whirls toward Sal's hut—and the invaluable cameras trapped inside it.

That's the moment my body collides with hers. I may be suffering from a terminal illness, but an all-district linebacker doesn't forget a decent form tackle. I lead with my shoulder, hitting her square in the breadbasket, and hear that familiar *ooofff* as the air rushes from her lungs.

More importantly, I hear her pistol clattering against the stony ground. My perfect hit forced a critical fumble.

I don't take Ameliana down to the dirt. That would be too merciful. That's what I would do to my high-school opponents, people I was play-ing a game against. It's not suitable treatment for psycho killers like her.

As I drive Ameliana forward, I hoist her onto my shoulder. Though every ounce of my burning nerves, sinews, ligaments, and muscles screams in retaliation, I sprint toward the tree line, hauling Ameliana along like she's a sack of fertilizer I've been tasked with spreading over the grove.

"Let me go, you bastard!" she shrieks.

Each stride feels like a mile, but this bastard somehow keeps going. I have to. If Ameliana manages to free herself, she'll beat me to the pistol she dropped. Then I'm a dead man.

Not if she's dead first.

Ameliana shrieks like the Furies of hell. She thrashes. She knees me in the chest, punches my back and ribs, elbows the side of my head. She does everything she can to shake herself loose. Everything in her power to keep us from reaching the forest.

My vision is swimming with black spots when we break the tree line. Ameliana continues her thrashing, but it's different now. More of a shudder, an involuntary convulsion. Her screams change too, no longer born of rage but of incomprehensible agony.

I sense something creeping along my shoulder blade, almost like a finger caressing my skin. Summoning my final reserves of strength, I shotput Ameliana as far as I can. Twisting, writhing, howling, she sails through the air.

She lands among a tangle of roots, near the trunk of one of Eden's legendary trees.

I sink to my knees. The dark spots have overtaken most of my vision, yet I watch on, praying for my friends' sake that Ameliana does not rise again.

For me, it makes no difference. I'm dying either way.

I teeter forward and fall onto my stomach. Beneath me, the ground feels strangely warm.

The darkness closes in. But I'm not scared. Everyone has to die sometime, right?

The last thing I see is the monarch. *My* monarch, tattooed into the flesh of my forearm.

Its wings are spread, ready to soar upon the skies.

THE EMPRESS GROVE

Unknown Days to Payment

"JER! HEY, JER!"

Ugh. Is that *really* the first voice I have to hear in the afterlife? Hasn't it put me through enough already?

Maybe this is my hell ...

"Jer, come on, buddy, wake up." The voice is strained with emotion. With distress.

Well. There's something new.

My eyelids flutter. The dark spots are still there, but they seem to be migrating back beyond the boundaries of my vision, where they belong.

Groaning, I turn onto my back. Above me is a canopy of silvery leaves and glowing branches, mottled black by the sky beyond. And, in the middle of it all—

"Cay," I whisper. "Did you die too?"

"Nah," he says, with the same lackadaisical nonchalance that always makes me want to strangle him. "After everything we've been through, I'm starting to think I'm unkillable."

"Let's hope ... the Malvudians ... feel the same way," I reply, sucking in deep breaths of life. "What happened ... to Drum?"

"Toast. Literally. When he started shooting at you, Galena ran right out into the open. Turns out she's dead accurate when she's got a clear shot. Or maybe," he adds with a wink, "she just needed the right motivation."

"And PAD?" I wonder. Robot that he is, I still feel responsible for what happened to him.

"He's down a rotor and a half," Cay says, "but otherwise alright. Last I saw, he was limping back to Sal's hut."

I try to sit but immediately collapse back to the ground. "Shit, Cay, I don't think I'm leaving here without a stretcher."

He chuckles and helps me up, throwing my arm over his shoulders for added support. He asks, "How many times have you passed out on this trip?"

"Four, I think."

"That's what I thought," Cay says. "You might want to have your head examined when we get home."

Now on my feet, I have a clear view of Ameliana. She herself is dead, though I wouldn't exactly say *lifeless*. A fresh system of roots has sprouted out her back and is burrowing into the ground like a family of tiny serpents. Up from her chest, the trunk of a small sapling climbs slowly toward Eden's dark sky. New twigs are uncurling before my very eyes.

It's a grotesque, yet strangely beautiful, sight.

"Sorry 'bout your girlfriend," I mutter.

"No worries," says Cay. "Besides, I've always preferred my girls a little less cousin-y than her."

THE COURTYARD OF THE MATRIARCH

Unknown Days to Payment

WE'RE ALMOST BACK to Sal's hut when I notice a lone figure standing in front of the Matriarch's glowing veil.

It's Galena. The rifle she used to kill Drum—to save my life, most likely—is on the ground beside her. But she isn't looking at me and Cay, returning from our triumph over Ameliana. She's staring at the branches, heavy with fruit.

Not a muscle moves in her entire body.

I remove my arm from Cay's shoulders and limp away from him.

"You sure you're alright?" he asks.

"It's cute you're finally concerned about me," I answer. "But, yeah, I'm fine. I ... think I should talk to Galena alone."

"Okay. I'll meet you back at Sal's."

I pass Drum's mutilated body as I go. A sickly-sweet aroma lingers in the air around him, reminding me of the Maillard effect Cay explained while searing a hunk of gurrffa meat. Galena must have unloaded on him big time.

I shudder and hurry along.

Galena doesn't hear me coming. Or, if she does, she ignores me. She's fixated on the Eden apples. She plucks one off its branch and stares at the fruit in her hand, turning it over this way and that, like it might hold the answers to all her life's most troublesome questions.

Then, I realize ... it *does*.

"Galena, stop!" I cry. Ignoring the incredible pain of the effort, I run toward her. "Don't!"

She turns at the sound of my voice. Her eyes glisten with blossoming tears. Then she opens her mouth wide and bites into the Eden apple.

When she has wolfed down the first bite, she takes another. And another. And another, until all that's left in her palm is a small, silvery stem.

My heart bursts, and with it, my tears.

"Why?" I sob. "Why, Galena? Oh, what did you do?"

"I set myself free," she answers simply.

"Free? You'll be trapped here forever!"

"All my life, I've been a pawn," she replies. "Used and abused in whatever ways Geiger wished. Not anymore. Not by him. Not by anyone."

Still crying, I step past her and pick an Eden apple for myself. "Then—then I'll stay too," I declare. "With you."

Before I can bite into it, Galena lays a firm hand upon my wrist.

"No, Jerricho," she says. "I will not let myself belong to anyone. Not even you. If I've learned anything at all in life, it's that the bondage of the heart can be the strongest and most painful of all."

"What do you mean?" I ask. The pain of my death sprint with Ameliana is nothing compared to this final, gutting rejection from Galena's lips.

"My heart led me to betray even you and Cay," she answers, "because of its bond of love with my mother."

Finally, it all makes sense. In my mind's eye, I see the older Vandreek castrata at the funeral, and in the Third Planet Entertainment lobby, and again during dinner aboard the *Royal Austrian*.

Galena's mother.

"He forced me to do it," she continues. "Geiger told me he'd kill her if I didn't. He used the one person I loved to make me do those horrible things."

Galena stares at the stem in her hand, liberated from its place between branch and fruit. "Now, no one can take me away from here. No one can use me for their own twisted pleasure or evil ends ever again. If that means belonging to one of these incredible trees, it's a slavery I happily accept."

"So ... what? I'm supposed to leave you here, all alone?" I shake my head. "I won't do it."

Behind me, a voice says, "If you stay, you're dooming me too."

I turn. Cay is strolling lazily toward us.

"I can't get home on my own," he says. "I need you in the cockpit to work the QRD, remember?"

He stops in front of me. There's something like sincerity in his sympathizing grin. "I can't imagine how hard this is for you, but Eden isn't your home, Jer. What would your parents do if you never came back? What would your sister think of me leaving you here?"

Even in a moment as dire as this, Cay has a way of making me roll my eyes.

"More importantly," he adds, "what would *Gram* do to me if I came back without you? There isn't a lucky crystal in this whole wide galaxy that could save me from her wrath."

Cay looks down, scuffing the ground with his toe. In a voice as small as the seeds of an Eden apple, he says, "And what would *I* do without my best friend? Who would save me from Hekkra thugs or angry Malvudians? So, you see, you *have* to come back, Jer. You just ... do."

I have no response other than a fresh wave of weeping. Galena likewise has nothing more to say. Instead, she wraps her lovely arms around me, presses her face against my own, and speaks sorrow's language by mingling her tears with mine.

When we're both cried out, I ask, "Is there anything I can do for you before we leave? Anything at all?"

Galena nods. She takes the Eden apple I picked into her own hand and says, "Go to the *Royal Austrian* and bring my mother here. Tell her I found something she might want."

SAL CANTORE'S HOME

Unknown Days to Payment

THERE WAS STILL the small matter of Geiger's remaining army to deal with—or so we thought. But when we returned to the *Royal Austrian* with photos of the dead on Cay's tel to prove the mission's failure, we discovered a different army mobilized and ready to deploy. Hundreds of black-robed Children of Eden had already subdued the soldiers, apparently without a single shot fired. The whole company was preparing to march to their Matriarch's rescue.

It didn't take long to find Galena's mother, locked in a holding cell aboard the *Royal Austrian*. After a hike through the grove and a tearful reunion with her daughter, she submitted herself to the same new slavery by eating the Matriarch's forbidden fruit.

The Children of Eden weren't too happy when they found out about it, but they must forgive quickly. Hardly five minutes had passed before they were laying the foundations of another hut among the great tree's roots. A home for their planet's two newest residents.

Then, I slept. Time-shift and Malvudian payment be damned, I slept.

At present, Cay is standing in Sal's doorway. He's making me nervous, tucking a multi-thousand-current camera under his arm like it's a case of beer he didn't have enough hands to carry.

Just this once, I'll give him a pass. After all, he's saying his first—and probably last—goodbye to his grandmother.

"I wish we could stay longer," he says. "But, as a wise woman once told me, 'Time-shift is a bitch,' and I've got a debt to settle. I imagine Bloodgout and Sawtooth would even manage to track me here sooner or later."

With an ear-to-ear grin, Sal throws her arms around Cay's neck and embraces him tightly. I imagine in doing so, she's making up for a lifetime's worth of hugs she never got to share with Marq. The glassy eyes and tremble in her chin all but confirm it.

"Thank you for finding me," she whispers, stroking Cay's cheek with her thumb. "And thank you for bringing my story back to the galaxy."

"It's still hard to believe, after all this, that the famous fruits of Eden don't taste like anything," Cay says.

Sal frowns, hesitant in her response. Finally, she says, "It's funny, isn't it?"

"Funny? What do you mean?"

"How the things we most pursue seldom give us what we think they will."

"You found that out the hard way," Cay says, "but not as hard as my grandpappy and my cousin."

Sal's eyes widen. "Oh! That! Yeah ... Gustav wasn't your grandpa."

"He's not?" Cay sounds more surprised by the undoing of Sal's earlier revelation than he was by the revelation itself.

"Nope," Sal confirms with a proud grin. "I just said that so he wouldn't shoot you. I always regretted my one-night stand with that twat, but it came in handy in the end. Everything happens for a reason, right?"

The door opens next to them. They step aside as Galena enters the hut.

Until now, I've been sitting on Sal's bed. I stand at once for Galena, gaping at her with absolutely no idea what I should say.

Fortunately, she has learned to recognize when I'm flustered. Giving me a gracious minute to gather my thoughts, she turns to Cay instead.

"A deal's a deal," he says. "You helped shoot my episodes, and I brought you somewhere no one will ever find you. You aren't exactly 'free,' I suppose, but let's not split hairs."

Galena chokes out a meager laugh. "Close enough," she agrees.

Cay looks over at PAD. The drone—what's left of him anyway—hovers quietly in the corner.

"Come out with me, PAD," he says. "We'll let these two share a proper goodbye."

Sal hobbles after him too, leaving me alone with Galena in the silent hut.

Once more, tears cloud my vision as I take her into my arms. "I'm gonna miss you like crazy," I whisper. "I can't imagine I'll meet anyone like you ever again. Not even if I spent the rest of my life flying from one end of the galaxy to the other."

"Thank you, Jerricho, for everything," she says. "For your kindness, most of all. Other than my mother, I didn't believe there was much good in this galaxy. Now that I've met you, I know better. That in just one person, there can be a whole galaxy's worth of goodness."

Galena reaches behind her neck. She unclasps the gold chain with its Azazule diamond.

"I don't need this anymore," she says, looping the necklace over my head.

The diamond, warmed by her rosy skin, feels heavy against my breastbone.

"It worked for me," Galena says. "But it has one more job left to do. Get home safe, okay?"

When I embrace her again, I know it's for the last time.

"I'll be back," I say, trying my best—and failing—to sound brave. "Someday, I'll be back. Maybe then you'll be ready for me."

Galena laughs sweetly. She cups my face in her hands and beams up at me with those perfect amethyst eyes.

"I can't stop you from trying," she says. "After all, it *is* a free galaxy."

THE *TANTALUS*

Unknown Days to Payment

I'M STARING OUT the windscreen as the *Tantalus* begins its ascent into Eden's airspace. Below us, the area around the *Royal Austrian* is abuzz with activity. After plundering the ship of whatever they thought they could use, the Children of Eden made a deal with the rest of Geiger's security team. The weapons would stay on the planet, and the people would leave. The soldiers agreed heartily to those terms.

Cay briefly joined the looting party before we left. I waited for him outside, wondering what he could possibly need from the *Royal Austrian*.

Now there's a brand-new, top-of-the-line fuel rod powering the *Tantalus*. It holds enough juice to make a thousand X-space jumps.

Technically, it means I could say farewell to Cay and stay here with Galena. But my best friend is right. This isn't home. Not yet, anyway. There are too many people waiting for me on Terra, counting on me to come home to them. After all, *someone* has to throw Oakey Greaves a retirement party.

The *Tantalus* climbs higher into the lost planet's atmosphere. Above me are the myriad stars of our galaxy. Below, the Trees of Eden, arranged in their circular grove. In the middle of that luminous sea of blue and silver, tall above them all, glowing molten bronze with her unique and tasteless fruits, is the Matriarch.

And, somewhere beneath her, is my heart. Eternally enslaved, yet free at last.

Cay offers me a condoling grin.

"Do you think she'll be happy here?" I quietly ask.

"Of course I do," he says, clapping me on the shoulder with his three-fingered hand. "She's finally home. Now, let's get back to ours."

SUNSET CITY, TERRA

– ORION SPUR –

CULLAN JONAS'S OFFICE

2 Days to Payment

"I HOPE YOU'VE enjoyed our interstellar adventure as much as I have during this flagship season of *Galactic Eats Reheated*. I can't wait to share more tasty food with you in the future. Until then, eat well, friends."

The wall monitor goes dark. In his high-backed leather chair, the half-Rouzh, half-human remains silent. He leans back, unblinking, staring at the black screen. His meaty hand lifts a sweating crystal glass from the desk to his lips, and he swishes a mouthful of bourbon across his teeth.

"Well? Whaddya think?" Cay asks anxiously.

Everything rides upon this moment. We've spent the past two hours watching all five episodes of *Galactic Eats Reheated*. If Cullan Jonas was going to reject them, certainly he would have done it already. Right?

Still, I can't help seeing the grisly image of the Hekkra tearing my limbs off one by one.

Finally, Jonas speaks. "It's ... unbelievable," he says. "I have to hand it to you boys—I didn't think you could pull it off. Hell, I didn't think you had much chance of coming back in one piece. But I'll be damned if that isn't some of the greatest programming I've seen during my sixty years in this business."

"I can't take all the credit," says Cay. "Jer deserves some too. Whaddya think, pal? Five percent? Ten?"

I scowl. "A helluva lot more than that, Cay. I worked my ass off editing that footage. All you did was stand in front of a camera and talk."

"Not only did you find Sal and the Trees of Eden," says Jonas, ignoring our squabble, "but you also caught all that Geiger drama on film. His reunion with Sal, Ameliana's double-cross, and *both* of their comeuppance! Don't get me wrong, the Food Fürst will be tough to replace, but ... Wow! We couldn't have killed him off better if we'd scripted it! This is program gold, boys. Program gold! It'll be the most watched event of the year for sure!"

Cay beams at me. I can almost see the cartoon money signs in his eyes.

"I don't mean to start talking currents and pips right away," Cay says, "but since you seem pleased with the product ..."

Jonas's laugh is like the booming of a cannon. The whiskey glass rattles on his desk, and he takes this as a sign that he needs another sip.

"The money's yours, of course," he assures us. "You earned it. Five million, was it?"

"I'll take two and a half," says Cay. "Jer here deserves the other half. Send it to him."

Cullan wags a finger at Cay. With a greedy glimmer in his eye, he says, "Two-point-five is only the beginning for you, Cantore. Oh, yes, I've got big plans for you. Losing Geiger is a bit of a financial setback for Third Planet, but you'll replace him in a heartbeat. In fact, I imagine you'll be even bigger! I'll talk to legal, and they'll have a contract written up by tomorrow afternoon. How 'bout ten million for another twenty episodes? Fully staffed this time!"

"I appreciate the offer," Cay replies, "but I have to turn you down. For now, anyway."

The folks in the lobby sixty floors below must hear my jaw hit the floor.

"Are you sure?" Jonas says. He's looking at Cay like he must have lost a few brain cells during our adventures. "We're talking *ten million currents*, boy."

"I'm sure," Cay confirms. "There's a couple other things I need to do first."

THIRD PLANET ENTERTAINMENT
Elevator

THE MOMENT THE elevator doors are closed, I all but scream, "I can't believe you're passing on Jonas's offer! Isn't that what you always wanted? To be a galaxy-famous chef, loved and adored by all?"

"It was never about the fame," Cay calmly replies.

"Really?"

"Okay, maybe it *was* about the fame," he concedes. "But *now* it's about the money. Saying 'No' today will only make him want me more tomorrow. A lesson you could apply to your love life, by the way."

I give him a bitter grunt. "Not sure there'll be much love to speak of in my life. Not for a while, anyway."

"Good. It's about time you stopped chasing skirts. Maybe it means you'll start chasing something bigger."

We descend a few floors in silence. Then I ask, "What'll you do? Once you pay off the Malvudians?"

"Prepare my wedding toast for Bloodgout's daughter," Cay answers. "That was part of the deal, and I'm holding him to it."

I roll my eyes. "And then? Where's your next scheme taking you?"

"Not far," he answers vaguely. "I figure I need to stop chasing things too. Maybe it's time to enjoy the beautiful thing I already have."

"What does *that* mean?"

"I hear there's an opening for head chef at my dad's restaurant," he says. "Figured it couldn't hurt to apply."

I flash him a mischievous smirk. "I think you mean *my* restaurant, Cay."

The elevator door opens. We pass through the Third Planet Entertainment lobby and exit onto the street.

That's when I realize I have no place to go. I've got a snowball's chance on Nabishna of Dirk Plath welcoming me back to his set, and my adventures with Cay have reached their end.

Where to now?

Cay must not have the same inner dilemma going on. Without a hitch in his step, he hails an ATC.

"Where are you going?" I ask.

I hate admitting it to myself, but I hope he invites me along.

"*We* are going to the suburbs," he says. "Each of us has one last debt to pay."

1300 PINEWOOD TRAIL

"HOLD ON TO your panties, I'm coming. Give an old lady half a second, would you?"

Half a second later, the front door opens a crack. Gram's wrinkled brown face peers out at us.

"I wanted to drop by before you sent any Hekkra after me," says Cay. Hopeful, he adds, "Unless you decided to cancel my debt while I was away?"

Gram cackles with unbridled mirth and throws open the door. Wrapping Cay in a frail but warm hug, she says, "I'm not taking a pip below the ninety thousand we agreed on. And I expect nothing less than Michelin-quality meals for the next week of my life."

"And I'm here to return this," I say. I hold out the necklace. The Azazule diamond dangles from the end of its gold chain. "After what I survived, I think there might be some good luck there after all."

Gram looks at the necklace and trembles. Then she swats it aside and pulls me into her embrace—one *much* tighter than the hug she gave Cay, I might add.

"I never needed that silly crystal," she whispers, burying her head in my shoulder. "I just needed my grandbaby to come home."

Gram steps back. She sizes me up, looking for damage.

"I'm alright, Gram," I assure her. "Really."

"I can't tell you how scared your family was—how scared *I* was— when we didn't hear from you all those weeks," Gram admits. "We assumed the worst. I can't tell you how relieved we were to hear your voice yesterday."

"This is a beautiful reunion and all," interrupts Cay, "but I'm starved. I'm gonna go on a pantry raid."

In the kitchen, Cay sets to work on a simple beef stroganoff. I can't help but notice the jade-handled knife he's using to slice mushrooms.

"Alright, but I already ate dinner," says Gram, taking a seat at the table. "No way I'm counting this as part of my personal chef week."

"Call it a bonus," Cay replies. "Especially since I'm not only cooking for you two."

"You're not?" I ask, sitting across from Gram.

Cay grins sideways at me. "Nope. We have a special guest on the way."

I scowl. "Cay, I swear to Cosmos, if it's Josephina, I'm gonna strangle you."

"No prying!" he says. "I don't want to spoil the surprise."

As Cay focuses in the kitchen, I regale Gram with the tale of our epic, cross-galactic journey. When I come to the harrowing chapters of the story, she doesn't react like I expect. She remains impassive, absorbing everything thoughtfully.

Maybe I'm not a good storyteller. Or maybe the scary parts aren't so frightening when you know there's a happy ending waiting for you.

I'm in the middle of the Bellamina chapter when we hear another ship landing outside. I assume it's one of the neighbors returning home from the workday.

Cay assumes different. Looking up from his simmering sauce, he says, "Be a dear and let our guest inside, would you, Jerricho?"

It isn't Josephina I find on the other side of Gram's front door. It is, instead, a tiny woman about Gram's age herself.

"Mei-Li!" I greet in surprise. "You came all the way here for dinner?"

Stoic as always, Mei-Li brushes past me into the house and says, "I pray I came for more than *that*."

Cay is pouring egg noodles into a boiling pot when we enter the kitchen.

"Good evening, Mei-Li!" he cheerfully exclaims. "Dinner is just about ready. We're having beef stroganoff. You're Russian, right?"

Ignoring the asinine question of ethnicity, Mei-Li says, "I'm glad to see you alive, Cay. When I awoke to discover that all my QRDs were missing, and that you were missing with them, I almost *hoped* the black hole would kill you so I wouldn't have to do it myself."

"Long story about those QRDs," Cay replies, giving the noodles a quick stir. "Care to take a seat?"

After introducing Mei-Li and Gram, Cay shares the rest of our tale. Every time he arrives at one of the harrowing moments, he pauses, leaving brief cliffhangers as he checks on the food.

When it comes to the spoken word, he's a much better storyteller. But that's okay. I prefer telling mine with a camera.

By the end, Mei-Li's eyes are shining with tears.

"She's alive," the old woman whispers. "I can't believe she's still alive."

Cay reaches into the bag at his feet. He sets a quartet of navigation cartridges in front of Mei-Li.

"Whenever the timing is right," he says, "there's your ticket to Eden. Do me a favor? Give me and Jer a call before you go."

Speechless, Mei-Li gathers the cartridges. Cay's story hasn't been without effect. In Mei-Li's eyes, I see that the embers of an age-old struggle have reignited.

"I also brought back a souvenir," says Cay. He reaches again into his bag.

Even I'm shocked by what he sets on the table.

"Is—is that—?" Mei-Li can't finish her question. Trembling, she takes the bronze, pear-shaped fruit into her hands.

"It is indeed!" says Cay. "A whole Eden apple, just for you. Although I'd strongly advise against eating it."

Cay notices my accusatory glare and raises his hands into a defensive posture. "What?" he says.

"What if that thing would've grown into a giant tree onboard the *Tantalus,* Cay? Did you ever think of that?" I say.

"I figured we'd be fine if it didn't have a host to feed on," Cay argues. "And see? Once again, my instincts have proven infallible."

At that moment, Cay's tel chimes, sparing everyone from further bickering. After a quick glance at it, Cay pushes back his chair and stands.

"Drain that pasta, would you, Jerricho?" he asks sweetly. "Jonas's payment just came through, and I have some very eager Malvudians waiting to hear from me."

PATIO, MARQ'S EATS
242 Days after Payment

CAY'S CHEF'S WHITES are blinding as they reflect the midafternoon sun. He's on the dining patio at Marq's Eats, leaning back in his chair, fingers laced behind his head. He must be taking advantage of the post-lunch lull to soak in a few of our star's warm rays. His eyes are closed, and I can hear him snoring lightly as I approach on the sidewalk.

"Still lazy as ever," I remark, sliding into the chair across the table.

Cay's eyelids flutter. We haven't seen each other for seven months, but when he looks at me, it's as if we got coffee together this very morning.

"Well, there he is, the Lord of the Butterflies." Cay points at my forearm. "Or maybe you prefer *Monarch* of the Butterflies?"

I laugh. Despite all the problems ravaging my body, it's tough not to find joy these days.

"How was the migration? Everything you hoped and dreamed?" Cay asks.

He's referring to the monarchs I've been following. Armed with my camera, an assistant I hired with my *Galactic Eats* earnings, and the same trusty PAD unit who traveled the galaxy with me, I've spent the last four months creating my own documentary. The subject? The majestic migration of the monarch butterfly.

"We wrapped up shooting last month," I answer. "Spent the last few weeks on the cutting floor."

"And?"

"Just got done showing it to Jonas."

"And?"

"He said it was some of the most boring programming he's ever seen. Still, he thought it was well done. Said there might be an early-*early*-morning time slot in its future, for elderly folks who need help falling back asleep."

"So he bought it?"

I nod. "And for a lot more than I spent making it. I think he wants to keep me buttered up so I'll help him butter *you* up someday. But if I'm being honest, the money doesn't mean much to me. I'll probably donate it to the Butterfly Oasis back home. I was doing this one for me."

Cay graces me with his familiar, cockeyed grin and says, "Good for you, Jer."

"What about you?" I say, jerking a thumb toward the building beside us. "How's the restaurant biz working out? Got any profit-loss reports you'd like to share with your owner?"

"Oh, you know, it can be a little tense working with your significant other," he replies, "but Trini might be worth the headache. We'll see."

I chuckle. I can't imagine Cay dating the same young woman who, just last year, escorted the Hekkra to our doorstep.

"She forgave you, I assume?"

"Daily."

"I'm glad you're happy here, Cay. Really, I am."

He stares at me, sizing me up with a scrutinizing eye, before asking, "You still think about her? Galena?"

"Daily." I frown and nibble at the inside of my cheek. "I can't see a star without thinking of her. Without wondering if she's anywhere near it. I just ... hope she's happy. I hope she found the peace she was looking for."

"Me too," Cay says, but he suddenly sounds distracted. His line of sight is no longer directed *at* me, but *over*.

"Excuse me," speaks a male voice.

I turn. The man interrupting our reunion is middle-aged, dressed well in a tailored gray suit and lavender button-down. His wavy mane of salt-and-pepper hair kisses the suit's collar, giving him the appearance of a billionaire playboy who knows how to walk the line between casual and professional.

"My name is Zinn Teal," the man says, introducing himself.

But for me, he's a man who needs no introduction. I've seen his name a thousand times—at the zoo, on nature programs, and in my National

Geographic magazines, to name a few. He may have even earned a mention or two at the Coral Sands Butterfly Oasis.

His name also came up during a memorable conversation on Bellamina.

A conversation Cay has apparently forgotten. "You can go back to Jonas and tell him what I've told all the others," he says irritably. "Still not interested in making the show. I'm happy here."

Zinn Teal raises a perplexed eyebrow. "I'm ... glad for your happiness. Truly. But I was actually looking for *you*."

To my shock, I realize he's pointing at me.

"You *are* Jerricho Hatch, are you not?" he says.

"I ... am?" I reply uncertainly. "But what do you want with me?"

"Mei-Li Tan—a mutual friend to us both, I believe—recommended you," he answers, sitting in the empty seat beside me. "And when I heard about your work with the monarchs, my gut told me you might be the man for the job."

"What job is that?"

"I'm a cosmic zoologist," he explains, "working on a new program called *Galactic Zoo*. A few weeks ago, my head cameraman went MIA—up and disappeared without a trace!—and I would like you to take his place. I'll pay you well, of course, and the job would mean plenty of intergalactic travel. What do you think?"

I sit up straight. I see in his piercing gaze how determined he is to bring me on board.

Suddenly, I'm hyperconscious of how terribly my forearms and fingers ache. And everything from my calves to my toenails feels a bit like a trollum has been using them for toothpicks. I've put my body through holy hell over the last year, and, truthfully, I don't know how much more it can take.

Which is why, confidently and without hesitation, I give him my answer.

"Absolutely."

DENALI MAJESTO spent his earlier years in the private business sector, yet he never felt quite at home in what he was doing. After an early retirement from the world of business, Majesto dedicated his life to the three activities he treasures most: loving his family, exploring the globe, and writing. He has since written a small library's worth of stories, which he has begun unveiling to the world—one story at a time. Through both his writing and the tireless work of his ambassadors, it is Majesto's wish that he might entertain and bring hope to the lives of countless others.

To learn more about the man behind the stories, or to view his free content, please visit www.DenaliMajesto.com.

Journey to an island where the *magic* is real, *hope* is reborn, and the dead *live on*...

"Emotional, nostalgic, magical, beautifully written. This story was absolutely captivating."

The year is 1918. War rages across Europe. A strange and deadly new disease has struck fear into the heart of a nation. But for Walter, Peter, and Pip, the three young Luther boys, life in Pennsylvania coal-mining country means blissful days playing in the glade and forests along the shores of Lake Acheron. Together with their best friend Hattie, they partake of the wonder and magic of the whimsical games Rosalie Luther—better known as "Mama"—invents for them. When the schools are closed to protect the students from contracting the deadly virus, the children rejoice at the promise of an indefinite holiday.

After "The Flu" claims the life of someone close to them, their world seems shattered beyond repair—until they discover an impossible island where the dead live on. In this place of goblins, dragons, and enchanted gardens, the magic which used to exist only in imagination is made real. Yet even as they bask in the light of hope reborn, a new darkness settles over their home, threatening to send their family into an even deeper ruin ...

AVAILABLE IN E-BOOK AND PRINT

Learn more at:
DENALIMAJESTO.COM

HIS STORIES ~ OUR LIBRARY

www.DenaliMajesto.com

www.ingramcontent.com/pod-product-compliance
Lightning Source LLC
Chambersburg PA
CBHW011914130726
47903CB00016B/2831